OCTET

MICHAEL'S STORY IN EIGHT VOICES

OCTET

MICHAEL'S STORY IN EIGHT VOICES

JAMES WIELAND

ARCADIA

© James Wieland 2018

First published 2018 by Arcadia
the general books imprint of
Australian Scholarly Publishing Ltd
7 Lt Lothian St Nth, North Melbourne, Vic 3051

Tel: 03 9329 6963 / Fax: 03 9329 5452
enquiry@scholarly.info / www.scholarly.info

ISBN 978-1-925801-30-9

Cover design Wayne Saunders

For Ian Templeman

Wherever your life ends, it is all there. The advantage of living is not measured by length, but by use! Some men have lived long, and lived little; attend to it while you are in it. It lies in your will, not in the number of years, for you to have lived enough.

Montaigne, *Essais*

A Word to the Reader

Although *Octet* is a novel in eight voices, with Michael O'Connell's being carried in italics through others' memories, correspondence and various written artefacts; there is also a discrete and ever present narrative voice in the background. For this is a novel of character in which the plot emerges out of their action and interaction. The story is not foretold or predetermined and the narrator, unobtrusive and unopinionated, having a limited omniscience not available to the other characters, helps to weave a path through the maze of voices. Should the reader question who is speaking, it is the voice of that embedded witness to Michael's unfolding story.

Charlie Greenwood:
The Heart's Ease

The church bell tolls. The grey morning of gusty showers absorbs its melancholy hymn. Across the countryside of sharp apple-green valleys and purpled mountains, shading from violet into the blue-grey of the ridges as the eye ascends, spanning over giant basalt boulders and the many runnels and creeks given a new lease of life by these late rains, I imagine people pausing; the dense, almost black clouds seem to be stilled and hang on the ranges as though held by giant hands, their busy scurrying ceased for the moment.

The bell is a call to the funeral that is to take place in the withered weatherboard church this shadow-punching September morning. The friend, constant companion, confidante and love of my childhood is being buried today. I need no reminder. And then it stops, its dying sounds fill the quiet, for although it is a Friday, the bell will ring on the hour until its final exclamation at twelve, when the service begins. For some around town the customary business of a Friday is suspended, if not in reverence, then at least in deference to the deceased. I am not at the *Stud*. Bran had one or two calves to look after but he said he could manage, and I am lingering, watching rain make patterns down the windows that frame views of my place, so intimately known. Ben and I are catching up later in the morning and Susannah has asked me to drop by. But I cannot relax; I feel anxious, as though someone is walking on my grave. My mind is working like the sea; washing up memories, sweeping them back, linking them to others as they surge in again.

It had been a bleak night when the stars are hidden as if shielding from the argumentative elements, and I rose early, unrested; my exhaustion seems reciprocated by the washed-out dawn, as if it was a poetic metaphor. I had spent the night re-hashing Michael's story the best I could. Tossing and turning my way through the night, I had been captured by the uncertainty of night thoughts: solving, un-solving, *resolving, and re-resolving.*

***

Up early I stood at the window; feel the slate-grey sky as cold as metal mirroring my mood, as my attention turns to the source of the now quiescent bell, hanging in the wooden belfry atop of St Michael and All Angels. 'Saint Mick's' to the locals, it is propped up by hope and a flicker of faith on the willow-fringed banks of the creek. The only church in Celtic Ponds; it was Michael's church.

Together with the tiny wooden primary school, the pub, and the old brick shire building set in a manicured rose garden and marked as distinctive by its colonial shutters, all facing onto Wellington Street, the church is in 'the old town'. The 'new town' which has a footpath, is made up of a string of weathered fronted shops and cottages that straggle down Blunt Street in a bent line to the bridge. It faces across the sand-flats and the ponds, now, so carefully tended as a part of the gully garden, to the 'old' side. The bridge, only ever 'The Bridge': to distinguish it from the Hump Bridge a little further out of town towards Broadwater, pins the two parts of town together. I know the place like the back of my hand. The little blue and white cottage on the other side of the road abutting the creek, is Susannah Beaumont's, the resident music teacher who has taught me from when I was a teenager and, together with Ben Temple, who I make gardens with, we've whiled away hours on her verandah, yarning. 'Our university in the sticks,' Ben calls it.

As to the significance of this day, it's difficult not to wonder about the many visitors who will find their way here. Like others before them they may think it quaint as they coast down the rise from east or west, but the locals are under no illusions. They reckon those who think so are on their way to somewhere else. It's always had a tea rooms and although May Diller now calls it a café little has changed, except that the coffee no longer comes out of a jar. Although her Devonshire Tea is worth stopping for. I'm on my way there now, past Nelson's News agency, offering everything from lottery tickets and magazines to faded stationery and a few fly-blown cards for 'That Special Occasion', but its main lure is the arrival of the Sydney papers at about 10.00 in the morning. It doubles as the post office and the local TAB, which means the proprietor, Peter Nelson, could know everyone's business if that sort of scuttlebutt interested him, but it doesn't, unless it's a tip on the ponies or anyone talking rugby.

Marjorie, his wife, is another thing altogether! The local gossip, her life is rife with rumour and innuendo; she harbours slights and conducts vendettas and encourages the formation of cliques. She is a bit of a joke now, but there are few in town who haven't been infected by her tongue. Oh, I know of her invective, but that's behind me now! Apart from Ted Wright's garage and attached general 'snore', as they call it, at the top end of town welcoming travellers from the west, there's Nina Oakley's *Softly Lit* craft shop and gallery at the town's eastern corner. Showing mostly local art: landscapes and washed out water colours, needle work, crocheting and quilts of varying quality, usually on consignment, it holds few surprises for even the most avid of passing scavengers who might also pause at Ernie and Alice Piggins' *Brick 'n' Brack* shop. When it's open that is, for Alice has three toddlers under five and, a good worker, Ernie's in demand as a labourer or farm-hand. The town's lost its grocery and vegie stores; starved out by the majors in Bega they left a couple of vacant spots although, when the new doctor arrived he opened his surgery in the row instead of at his home like old Doc Eddington before him.

You can't miss the pub: *The Clover and Thistle*, which is ideally located opposite St Mick's on Napoleon Street, offering a different kind of nourishment. It's been there since the turn of the last century. Standing with a faded knock-about elegance at the cross-roads, it has a couple of rooms for rent, but apart from a farm-stay or two, there was little incentive to stay there until they spruced up a couple of rooms. Natasha is staying there this weekend, but it's unlikely that any of the many dignitaries who are expected will stay over. In the past, visitors often preferred to stay in Broadwater and make the drive up, but they won't be bothered with that either: the footy finals have started.

For most of its existence, it's been a battle to find the Ponds on the map or remember its name. But the place has always done its job for the surrounding district of farmers, cattlemen, townies and a few itinerants and their families and, what with the *Stud* sales and open days at *Clifton*, the opening of the Memorial Gardens in '88' where the Anzac Day ceremony is now held, and our latest venture: the 'Cool and Classic' music festival which is to be held on the March long weekend, the appeal of the place is steadily growing. However, thinking about the town like this, I'm brought back to Michael, for O'Connell stories are woven into its fabric.

It should be a luxury not to be rushing! As a rule, I've put in a couple of hours at the stud by now; might be having the cuppa that shortly I'm going to treat myself to at the *cafe*. But, as I wander down the worn gravel path that winds its way to Blunt Street, splashing as I go, protected by my old galoshes from the puddles running together now into streamlets, I'm overcome with a numbing fatigue; to move is almost heroic. Michael, and thoughts of our intertwined lives in the village, have taken possession of my mind.

* * *

'Hello Charlie.' Mrs Diller paused. 'Don't usually see you in here, not on a Friday.'

'No May.' Could never call her 'Phyllis' like the locals. 'Change of routine today.'

'Of course, love. Guess it's a weird day for you, eh?' She wasn't prying, concern coloured her voice.

'Yes ... Michael and I: a part of the place when we were nippers, weren't we? I used to think all my Christmases had come at once, though, when you or your Mum were at the door and you'd give us a piece of cake or a scone on our way to school.'

'You remember that do you? Bet the other one just expected it! I was helping mum out; she was pretty crook. Used to love seeing you kids traipsing home from school, and if I had any left-overs I'd let you have something.' She had a faraway look in her eye. 'What a sight you two were. Chalk 'n cheese! Michael was a looker even then; everything, from those flashing dark eyes beneath a shock of hair as black as pitch, always spick 'n span, down to his designer body and legs, even then! Oh, I remember him putting on such a show at Mass. Struttin' around. And you? Well love, you were all arms 'n legs 'n skin 'n bone, but, oh, ... I've never forgotten them, you had the loveliest hands. It was as though the good Lord had made them, was very satisfied with the job, and didn't bother too much about the rest. But, oh love, those hands!'

'Well, well, May! ... They're not so hot now are they? Work!' He mumbled as he placed them on the table, one palm up, one down.

'Maybe so ... you might think they are weary and worn, but to me they look like the fingers of God in that man Mister Blake's paintings. There!'

'You know, on the way down I was thinking about how as little tykes we used to meet up at the bridge, before we built one of our first bridges across the creek upstream. It's still there, that old bridge. Ben and I rebuilt it when we did the gardens, you know, but that's another local story.'

'You could have left I guess, but ...? C'mon now ... what'll you have?'

'Coffee thanks, can I have a mug, and oh, a scone and jam would be lovely?

'I'll be right back.'

Ah the Ponds, why am I still here? May as good as asked the question, but then she was back carrying a cup for herself and a biscuit. 'Do you mind?'

'Oh please do, it's nice to chat.'

'I fancy you don't do this sort of thing very often, except p'raps with

5

Susannah and that gorgeous Ben. You all seem like good pals.'

'Yes, we are. ... Anyway, we were talking about the Ponds. I'm still here, because ... well, I'm knitted into its people and deeply into this landscape. Look!' She couldn't take her eyes off this reticent man opening up. 'Look! Look out there! I make my music and art out of it. Can't think of it without thinking of its land and weather scapes. Even today, dressed in sombre tones, it takes my breath away.'

She followed his gaze out towards the deep blue flannel-wrapped mountains, source of the creek that runs past her door. He was caught up in his thoughts. Oh, the joy of it. The creek rattling down now after the rain. And the call of the birds across the gully, from the day-break conversations of the magpies, as if setting their day's agenda and the cah-caawing of a gang of crows cracking the day open, the whip-crack call of the shy whip birds in unison and the larrikin scream and squawk of the rioting sulphur crested cockatoos, hanging about, putting on a show for everyone later in the day. They have a place in my dreaming. 'Ah, May, I'm very fortunate.'

'Really!' Having cast him as a figure of sorrow she'd never thought of him as a lucky man, what with his problem and after what had happened.

'So lucky, this place written upon by the generations ... Sure I'm not boring you May?'

'God no love; it's lovely to chat. What generations?'

'I was thinking of Michael's family actually. Timothy, who I didn't know, but ... come to think of it, did you?'

'Died, when I was tiny, he did. God forbid, I'm not that old Charlie.' She laughed. 'I'm a '35 drop. Never heard a bad word said about him you know; not like that son of his: the *Absentee Squire* we all used to call him. We didn't go for him. But, Mum reckoned Mr Timothy was salt o' the earth, if you can say that about a Toff! Where'd we be without the O'Connells though eh?' But old Timothy, tell me bit about him.'

'Well, he grew up in sight of the Wicklow Hills in Ireland. It's beautiful country they say, with great granite outcrops running down the Eastern hinterland from south of Dublin just like ours, with a shallow plain to the sea. He was the second son you know, had no prospect of inheriting the estate so he came to Australia as a young fellow. A piece of his heart must've been in the old place though, because as soon as he found this bit of country he named it after Wicklow. Story is it was about '95 and once he was here he got to work. There'd be no St Mick's or its bell without him. He shipped the bell out, a gift from *Rathnew*, his family estate; and, with all the Catholic hands in the village putting their faith into building the church, he joined them with his O'Connell money, desire and labour, and let his roots go deep.'

'It's the truth, bless him. Mum said his business interests was in the city but he and his lady wife were at home here, building the *Stud* and making that beautiful garden you know all about God bless you; oh dear, there I go' she laughed, 'I'm blessing everyone today They were a part o' the town alright. Even if it was just a way of making money for that son of his, Edward; who used to lord it over us, but old Timothy wasn't like that I believe.'

'I've heard stories that go back to the start of the town, but you know May, in fossicking around I've also found pieces of shaped stone that hint at a much older presence in these hills and valleys. Ethel Williams has a story for nearly every track I've taken, every rock outcrop or creek that I've passed and with her daughter Alwyn's help, Ben and I had them shape some of the tracks in the Memorial Garden. Did you know that?'

'Well I never. So it's real ancient eh? Old Ethel and Ally ... pretty little kid wasn't she!'

'Yes, Alwyn and I've been friends since schooldays and Ethel's the keeper of the local Yuin stories that are seeded into this country. While I believe the first white settlers might have been a couple of Italian boys who called the place Biella after their home town; they barely scratched the surface before they upped stakes. Good coffee, May.'

'Ta, the old boy's finally got the knack of the machine now he's retired from the timber mill.'

'Anyway, the Italian boys were gone by the 1870s when a more permanent wave of settlers arrived from Ireland and Scotland with purpose and intention and laid down their roots, turning Biella into Celtic Ponds.

Although, it's *Yarrah* to the Yuin people: water place.'

'Well I never! And it should be: those gorgeous ponds and the beautiful Crepe Myrtle sown all along their edges; lovely, firing the landscape with their red blossom;' she had a dreamy look in her eye again as he continued.

'Folk like the James clan and the old Scottish families who may have smelled heather in their dreams but were hardy stock; dug in no less than the Irish who came, starved out of their homeland. The O'Mahoneys, the Duggans, and the Dwyers had nothing but their religion to cling to, but they got in first and built the old church leaving the God fearing Presbyterians to feed their religious hunger at a Kirk on the coast or in the hall. Gee, May, look at the time; I'd better get cracking.'

May was smiling. 'Took me right back Charlie.' She was whispering, 'like fragments for a patchwork quilt; it's been just lovely. You should put all this down:

... at least you could tell Michael's story.'

***

I thought about our conversation as I dawdled towards the bridge. I've always been a listener – only child syndrome I guess! – interested in these tales, picking up a word here a speculation there, which has hardened into a fact to be traded in gossip or yarns around the dinner table or over the fence in town, at the news agency or the front bar at the pub. They may contain genuine expressions of concern about actual events, may hold deep knowledge and shape how a place is imagined, particularly when they are associated with joy or sorrow: the grand emotions.

Tales of how the Dwyers started the pub in the front room of their cottage serving home brew, before old Sean, confident of steady traffic along the mail route, built the two-story place using left-overs from the construction of the church. The pub's been associated with the family for four generations and with Joe Wellham marrying Sean's granddaughter, it stayed that way even though *O'Connell* owns it. Stories about the names on the War Memorial; there was hardly a family in the district that wasn't touched by it, and now the reverence that's attached to this small obelisk has a new resonance, with its transfer from an inconspicuous spot near the oval to the Memorial Garden. Stories of road accidents, of unwanted pregnancies, of arrivals and departures salaciously speculated about, of floods, of good seasons and bad, of folk lost to alcohol or drugs, to madness from loneliness or war. Then of course, there was Mrs O'Connell's death after giving birth to Michael and her husband Edward's hasty departure to London leaving the Doogues to run the *Stud* and raise the beautiful boy.

These echoes, migrating between the sunlight and shadows of lives are poignantly caught in the O'Connell's tragedy of that little boy, Michael, born in the same year as me, and surrounded by such sadness, not only gives this tale its shape and direction, but, sometimes I wonder if they didn't shape mine as well. But that's too simple!

***

Leaning on the railing of the old bridge, I find it extraordinary that I'm able to embrace my past with pleasure and even now, at forty-seven, can face the future with anticipation. For when I came back from the Conservatorium, a mediocre degree in my hand and a career in music all but dashed, I was a shell of the boy I was at seventeen and a shadow of the man I am now. A few would have reckoned Marj Nelson's disparaging remark – 'little poof's come slinking home' – wasn't all that wide of the mark, others might recall that after leaving school I was away studying in the city, but I doubt many knew or cared what I was doing. I wasn't the sort of kid who had a lot of mates. Michael was enough for me and I always liked playing with Ally and Karen, even as Michael told me I must be *bloody crazy bothering with them*. Many years later Karen told me how much they'd enjoyed it: 'it was like having a sister. Not like that arrogant bully, Michael.'

My settling here and working the orchard started by my grandfather was my choice. I felt as though I'd failed and had no alternative but to knuckle down at *Glen Cannich* and learn the ropes from my ailing Dad. These decisions are not as unalloyed as that of course; mine was fraught but I haven't lost music or art. They are very real and when I'm at the cello, working on a score, or on the concert stage with Sue, or in front of an easel, I'm in another world.

Lingering, watching the creek tumble beneath me, the chiming bell breaks into my reverie. For you Michael the bell tolls today; the nine o'clock chimes fill the air. Close by now it is almost physical, hammering away at questions inside my head. Oh, I know I'm not on my own, that others too will pause and reflect. Individual tasks in kitchen, field or shed; out in the paddock, or behind shop counters may be set aside for a moment or be subtly changed as they gaze into the middle distance of memory, recalling the man we knew as a boy nearly fifty years ago.

Glancing over my shoulder towards *The Clover and Thistle*, I can't help wondering how Natasha is feeling. All eyes will be on her today, for not only does she bring a hint of the exotic to our isolated hamlet, but there's a certain fascination that one of the nation's richest and most influential men should have requested he be buried in the churchyard of our dilapidated little church. Curiously I remember him joking once how *the old Ponds was a good dump to die in*, I didn't think he meant it quite so literally!

News of his death and the plans for the funeral had excited the town which is already invaded by the media. Folk are gathering. Marj has taken up a strategic position and May is on her verandah, hoping to entice a few in for a Devonshire Tea; while Alice Piggins and several of the local Mums with toddlers on the hip, congregate on the curb. Nina Oakley is there, chasing snapshots which she'll display in the Gallery and the James' and a few other cow cockies have come into town. There's also the odd grazier from further out in tie and tweeds, their wives in hats and gloves as though they are off to the Royal Easter Show. The Queen could have been visiting! Journalists, photographers, television crews and men eating microphones are scurrying around, and over the next couple of hours a stream of cars, like a line of toiling ants, will be rolling into town cluttering the main street, shunting here and there, until Sergeant Heenan directs them to the make-shift parking area at the school giving its coffers an unexpected boost. Pollies, and movers and shakers and a minder or two from Canberra and Sydney will have been on the road at cock-crow, but, then, funerals are great photo opportunities, and this one has the added frisson of being linked to money and power.

I can't help wondering what they know of Michael. Most will have the barest outline; press secretaries and PAs may have sent juniors off to sift through newspaper back files to put a little flesh on the bones and the obituary published on Monday would have given them plenty of hooks to hang a sound-bite on or fill the back of an envelope! *A Great Australian. The Model Philanthropist. Titan of Business. Sportsman and Scholar. Doyen of the Arts. The International.* Something there for everyone, from Ministers of the Crown to merchant bankers and big business; for everyone who strode the corridors of power. Michael had given them a Michelangelo, while to those who knew him, he'd left a Machiavelli. Although I did wonder if a few might be hoping he'd made good use of the shredder!

The tabloids and magazines had taken a little license with what he'd given them, embellished this sketch of his public self after some cursory research, inevitably dwelling on his British knighthood and reputation as an international businessman, aligning him with Australia's other expats whose achievements are supposed to bestow on those left at home a faint glow of warmth and recognition. I knew he'd kept a low profile in the UK where most of his business operations took place, but such was his glamour and appeal to an Australian readership hungry for heroes that he simply could not be ignored. Michael O'Connell was news; fodder for a fawning media. Oh, I'd kept track of him. The darling of both the Sydney and national broadsheets and coveted by television journalists. Even though his brief, but stellar, rugby career was cut short by a crippling accident, he seemed to travel through life undaunted. Handsome, articulate, cultured, and energetic, a doyen of business and lion in the boardroom, a fixture in London society, his dinner parties at Cadogan Place some thought, were not to be missed. He had also added glamour and mystique to his profile, marrying the exquisite Russian ballerina, Natasha Yakovlevna Levinskaya, an incomparable trophy. Sir Michael O'Connell was a presence and like the most photogenic of fashion models, the camera seemed to love him! His one short-coming for the hungry editor, may have been that no scandal stuck to his polished veneer; try as they might to expose it. When it came to his personal life, he was an enigmatic figure and with an appetite for litigation, no editor probed too deeply the glossy outer facade that he presented with practiced skill.

He had about him a certain thrill and panache, while his company's philanthropic arms, regularly announcing endowments to universities and hospitals or providing funds in trust to support cultural projects, large and small, gave him a human face and ultimately earned him an AM in recognition of his contribution to the Bi-Centennial celebrations. Later he became a Companion in the Australian list for his significant donation to The Children's Cancer Clinic and the gift to the State of his remarkable collection of Australian landscape art. Some of the cynics around town reckoned he'd spent his money well but I didn't subscribe to that. He had been generous to the local community, the State, and the Nation, but it did cross my mind, that *O'Connell's* business operations and a darker personal side were protected from scrutiny behind this public face of benefaction.

'You could tell his story Charlie, no-one better.' I was musing again on May's suggestion as I wandered up the main gully garden walk. Could I? Sometimes I wondered if I knew him at all. Oh, I could manage the physical likeness I guess. Could catch him as a striking sixteen-year-old, his dark hair shining, his naked body rippling with energy and promise. I can still feel him, breath of my breath, flesh of my flesh. For seventeen years he was my emotional north: together from infancy, we played with our first building blocks together, read the same books, painted the same scenes, built, dug, explored our place in tandem, head to head, eye to eye. For all that I could offer only the most partial view. I realized I rarely knew what he thought, was never sure if he was being sincere or if there was an ulterior motive known only to himself, as though he was a clever Secret Agent playing me. Or is a rugby metaphor closer to the point? Like a good half-back, he'd show the ball, sway, baulk, and leave me – me? Anyone trying to get a grip of him grasping at thin air while he kept the ball and then the game was over. Why? Did he think we wanted to bring him to ground? The very opposite was true. We all loved him, but he didn't want to share the game with us.

Who was he? He grew up in Celtic Ponds. The cattle property started by his grandfather shared the Myrtle Creek boundary with *Glen Cannich* from which my family toiled a modest living. Unlike our orchard which had been a family business from the outset, *Wicklow Stud* has always had managers responsible for the everyday running of the property. The last manager was appointed in 1946 when Michael's father, Edward, invited Bran Doogue and his new bride Claire, to run it. They have earned their keep! Edward had only a passing interest in the place, was absent for long periods in Sydney or oversea and rarely visited, even when he was in the country. When Michael's mother died from complications after his delivery by caesarean section, Edward asked the Doogues to raise the child.

He and I were the same age. 1953 drops, we attended Claire's little makeshift kindergarten with Ally Williams and Karen Brown, started at the local three teacher school together and then went onto *St Patrick's College* in Broadwater, down on the coast, an hour away by bus. I wasn't a Catholic and the decision to send me to *St Pat's*, which I later learnt was based on convenience and the sound reputation of the school, spelt the end of my dad's Masonic days. For Michael however, his attendance had to do with the family faith, but the school wasn't his choice. He wanted to go to *St Ignatius*, *Riverview*, the great Jesuit College in Sydney. It was his father's school and he had expected to follow him there; it was no secret that he coveted putting on the blue and white. He never forgave his father for letting Bran and Claire persuade him not to send him there to board. I know he was precious to the couple and they didn't want him flying the coop so early. With his father no model, I think they believed he needed the love and, dare I say it, the guidance, they could provide. Perhaps they were being selfish. I was certainly pleased he didn't go and I can still say, despite what happened, we had a wonderful childhood. Perhaps what happened was a result of it!

Yet, as if to assert himself, Edward had sought a guarantee that his son's religious education would be maintained. I laughed when Michael told me Claire's response: 'I believe the Jesuits and the Christian Brothers still pray to the same God!' But Bran, who rarely missed Mass, although his earlier blind faith had been shattered in the war, gave his earnest promise and encouraged Michael to serve at the altar. I'm not suggesting that Edward had any great respect for the Church, from all reports, his Catholicism was a matter of convenience – a card he played when it could be useful to him. None of this was lost on Claire who drew the comparison with stories of old Timothy: a pillar of St Mick's, his religion was a living entity. I know Edward scoffed when Bran told him Michael had become an altar boy. 'Christ Almighty Doogue, don't overdo it. The lad'll follow me into the business when the time's right. The Church!' As for Michael, assisting the priest had little to do with religion or faith and a lot to do with a performance. With his shining black hair offset by a pearly white surplice and black cassock and being centre-stage during the celebration of the Mass, he knew he looked impressive. *I wish you'd come one day Charlie and see me waving the thurible and spreading incense around, tinkling the altar bells, holding the books for Father Patrick.*

As kids, we were hardly out of each other's sight. We would walk to school together and, afterwards, race home and head off into 'our country': *like the black fellas reckon they know it Charlie, this is our country too*, he would say, *and nobody, … nobody needs to know what we're doing*. We climbed over and around the hilly slopes, made bracken forts, dammed streams, built wooden bridges and constructed secret tracks. It wasn't the Mississippi but I often felt that I was Huck to Michael's Tom, as we explored our place. Yet place to him was only ever physical I think, whereas, I felt it in my blood, my heart and soul.

These memories come back to me as a kaleidoscope of scenes out of sequence, but clear and sharp. In contrast to those monochrome years at the Con, they have their own sound and colour imagery. One of the first is of a narrow canyon carved out by a creek and hidden behind a spill of huge basalt rocks and a dense thatch of tall grass and scrub we'd found during the long summer holidays; we were fourteen. We christened it *Apple Pocket*. It's no longer there, Ben and I blasted it when creating a waterfall for the Memorial Garden, but at the time it was a source of extended delight and came to me when I thought of it in shades of joyous green. The day we found it was steamy and hot, Michael's body was glistening with sweat. I remember taking a photo of him and our exciting discovery. Clambering over some boulders, there it was: green, and black at its depth, sparkling in the sunlight, with willows, wattles and fiery myrtles flanking the edges. Pristine, we thought, virginal: *no-one's ever seen this Charlie, not ever*. It was ours, our apple-shaped sanctuary.

In the long reaches of that summer we spent whole days there, letting the sun play on our bodies, sometimes basking in it, stretching and rolling over like cats, at other times seeking out the filtered light beneath the overhanging trees. We'd fall into the cooling waters, ducking, diving, abandoned. Lying naked on the warm boulders, we'd eat fruit I'd plucked from the orchard.

I had started carting my old camera about with me but, although he had a good camera, Michael never brought his along and ridiculed my interest. In what was to become a lifetime practice that I would later share with Sue, I snapped various scenes which I thought I might be able to turn into a painting, or music. I liked the intimacy of a camera, whereas he reckoned it wanted to know too much; and yet he wanted copies of any I took, particularly if he was in them, which he often was especially at the pool. *Don't want these getting around*, he'd say, smirking: *Just for us*. We were also voracious readers, but while I saw it as a shared interest, he seemed to want to turn it into a contest. The big house had a fabulous library of classics which he was working his way through. *I read three novels this week, Charlie*. I found plenty I wanted to read in the school library or in the public library at Broadwater, which Michael thought had only *junk stuff for the yobbos*, but I wasn't counting. Brother Tippett, our English master, often lent me books that he thought I might like. But if I said I was enjoying someone, Michael could go one better: *You're not reading morbid old Irish Joyce? Pah, you should get into Lawrence; he tells a tale! I could be*

Gerald and you Rupert, he winked. *You should see the terrific fight they have. They were all over each other, going at it.* He licked his lips, watching me. *Anyway*, he said, his face shifting into an ugly grin, *Gerald fucks Gudrun; it's terrific!*

Michael also started reading me some of the poems he'd been writing. At the time I liked them. My music was coming along as well, but I couldn't very well drag my piano out there. Anyway, I was the audience! I would lie down, my head on a rock, close my eyes and let his voice roll over me. I particularly liked one that he called 'Scapula'; I thought of it as 'Apple Pocket'. I still remember the opening verse:

> *I imagine our meeting place*
> *behind your house on the sickle shoulder of hill*
> *In the thin bleached grass*
> *Braided flat against the dark scapula of rock.*

There was a later line I particularly liked: '*We, spread-eagled on the earth, / ears to the ground to hear the landscape's heavy breathing.*' Even as I read the poems now, while I can put many of them aside as adolescent pastiche, this poem, with its complex half-rhymes and insinuating sibilant sounds, and the double entendre of 'heavy breathing', which catches the nascent sexual blooming that was a dimension of our lives at Apple Pocket, fills me with sad delight. But, now, I wonder who was that 'I' at the centre of these poems.

Memories! Here they come as I wander across our gully garden. I remember an early December weekend. It was one of our first sorties out to Apple Pocket the next summer and with all arms and legs and yelling we threw ourselves into the water. Michael surfacing first was waiting for me when I came up. Catching me around the shoulders he turned me so that my back was to him, he held me against his body. This was not a playful scuffle. It took place as if in slow motion as his hand slid across my belly and settled at my cock, holding me, just for a moment. Then he pushed me away watching me closely: *Gotcha!* When I got out of the water still excited, he dried me, brushed my cock again, watching. What did he want?

This'd make a good painting: me, wrapping you up in a towel: Lovers.

I tried to think of the composition, but my head was elsewhere. Did he mean it I wondered.

You'd have to do it though ... the painting. But he was so composed: *I'll drop art next year; you can't get high marks for it unless you're Picasso!* He'd brought me back to ground and then was off on another tangent. Had he forgotten about what had just happened? My pulse was racing and he was talking about going to Cambridge: *If my Father loosens the purse strings.*

I kept on with art, finding it a useful counterpoint to my music and literary studies, lead these where they might. Michael wanted to be more instrumental in that kind of shaping. *Don't know why you muck about with that stuff. They won't help you make a fortune! Bloody useless, like poetry.* One of the first art works I did that year however, was a cubist treatment: *Taking our pleasure at Apple Pocket.* But it was misplaced before I had a chance to include it in my portfolio. Natasha told me it found its way to Michael's house in Sydney!

But, I digress. There was hardly a day up to Christmas that summer when we didn't rush out to the Pocket. Sunbaking, swimming, diving, ducking each other, our hands alive. We had always touched, innocently explored our bodies from when we were little kids, but now there seemed to be a different intensity or was it intention? I was too innocent to know, but was he? He would touch me, lingering on my body, brushing my prick and watching my reaction as it swelled. I was happy to be captured by this adventure and responded, I suppose you could say, romantically to it and in retrospect, quite artlessly. However, Michael was more matter-of-fact as he seemed to be clinically appraising my response ... yet where was he leading me?

And then, abruptly it stopped. *Swimming's getting boring anyway, we ought to find something better to do* he said one afternoon, stifling a yawn as I dried him down, knocking me off balance. *Don't know why we spend so much time out here,* he muttered into the air, leaving me bewildered and disconcerted. Was it even then, a premonition?

Later that year – I guess it was September, because we had an assignment on spring flowers to do – he found one of his grandfather's books in the *Clifton* library on landscape gardening, by Lancelot Brown. *They called him Capability. How about that for a name?* He laughed. *We should map the Myrtle Creek gully between your place and mine and build our own landscape!*

I was excited. In my mind's eye, it soon became the Gully Garden, and I was off chasing books on other landscapers, gathering ideas about what we could do: 'these are true "artists", Michael.'

OK! Michael bellowed. *Let's get cracking. I'll draw up a budget, and a list of plants and shrubs.* Then he paused. *But, er … what do we include? I'll see what old Capability planted.*

'Well, not so fast Michael! That's where we come in! We show our capabilities! We'll make our garden; not his! I don't want to copy him; I want to learn from him.'

So, having steered him away from replicating one of Brown's gardens we agreed that our 'landscape' would include a mix of local native plants and exotics from elsewhere. We also planted a copse of Japanese Maples, to give them time to mature so that we would create great drama in the autumn. As I explained what I had in mind, Michael looked at me strangely as though he was studying me. Was there admiration in his voice? *You really understand it, don't you Charlie. I look at it in a book and I want to reproduce what I see, but you're creating your own view – they often called it a 'view', you know – but, hey. Aargh, you'll go far, lad,* he joked, sounding like Brother Tibbet from school as he lay his arm across my shoulders.

I wondered if a shift in the dynamic was occurring. But he didn't let me get ahead of myself, it was his show. *I'll do the research, you measure and map the gully.* We began making plans to *advance the project* – his word – in the next term break.

Looking down the gully now as I can from where I am sitting, I smile, for although it took almost twenty years to come to fruition and then with Ben as my collaborator, the garden lays before me, serene and beautiful and ever-changing, certainly a long way from 'Old Capability'!

As the memorable summer of 1967 was brought to a close, it didn't seem enough for Michael. *I'm going to keep an eye on you*, he told me. *I've got Bra's old bird-watching binoculars. I can see right into your bedroom, you know ... better be careful what you do*, he'd sniggered, pausing and licking his lips. *You have no secrets from me!* Was this a warning or a tease?

It wasn't unusual now for him to stand in his bedroom window so that I could see him from *Glen Cannich*, sometimes he would be naked. It meant of course that I checked to see if he was there; wanting him to be! On one particular night he told me to watch for him in the window and come over. I remember the night well. The wind was up, bending the trees, opening and shutting anything loose and the sheds were rattling. I was on edge: keen, alert. At last, the bedroom light came on, it was about ten o'clock but it was Claire who appeared in the window. Disappointed, I spent a restless night. When I asked Michael about it at school the next day, he said he'd forgotten.

You must have imagined it. He scoffed, dismissing the subject. *Pretty bloody stupid anyway: Childish.* I was surprised by the reaction; had he been caught out?

* * *

By the time we were sixteen I was still fresh-faced with only the hint of facial hair, my voice having just broken. I was in the midst of a growth spurt that took me, all bones and sharp edges, up to Michael's height. He was striking and was growing comfortably into his superb frame. With the hint of a beard line and a tanned body, I thought he looked like a young god. But he seemed to accept it as a given. Always good at sports, he'd been selected to train with the school First XV, making his debut in the opening game and expressing himself superbly on the wing. Even at this early stage, his school coach Brother Liam and Father Patrick, a former Irish international from St Michael's, were grooming him to play lock, as long as he continued to fill out. He was sure he would: 'Made for Union, Claire.' Father Patrick had offered.

My development was taking a different turn. Games didn't really interest me. I could run and jump like any ordinary kid and played a bit of hockey on Saturday mornings but I was only making up the numbers. However, about this time, Mum had joined the World Record Club and along with Dad, we were listening to some fantastic music – how I remember the set of Beethoven *Concerti* – and I was really enjoying the piano; I'd even played in a couple of the school concerts. Having taught me at home, where I'd been clunking around on Grandpa's old upright piano since I could reach the keys, Mum thought I was ready for 'a proper teacher.' We'd had lots of fun at the keyboard, but she'd taken me as far as she could: 'Now, you know I advertised for someone. Well, we might be in luck. Her name is Miss Susannah Beaumont. She's young, has wonderful qualifications and seems serious about coming. I've invited her for dinner tonight and with Bran's help we've got a place for her in the *Punt House* down by the bridge; you know, looks like a wilderness in the front garden? What do you think?'

Miss Beaumont who didn't stand on any ceremony was soon 'Susannah', and although her pupils were mostly learning the piano, her instrument of choice was the cello. She played the piano beautifully I thought and could easily turn her hand to the violin, but I loved to hear her on the cello. I would arrive early for my lesson and sit on the worn wooden bench on her verandah, listening to her practice. Some days she brought tears to my eyes; the music was so exquisite, but when she discovered that it was my habit to wait outside, she insisted I come straight in while she finished. It wasn't long before I added the cello to my piano studies. *But you haven't got a cello, Charlie; how do you get on?* Michael asked.

'I play one of hers; I'm at it all the time. She lets me take it home, but Mum and Dad are saving up.'

I liked Susannah Beaumont from the start; liked the way she didn't get dressed up for classes, wore jeans and T-shirts and jumpers and flat shoes and let me call her by her first name. I liked that she was only in her early twenties and that she wore cute glasses with round frames before John Lennon made them fashionable again and loved the way they sat on the end of her nose when she played. I don't think she was particularly beautiful, different, perhaps describes her best. She was slim, not skinny: lissom, with dark blonde hair cut short like a boy's, rarely bothering with make-up, her face which showed its moods and her beautiful fingers made her cello sing; I loved to feel them on mine when she was correcting my grip on the bow or on the finger board. She was wonderful and in my world. Although I was not a possessive kid, I felt as though I didn't have to share her with anyone. To be honest I liked the way Michael dismissed her: *She can't be much good if she's here.* On my inner palette, I painted her in shades of blue for the clarity and purity of her intellect and I could never separate her from the complex beauty of the Bach *Cello Suites.* When I told her later of how I saw her in the abstract through colour and music, she laughed: 'Oh, Charles, at that time I was pretty damaged. Not Bach, something violently wrecked: Goreçki, the sacking of Poland, shades of purple!'

I didn't know much about her, but what teenager inquires about those kinds of things? I heard she'd come here after studying in Europe and that she was from a prestigious Melbourne musical family. Mum said she was here to see if she could make her way as a composer. 'Fancy that, perhaps she'll put us on the musical map. God knows we're hardly on the road map!'

Apart from the time I spent with Michael, my music lessons were among the most anticipated hours of the week. At night, before falling asleep, I'd lie in bed and rehearse the conversation I would have with Susannah at my next lesson. Slowly, she wasn't one to wear her heart on her sleeve, and as she became more confident of my interest (was I authentic?), a kind of friendship began to develop and she would suggest pieces for two cellos that we could play together. Starting with simple scores that she had transcribed, she gradually increased the difficulty: 'walk before you can run Charles, even if you are in a hurry. And that's alright too!'

We often talked about poetry. When she asked if Michael shared my interest I said I found it strange because although he did, he saw it as something to imitate, to take over as if it was his own. 'You know, the more I try to write music or make anything, the more I understand the difference between what's given, what comes from a level beyond thought and what's made, which has to do with craft and the labour of thought. Does that make sense?' Susannah was nodding: intent.

'I don't want to remake other peoples' poems, music, art; I want to "live" through my own. I know I can't force a line or an idea, I need to be still and open up myself: trance-like.' We smiled at each other. 'Now that is far too risky for Michael, he wants to dominate the pen; finds it safer perhaps to steal someone else's idea.' I had in mind a pastiche he'd done of *Under Milkwood* but didn't go there. 'It's the same with silence. I'm not afraid of it, but I think he is. When I listen to you playing the Bach *Adagio*, it seems as though the silence at the end of a phrase is filled with what has gone before, making it vibrantly alive in the moment; the space between the notes seems to open up and we have that breathtaking sense that the next note may never arrive. We can enter this silence without any fear and if we're lucky, it will echo in the mind for what seems an eternity. Michael would close it off.'

'Oh, those echoes in silence, what a beautiful idea. Who is teaching whom,' she murmured!

* * *

The plans for the gully garden lay untouched in the *Clifton* library. I stole a glance at them occasionally, but I was absorbed by my music, and Michael was the talk of the school in rugby. He was even invited to the State Schoolboys' trials, which were held at *Riverview*. Mr Doogue invited me to join them, thought it might help calm Michael down, but he didn't need it and, although one of the younger boys in the trial, he made the team.

There's guys from all the great schools in the team, he told me. Even some from the State Schools, but I didn't see much of them. We had a gas time. There's this great guy, Angus. Boy, is he hot! A Scots fellow, lives in Belleview

Hill. God, he looks like that sculpture of David! He smirked, as he mocked mopping his brow. *We played in front of big crowds, too, and a lot of girls seem to like rugby! There were plenty at the games. Not like down here.*

Although he hinted at what they got up to socially he didn't elaborate, leaving it in salacious hints and innuendo. I didn't know what I could ask him anyway. He was invited to one of the school dances towards the end of the year just before the holiday recess: *one of the chicks I met during the rugby trip, ooh a real doll*, he said, grinning. *Of course, I'll have to stay overnight at her place.* He made me feel like a yokel. Or was I being too sensitive? It turned out that there was an element of fabrication about the whole thing. He did go to the *Ascham* dance with a girl he called Madeleine, but I found out much later he stayed over with another new friend, Jeremy, and Angus didn't exist!

Social life? What did I have that amounted to one? I went to the school dance and of course I took Ally, she was really my best girl friend, but Michael thought I must have been off my rocker! *What did your folks say?* They thought she looked lovely; Mum and her Mum got together and made her a beautiful cream dress. I knew what he was getting at, but she was my friend. I didn't think about her physically the way I did about him, but I liked her. As for Michael, he didn't come to the dance: told me he couldn't bring his chick to our *hick show*!

Any concerns I had that Michael had gone cold on me however, were swept away once we went back to Apple Pocket after Christmas. A full year had passed since we'd relaxed like this, as we spent blissful day after day at our pool. I would never turn heads like him but I'd put on a few pounds. Stripping off, we lay in the sun letting it play on our bodies, then collapsed into the water. And as he'd done before, drying me off or romping in the pool, Michael would run his hands over me watching my reaction as I trembled involuntarily. Watching me: watching, watching! Although, as I thought about it later his eyes were cold and his beautiful body was taut. It made for a curious tension because there was nothing accidental or tentative in his attention. A question seemed to hover on his lips. For my part, I gave myself to the advances and afterwards, drew enormous pleasure from reliving them when I masturbated. I remember being exquisitely alert, as though everything was happening to someone else and Michael, running his hands over me, was also excited as he rolled me into the pool. 'Come on, you too!' I called and he did, feeling for me; I was excited by his naked body. Poignantly and then quite pointedly, I began to think about my 'difference'. How I hated the word, for my reactions felt so natural. Yet instead of making me feel more vulnerable – God knows, I'd felt that often enough – by naming it, I gained a kind of strength and could look the teasers and taunters in the eye, could tell them in their own language to 'piss off and find somebody worth picking on.' Fortunately, Michael was never around to back me up, I couldn't have tolerated that as I told Mum later; or if he was, he chose to ignore it. When I was with him though, I felt my blood warm and I was vividly alive.

Reflecting on our relationship at that time, I suspect Michael thought he was exerting his control over me, indulging himself perhaps, but I knew in an inchoate way the opposite was happening. It was as though he found it difficult not to touch me, was drawn to me almost against his will. Was the nature of the relationship changing I wondered and as reluctant as I was to use the word 'love', because I knew nothing of sexual love, I began to feel that my feelings for him were being reciprocated, that he was getting genuine pleasure from our contact. At other times however, his altered reaction and my openness about my emotions seemed to throw him off balance. He was so accustomed to being in control of himself and of any situation in which he found himself that I wondered if these potentially unbidden impulses unsettled him. Was he afraid of them. Were they foreign to him? Or were they, like mine: natural, spontaneous, genuine feelings? It was impossible to know; he never spoke of them. I adored him and made no secret of it, but I wasn't sure what he wanted. At times, in my most abject moments, when he was cool and distant, I wondered if he wasn't simply trying to get things back into equilibrium.

It was tacitly understood that we would avoid each other at school; he put on quite an act and imposed an aggressive distance between us as he spun off to all and sundry at school some of his rugby escapades, usually embellished with tales of Madeleine. And yet, as soon as we were away from school he seemed anxious – not a word I often associated with Michael – to see me and would come over when he knew I was at home and we'd steal whatever we could out of our busy schedules; but to what end I now wonder? And as soon as school broke up with the summer holidays stretching out before us, a respite before the next big year at school, we picked up the threads. Racing to Apple Pocket that first morning, tossing our towels onto the rock, Michael was yelling, *Okay, get yer gear off.*

Watching him strip down, I couldn't resist running my hand over his flank, firm but still relatively free of hair, intentionally sliding it higher, brushing his prick as he lay back. He was talking about something but almost involuntarily his face bloomed red and he avoided my eye as I gazed at him. When we were both stretched out, I turned towards him, ran my hand across his chest to his far shoulder, rolling him gently to me and kissed him. Michael looked startled, he arched his back, resistant, then pulled away from me. I smiled at him; the silence was deafening, intense, broken only by the lisp of a breeze rocking the myrtles and rippling the pool. Then he yawned: *I must go, things to do.* His rejection was like a physical blow.

'Stay a while longer.' It was neither a plea nor a command. I touched his arm: 'It's ... it's okay to show how we feel.' But he grew more agitated: *It's our secret, Charlie; don't for Christ's sake tell anyone. You mustn't.* In an instant, I was in despair; felt abandoned; was cast back to the confusion and doubts I'd anguished over before the summer break. My pastoral canvas was splashed with the ugliest vermilion! 'Who would I tell. Go on, then ... get going.' I wanted him to go. Was screaming inwardly: 'Fuck off! Go on, piss off!' But ... mumbled: 'don't worry, hey! ... See you here tomorrow?'

Later in life I wondered if he had been engaging in a careless grooming, an indulgent foreplay of which he'd nearly lost control and his reaction, which I was appalled to think was designed to destabilise me in the relationship, was his means of regaining the upper hand. These reflections, sordid and calculating, suggest the boy who I thought of as my lover was toying with me. Whereas, at the time, in my innocence and out of my love, I was worried I'd shocked him; that with neither the experience nor the language to explore it, I'd got it wrong. If his approaches were genuine, then why reject me? At sixteen or seventeen, I knew these were huge, potentially traumatic questions and were not to be trifled with.

I remember going home that afternoon in turmoil. Re-playing the events in my head, I felt completely disoriented. Poor Mum didn't know what was wrong. 'Did you have a fight?'

'Worse than that, but ... I don't want to talk about it.'

He was at the pool the next day. Having arrived early, he'd posed composing himself on his side, resting on his bent arm, naked, he was facing in the direction I would come. *Sorry about yesterday; I wasn't myself. I am today, as you can see.* He smiled, nonchalantly. *All is forgiven.* Forgiven! Was I out of order? But my heart was thumping.

Thereafter, it was a delicious holiday, heady with summer scents and the vibrating echoes of crickets; I was lost in our pleasures. We'd swim and loll at the pool, ducking and diving, dry each other, linger on each other's body, have picnics, sketch in grand plans for the garden or an art collection, make poems and share them. Was I imagining it? I would catch him looking intensely at me, watching my every reaction, as if measuring his own emotional reaction as much as mine. But I was in no mood to let any small anxiety soil the pleasure of what I thought of as that endless summer; yet, I couldn't account for the occasional umbra of despair.

There were to be many occasions over the next few years when I would revisit that summer, interrogating entire conversations and reactions, trying to probe to the truth of them. What was surprising was that, in characterising it as that 'endless summer', I'd lifted the phrase from a Surfie movie doing the rounds at the time. It was second hand, its sense of romance was trite, as if I unconsciously recognised that the relationship was fraudulent.

* * *

When this is over, Charlie, when we've shown the world how clever we are ... He was looking at me, as if eager for my reaction. *Why don't we make a break for it, and go overseas.*

'You mean, together? God, but ... er, I don't know how I could afford it, and ... oh shit, I don't know what Mum will say.'

Well, first things first, you great bag o' bones. Michael's voice was soft, soothing, as he rested his hand on my arm. *Your mother doesn't need to know anything. These are our plans; right!* His grip tightened, momentarily. *It's you and me! I'll pick up the tab for accommodation and that sort of thing. I mean we won't be staying at the Ritz, but we sure as hell won't be camping out either. My father owes me, really owes me and I'll ... anyway, don't you worry about that. I'll fix that stuff. You'd better give me a copy of your birth certificate.* Smiling, at his charming best, Michael laid out his scheme. *It'll be like a Grand Tour; think Shelley and Byron swooning their way around Europe; brush up on your French.*

Who could deny him! My mind was racing. Then, he was off again: *Now, how can you afford it? You'll need a job? What about old Wright's; you know, pumping petrol or working on cars?*

I couldn't help laughing. 'Oh, yeah; see me in the garage! Come on! I can't tell a clutch from a cucumber. No, I'll find something.' I was surprised by the suggestion.

You're right, don't want to spoil those beautiful hands; best left caressing a cello, eh? Or me. He whispered, leaving it unexplored. *Anyway, give it some thought. You might have to give up a few things, but that'd be okay, wouldn't it? It'll be fabulous –* (tossing in that new word floating around) *– it'll be our debut on an international stage!*

I landed a job in the fish shop in Broadwater – good old *Sweet Lips* – from Wednesday to Friday after school, and Saturdays, which meant a complete reorganisation of my week. I lost Saturday, but my bank account grew.

'You never have any free time.' Mum remarked. 'When did you last go

27

over to Michael's after school, or just have some fun? Anyway, what are you going to do with all this loot?'

'I'm saving up. Maybe I can help you out a bit next year.' I wished I hadn't said that. It was cheap, but I didn't like talking about it. Cheating on her took the edge off my excitement.

As the year went on, Michael and I hardly saw each other except for the odd Sunday afternoon, and a kind of pattern developed; with Michael, alluding to the fun we were going to have and encouraging me to imagine myself into various exotic locations, while chatting about his rugby and new Sydney crowd, talking up a world to which I had no access. Yet, even as he prattled on, he would put his arm over my shoulders or hold my eyes with his, leaving me unsettled, but no less eager. While, at school, he turned evasion into an art form.

When the exams were out of the way – not a bad set of papers I thought, despite the distractions and my fatigue, I turned my attention, properly, to the trip. I had only one misgiving: that I'd been sworn to absolute secrecy. *Far out! Don't be a spaz, Charlie, it would wreck it; this will be a gas trip, just for us guys. Don't blow our cover. Your folks'd probably go berserk or they'd bugger it up in in some way. Just be cool!*

'Far out. Spaz. Gas. Guys. Berserk. Cool'! Ever since the Rugby trips, his speech had been sprinkled with this trendy stuff. And he swore more, used it as a kind of weapon and I'd hear about the '*cool city chicks and guys*'. Claire called it his 'Pan-Pacific drift'. It got up her nose as well: 'He hides behind it; uses it as a kind of distraction, I think!'

When school broke up he told me everything was set. We had a couple of swims at the Pocket. *We'll grow up as men together,* he whispered to me one day as he dried me down. On the Monday before we were scheduled to leave he told me he had the tickets and passports: *all we need. And Ben, you know the guy that drives the pick-up truck, will pick us up at the Hump Bridge at 5 am on the dot and drive us down to the Broadwater bus. Don't be late. Wait under the bridge so no-one can see you. Here, leave this note for your Mum and Dad.*

Hi Mum and Dad: I've gone away with Michael. Everything will be fine, so don't try to follow us. I'll be back before you know it and it should be lots of fun. I'm sorry I had to keep it a secret but we agreed that it had to be like that. Don't worry about us; Michael will look after me.

Furtive; I slunk around the place the night before our rendezvous, packed my bag, stowed it under the bed and composed my own note.

Dear Mum and Dad, I love you both and am so lucky to have such wonderful parents. Thank you for loving me and for giving me such a good education and showing me the way.

I don't want you to worry. Michael and I have decided to go overseas for the year, it's all organized; Michael has seen to that. I know you'll be concerned so I will write often I promise. You might be angry with me but we were sworn to secrecy in case our plans were discovered and everyone tried to stop us. We've tried to think of everything and honestly, my only concern is that I will miss you both. But I'll be back, and we can have a good reunion then. Think of all the stories I'll have to tell! I'm not flying the coop forever, just testing my wings, learning to fly and I'm so lucky to be able to do it with Michael.

You loving son, Charlie xoxoxo

I hardly slept that night, left the note on the table, slipped out at 4.40, and hurried across the paddocks to the Hump Bridge. Ben arrived in the old truck at five sharp and tossing my ruck-sack in the back, I leapt into the cabin, 'Michael'll be here any mo.' A minute became five then ten; 'must be having trouble getting away, Bran gets up early, hope he's okay', then fifteen; 'perhaps I should have a look for him? Jeez, I hope he's not in trouble.'

'Gee, Charlie. Mick set it up. Would he muck you around?'

'No, no; I'd trust him with my life. Something's wrong. We've planned it, just him and me, for ages.' After an hour, I couldn't sit still, I had trawled up the road a couple of times and knew Ben had to go. Blinking away tears, I felt like vomiting.

'Jesus, you look like you've seen a bloody ghost, mate. I'll drive you home if you like.'

'No, Ben. No. You've been great. You'd better go. It's too late anyway. Oh God, he must be in the shit with his folks.' I was whispering as I clambered out of the truck, collected my bag and slunk back the way I'd come. 'God, I felt sorry for him,' Ben later told Molly, 'he looked like someone trudging out of an earthquake or a violent explosion. Normally in this sort of situation, you might be cut up for yourself, for the embarrassment of it all, the abandonment. But all Charlie could think only of was Michael; he shook with anxiety for him.'

Mum was in the kitchen when I got back, head in hands, fingering the note, she was crying softly.

'He didn't turn up.' My voice stuck in my throat and I was shaking when she hugged me, sleep still in the smell of her. 'Hush, hush, darling. Oh, you poor thing ... didn't turn up?'

'No; must've got caught at home. Hope he's not in trouble. I'm worried about him, Mum.'

'I'll go over and see, but I've got a funny feeling ...,' she left it unspoken. Now ... go and lie down, you look dreadful. Do you love him so much?' I nodded: abject. 'I won't be long. And ... not a word to Herb.'

I didn't go to sleep. The painful beauty of the massed voices in Saint-Saëns' *Requiem* was rolling through my head until hearing Mum on her way back. I was at the table when she came through the door: 'That friend of yours is in Sydney, getting ready to play rugby.' Her voice was dark with anger.

'What's this all about Mol, what's going on?'

'I'll tell you in a minute Herb.' She took his hand, she wasn't brushing him off. 'For the moment,' her eyes lingering on my face, she drew us both to her: 'I think we've just got to give our beautiful boy all the love we can.'

After talking to Dad, she found me on the verandah. I was gutted. 'He had no intention of turning up dear. The priest drove him up. He might be away for the summer. Don't beat yourself up, Claire told me Father Patrick had been setting up a trial with Randwick since early in the year. Hadn't Michael told you?' She held me to her, cheek to ashen cheek. 'Why was Ben involved, you ask? Well, I can only think he was there as witness of Michael's public rejection of you, was callously telling you that this is the end of your very private affair.'

'But we loved each other, Mum.'

'You love him, my dear. But he wouldn't have treated you like this if he loved you. The only thing I can offer in his defence,' and she hesitated, 'look, I think you're coming to terms with your difference. But he hasn't even begun to face his.' She put her arm around me, 'By rejecting you, it is as if he is lopping off a part of his being that he is uncomfortable with. It's not that easy; it's like trees darling, by cutting off branches the tree is left misshapen. He has a long way to go and I don't think the rugby change rooms will help him work it out! Nor is it easy growing up in a country town. Am I being too … too … intrusive, darling? We don't have to talk about this now if you don't want to, but sometimes it's good to get it out in the open. I've suspected it for years: the way you play, share, care. The selfless love you give… my beautiful boy. Dad and I so love you.'

'I need to talk about it Mum. I've known I wasn't the same as most of the other kids … agh; I hate being called queer like they call me – but I know I'm different. I thought Michael was … you know, finding out about it along with me.'

'It takes guts Charlie. I think you're facing the reality of who you are with greater honesty than our tough rugby player. It's not an easy journey I'll wager, and my darling boy you'll find it a bumpy road, but we'll help you and, as I think you are finding out, you haven't really got any choice anyway! *Vive la différence*! 'But her gentle chuckle stuck in her throat.

'I'd never do to anyone what he's done to me. I feel like rubbish …!'

'Don't lash yourself darling, it's wasted. Look, pop down to the bottom trees will you, see how they're off for water? Save Dad the trouble.'

What was there to say? He had abandoned me. What did I do wrong?

I was obliterated. My mind kept churning through conversation after conversation, kneading away in that strange nightmare netherworld in which, for the next few weeks, I resided, barely able to move.

* * *

As I wandered along the Memorial Garden path, I thought about that earlier walk Mum had sent me on through the orchard. Had to stop, just as I had thirty years ago, under the weight of my sadness, but it was no longer bone-aching and I didn't, as I had at that time, wish to be buried beneath the soil I was rambling over. Time doesn't heal all. With any savage wound, there is always some scar tissue left behind. Today, almost involuntarily, I'm picking away at that old sore. Yet, is it strange; Michael still has a place in my heart. I am who I am, and have few regrets, although at the time I was shattered and couldn't imagine a tomorrow.

When I staggered home from the bottom of the orchard that day, Mum told me she and Claire had been mulling over how they could help. Mum said she felt a bit like the coach of a team, looking after the new boy who is fumbling around making a mess of all the set drills, when, really he's carrying an injury and needs the club physio to try and soften up the bruising; in this case … to your heart and soul.'

'So, who's going to rub me down?' It might be a serviceable joke now, but then it was just grim.

'Well, Claire wondered if Susannah could help. She thought Bran would probably suggest the Church, but we don't think there's much comfort there for a boy like you darling. Patrick could help I'm sure, but, having arranged the trials with Randwick, he's too involved; be like salt in a wound. We thought music might nourish the soul; help lift you out of the abyss.'

Claire put her hand on my arm. 'What do you think?

I don't know what would have happened if they hadn't enlisted Susannah Beaumont.

'What's happened is really shitty Charlie but it gives you a choice. You can curl up and withdraw from life, or you can accept the challenge he's thrown to you, because I think that's how he sees the world, in purely combative terms: you either win or you lose. It's easy to retreat. The alternative is harder … believe me; it requires an act of will to stand up to an emotional battering. Oh, Michael can take the physical stuff, welcomes it, but I don't think he wants to put his emotional self on the line; don't let him seduce you into the same response. But you? You fortunate young man have, literally at your fingertips, the perfect foil. Is there a better one than music? Believe me, I've been there. It invites engagement, enables you to speak in your own voice or express yourself through interpreting others. It can surround you with beauty or in fact any emotion you want, but it's not a shell like I think he has erected over himself, it's a gossamer film that you can pass through whenever you wish. I want to make music with you but … I want your heart and soul in it when we are doing it. Choose life, Charles.' She held my eyes. 'If you give up now, you'll regret it for the rest of your life. But, being a musician Charlie, is a little like being in love, if that analogy isn't too close to the bone; you can't just do a bit of it. So, you tell me. It's not a choice between Michael and me; it's between the darkness and the light.'

The choice was the easy bit and she knew it and would know with every note I played, whether I believed it or not. 'I'll let you know after Christmas whether I want to waste your time.'

'It's not a waste of anyone's time, if you mean it,' she said, as I continued: 'but … at the moment, do you think you could help me get my place back at the Con, I told them I'd be taking a leave of absence for a year? Oh God!' I didn't even know if that was what I wanted to do; but it was something.

'That bloody Michael O'Connell!' She cursed. 'I'd have his guts for garters! Well anyway, you've given me a kind of answer. Let's start with the

Con. It won't be difficult Charles, no more diminutives, you present with an interesting portfolio for a novice, original and technically sound, like your playing; so I don't think it will be difficult resurrecting your place, although like me, they might want some guarantee that you are dinkum.'

Was I dinkum? I didn't have a clue; my head was filled with thoughts of Michael. But I had to do something! And while, like old Dr Eddington oiling the water for fish, Sue was putting out a lure to see if I would bite, I felt disembodied, as though I was looking at myself in the third person watching to see how I would respond.

I was playing muck and Sue let me. All she did was give me heaps of music to play and we worked on technique, bowing, passive fingering in the bow hand, loose fingering on the cello; practiced through the range of strokes directed at reducing the tension in my hands and shoulders. Relaxing me, shit! I'm wound as tight as a spring, and Sue's talking about loose hands! But, I tried.

* * *

Honestly, I have few recollections of that summer. I heard that Michael came down to collect his belongings. 'Took just about everything that wasn't nailed down, Mol', Claire had said, but she was distraught. I felt for her: a mother and her child. No less than me, he was all she could think of, constantly churning over their relationship. Mum thought Claire loved him too much: 'showed your hand love, like Charlie.' It was tearing her apart, she could find no solace.

'Oh, Mol, I'm neglecting Bran, the Girls at the CWA and the *Stud* books. Can't recall ever dropping my bundle like this. You know, even during the war when B was going through hell in New Guinea, or when we were losing our babies, it wasn't as bad as this. I knew we'd get by because we cared so much for each other; in Michael's case though, there's an air of futility about it, he absorbs our love, all of us, but gives nothing back. One day', her smile was bitter: 'he'll have to wring out that sponge; it won't be a pretty sight.'

'He didn't even leave a note,' Claire confided to Mum and me. 'He's seen Father Patrick off. I had a letter from him. What with the awful rumour and innuendo floating around about him and Michael, he's going back to Ireland. The dreadful Marj Nelson is orgasmic, serving the story over the counter at the News agency! He's a beautiful man, Patrick; he was trying to help the boy. Pah! Makes my blood boil! Even Bran can't get rid of him quickly enough, thinks he shouldn't have been involved, blames him for everything that's happened and like some of the other fellows around here, insinuates all sorts of filthy rubbish about him. Oh, in Bran's case, I'm sure it's a part of alleviating his own pain. But that's no excuse. I've no sympathy for him on this one. Thank God we don't disagree on much. You could cut the air with a knife at home at the moment. How's Herb?'

'Well, how's Herb? He's a Mason, if defrocked,' she laughed; 'he's never had a good word to say for Paddy, of course. But honestly Claire, he's so ill it exhausts him even to get involved.'

***

I went through my undergraduate studies in a kind of fog. It was as though I'd lost my mind. Week after silent week when I started at the Con I'd creep out of my room in Surry Hills only to attend classes. The rest of the time, hardly eating, I moldered away in my melancholy, rewinding it all. Hands caressing my shoulders and back, slipping into my bony blades. More! Tracing the nodules of my spine, running over them. Lower! As though my body is worth touching! My flesh sings. Don't stop. Turning me gently. My lips brushing his shoulder. Bodies close. I would fit my body into his if I could; open him to take me in. But … his eyes? Black pools. Watching me but no glimmer there to affirm what his hands are offering. What does he want of me? I seek his lips, but he evades me. 'No! Our secret. No!'

Over and over. This re-creation. I live it. My hands sliding over his hips. Brush the prickling hairs; his prick, rising to greet me. His eyes watching,

watching. A thin smile cuts his face in two. I look for his response, hardly a flicker enlivens his face. Turning again from my hand as I trace his cheek, his lips – searching for him? – feel his beard stubble; even as young as we are, his jowl darkening. Intimate, find my way to his neck. His adorable body. Where do I turn? Slides too easily into Spurn. Spurned. Overturned. The jumble of thought. Sloughed off. Skin. His skin. I can still feel his skin; would wear it. But his black eyes, blank as if he didn't recognize me. Aren't they curious? That mirthless smile, but he touches me; isn't he seeking a reaction? Which I give, I give, I give: with nothing to hide.

Night after night and into day after aching day, these dreams ... dreams? (am I awake or asleep?) overtake me, curled in my misery. Looking for clues, traces of what it meant: this abandonment. His mind, sharp as a knife: the exhilaration in the thrust and parry of our conversation, as intimate as sex, his beautiful body, voice, hair, thick and as black as coal. There is no play in this re-play, nothing creative in this re-creation.

Memory, like a barricade, stops sleep. My mind working its way in and out, over and under, burrowing deeper, searching for the centre: but nothing. There is no centre! Screaming! I find nothing and start again: revolving, resolving ... nothing. Get out! Cannot presume tomorrow's dawn. I can see no first light. Those 'mountain hopes ... eternal schemes' spun from ambition and desire, 'expire.' Get out! With your fucking night thoughts. I am there. Searching for his heart's desire, I find nothing, emptiness, absence. Did he not mean it? Did I love him too much or not enough, expose myself too fully? I hid nothing, went to him naked in my innocence and love of him, why not? I flowered, blossomed with him.

* * *

Had I over-reached? When I applied to the Con I wanted to see if I could make it as a solo performer. But by the time I got there, I'm only talking three months mind you: all that bravura and confidence had foundered. The budding virtuoso cellist who they thought they had on their hands, as tutor after tutor remarked; was now noted only for his passionless application. What they didn't know was that in my disorientation and grief, there were times when I didn't have a note in me. Me, yet not me. It was as though I was looking at a photographic negative.

I had become timid. Some scoffed that at the time there was such an excess of melancholy, scoffed that I let myself become so overwrought, my emotional reaction over-blown, when in the context of things, all I had suffered was little more than a minor car crash in the road of life. But from my position now, I am sympathetic. Think on it: I was devastated, I wondered if my judgment had been so wrong in this matter, why should my other dreams and aspirations have any foundation? Overwrought? Melodramatic? Yes, all of that, but I had adored Michael O'Connell with the absolute intensity and passion of first love. As I look back on that critical, disjointed moment, I felt as though I'd lost my mind, my voice. Abandoned … I was without hope and left no mark behind me.

And yet I didn't lose contact with Susannah while I was at the Con. I sought her out during each long vacation and the many weekends when I escaped from Sydney. I'd wander over to her cottage to talk, listen to what she was working on and play duets. The tone of these meetings was set during the first vacation. She suggested we walk to the top of the hill behind our house. Ironically, that's where I've built my house. Talking as we climbed the rocky path, we found a spot on a flat rock and Sue produced a thermos of coffee, two mugs, and some Anzacs biscuits and started to talk to me about the language of music. This wasn't the professor casting down her pearls from on high, she was sharing her musical problems and giving music a locus as she set me simple compositional tasks; it might be to respond to an aspect of the landscape, or a piece of poetry, or both. One afternoon as the sun was setting, she recited a piece of Rosemary Dobson; 'lives just up the way, you know.' Listen to this, and look:

> … *the day slowly drains away*
> *Or strides from hill to hill and strikes*
> *A match against the friendly stars.*

She was helping me to see, really see, the shifting colours of the sky, valley, and mountains; we'd touch and feel the texture of leaves, bark, and rocks, renewing what might be called an intimate, tactile knowledge of place. I was being taken beyond silence as she put it; not to hide behind it, but to enter into it. She was inviting me to listen for the whispering patterns of the wind, the rustle and whisper of leaves. There was no reference to my unhappiness, depression, or even my progress at the Con; she was taking me back to music at the fundamental level of sound. Why was my mood now so different from how I felt in Sydney?

* * *

It was different at the Con however, and by the time I'd finished and I say it ruefully, they were done with me. 'The degree will be useful if you go teaching.' But Honours was out of the question. I came home, wearing my loneliness like a coat.

For some in the village it was taken for granted I'd be back to take over the orchard.

'You watch, he'll be back! Good Lord, it's been in the family since old George Greenwood cleared the land in the twenties. He's the only son: a musician? Get away! Bloke's got a get a real job sometime.' For them, the choice was predetermined by a kind of rural logic, I was simply playing out the inevitable; but in fact I came back because I had no choice. As far as I was concerned I was so emptied out over the love of him, the loss of him, that phase of my life was over. The cupboard was bare: not even a bone for this poor dog!

Ironically, this was one of the great periods to be alive in Sydney, as the social and sexual revolution of the sixties flowed into the country and the Emerald City gobbled it up, as Jay used to say; but I found no place in it and the more these liberating crackers were exploding around me the further I retreated. Oh, I had a couple of friends who bothered, Cass Bingham and Ruth Levy were great mates: 'We love you Charlie, you're the sweetest guy, you're one of us! But you're so bloody straight,' these outrageously gay girls laughed. And through them I met Jamie – Jay – Luscombe and although we were not lovers: 'dreadful waste, Charlie!' – we were friends and he gave me a vicarious glimpse into the gay scene which he was sampling with flair and gusto! That was not my scene. I was not nor have ever been: promiscuous. I didn't look for one-night stands or hang out to be picked up. With Jay it was as though I was looking through a one-way mirror: I saw what was going on but I was separated from it. I was drifting in and out of depression.

Dr Eddington prescribed anti-depressants; that is, he didn't really engage with my problem. God, I took myself off the tablets before I slashed my wrists. I was shaking with nervous anxiety by lunch time when I was on them. At moments like this, the distortions, the exaggerations took over reason. I felt like a castaway. I wasn't of course, there was love all around me. Mum and Dad, as ill as he was, were there for me unequivocally, and others: Claire was marvellous, and Ethel Williams and Ally, even Ben, dropping by now and then and old May Diller, in her funny abrupt way, lent support; all of which were supplemented with what Sue called our collaborations. Ah, dear Sue, even though I was disappointing her, she still talked about us making music. Make music? At times I felt it was leeched from my soul. Asleep or awake, I am not free of him, of thoughts of him. It's as though he's stolen my music. I stare in terror at the blank score sheet, the empty canvas on my easel. In losing Michael, I am dumb.

Michael, Michael! My only contact with him – we were only a few miles apart when I was in Sydney – was to send him a note after his accident. I knew he'd had two spectacular seasons with University and was being freely talked about in the press as a *Wallaby*. The wider press couldn't get enough of him on and off the field and *Honi Soit's* photographer on campus seemed to love his body. But I took no pleasure from his injury. He may not have been able to understand that. The note opened and resealed, was returned to me at the orchard.

Dear Michael: I was shocked to hear of your accident. Please accept my deepest sympathy.

I could offer various platitudes about your recovery and the future, but I won't even try. You have a tremendous will to succeed and while those who love you as I do, wish you every piece of good luck as you take on the challenge, it will be your determination and application that will carry you through.

Should there be anything that I can do to help as a friend, or in more practical ways, please let me know. I would like to help. Good luck.

In friendship

Claire told me there was a rumour being gleefully circulated by Marj Nelson that Michael was in a bad way after the accident, had become reclusive, had gone back to writing poetry and was using the family money: 'great wads of it, Mol', to put together a collection of Australian landscape art, 'a sort of therapy, I s'pose. Alright if you've got the money!'

Ben, on the other hand, having visited Michael during his rehabilitation had an entirely different take on it. 'Therapy? Work might have been his solution. Of course he was flattened at first, but the turn-around was pretty quick. I saw it! Didn't see too much art on his walls, and one bit was pretty strange, I can tell you, and he seemed to have little patience for poetry: *Poetry? What bloody use is that?* he'd bellowed at one point as he told me of the hours he was spending in the gym, when not *sorting things out in the firm* and finishing off Honours. 'I don't think you have to worry too much about him. It's an awful business, but he's damned determined. This won't bring him down. He'll show us.'

That last remark captured Claire's attention; it was, she thought, very perceptive and made her look at Ben in a slightly different light.

***

Sue was away for my first summer back on the farm after finishing at the Con, but I received a long letter from her. In a perverse way it gave me a lift, the kind I received from being with her, but in explaining how she felt cut off from her inspiration, from what had become the well-springs of her imagination, this time in Europe, I could empathise with her. She told me several of the male staff were bullying and ridiculing her aspirations, making her feel 'unwanted and inadequate, although,' she wrote: 'I am not incompetent. That's how they want me to feel!' But then she cast off all doubt and equivocation and drawing me in, she began mapping out a way forward: for us both if I wanted it. I was caught up in her enthusiasm and for the first time in more than three years I composed a small etude for two cellos and sent it to her. It consisted of little more than cello exercises in its entirety; however, it was more than that, for it was duets that we most cherished when playing together and I had tried to explore themes that interested us. The simple score took its tonal shifts from the daily sounds of the town, from cars and horns, trucks changing gear as they made the climb out of town, from the wind rustling in her garden. For the first time in what seemed an eternity, the blank score sheet didn't terrify me; once written on, it gave me great satisfaction.

I missed her but that small study, minor as it was, set me thinking more creatively than had been the case for several years. She liked it.

What you've done in this little (but not minor) piece Charles, is tap into what I'm thinking about. You've begun to give your music 'a local habitation' as Mr Wordsworth put it. What makes me so dis-comforted over here, amongst the chandeliers, the gold plate and baroque grandeur of high Europe, is that I feel somewhat discombobulated. It's not my place. I can love its music and play it, but I can't make my own music out of it. You have helped me to see more clearly! Bravo, Bravo, Charles!

Can you imagine how I felt after that? I began to understand that my sadness, breaking down periodically into a grinding grief, could not be blamed solely on the collapse of my relationship, nor on the academic nature of my studies, for I needed that core of knowledge; but, rather, it had also to do with the accidental separation from my place. In Sydney I was cut off from the sources of my inspiration. The music of *my* spheres I thought rather grandly, comes as much from my 'country', as it does from Bach or Handel. I wished Susannah was here, but Mum and Claire were all ears. Almost as I spoke, Claire rushed off, came back with a dog-eared book and began to read:

> *... Therefore am I still*
> *A lover of the meadows and the woods,*
> *And mountains; and of all that we behold*
> *From this green earth; of all the mighty world*
> *Of eye, and ear, – both what they half create,*
> *And what perceive; well pleased to recognise*
> *In nature and the language of the sense,*
> *The anchor of my purest thoughts, the nurse,*
> *The guide, the guardian of my heart, and soul*
> *Of all my moral being.*

'Wordsworth, eh. Yes, it's very beautiful. It's the kind of personal interchange I'm seeking. I think Susannah and I can make together. Oh, I know she's in another league to me, I'll only ever be a minor voice, but at least I have a voice, expressible in my performance and composition and I want to release it. So,' I said, laughing, and sounding like a footballer, 'I'm on the comeback trail!'

When Sue returned from overseas, I thought she seemed different, more relaxed. I was delighted to see her; I trusted her, she was my still point. And we seemed to have broken new ground in our relationship, for my pleasure in seeing her was reciprocated and, in a moment of candour, she confessed, she'd rid herself of a few demons and was ready to get on with her life and our music!

* * *

Dad died in 1975. It was the end of a long illness and, sad as it was – he was so gentle and stoic – no-one begrudged his passing. A friend of the town, we buried him with a minimum of ceremony and fuss in the old cemetery and held the wake, just for a few, at *Clifton*. Michael sent me a stylishly designed book of his verse, *The Partnership of Shadows*.

I looked for a note, there wasn't one, except for a few lines scribbled inside the cover: *Sorry to hear of your father's death. Treasure the music and sing the graffiti of my words. Michael.*

What did he mean? The perfunctory opening is followed by the injunction that my consolation is to be found in his 'words'? I took little comfort from the gift. Was it sent as a genuine condolence or was it, as Claire suggested a sign he'd returned to poetry as an outlet for his own sadness after the accident? But when I looked closely at the collection, there was little new writing and with a couple of notable exceptions many of the poems were derivative and fed directly off his sources. I don't think I was being too harsh. There was a kind of impotence about his language. I couldn't help wondering if it didn't stem from an inner vacancy.

As to atonement, he showed no interest in making contact. I resisted writing to thank him, it seemed so inappropriate, given his seeming diffidence. I've returned to the collection in these recent days since his death, even glanced over it this morning and for all their second-handedness, I appreciate they were trying to evoke a certain time and place in which we both participated; but there is a dis-connect, a slippage, between the images, sentiment, and imaginative world these poems explore and the man for whom the bell now tolls.

I did write to him however, a year later, on the death of his father who, unlike his son, had no desire to be buried in Celtic Ponds nor did we have any wish to do the remembering; but Bran and Claire made the trip up to Sydney to see Michael. He would have received my condolences by then, although he made no mention of it.

Dear Michael: please accept my condolences on your father's passing. If you are anything like me, it will leave a hole in

your life that will take time to fill; if it is ever fully replaced.
Sometimes, however, it can be a release; perhaps it will be that
for you.

You are in my thoughts. Fond regards.

Why I included the second sentence I do not know. To flesh out the note, perhaps? There was little to say. I knew Michael had no regard for his father and that he was not like me!

* * *

Change was happening around me as I adjusted to being back to the Ponds. Bran and Claire were in the big house at *Clifton*, and Ben, having been set up in a gardening business which included care of the large garden at *Clifton*, was in their old place. Bran was managing these arrangements, but Michael's hand was behind it. Claire told mum that they now had complete control of *Wicklow Hills*. O'Connell continued to hold the freehold and drew a 7% dividend, if the season permitted, but the Stud Account which was used for all stud and estate developments was left unchanged. While, true to his word, as a consequence of Edward's death, Bran and Claire each held 15% shares in *O'Connell,* which provided them with significant annual dividends. The other *O'Connell* tenants in the town were also released from the rental obligations imposed by Edward when he took over from Timothy.

'My word,' Molly gasped. 'So thorough. But, oh, I know I sound like an old shrew; there's no place for Charlie among all this largesse?'

'Oh, Mol!' Claire hugged her.

As for myself; I was glad. By then, I was settled at *Glen Cannich* and, if initially, almost everything I touched or thought about was marked by the impress of my former friend, my friendship with Ben was comfortable. And, with his new living arrangements placing us on adjacent properties, but with no need to keep an eye on each other, with our dogs at our feet – my glorious green-eyed Ruby and his Tucker and Bib; Tucks, a sweet-tempered dog with a white splash on his chest – we often shared a sundowner at his place or mine: a few beers or a bottle of wine, sometimes a meal, which one or other of us would cook.

It wasn't unusual for us to listen to music. Ben was untutored, but he liked music and responded to it viscerally and he had an appetite for knowledge. God knows what sort of rubbishing he got at the Rugby Club over his friendship with the resident queer, but it didn't seem to bother him and I didn't ask. There was an authenticity in our relationship such that, if it was a problem, he would have mentioned it. He was playing tremendous football at the time and seemed comfortable in his skill and skin, and in fact, he used to tell me a little about the finer points of the game. From memory this was when he won a couple of trophies.

Really, I was more interested in his gardening and helped out to the extent that *Clifton* was soon a joint project. It was good work. We transformed a rather tired formal garden into a vibrant hybrid country garden that folk would come miles to see and he paid me well.

I'd read somewhere that gardening is the most difficult of arts; difficult because, of course, plants are living things and are subject to all manner of variables: soil, weather, attention or its lack, too much space, not enough, and as such are rather like humans: they can flourish, or fade, respond or resist, but as I got to know myself better, it was this unpredictability, this changeability that I valued. It began to inform my arts practice, for I found that a work: a painting or composition is never finished. I couldn't write nor even imagine a concluding note or paint the last brush stroke. A piece may stop, but it's never finished. It's not the completion of an idea, rather a hint, an intimation. I was seeking a music in search of the sublime. Couldn't a garden be like that? Michael would have said it was *a cop out*. He had to have resolution: a conclusion. But I came to learn there is a great profundity in a garden.

As I told Ben, to some eyes I may fail in my aspiration but that doesn't frighten me and of course, failure is a 'Michael' word; one of those front-brain words. I haven't failed; I simply haven't found what I want yet! *Bah, what bullshit!* I can hear him saying it. I don't even know what failure is any more. In my music and art and everywhere in my gardening, I'm after the inexpressible.

I still laboured on the orchard but with Coles and Woollies screwing down harder and harder terms, Mum and I were battling to keep out of debt. Susannah and I however, were sparking off each other and although my daily work often left me exhausted, she found ways of musically extending and reviving me. We met twice a week for what she called reciprocals: shared music lessons. I joined the Celtic Ponds Music Club which she had started and as the *Highly Strung String Duo*, she and I gave regular recitals in the towns around the region, gaining confidence that we had something to offer and growing an audience. An unforeseen bonus was that we began to meet and socialise as a threesome with Ben. That of course set off derisive jokes about groups of three and gender roles; but we were good for each other. And yet, as I watched the other two getting closer, I felt the absence in my own life of that kind of singular and intense interest in another that made my pulse leap and the hairs on the back of my neck prickle in delighted anticipation.

It wasn't long after this that I received a post card: 'that's out of the blue' Mum said, from Michael: from Rome. Rather than carrying the kind of ephemeral message that one might expect from a friend after an absence, the note was sharp-edged as if, I thought, to hold his mirror up to me.

> *You have retreated from the stage as a gifted musician, with the potential for an international and celebrated career, to become an apple farmer growing chook food and fodder for cows, an untrained landscape painter who does not exhibit, a composer who refuses publication and a soloist who plays in a community band.*

I was annoyed more than hurt, as I felt him trying to have his way with me psychologically; trying to put me into what he thought was my place. At first sight I wondered if the intent of the note was malicious and yet I read it as petty; if it set out to hurt, it carried instead I thought, the voice of the bully, flailing around for a target. What could have generated the note? Was he throwing his success at me, implicit in a card from Rome, tourist's delight and well-spring of Western Civilisation, inviting me to compare it with my own life? Surely, there was more behind it than that! As a reply, I sent him a line from a recent composition, a piece I'd called *The Heart's Ease,* inscribed on a blank card with the note: 'Hope Rome satisfies your every need. As Celtic Ponds does mine.' My point, would it escape Michael, I wondered, was that I was now so physically, emotionally and imaginatively embedded in this place that, rather than a prison, it was a point of creative departure; it gave my *heart ease.*

I later learned that this was when Michael met Natasha. But in a way which I hadn't previously considered, this little exchange forced me to confront what Michael meant to me. It's not that I wanted to forget the affair, but I realised that any emotional hold he had over me was loosening and in what must surely have been an unconscious reaction, I contacted Cass and Ruth and made arrangements to go up to Sydney. 'Well, we're not a unit anymore, but we're mates and love each other; I've got a bloke actually,' Ruth explained, 'gone back to the fold and show my head in Dover Heights, but Cass is the genuine dyke. We'd love to see you; are you okay?' She was gushing, but it was genuine. 'I still see darling Jay, naughty as ever and full of shit,' she laughed. 'I'll see if we can hook up with him as well. He thought your celibacy at Uni was a dreadful waste, very debilitating!' She guffawed, flirting for Jay: 'reckoned it stalls emotional growth.'

I had a tremendous weekend. We laughed and joked, told our stories, even me! 'O'Connell eh, didn't pick him as one of us; your old man says he's a difficult bastard doesn't he Ruth? Hard as nails, and that's something coming from old Sol, but even worse, he's not always good for his word.' We made plans to catch up again.

I wasn't deserting Susannah and Ben, simply opening up other dimensions to my life. Soon, thanks to Jay, I began to make new friends and if he wasn't out on the town we spent the night together. I liked him. We had a bit of shared history, made each other laugh and mutually...how can I speak for him... enjoyed our sex. Although, with what was happening on the wider scene – and Jay brought me regular reports and the juiciest gossip from the front, as he liked to call the Sydney gay scene where AIDS was beginning to take its toll – we always took precautions. 'I want to fuck you, Charlie, but I don't want to fuck you up.'

I still had the occasional depressive incident, but the gaps between them widened and I felt as though I was reclaiming my life. Yet I was rarely without the sense that Michael had his eye on me, even over distance and time. This uncanny sense of Michael's presence was never more apparent than when I returned to our old idea of developing the gully that joined *Wicklow* and *Glen Cannich,* running from the heights above both blocks, through the town on its way to the coast. I spoke to Ethel and Claire and Bran about it; got their approval: approval? Knowing we were serious, Ethel was delighted to give us access to her country, while Claire was ecstatic. She remembered the plans, could lay her hands on them, she thought.

As it happened, she couldn't find the old drawings: 'lost in the move, I guess.' I wanted to start afresh anyway and saw at once how it might work. I remember it well. I was tracing out a zig-zag path running from the side veranda of my place, past the old packing shed that had been our 'theatre', through the orchard to the log bridge which, as kids, Michael and I had built over the bend in the creek. I'd just finished when I heard Ben calling from his verandah: 'What'ya up to?' And over a beer I explained my plan to landscape the gully. 'Want to be in it?'

***

And here I am, rambling through that garden we made; stopping every now and again to take in a vista, check a new bed; fixing and fussing. In my element.

Once we started, there was hardly a Saturday for the next few years Ben and I didn't devote to the project. Oh, I worked the orchard, but that was just to pay the bills. Together with music and art, landscape gardening became what I did, and Ben was a constant source of surprise. His knowledge of plants and shrubs and their growing habits, acquired by experiment, practice, and study over the previous fifteen years, was compendious. We worked so well together. He is an intrepid explorer, searches everywhere for plants to enhance our garden – I imagine him in the eighteenth century, climbing mountains, withstanding all kinds of privation in China or India, perhaps, searching for specimens – and never ceases his explorations. It is such a joy. I love him like the brother I never had.

Unlike the way it had been when Michael and I first began to plan the project, where he assigned the roles as his right, there was now no simple division of responsibilities, we worked collaboratively on all aspects of the garden. Thinking about the site's terrain, mulling over how to balance the planted areas with the open space, rock and water areas, and the natural bush, Ben said he'd been drawn to a book on the design of Japanese Gardens, which might be worth exploring. 'It might solve your problem as well, Charlie. 'I know you don't want a "Hooray Australia" garden!'

'Precisely. We'd better have a gander at the gardens being built at Cowra, then. What do you say?' I replied, while to myself I was admiring Ben's wonderfully open and practical mind. He might have been dragged up by his boot straps but his feet are firmly planted on the ground. Before we took the plan too far however, Claire suggested I talk to Bran.

'Well son,' he said, 'funny you should mention this grand gully scheme because, at our last meeting, Michael indicated he was prepared to put money on the table to bring it about. *My contribution to the town for the Bi-centenary in '88.*' He said.

Speechless at first, my reaction matured into a simmering uncontained anger. 'Have you been telling him what I've been doing?' Looking at the ground, his face said it all. 'I'm sorry Bran, you're a great bloke but this is a bit rich. Please don't talk to him about me. "His Bi-centennial gift!" Our Myrtle Gully project is his to gift? I was shaking with anger. 'Steady on, mate! He's only interested in it if you do it.'

'Steady on; steady fucking on! Only if I do it? Of course. Don't you get it? Don't you see what he's doing, what he does: he's taking over, calling the shots from afar, buying us and the project; everything has a price. His project: we do the work! And he's making sure he ties us down to the Ponds. Now, I don't have plans to leave, but that's beside the point. He's making sure I don't. He's the only one who can play on the big stage.' Later, I wondered if I had over-reacted.

'Why see it in that light, Charlie? Isn't he trying to make it happen?'

'Oh, you're a generous man, Bran. I'm not so sanguine. Let me think about it.'

Bran was pretty sheepish when I called into *Clifton* the next morning. Claire was by his side in the kitchen, but I could tell she was not with him in spirit. 'Got to hand it to him.' I said. 'He's a shrewd bugger. You're not likely to argue with him are you? And nor is Ben! God, for his entire livelihood since, since … oh since he rolled up in the Ponds with his footy boots around his neck, he's been beholden to Michael. Old trick! And now look how you're placed.'

'You're not entirely on your own, Charlie.' Claire's voice was soft, but firm.

'I know Claire, but I'm not going to put you on the spot. Look, I'll tell you what I'm prepared to do, but if Michael asks … should he happen to inquire, I'll only proceed on the condition that no part of the project has his name associated with it; nor will he have any say in its design. I'm not happy. I feel compromised and a little soiled.'

The three of us subsequently made the trip to the Cowra gardens, although, for his own separate reasons Bran joined us under duress: 'Anyone who saw the Japanese in action in New Guinea as I have, can neither forgive them nor have any desire to understand their culture.' His face was strained. 'That's for subsequent generations to do and for them to earn our respect.' Then he stopped. 'But, look, hang on! What am I? I'm the overseer, I dole out the funds. Okay, if you want me to come, I'll tag along. Don't expect me to be the life of the party.'

Ben and I got a lot out of the trip. And, if somewhat incongruously, I think Bran found the place beautiful and serene in a confusing contrast to the horrors impressed upon his memory. While, in accepting the situation, I realised I was giving tacit agreement to a range of other conditions that would have to be met to complete the project; not the least of which was the compressed time-line. Whereas Ben and I had set no deadline; we now had only four years, although I understood that Michael's notion of completion and mine would greatly differ, but I didn't raise that! This was only the start of it. For although Bran passed on our conditions to Michael, it sounds as though he disregarded them. As Bran told me, their next conversation was perfunctory: 'They are on board. This is what you'll do. Excise the *Wicklow* land and the corresponding stretch from the Greenwood's: the tracts that run along the creek. Straight-forward really. See any problems?'

I saw two rather large contingencies, since, in a sweep, the proposed excisions took in both the *Wicklow* Manager's cottage and our farmhouse. And there was the question of Native Title. Yet Bran said Michael seemed somewhat surprised when he raised the matters.

I know about the houses for Christ's sake, Bran. Of course they do; they are on those parcels of land. We'll fix them up. The project can't go ahead if they disagree. And, on that other matter about naming etc, I don't give a fig. Never did! As for the aboriginal question, why open that can of worms? Ignore it! I'll deal with it.

I was speechless. He was calling our bluff and if not having the final say on the detail, was determining the scope of the project, while ironically, enabling us to give it the grandeur which, all along I had wanted but did not have the resources to provide! I had to admit to an absurd but grudging admiration for his nerve and arrogance and damn it, his drive. He took my breath away. I had few illusions left of this man who I had loved so unconditionally: his ego however, intrigued me. He'd thought of most contingencies, just hadn't bothered to discuss them! Not only were the two houses along with the extended creek lands being donated to the people of Celtic Ponds, but the matter was a *fait accompli*. When I protested to Bran about the peremptory nature of these decisions, he could only splutter that the budget allocation for the appropriations was considerable. Houses were to be built for me and Ben, according to our specifications, on land on either side of the upper gully. I had to laugh bitter and bemused. But I sure as hell wouldn't leave Native Title to him to *resolve!*

The ramifications of Michael's decision penetrated deep! But did he care? His rejoinder, as Bran told me when my concerns were raised, suggests not a jot! *Problems? You're the CEO Bran; give you something to do!*

And that was the last we heard of Michael O'Connell's involvement. He didn't visit; didn't even attend the opening. Ben and I went onto the Shire payroll on a generous contract funded out of the *O'Connell* package. Yes, I buckled, I let him buy me! I wasn't happy about it, but it meant the garden was expanded in scope and fully funded and Ben and I would get new houses. As a consequence I virtually put *Glen Cannich* on care and maintenance, giving Sundays over to it. I couldn't afford to employ anyone.

Don't get me wrong, I'm not complaining about the outcome; just how it was arrived at! He'd done me over again, but as I argued myself through the compromise, I turned him into a patron not a puppeteer. My life underwent subtle changes. Having begun to find my feet and develop modest or occasional alternatives to Celtic Ponds,

I was once again fully occupied here. I couldn't help thinking, if he cared, Michael might have thought he'd had another victory.

* * *

With the appropriation of our house into the greater Pioneer project and the associated disruption, mum moved to Broadwater. It had always been planned but now, she was just on sixty-nine, she and her sister, Beryl, whose husband had passed away a couple of years earlier, decided that the time was right. Beryl moved from Adelaide. They bought a duplex and got on with things, which didn't mean that she didn't spend some time in the Ponds – they loved to visit – but they had other lives. And mine took a dramatic shift.

I had Andy's friend, Stefan Holderlin, design me a wood, stone, steel and glass, two-bedroom, open plan cottage among the trees on the upper reaches of our old block. Named *Glen Cannich* after the orchard, it was a simple place, with the front half of the house raised on stilts. I felt as though I was nestling in the trees. My only indulgence was a huge book-lined, music-cum-painting studio. One corner was dominated by a massive sofa and lounge chairs with coloured cushions and rugs thrown across the wooden floor. The back corner of this grand room was the engine room. Containing a small computer desk, a large cedar solicitor's desk and filing cabinets, it abutted the 'Specialist' end of the library, with shelves loaded with books on gardens and gardening, art and music, novels and poetry, dictionaries and compendia of various kinds, and albums of photographs. Elsewhere, there were a couple of easels and a bench of oils, music racks and stands, and there was even a place for the old iron piano, clunky as it was; while my other world was framed by the massive windows across the living room. As if to complement the external landscape, I hung a large triptych of mine: *Dusk to Night: Celtic Ponds; 5 pm; 6 pm; 7 pm* along the back wall. An unfinished abstract landscape symphony in colour, it had its genesis in one of my earliest musical compositions, *Weeping of the Mountain Clouds,* which I'd lost. Every now and again, I take it down to make some minor tonal change to it; always trying to get the light right. It's down at the moment; in exploring some indigos, I'd found an extraordinary shade of deepest lazuli, which I wanted to introduce into the third panel, replacing my previous deep blue, making subtle, barely discernible changes to some of the tonings in the earlier two panels as I went. Some say I'm obsessive.

Jamie became a regular visitor. 'And bring that big-bellied violin with you. I know you think we're country bumpkins but, actually, we have a bit of fun.'

Having him around was good for me. I trusted him and knew he cared for me. We were good together; it wasn't heavy; there was no jealousy or spite, or manipulation; he relaxed, and I was taken out of myself. R & R, he used to call it. Claire liked him; perhaps for the very reason that Bran had a bit of trouble and when she met him, Natasha said he reminded her of Rudi! While Susannah was delighted to have him around. 'A double bass player. Couldn't we turn the *Highly Strung String Duo* into the *More Highly Strung Trio*, when he's down?' Poor old Marj was apoplectic of course, fuming about consorting adults! 'Consenting, love?' Hubby laughed.

Glen Cannich became an alternative creative space for Susannah and me; we were often here, exploring ideas, or just enjoying our eyrie with Ben. After he arrived, Andy Buchanan, the new doctor, would also come up and tinker around on the piano, which reminded him, he said, whimsically, of an old upright he'd had in Edinburgh. Ally, who was open to her culture like her mother, was often here and we started doing some interesting things together as I explored musical pathways through her renderings of this landscape. We'd never lost touch. I got her a position as a guide on the Myrtle Gully project and, in fact, in its meanderings, our garden follows some of her 'tracks'. I'm on one now, as I cut diagonally across the garden and am overtaken by another memory.

* * *

'Can you hang on here, Charlie?' It was Claire. We were standing on my back verandah looking down across the orchard; weeds rustled in the breeze: 'looks like a Sunday morning hangover,' she giggled.

'Just can't give it the time. I try, but it's running me ragged. Hard to let go, though.'

A couple of weeks later, Bran raised the subject again. 'Claire tells me, and I can see with my own beady eyes that you're battling. What would you think if we, *Wicklow*, bought you out? We could do with the land.'

'Jeez; what can I say? My immediate reaction is to fall at your feet and kiss 'em! But, let me talk it over with mum and channel grandpa. Hell, I'm interested. A little piece of Glen *Cannich* in *Wicklow Hills*,' he chortled, open to the irony. 'I like that.'

Mum burst out laughing when I told her of the offer. 'Snap it up, darling! You've never had two bob. You deserve it.'

'What do you mean; it's your money, Mum.'

'What am I going to do with a quarter of a million, Charlie? I've got everything I need. Go and find a clever accountant, sort it out, and enjoy it. I want for nothing.'

For the first time in my life I had money in my pocket. That wasn't all! With the incorporation of the two properties completed, the Dougues said they'd been thinking about a succession plan and offered me a position as the deputy-manager of the *Stud*, on the clear understanding I would succeed them. 'We thought we could work together for a few years and then you take over?'

'I'd started thinking about what I was going to do, Bran. I'm very touched by this offer. ... Jamie would like me to move to Sydney, but to be honest this is my place. Yes, I'd like to see if it could work. But, have you thought it through? You'll have to be my mentor. Would that be a problem?' It wasn't an entirely innocent question.

'We'd like to try it, Charlie.'

'That's not what I asked, Bran. Would YOU like to?'

'Ah, I see! Yes, most definitely I would. Charlie... Charlie...' Bran was groping for words, 'you're like family mate,' he said, putting his arm across my shoulder, 'who, ... oh, shit, I'm making a nice old mess of this: who, I'm not saying I felt sorry for you, but I knew life wasn't a bed of roses. And, I didn't want it for Michael.'

'Not a lot of choice about it, Bran! Although,' his voice was trailing off, flowing a train of thought: '... he seemed to think he had one. Perhaps that was his problem? Anyway, I'll be surprised if it was Patrick who was doing the grooming!' I looked at him. 'My other concern is not unrelated. Sorry to be a stickler, but I need to know the degree of independence I would have if I took over as manager. Where in the scheme is Sir Michael?'

'He owns the land Charlie; that won't change! But I, you, if you agree, make all the decisions relating to its running without consultation with him. You need have no contact with him if that's how you would prefer it.'

'That's how he may want it, given his reluctance to have any contact over the last twenty years. Have you discussed it with him?'

'Of course. He agreed with one condition: Claire and I, if we wish, continue to live at *Clifton*.' Bran was never one to dissemble, but he didn't bother relating the conversation in depth since like many dealings with Michael it was riddled with contradictions and ambiguity. Greeted at first with a steely eye when he put the proposition to him, it went full circle!

It's not your gift to bestow. That'll be mine when the time comes. Although you're an enduring bugger, I'll grant you that, so I think this is a smart stop-gap and since he still hasn't made much of his life, it will give him something useful to do. You'll be paying him.

'I wouldn't have it otherwise.'

Good. Solves my next decision about Charlie, Bran; good thinking. Gets Ben off the hook too. A good servant to the cause over all this time.

Bran never failed to be surprised by Michael. Ben was a 'servant'; Charlie, a 'cause'? But he didn't need to go into that. 'So, it's yours if you want it, and from what I've seen, without pissing unnecessarily in your pocket, you'll be a great fit. And I thought we might make Ernie Piggins permanent to give you a hand; he's a good worker.'

So it was, on my forty-second birthday in September 1995 I took over as the fifth manager of *Wicklow Hills Stud;* and what a party we had in my 'play' room! The Sydney girls all over each other and dressed like they'd got lost in the Opera house costume department, plus Ruth's gorgeous Hymie who, although he was born here, looked as though he'd just got off the plane from Israel, came down with Jay and his entourage of selected lovers and hangers-on from Canberra and Sydney; all known to me. All of my immediate friends and family, including Sue's friend Cynthia, Stef Holderlin, Ally, Karen and Amy and their hubbies and the old families were there to open the first bottle. Mum and Beryl, who were all eyes, came up from the coast, Andrew Buchanan, the new doctor who was just getting to know everyone, fitted in easily and even a few of the old hands from the Rugby Club dropped in.

It was a night of music and hilarity shared by all and sundry alike. Accompanied by Andy on the piano, Susannah sang me a birthday song; the jazz standard: *Someone to Watch over me,* which she changed to *'you',* and in so doing opened up the delicious irony of just who was doing the watching, an irony open only to the most intimate of my friends and even then it was only partially exposed to each of them. I know Claire thought it was an appropriate choice, for while the message that was intended was to speak of the delight Sue and Ben took in watching over me, it opened up other possibilities, some of them more sinister and oblique.

I also received a card from Michael's wife Natasha, who was a thing of wonder and gossip, for only Andrew had met her. They'd been together for seven years now, but Michael had let us find out through the magazines.

> *Dear Charles: We haven't met. I look forward to the day when we can but for the moment, I have to make do with the pen. I know Michael would not want your birthday to pass without sending his best wishes to his childhood friend, and I gladly add my name.*
>
> *I have met none of Michael's old friends, among all of whom, I know you were very special; but I plan to escape one day to Celtic Ponds and meet you all. May I call you 'dear Charles' in anticipation, for you will be my first stop. We might have a drink together. For the time being though, I have to raise my glass in isolation. Happy Birthday.*
>
> *Eagerly, Natasha, and Michael*

How sweet of her I thought, even as I realised Michael may have known nothing of the note. It was to be three years before I met her.

But those few years flew. Bran and I were a good team. I planned our weeks while Bran was more spontaneous, but generally one did what the other couldn't. He cut back a bit but he never retired although his ticker is a bit dodgy. I tried to do the heavy lifting and took the farther paddocks or left them to Ernie while Bran cast his by now extraordinarily astute eye over every last detail of the herd. It wasn't unusual for Claire, waving to us from the verandah of the big house, to greet us as we wandered in almost like father and son, chatting until we'd look up and wave in return. And we'd sit, the three of us, over a bottle of red until those glorious evening tonings of blue I still marvelled at, wondering how to catch in colour and sound, shaded from azure and gently deepened through that fabulous lazuli until there was no colour left and it was night.

Susannah and I continued 'classes' together and *Highly Strung* gave concerts from Canberra to Eden, trying to extend our audiences by the repertoire we chose. I found our explorations in music thrilling, even though Sue had less time for them as she became more widely in demand as a composer. While my own composition, modest as it was, had become inseparable now from my painting and our work on the gardens, and had taken me in another direction to Susannah. Just as she basically wanted to tell stories and explore ideas, my explorations were into pure sound and colour. I'd already made seven versions of the large triptych, as I tried to reproduce that exquisite time of day. And there'll be many more! Am I just a little too intense? Is that what frightened him off?

Claire and Bran:
Dancing with the Lady in Red

I was in the kitchen, lifting a tray of scones out of the oven, when Bran wandered in. He smiled. 'Ah! Just what I need.' He had never complained about his tucker! 'Sometimes I think it's my cooking that's kept you around you old lump. Good in the kitchen? Well I'm a country woman love, that's one of the things I do!'

'Oh, it's more than that; there's these wonderful melons as well!' He was smiling as put his huge stockman's hands around her from behind: 'Never tire of them.' A wry smile creasing his face: 'Got half-an-hour?'

'Who are you kidding; couldn't stir the dough with that old thing.' I snuggled into his hands and wriggled my bum against his prick: 'Hmm, I think you're dreaming! By the feel of it, the heart's willing but the flesh is weak! There's the door. Out! Before we try the nigh-on impossible;' I'd never stopped loving him. And here we are, the greatly loved seniors of our village.

They'd arrived as young newlyweds, in 1946. He, straight from a terrible war:

> *Rotting corpses strewn everywhere; do you ever get over the frozen stare of the dead, the awful mutilations of a body and the ghastly sweet-smelling stench of death that fills your nostrils? Buna! Human flesh in the enemy's pannikins. I'm in shock at what I've witnessed, and it makes me think: too much! There is no purification in war. What a whale of a time the maggots are having!!*

I was a school teacher from Bathurst and was in his war from the moment we met. Hardly a day went by now that I didn't buy a paper on the way to school, it was as though I'd entered the adult world. Was Mr Forde the right man for the army, and what about Mr Curtin? He's a wonderful speaker on the radio, but can a pacifist look after our boys? Headlines and lead articles seemed to be addressed directly to me and I got angry when I saw young men kicking balls around a park: 'Why aren't they doing their bit,' unconsciously slipping into the language of propaganda. But I wasn't a maudlin woman; I got on with things, always have. At times however, I knew he was being taken to the edge of existence.

> *Secured 150 yards. What a day! It's scorched into my brain. How do I describe it? My simple education hasn't given me the language to do it justice; someone will one day. With Wootten's words – 'There'll be no turning back tomorrow!' – ringing in our ears and our reputation going before us, we knew by now we were a good fighting unit as we went forward into a world that was exploding around us under the unrelenting Jap fire.*

Oh God; life at the extremities! How do I comfort a shocked soul?

We'd met at a CWA dance. I was on the desk when, on leave after Tobruk – muscular, tall, decked out in his uniform, sky-blue eyes and with a mop of blonde hair just contained – he filled the doorway, seeking shyly to come in.

As for him, he'd always remembered her as a figure in red, with glorious amber eyes. He grew up in the Depression, doing odd jobs for a few shillings a time from when he was a nipper; doing his bit, but his childhood became a casualty of their circumstance. Even his name got muddled; he should have been Brian of course, but Reg got flustered when he registered him! He loved school, but the family didn't have two bob and when he was fourteen, his dad's old army major gave him a job as a rouseabout on *Wembley Downs*, in western New South Wales. Tremendous property, stretching as far as the eye could see; he liked it and felt pretty lucky to have a job. 'Least I could do for your old man lad; he was a good soldier,' Major Carmody had said. 'He just got knocked around a bit. You make a go of this and who knows …' It meant he could send a few quid home to his mother and by the time he enlisted he was doing a lot of stock work. 'There's a place for you here when you get back, son.'

I was a bit luckier; old money, although I always laughed that the way my darling Grandmother, the wonderful Elspeth Carrington, was going it wouldn't last forever! Always comfortably off: a Sebag, Elspeth had lived a life of genial indulgence. Whereas my father's promising career as a banker was ambushed by the Great War; and when he got back he found those who hadn't gone had leap-frogged over him and he was left with minor managerial roles which saw them carted all over country New South Wales. It was two years here, three years there, until broken by the Depression and surrounded by the futility of it all, he dropped dead of a massive heart attack at forty-five, having just taken over the Parkes branch. I was sixteen, and while I finished boarding school and went to Teacher's College Mum, born to another life, gave in and moved in with Elspeth in Bowral and never left.

Bran was shy, awkward and socially apprehensive. He'd never really had any playmates; kicked footies with other kids, or gone skidding around on bikes. Off to deliver papers as soon as school finished, there wasn't time for that. Meeting Claire ushered him into the unknown and not without thought, nor hesitation, he accepted the invitation to enter her world. It was almost heroic! 'You've got such grace and confidence,' he said. I think he meant I had Elspeth's panache; nothing seemed to daunt her.

I'd had boyfriends and had a few crushes, but I'd never been in love before and I embraced it, but like him, not thoughtlessly. I knew he was a decent man from the moment I met him and would never let me down. Besides, the very thought of him made my nipples offer a welcome!

* * *

Our love grew through the war, finding each other through letters until, rushed as it was, we were married on 21 June 1943; a brief respite before he was back to New Guinea and our epistolary existence continued. Our initial letters overlapped.

Bran, darling heart

Is it possible to miss you from the second you left? To long to touch you and feel the warmth of your body pleasuring mine and to check our hearts in unison? I did, and do; how can I tell you, however, in contradiction to this aching sadness, how happy I am in my soul. To have found my mate. I hope one of the first things you do when you arrive is read of my love. I realise there won't be much time for these indulgences – is our love an indulgence? I don't think so! But you know what I mean – once you are organised but I just hope, and it's the simplest of wishes, that you can linger over this page. I love you, 'B'; can I say, my Big B?

Your father was wonderful after you left; so careful that I was alright. (One of your words, you see, how embedded you are, even in my language.) He walked between us, Maude and me, and took our arms, and chatted about this and that around us at the dock. Maude was kind as well but, like me, she was quiet, searching her soul perhaps, although I saw no obvious balm from her feverish ticking of her rosary. Still, who am I to say. They both love you very much, and are very proud of you. We spoke [a long section obliterated]

… [news of?] … Edith Lyons and … Tangney who were elected and are the first women in the Federal Parliament. That's an achievement for women. They say that Mrs Lyons has always [section lost, apart from a few words: poli[tics], husband, put the case …, there was then some discussion of the Election, with John Curtin, Menzies, and 'poor old Fadden' appearing in an extended discussion.] The size of Mr Curtin's [victory?] surprised [everyone?], not least my Mo[ther] who thinks Mr Menzies is without fa[ult], and not a good word [about] Arthur Fadden?

I will see Beth [section lost] very sweet and is intrigued by our love affair and marriage, while young Don floats around in his own world [section lost] creepy crawlies which makes me think of some of your tales of ... the jungle; [lost.] I write 'jungle', and it sets me off; take care my darling boy. We have the world in front [of us]. [The rest of the letter is lost.]

As for Bran, it was as though he was simply writing to name me.

Dearest Claire

Oh, to think of you as my Wife; I can't quite believe it! We've settled in and are not being called on. Camp is ship-shape after we scrubbed it up, and, apart from the usual military things, we are busy with chess, chinese checkers, bridge, I've even been in a debate, and joined the choir; evidently I have a passable baritone; perhaps I will be able to sing to you when I get home, or lull our babies to sleep? I am enjoying the choir; there are forty of us doing harmonies in which I manage to keep up most of the time.

You vote tomorrow; good luck. I hope everyone does what's best for Australia and throws out those UAP loafers. At least Mr 'Ming' won't be there. I'm not surprised he was seduced by the Poms!

All my love, darling, your husband, Bran.

Having had it offered to him twice before, he eventually took a corporal's stripe. He now had 8 men under his charge, four of whom were new to battle and two were in a bad way: Clarrie, a window dresser from Brisbane couldn't stop shaking, while Joe, a fisherman was pissing himself. 'You wouldn't be normal, boys, unless you're shit-scared. I'll tell you how I feel. At first, it's very bloody scary, no less than you're feeling I reckon; so ... it's common and it's alright. None of us'll have any trouble having a piss before we go. Speaking for myself, when I'm in the thick of it, all that fear is temporarily buried, I become extremely alert, as though I'm out of my body; I can't account for it. You both are and are not your usual self, and if your training has been good: you'll just act and re-act. Others have told me they have no idea what they are doing. I know what I'm doing, but it's as if someone else is *doing* it. When it's all over, be careful, there can be a horrible let-down; perhaps you smile that you didn't cop one, but for me: I'm exhausted, drained, emptied. I don't like it. Now when we go forward tomorrow, I want you, Joe and Clarrie, so close behind me, I can feel you breathing. Is that clear? Fred, you and your scaly mates: 'Tosser' and Roldy, also right behind me. I'll lead us into the action; should anything happen to me Ray, you've been around as long as me, you take over. Good luck, and … stay together. For the moment, go and stretch your legs; they're goin' to be between you and death tomorrow.'

This was a Bran that few knew. There was never any question about his nerve or competence in the ranks, but now he was talking with such authority and showing leadership.

> *Had my wounds dressed.* [He had taken a shrapnel wound in the shoulder.] *They were clean and did not cause much inconvenience. Under cover of a mortar bombardment, I had my small group. 'Don't leave my side, lads' – infiltrate their position – and, on the signal, bayonets fixed and covered by a hand grenade barrage, we were upon the enemy in a mad melee of noise, flailing bodies and the dead and wounded. It was ghastly; a crude and callous mission.*

And so it went on, as he struggled to find a language to describe what was happening; he knew in his blood, day after day, that he was on that hairline between life and death.

> *Night of 20th, awful; couldn't dig pits, had to be on the alert. Sleep? Forty winks at best. Had a hot meal, though; bloody brilliant; cooks outdoing themselves; brought up to us from*

Cape Endaiadaire (sounds like 'Endoftheworld', which it is!), followed by hot, sweet tea; good for the morale and needed. Strange? Amidst all this carnage and death, we celebrate a hot meal!

Only a few patrols on 21ʰ; cleaning out, but still bloody hot, and I don't mean the weather. By mid-afternoon, we'd lost all four of our Company officers killed or wounded, and. I was temporarily 2 I-C! Diary, how was I still alive? I still had six of my lads with me. As the day closed in on the 22ⁿᵈ, we'd taken the stinking, muddy Creek. Stuffed with the dead, it was alive with rats and bloated vermin. What spoils to the victor! At times like this, you can't help reflecting on luck; why one cops it and another doesn't. Some of the fellows want to talk about Divine Providence; that's rubbish; sometimes you are just in the wrong place at the wrong time, or, if you get through, the right time and place!

Can't believe I wrote that; I'm becoming a pagan! I am shocked to the depth of my soul by the fate of two missionary women who, when the japs had landed at Gona, were humiliated and then bayoneted to death.

In his next letter, still reflecting on the absurdity of war – how one survives and not another – he took me into his confidence in a moment of spiritual exposure: *It's come to this, I've been brought to the last vestiges of hope. I have faith in nothing now but myself and my men (and you); but, we will survive.* I wept for him.

He endured; and for his furlough we honeymooned at Mission Beach. Bran had the loan of a cottage on the beach from one of the blokes in his battalion and we swam, made delicious love, lolled around in the shallows and wandered in the rainforest that grew almost to the dunes; caught fish and cooked them, washing it all down with good white wine, as we tried to forget he'd be away again sometime soon. 'Oh, my darling, I gaze at your beautiful body, run my rough hands hardened by labour and combat and they come alive, as though a current is running through them. Where did you get that glorious olive skin?'

'Thanks to Granny,' Id grinned when he confessed his love of it. 'A hint of the Levant passed on!' As carnal as these pleasures were however, he told me, this shy man, he felt a deep joy touching his spirit. We played and laughed the days away: a new world. We nearly wore out *L'Isle joyeuse:* 'he's spying on us my darling, that Debussy knows just how we feel. … Oh, how I've lusted after you, B. Glad my little kids can't read my mind!'

From that point on, when he is away again, his letters were written, written solely to let me know he was alive, he said, and his diary entries were brief.

> *1 January: leave Gili-Gili, for a spot in the Finisterre Ranges called Shaggy Ridge, which unleashed a few jokes. But it's no laughing matter! The natives call Ramu Valley, 'the valley of death.' We are in it now. The Ridge rises sheer above us, disappears into the mist.*
>
> *9 January: In place by 3 January, On the plateau. We have few secrets from the enemy, who is well entrenched as he rains constant fire down on us from a hidden mountain gun (or two?). We'll find it! Reminds me of the old stories of Gallipoli.*

By the end of January, he's talking into his diary: *proud of the lads, we have the enemy sandwiched, but he still has the high ground.* He knows it is not over yet and is lamenting the contrast in human behaviour between our recent blissful days and the dreadful action he is engaged in as they mop up the enemy. He took no relish from it.

> *2 February: enemy over-run on Crater Hill. Took several pillboxes – Dear God, they were filthy! 'Silenced' a counter attack. Hindered by the conditions and terrain: mud, steep slopes, undergrowth, enemy fire, and the scattered dead, we are on the top of the world!*

4 February: visited again by the dysentery, violent evacuations; from the filthy Jap pillboxes. Pretty crook; native carriers help me. Two fresh men due. Hope I'm alright to welcome them. Passed out twice in last 24 hours.

8 February: feel really crook!

16 February: relieved (understatement!) to Guy's Post. Had a hot meal; it didn't stay long with me.

I learned later that there had been great concern about his health. Invalided out on the *Duntroon* on 17 May, arriving back in Australia on the 20th, he was taken straight to the Kalinga Camp near Brisbane. Maude and Reg told me he looked like an escapee from Hell. Barely able to stand, his eyes sunken into their bony caverns, his flesh a sickly green, he was slumped across his kit when he saw them. Acknowledging them with a flick of his eyes only, he was mumbling: repeating over and over the names of his lost mates, 'gone forever.' It was another two weeks before he was released into my care in Bathurst. Trembling in fearful anticipation, I felt skin and bone when he fell into my arms at the station; we gripped and held each other: each whispering the other's name.

'Oh, my darling, darling girl.' He was weeping now.

'There, there; you'll be as good as gold in a few days. Now …', but I didn't finish, wiped my eyes and his; kissing him, caressing his face. 'Yes, now… a surprise I think we'll take a taxi.' In five minutes we were outside a tiny white weatherboard cottage with a huge '*Welcome*' emblazoned on the door, festooned with balloons, black and blue streamers for his regimental colours and drawings of hearts and lovers and soldiers. His face lit up!

'Oh, my kids have had such fun making the banner and suggesting all kinds of things they could put on it. They are so excited you are coming; and as for me, my darling husband; I'm beside myself. Welcome! It's ours for a month. What do you think?'

Holding his hand, overcome with want of him we kissed, slowly, opening our lips, in search of each other. I put my arms around his neck and held my boy. 'Given that I'm probably heavier than you, sweetheart; I think we'll do away with the convention; just hold me and claim our love nest.'

'Oh, yes, please ...' He said, almost shy again. We didn't get any further than the bedroom. No, it wasn't like that; we simply lay in each other's arms. While Bran slept, I dozed, waking regularly and soothing his wasted body, anxiously watching the twitches and vibrations, the nightmare jolts; listening to the grunts and groans, calls from some ancient deep that erupted and disturbed his sleep. His dreams taking him back into the thick of it.

It was as though I was listening to his soul issuing the awful trauma of war. Occasionally, I would calm him: cradle his head, kiss his closed eyes, brushing my lips across his cheek, consoling him, bringing him back from the brink. What places had he explored? And, all the time, there was his exhausted body. Slowly, I brought him back and he let me. One memorable evening stayed with me. He'd set up a picnic on the lounge room floor: salads, a chicken leg each, some cheeses, a sweet white wine, and her Grannie's delicious bottled mixed berries. Kissing now and licking scraps of food away and caressing, gently touching. And he lay back' – 'Ah, that's the entrée' – and I lay across his chest and we shared a peach? 'And, and?' I loosened my breasts to fall across him. A memory, so vivid. Did we say anything? Nothing coherent, apart from sighs and sounds of pleasure, all self-explanatory. 'What are you doing?' I'd squealed as he slipped his hand, dripping with berries and their juices, down between my legs. Ohhhh, I'd kissed him deeply, feeling herself arch in pleasure. 'Oh, berry nice!'

I also dipped my hand into the berries and fed them, dripping, into his mouth, my fingers finding his tongue. Rolling around in delight, his lips lipping my breasts and my hand finding him, erect. 'Ahhh,' how does it go, that piece of Donne we were innocently, and with great joy, enacting: *Licence those moving hands, and let them go / Behind, before, above, between, below ...* Ah, that's right. *My America, my new found land.'*

Yet, Borneo awaited him and in its awful way, me.

* * *

Still conscious of Bran's presence in every part of my being, I was with the 2/9th as they took Khandasan, forced the enemy off Santosa Hill, and swept inland to Pamaluan. But I understood that, as easily as these operations read, or rolled off the tongue in the nightly radio news bulletin, on the ground it was a different matter: my man was in constant danger.

By 3 July, he was logging their systematic movement towards *Balikpapan*. In the process he was exposed again, to the grim Japanese *memento mori, straining mercy to the limit,* as the mutilated bodies of local men and women were found on the beaches. But, by now, with the enemy retreat under enormous pressure, as he told his father, he felt under greater threat from anxious American fire. And as much as he loathed the Japanese, he was also shocked to his core at the use of the Atomic Bomb on Hiroshima and Nagasaki. Appalled: what had humanity come to?

After the Japanese surrender on the 15th, the wind-down was rapid. In my prayers since we met, his survival filled my fervent orison the next Sunday when I attended the little weatherboard church. I was not deeply religious, but on this momentous occasion, I gave blessed thanks.

* * *

I didn't know whether to laugh or cry? Inevitably it was a bit of both when he disembarked but this time, he didn't fall exhausted and battle-drained into our arms. He had obviously been in the thick of it again, his face was still written on by what he'd seen and done. With a tear in his eye, hugging his son, Reg told him how proud he was of him; but with them all embracing, on this occasion, I lost all composure. Having tried always to be the strong one, I shook uncontrollably as three years of worrying about my man flowed from my body. Within a fortnight, having marvelled how quickly he was back into civvies, we were in our cottage and were being feted all over town; but I knew it would take years before he could put the war behind him and find a replacement for the horror that had scorched his soul. I wasn't surprised he spoke rarely of his experiences and although he recognised the need of some to do so, didn't take part in Anzac Day marches; but his mates – he could do the roll-call to this day – never left his mind. Each to their own, he'd say. Some days he might stop whatever he was doing and gaze up at the sky, that sky which for days on end in New Guinea he may not have glimpsed: as though seeing it for the first time. If I happened to see him I'd join him, put my arm around him and nuzzle under his arm.

He was alive! 'Oh, sweetheart, isn't it exciting to think we have a future.' It was something he'd rarely thought of, even before the war. 'First things first eh? I'd better high-tail it out to *Wembley Downs* to see if there's a job for me.'

'Don't bank on it, B. The drought's back with a vengeance; poor dears.'

'Oh, I know, but ...,' he smiled weakly, 'I said I'd go.'

* * *

'Bran, you're back!' Jacob Carmody slapped his arm across my shoulder. 'You don't look too bad, if I may say so; better than a couple of years ago I can tell you. Mother!' He called. 'Come and see who's here.' Mrs Carmody scuttled out of the kitchen, fussing with her apron. 'My, my: Bran Doogue, welcome home!'

'You're as good as your word son; said you'd come out to the *Downs* when you got back.'

Bran looked quizzically at him. 'How are things, Mr Carmody? Looks pretty crook.'

'Yes, we're battling; it's down to me and one of the old crew, might have to get the old girl out of the kitchen soon,' he joked, wryly. 'We're just caretaking really: waiting, hoping, praying for rain. Didn't bring any back with you, did you?'

Bran smiled. 'Could've though, plenty to spare up that way. I'm thinking you might have a bit of trouble putting me back on, am I right?'

The old major, aged by time and worry, looked up from under his eyebrows thinking: my, the army has matured this boy. 'Well, that's to the point, son: we'd have trouble; but I'd be pleased to put in a good word for you around the district. I'm sorry; I know you were banking on it.'

'Claire kept me up to date and God, I can see it.' It's not much better than that sea of sand in Tobruk, he thought, as he gazed across paddock after paddock of what looked like rubble.

'It's sad, I feel for you Mr Carmody.'

'Well, you make it easy for me Bran. How's Reg?'

'You wouldn't believe it if you saw him, he's a new man. He's held down a job for a couple of years and he's now the Dad I never had; I'm so happy for him and Mum. But, about work; just keep us in mind ...?' He didn't finish. The poor old bugger's exhausted Bran thought as he was ushered into the kitchen.

'Mother'll put the kettle on.' Sitting down, they yarned in a desultory way about the last phase of the war, but Bran didn't go anywhere he didn't want to. Hanging over everything were unstated questions about the future, as the conversation moved by fits and starts, the three of them preoccupied, eyes flicking around the room rather than holding a glance.

'Hmm, back to the drawing board,' Bran said over dinner that night. 'Meanwhile, I'll see if there's anything doing around town. A new chap's running the pub, he took over from Joe Wellham, perhaps he needs a yardman. I'll give him a go.'

'Joe's in town actually, cleaning up the last bits and pieces of his move. Did you know he's moved down south to run a pub that's been in his wife's family for years. I bumped into him, told him we were on the market. He might have something, wants to have a yarn tomorrow. I suggested after school at the hotel.'

'There's this chap: Mr O'Connell,' Wellham explained. 'He owns the *Wicklow Hills* (cattle) *Stud*, and the hotel, I'm only the licensee of course, and probably owns ... oh, about half the town. Anyway, he told me he was looking for a couple with a cattle background to manage the property.

Would you like to meet him? Could be a good fit. Whad'ya say?'

'I certainly don't mind you mentioning us! But, um, don't know if you could call me a cattleman. That might be a bit of an exaggeration,' he chortled. 'But yeah, I'm interested of course. What's the place like?' Bran was keen, but he was worried about uprooting Claire.

'I can only give you a rough sketch. It's a fair dinkum stud, runs about 250 head I reckon; pretty well half 'n half, breeders and commercial. I guess there might be 1,000 to 1,200 acres with some hay and lucerne. It's been let go a bit but everyone says it was once a terrific property. It's fairly old; the original homestead, a fine big house you could get lost in, was built before the turn of the century, and has a huge ornamental garden. Rainfall's a consistent: 27 to 30 inches a year, not like out west mate! The previous manager had been there nigh on twenty years. Edward O'Connell, the owner, is not there often; huge business interests in Sydney, and overseas. His wife, Rebecca comes down occasionally, but for the most part she travels with him.'

'What's she like?' They asked, almost in unison.

'The missus says she's pretty high maintenance: Blunt Street Celtic Ponds ain't Regent Street; if you know what I mean! Real pretty, raven-haired, young, twenty-five, maybe.'

Claire nodded, 'and the town: anything like Bowral where my Grandmother is?'

'Well no, Celtic Ponds is nothing like it and it sure as hell doesn't ooze old money, apart from Mr Edward that is! It's small; but I think it's a bonzer place.'

'Any larger towns nearby?'

'Bega's the regional centre, sorta like Bathurst, and Broadwater on the coast's not far away. Forty minutes to either place. Real nice community; no-one's in your pocket, but they'll help out at the drop of a hat. I settled in like that', he flicked his fingers, 'but then my wife's a Dwyer, old family: they've run the pub there since it was built, before the O'Connells bought 'em out for a pittance in the '30s when they were going broke. As managers nothin' much changed, except we don't own it anymore; we lease it from him, but we make a living.' Wellham looked at them. 'Be mad if you didn't come and look it over Missus. He's in Australia at present, I'll let him know I've spoken to you and we'll go from there.'

* * *

Within the month, Bran Doogue was *Wicklow Hills'* fourth Manager and had moved into the Manager's house on the property. Claire would follow as soon as school broke up for the long vacation. Rather than being reluctant to move, she was eager. 'It's a great opportunity B. I love my kids and am sorry to leave, but my darling' – those glorious golden eyes shining – 'I'm getting clucky! I want us to make a baby; sounds like a good place to start.' She wriggled her body into his and kissed his cheek.

'What's he like, B?'

'Bit of a cold fish. But he won't be a bother unless I'm mistaken; he seems to have only a passing interest in the *Stud*,' Bran told Claire. 'I didn't have to haggle over pay; extremely generous; more than double what I would have expected out West. 'And he reckons he can put us into that new Holden that's on the drawing board; depending how things go.' The only thing Mr O'Connell seemed to have a firm view about was that *Wicklow* continues to show at the Royal Easter, and the Melbourne Shows. 'Keeps our name up in lights, Doogue.'

'How old is he?'

'You'd think he was old enough be my father, with all that "Doogue" and stuff, but he might give me five years, not much more.' It was six, Edward was a 1913 drop.

It became clear as he brought himself up to pace with the *Stud* and got used to cattle breeding down South, as distinct from what he knew of the industry out West; that the place had been let go. The sheds were run down and the fencing around the yards needed replacing, everything was outdated. Bran wondered what the previous manager had done during his tenure. There was insufficient feed stock and, even at this early stage, he thought the herd needed expanding to be profitable, a view that was confirmed when Claire and he got into the books. The place had run at a loss for the last decade. Did O'Connell not care?

Something needed to be said: so just before Mr O'Connell returned to England for the Northern Summer; Bran went to Sydney and told him he'd have to spend some money. Not everything could continue as it had under Dalton. 'Good, good,' he'd mumbled, barely listening. 'New broom. Good. You've got a free rein on the *Stud* bank account: up to ten thousand a year. My accountant tells me it's been run right down. Should've kept more of an eye on Dalton I guess, but I top it up on 1 July every year anyway.' Like Bran's salary, this also exceeded expectations, but that wasn't what this conversation was about.

'I'm serious Mr O'Connell, if I'm to stay, things have to change.' He appeared surprised; it was obvious he didn't expect to be spoken to like that. 'I want you to come down and have a look: a proper look over the place. I need some kind of assurance from you that I don't run this as a hobby farm.'

'Well now don't get ahead of yourself, young man. Hobby farm?' He looked down his nose. 'Damned impertinent! Don't know what Dalton'd say. Ribbon in Melbourne last September you know. Hobby … indeed! If that's what you think Doogue, you'd damn well better prove your point.' He was elevating himself onto a very high horse.

'You'll come down then? It can't wait another six months?'

'Too damn right I will! End of the week eh? Day trip, do it? Mrs O'Connell will probably want to come so warn the wife.'

Two days later, they made the trip down. Edward was shocked. 'Bugger's let the place go to rack and ruin, the bloody scoundrel. Well you've got a job of work to do Dougue; better get cracking.' He was puffing his cheeks out as if inflating himself. 'Don't want the O'Connell name associated with a hobby farm. Show me what you can do, don't care if there's a bit of a budget over-run: but don't go off your trolley: get this place shipshape.'

Claire was excited, 'that's settled; sounds like he's given you *carte blanche* to fix it.'

'Yeah: I started to tell him what I planned to do you know, but he wasn't listening; just wanted it fixed! We'll start by expanding the herd and listening to some of the better local cattlemen. I want to move away from the Hereford base; they lay on too much fat for the kind of stock I want, what do you think?'

* * *

Rebecca O'Connell did come down and set herself up on the cane lounge on the verandah of the big house, eating chocolates and glancing at magazines she'd brought with her. 'None here, Claire? You should have a few lying around for guests, I'll leave these for a start.' She'd said, when Claire popped up to see her.

'Coping, dear?' Claire had asked, with no attempt to hide the irony.

'Yes, thank you, …' She'd forgotten Claire's name. 'Very peaceful; although I must say, the garden's looking a tad shabby. Hope you're not neglecting it? I've always loved it!'

'I'm not neglecting it, Rebecca.' At which, Rebecca looked up at her as if wondering if Claire should be so familiar. Returning the glance, Claire continued: 'It's not in our brief dear, your husband has made it quite clear *Clifton* is your domain. We wouldn't presume to interfere, but in answer to your query: yes, I think it is in need of care; perhaps you should speak to him about it. I believe it was a glorious garden when the previous Mrs O'Connell ran the house.' Touché.

Again, Rebecca looked sharply at Claire. 'I'll just have a salad for lunch, up here I think, then a nap; best room in the house. You have been airing them?' As Claire indicated to Bran later: she was being put firmly in her place, 'I didn't warm to her.'

After the O'Connells had gone, they got down to business, laying out a six-year plan for the expansion of the herd. As a first step they let two of the old bulls go, moved a mean Angus on and acquired a new bull: *Mittagong Major D101*. 'A real corker, first new breeder for years I'd say, Claire.' Bran scoured the state for the best quality stock as a first step in gradually shifting the balance of the herd and upgrading the quality of breed stock.

Although it couldn't be done overnight and there was a continual battle with Edward's accountant, Ronnie Threadgold, who complained as though it was his money that was being spent, Bran kept expanding the breeding programme. *Mittagong Major* relished his work and his first young bull, *Carte Blanche G2404*, was cast in his mold. The fencing had been repaired or replaced and a semi-circular raised walkway had been erected around the forcing yard. 'Ah, Doogue, very state of the art!' Edward snorted. But he was impressed and when Bran explained they needed more feed stock, he purchased the old Fitzgerald place down the road, making additional room at the *Stud* itself for the expanding herd. Bran had also named the paddocks – *Home, Creek, Timothy*, and *Gulaga* where they ran the breeders – while, more prosaically, the smaller holdings for the bulls were: *North, South, East, West*.

'Gulaga', Edward snorted; 'bloody idiotic name.'

'Not really, in the local Yuin language it means the mother.'

'Still, bloody stupid.' Bran ignored him, pleased he had only to deal with him occasionally. Their year now had a real shape and rhythm, Claire's was determined by the school year, although she had an increasing involvement in the Stud, while Bran's was shaped by the seasons and the breeding, calving and cropping regimes. As advances in artificial insemination and embryo transplants become more simplified, calving was greatly streamlined. Never one to run before he could walk, he began to feel as though they were getting to know what they were doing.

The only downside – and it devastated them – was that, although Claire could fall pregnant, they couldn't make one stick. They tried to make light of it; used to laugh that B only had to wave his willy anywhere near her and she'd get pregnant, but that's where the jokes ended. They'd been warned the Rhesus factor might be a problem but Bran reckoned he had enough blood for the two of them: 'Plenty of the very best juice, tried and tested in the jungles of New Guinea.' Pregnant in 1946 and '47, they lost both around 28 weeks and from there on, even with a Caesarean section on offer in '49, she simply couldn't carry one.

'Oh, Mol,' she said, able to share her anguish with her friend, 'it's harrowing. I can feel the sadness lapping at my very being but thank God, Bran's a darling; so understanding and gentle. I lie with him at night and he rocks me to sleep. Curled into his belly, I can feel his lips caressing my hairline, his hands gently wiping my tears. Told me he feels as though he shouldn't be listening to my sorrow, just gives me his time and his love. Won't let me talk of these things as failures, or take any blame. 'There's no-one to blame, it's just nature having its way with us,' says, eventually a certain peace will come, and I guess it will. But he doesn't rush me, the sadness will never be gone, but I'll bury it deep.'

After four attempts they decided to leave off trying and took precautions. 'Damn the Church, bloody ridiculous!' she roared. They had plenty to go on with, and if anything, they grew closer as he opened their world even wider.

**

Rebecca O'Connell had fallen pregnant during the previous Northern Summer – possibly conceived at the Helsinki Olympics – and despite Edward's apparent disregard for Celtic Ponds and its community, a large number of whom owed some or all of their livelihood to him, the possibility of an heir to the O'Connell Estate generated more than passing interest. Born in Sydney on the sixth of March 1953, his head was heartily wet by some, and more genteelly by others, at *Clifton* on the 7th which, as luck had it, was a Saturday. 'Well,' a few of them wondered as they tucked in, 'will we see more of this little tyke than of our *Absentee Squire?*'

Sadly, they had their answer within the month as Rebecca did not recover from the childbirth.

'The poor little blighter, not even a belly full of his mother's milk, nor even a cuddle I bet,' Marj clucked as she spread her views during the daily round in the village. 'What'll become of him? Can't see Mr Edward being much of a hand at it eh? Probably take him back to England and give him to a wet nurse.' Someone offered.

Mr Edward had other plans. Having gone to Sydney for the funeral, Claire and Bran were almost fussed over by him, as he invited them back to the Elizabeth Bay house for drinks after the burial. The wake, if it could be called that, there were so few there, was a desultory affair. 'So sad, she was only 28 you know,' seemed to be the point of reference.

'I wanted you here Doogue, and you Claire,' he said, putting his arm around her and drawing her a little closer than was necessary. 'I've a favour I want to ask of you. I can't bring the little bloke up you know, with my comings and goings, and being so flat out. It wouldn't be fair to him. I won't keep this big place. I'll find a flat that I can lock up when I'm not here. Do you think, ... er, would you be prepared to, ... to ... give it a go?'

'At least he felt a little sheepish asking B! And, ... "favour"? "Give it a go"?'

'It might help you with your own ... little problems. I believe it can!' he mumbled, at which Bran, feeling Claire react, held her hand while O'Connell continued. 'I'll cover all expenses of course, you and he would want for nothing. What do you think?'

He might have been asking them to look after the puppy for the weekend. 'You are asking us to raise your son; is that it? What are we to be; friendly uncle and aunt? What do you have in mind?' She had moved out of range of his invasive hands but was watching him intently.

'Frankly Claire my dear, I don't have much of an idea. I mean I'm still the lad's father but I want you, I guess, to be … Yes, I want you to raise him.'

'I see. All care and no responsibility?'

'That's pretty tough. You know how it is for me; I'm trying to work out what's best for the boy. Come,' he reached towards her, as if offering something as yet unstated.

'You obviously don't think you are …er, best for the boy?'

'It's not just Claire, Edward,' Bran dwelt on the Christian name; the first time he'd used it to Edward's face. 'We'll do it together if we do it and I want to know how you see it operating. Personally, I think we need the authority to act for all intents and purposes, as the little boy's parents, without undue interference.' The dynamic was changing. She held Bran's hand.

They were prepared to raise the boy, but they wanted O'Connell to understand what was being undertaken. He would be consulted on all the major decisions, relating to the boy's education and religious upbringing, but otherwise, he was not to interfere in matters of discipline, or in how Michael was raised. In particular, he was not to shower the boy with excessive gifts of toys or money. They were to be his sole God Parents – Edward must agree to that – and they would take responsibility for him up to the age of eighteen. Beyond that there would have to be further discussion. Inattentive, nodding his way through the conversation in which they laid out their terms, Edward was visibly relieved.

'The awful man would have agreed to anything; ooh, he makes my flesh creep,' Claire remarked. So it was settled; they would receive an annual un-audited allowance to be used for Michael's benefit as they saw fit. Edward would be invited and was welcome to join in celebratory occasions, and other special events that may have particular relevance to the boy and his father. He would have open visiting rights and, on those occasions when he visited the Estate, Michael could stay with him, but he could not take him away for extended holidays. The last condition, which would have anguished many a parent was again, greeted, with relief. 'He really is the limit; he doesn't want to have to bother with him.'

'On the question of money', Edward O'Connell said, winding up the conversation, 'you should be aware that, on his eighteenth birthday, Michael will automatically hold a 45% share in *O'Connell Global Holdings*. He need not know anything about this matter until he is much older; in fact I would prefer that he didn't know. So ...,' as if wiping his hands of the matter, 'can I express my thanks to you both then for agreeing to this undertaking. I will ask my solicitors to draw up the necessary papers.'

'Undertaking?' She spluttered later.

Within two weeks, Edward's driver, accompanied by a nurse, deposited Michael Edward Timothy O'Connell at the Manager's cottage. 'I can't believe he didn't make the trip,' Bran whispered to Claire as she held the little fellow in her arms, seeing the Humber off. 'Welcome, Michael my boy, you're home!'

Father Donegan received him into the Church in September, taking him from the arms of his God Parents for the blessing. Unfortunately, Edward had a horse running in the Spring Carnival and couldn't make it, although the Christening was organised around his availability. Claire kept his gift of a silver Christening mug for years, always polished, in the china cabinet so that Michael could see it. It has subsequently disappeared; she's looked everywhere for it.

Michael's head was wet again at a party at *Clifton*, although Claire, who was pregnant, took it quietly for not surprisingly they had tried soon after Michael's birth to provide him with a playmate. In fact, Claire kept Molly company during the party, as Molly was full term. 'Tight as a soccer ball she is Claire; any day now, I reckon,' Herb Greenwood said. Anyway, Doc Eddington was on hand if needed; indeed there weren't too many of the locals who weren't at this rare opening up of the big house.

It was a glorious spring evening and *Clifton* rippled with chatter and laughter, and everyone goo-ed over the new heir to half the town. And the talk: there was great excitement about the passing of a Television Act: 'bet we don't see it for yonks!' Bran remarked on Jim Scullen's death earlier in the year: 'Good Labor Man, poor devil, brought down by the depression; we never saw the best of him.' 'Not a patch on Menzies!' Someone said, probably Granny. 'Now, now; let's not go there,' the doctor cautioned. 'Who's in the FJ out the front?' Ted Wright inquired. 'It's ours,' Bran answered, trying not to look smug.' And so it went on, from hemlines, to South Sydney's success, to tit-bits about the recent Coronation, from baby clothes and hand-me-downs, the recent cold snaps, Doc Eddington's fishing tips, to stock prices. Everyone was overjoyed for Bran and Claire; the love in the house was palpable.

The sad footnote to these celebrations is that Claire once again lost her baby, while Molly and Herb's little bloke, Charles – Charlie, to most – popped out a week later, tempering their sadness. 'That's it, B, I think I'll pull up stumps. It's too traumatic; let's just be satisfied with our lot. Charlie and Michael will grow up together.'

'You're my lot my darling: my handful,' B whispered putting his arms around her. 'I don't need any more than you although of course, it's no trouble to make room for Michael.'

'Ahh my dear, dear man. I love you! Plenty of room for Master Michael. Perhaps he'll be a God-send as well as a God Son?'

* * *

By 1953 when Michael joined the family, the Doogues' other pride and joy, *Carte Blanche G2404*, had taken out repeated ribbons in both big Shows. There were only a few of the Herefords left among the Angus, and Simmentals were being acquired. The old stone manager's cottage had been turned into a home, instead of the bush shanty it had been during Dalton's time. They'd put in a huge country stove, like the one at *the big house*, decorated the sitting room where they often sat by the large open fire and talked over the day's activities or listened to the wireless. They made a beautiful nursery for Michael and converted one of the other bedrooms into an office. Bran even had Threadgold on side at last: 'Go ahead mate, you're doing a bloody marvelous job. Edward'll never tell you, but the place looks a treat.'

'Well that's terrific, Ronnie. By the time Michael's of age you know, we'll have something here that he might be fitted to very nicely. Make a genuine *Squire* out of him!' Threadgold smiled weakly, 'we'll see, I guess. Not sure what grand plans O'Connell has for the son and heir! Looking at what you've done, anyone would be very proud to own it.'

* * *

But that is to gaze into the future, Clare and Bran's immediate concern was to settle Michael in and spent hours with him. 'He's a strange little bloke, Bran. I don't think likes me cuddling him, there's an unspoken resistance: a restraint, as though he was holding up one of his tiny hands and keeping me at a distance. Have you noticed it? He seems unable to respond to the love I want to give him.'

'Oh, love don't rush him. Just let him get used to us.'

'Hmm. Surely, it's not an act of will at this young age? Honestly, I'm worried about it. I watch other mothers dandle their babies, watch the little thing return the affection, holding their finger in a little hand or giving tiny gifts of kisses. Michael seems determined to never give back that comfort, or allow himself the pleasure. Was there about Michael a certain spitefulness, as though he was carrying memories from beyond the womb? She wondered. He seemed hostile to affection. Visitors learned not to cuddle and fuss over him, as it seemed to unsettle him. There were so few moments when he was at peace. 'How odd to say that of a wee child.' Molly murmured, when she and Claire tried to fathom it out.

'I like to bring him into the kitchen to bathe and we'd make a wonderful mess with water and suds, him and me, laughing and gurgling but even then, when he gets out of the bath, it's over; he insists on drying himself, doesn't want me helping and smooging, or wrapping him up in the fluffy white towels I'd washed especially. Am I imagining it, B?'

'No, pet; all we can do is love him. Show him how. You can't make him!'

'Oh, my gentle, wise man. You're supposed to be the dumb jackeroo, remember!'

Molly Greenwood and Claire spent a lot of time together when the boys were small and they grew up as close as brothers, or were they Claire wondered, watching them at play. Whereas she had no doubt that Charlie would share a toy, a cake, a spot by the fire; from very early on, she noticed Michael always had a reason why he shouldn't do the same. So that for all his charm — and he could turn it on at will — he reaches a point where suddenly, he closes down and retracts every outward gesture. He is just as likely to sneer or snarl, instead of smile and you know it's all over, he's hiding himself again!

'He'll grow out of it, Claire,' Molly suggested. 'He's just finding his way.'

'So's Charlie!'

'Yes, but Michael's way was more traumatic; he lost his mother before he knew her and his father doesn't care tuppence about him. He must feel some of that, even if it's in his unconscious. I don't think you can underestimate that start. Trauma doesn't have a shape, doesn't show itself in any pattern, it may manifest as fear, anger, passivity or it may loom in front of the sufferer as an insurmountable wall.'

'Yes. That's what B says, anyway we'll see.'

Almost from the time he could walk, Bran took Michael out on the property with him; sometimes in the old *Commer* ute, or he might be seen traipsing around with him on his shoulders, talking about the cattle, telling him their names and breed; although strangely, the dog would have nothing to do with him. Later, when he was older, he took him as a pillion passenger on the *Harley* when they went to the back paddocks: 'Better not tell Clar, she'd worry.' At other times they might just rest under a tree and yarn.

Show me the scar on your shoulder, Bra. Did it hurt?

'Not as much as you might think you know; there was so much going on!'

I can't imagine it; fighting like that.

'I can't imagine it now, either, son.'

Did you get him? The one who shot you. All that stuff I've read about in your diary.

'So eh, … you've looked at the diaries have you? Now you know, when I look out across *Wicklow* it's as though it was someone else in those pages.'

Nah. It was you! Isn't that what happens in those thunder storms? Gives you memories, does it? Some of the things that happened?

He looked at the boy. It was years before he stopped quaking before torrential rain and the lightning slicing the night sky open, waiting in terror for the horror: the sky filled with debris; the undergrowth uprooted, leaves, bark, whole trees, tossed in fury, then raining down like shrapnel, forming a shroud over the rotting dead: the bloated carcasses of the dead.

What did you think about when you were fighting, Bra?

'After I'd met Clar my boy? I thought about her; she kept me from going mad.'

All those bodies and bayonets and bullets. … You thought of her? He stopped chattering; thought for a while: as though, for the first time, understanding war wasn't a great adventure.

'I was terrified most of the time me little mate. It was awful and I couldn't wait to get home to my beautiful girl, and that'll do for now, is that okay; these aren't happy memories.'

But you still did it. I'd have done that for my mother, you know…

'Enough!' Bran whisked him up and gave him a hug and a huge sloppy raspberry kiss. Thrrssspp! But he never got one back!

Some of these behaviours became more obvious when Claire started a small informal kindergarten up at *Clifton* for the two boys, Ally Williams and Edna Brown's daughter, Karen. Edward didn't mind them using the place but he couldn't see why she bothered with the Williams girl. 'You know what they're like; here one minute, gone the next, and bolt down your silver. I'm not sure it's good for my Michael.'

My Michael, indeed. Pah! 'She's a lovely kid; as sharp as a tack. Charlie and she are lovely friends. I think she's getting a lot out of it. And, … she's giving a lot.' Much more than Michael, she thought. While the other kids will show and tell their stories and painting, Michael keeps his stories private and protects his corner. Turned it into a kind of No Man's Land, fending off contact with the others. Thought it was more like combat than play.

'It's a problem, Mol. I'm trying to solve it by getting the kids to pass their work around mid-way through a task and ask questions of each other about it. Share, you know.'

'And Michael?'

'Well, he often refuses to distribute his work; seems suspicious of what the others might do or say about it. Or, he might screw it up or scribble all over it and if he did show it, wouldn't answer questions. It's not as though he doesn't have things to share. His language skills, like Charlie's, were highly developed, yet, more often than not, he just won't engage.' And although she was reluctant to admit it, she thought he was cunning, but she didn't mention that to Molly. Watching the four of them doing simple tasks she'd set them; while Michael would ignore Karen as superfluous, Ally had to be dealt with and whether verbally or physically, he would push her out of the way; making it clear there was no place for her around him and Charlie. Claire pulled him into line but behind her back he did whatever was necessary to let her know she wasn't wanted. Watching moments like this play out, she thought there was a brutality in his actions that Charlie never came to terms with, and it made him try to help Ally and share her pain. For he knew she was hurt; she was like a sister to him and they were great mates.

'She's only a boong, you know!' Where did he pick up these words?

'Gee, you're a shit sometimes! Why do you do it; she's not hurting you.'

Yet, he always made sure the boys patched it up.

Claire continued to job-share – a very early version of it – at the school, working three days a week when Edna Brown was having another baby, and two days when she returned. She was also running the monthly CWA dance and keeping an eye out for the needy, including calling in on the Williams' and their cousins, to make sure things were okay. Did Alwyn need new shoes; were the bigger boys going to school? Or, she'd pop down to the Temples, checking on the little bloke. At the same time, she was building up a data collection system for the *Stud*, following the lead from their West Australian cattle friends. Each animal was accounted for; birth weights were recorded and systematically updated. Assessments of calving ease were recorded, and a docility regime was developed. Vaccinations were logged, along with detail about the bulls' scrotal measurements, as they worked towards an ideal of docile cows and virile bulls. And then, with a grant from the Federal Government, they began exploring advances in artificial insemination as a way of controlling breeding and expanding production.

'Pity they haven't got one for us, love?' She murmured.

And Michael was cherished and loved and his interests, as far as he ever let them be known, were catered for and fostered. They'd often take the boys down to Broadwater for the day. Bran can't remember how many times he was buried in sand or how many sand castles and moats were built and demolished by Michael, *in case anyone takes them over!* In winter, they'd go to the pictures or concerts if any were on; or ramble in the bush or go up into the snow. Just occasionally, leaving Michael with the Greenwoods, they had what Claire liked to call a Mission Beach-weekend. 'Ohhh, aren't I naughty,' she'd giggle. The thought of them still made her shiver with delight.

* * *

There was enormous activity on the *Stud* throughout the sixties. I eventually gave up teaching, except for occasional relief work, and the three of us even had a holiday in the States, looking at what they were doing with their Simmentals and with artificial insemination. Bran had formed the view that by blending Simms with the Angus herd he could arrive at the more moderate frame he was after. 'Sounds like a study tour, mate. Don't be shy. It's a tax deduction,' Ronny had counselled. May be so, Bran thought, but all he wanted was beautifully structured animals. 'Ah, well,' he joked, putting his arms around her, 'that's what I've always loved! What do you think?'

'I'm not sure about likening me to one of your prize beasts! But, let's get cracking, it'll be so much fun! You've said it yourself, the US is where the latest research is going on in this breeding business. I'm sure we can go beyond that fellow sticking his hand up the poor old cow's behind to plant the seed,' she grinned. Bran's sole reservation had to do with his experience of 'the bludging Yanks during the war. A bloody waste of space on the ground up there.' He'd reflected on them in his diary.

> *Those bloody Americans ...; buggers have turned inactivity into an art-form. Pampered, they don't want to fight; what do they think they're bloody here for? I heard a rumour that MacArthur asked Blamey if he'd like some support from a couple of American battalions when the Aussies were doing it tough at Gona, and Blamey knocked him back; said, he preferred a weakened Aussie battalion, as he knew they'd fight! Didn't think I'd ever say a good word about Blamey, but there's one!*

'Just relax, B. I've got a feeling this is a gift and that we should take it.' And they were off, going first to Zach and Deb Kronenburg's *Double K Simmental Ranch in* in Minnesota, ogling their black beauties. 'He made me change my mind about Yanks' Bran reflected, 'smart, generous – they were always that – and damned hard-working. Salt of the earth; and a deal on a handshake.'

'What a time we had, Molly, I think I spent three years' clothing allowance in a day on 5th Avenue. And the bookshops! Michael even took us to the MoMa, MoMa! Said Charlie insisted that we mustn't miss it; and spent ages in front of the 'Guernica'. *Wait till I tell Charlie! He'll be so jealous.* He was so excited.'

'It must have been a wonderful holiday, Clare.'

'Yes, we also went to a baseball game but Michael wasn't impressed. *'There's so much yelling and screaming,' he grumbled, 'and that organ booming out; no-one watches the players. I wouldn't like that if I was one of them.'* After that, it was across the country to the new *Walt Disney's Land*. And that was terrific, laughed a lot (for him) and seemed to relax, tugging them here and there to see things. He found it *really great*; even thanked us for taking him but didn't let us take too much satisfaction. *It's all kid's stuff!'*

* * *

'He's a strange lad alright, love. But that's the way he is; let him be!'

By the time he was nine or ten, I noticed the boys were more often up at *Clifton,* than down at the cottage. I remember the first morning I found them up there; it was the May holidays. I'd gone up to give the place its weekly spruce up, running a duster over things, and there they were, spread out on the rug near the dear little Queen Anne dressing table in what I always thought of as Rebecca's bedroom. Michael was sitting in the line of sight of a photograph of his mother on the dressing table. It was one of those studio portraits where she has modelled a classic pose at the same table. She is very beautiful: seated in front of the mirror as though completing her make-up, her black hair with delicious curls, a la Elizabeth Taylor, is shining, a black onyx necklace hangs loosely at her throat and there is a companion ring on the centre finger of her left hand. She has on what is clearly a superbly cut black dress, leaving her left shoulder bare. She is looking back over that shoulder, smiling. It's a clever photograph, for not only is she looking out into the room, but the reflection in the mirror captures the other side of her head and the other shoulder. And Michael has positioned himself so that she appears to be looking directly at him. He would often look up at it, a hint of a smile shaping his lips. I was touched. Felt sure, this wasn't the first time he'd sat with her!

His growing library had also been transported to *Clifton.* We read to him from the start, but, as soon as he was able, he politely but quite firmly – like a cat sated with petting – made it clear he didn't need us anymore. Part of our pleasure of course derived from the indulgent delight we experienced when he cuddled into us, one or the other, sometimes together, before dropping off to sleep. He took less from it it seems; or he denied himself, but he read a lot.

The Adventures of Huckleberry Finn was a great favourite, where he identified with Tom Sawyer. *The smartest of them all, he said one day. Buck didn't have a clue what he was up to.* He read Dickens, some Kipling, and E.V. Timms, who she didn't think much of, but wondered if Michael wasn't titillated by the veiled sexual references in some of the convict and earlier historical novels. He didn't bother about comics or feel the need to emulate matinee heroes. But she did see him sneak some *National Geographics* out to one of their hidden nooks, perhaps to linger on naked bodies that decorated stories from parts of Africa and New Guinea.

He also made good use of the *Clifton* library. That's where he found the Dickens, among a reasonable cross section of nineteenth century novels. I know he read Conrad; read *Heart of Darkness* several times. I couldn't help wondering what he made of Kurtz. He'd also brought Bran's War diaries and his letters in the cedar box up to *Clifton*.

Oh yes, they're awesome! Bra was in some terrific battles.

'Yes, he was very brave, darling.' She was thinking of his inner scars, still healing.

They wanted to make him an officer, you know. He would have had pips on his shoulders, and given the orders. He never talks about it, but...

'He didn't want to leave his men you know, which he would have had to if he'd been made an officer.' I couldn't help thinking of one of the few occasions when he'd opened up to me about the war, told me of the intimacy and basic honesty of combat mateship when one's life literally, lay in a mate's hands. I thought of them as friendships at the edge of being; you didn't count the cost. 'I'm glad you've read them.'

Hmm, Captain O'Connell!

'Don't wish too hard my darling, it's truly awful; nearly scorched Bra's poor soul.'

Yes; that's what I love about him; he cares so much. Claire looked intensely at him.

***

By the time Michael and Charlie were ready to leave primary school they had explored and named every inch of 'their' place. They would come back each afternoon or on weekends, when it wasn't unusual for them to take picnics, and Charlie – always Charlie, I noticed – would excitedly talk about where they'd been, what they'd done, and what they'd named and made their own on the Resolute Mountains; 'you should see the bridge we built over Tin Pot Creek, Mrs Doogue.' Michael seemed unable or unwilling to share the excitement. *Shut up Charlie! These are our places.*

'Don't be rude, Michael. Thank you, Charlie for sharing, I think you should go home now. I want to talk to Michael.'

'That was rude, and … cruel, I'm disappointed in you.'

One glorious summer morning after the boys' first year at St Patrick's, just to make sure they were safe, I snuck out and followed them. As it happened, it was the day they stumbled across a narrow canyon carved out by a creek, banked by a thatch of scrub and hidden behind a spill of huge boulders, which she learned from Charlie, they christened 'Apple Pocket.' I saw them chattering away, arms across each other's shoulders, heads together, admiring their discovery before throwing themselves into the pool. When they returned home however, Michael brushed it aside: 'Oh, we found a new place; you wouldn't know it.' And, that summer, they spent hours at Apple Pocket. It was a rare afternoon that their laughter didn't echo through the kitchen. I'd never seen Charlie so happy and animated.

***

I knew Michael had found a book of 'Capability' Brown's garden designs in the *Clifton* library and was intrigued by the interest it generated. When he latched on to something, Michael's energy and commitment was intense. By the first long vacation after going to St Pat's they were sharing their time between the Pocket and mapping the Myrtle Creek gully between the orchard and the *Stud*. In a rare disclosure, Michael told me he wanted to build a landscape garden. He wanted, he explained, *a deliberately shaped but informal naturalism*, which, I later learned by accident from Charlie was straight from Brown.

'And Charlie?' I asked.

Yes, the two of us, but, and he grinned, … *but it's my garden.*

'Of course. Must you always be in charge!'

He peered sideways at me. *Well, it has to be done properly.*

'It's a fabulous idea, Michael. Bra and I can help you buy the plants if you want.'

That won't be necessary. I've been putting together a budget, and, besides – he'd never let on before that he knew all about it – *there's my inheritance; I could draw down on that.*

'Draw down'? Where does he get that from? A little surprised, I told him I'd be happy to tell him about his mother's Will if ever he needed to talk about it.

No need, he said, pausing before taking over Charlie's ideas and detouring around the subject: *we want a mix of exotic and native trees and plants; must have our own plants don't you think*? It wasn't a genuine question; merely part of the smokescreen he was sending up.

By the end of that summer they had a set of drawings, a list of essential plantings, a budget and, to my considerable interest, since for all Michael's bluster about being the boss, at Charlie's urging they had planted a copse of Japanese Maples. I began to notice Charlie led as often as he was led but made no show of it.

It was about this time, to my delight, Michael began reading and writing poetry and the *Palgrave*, which I'd bought for him anyway, was soon at *Clifton!* I'd see pastiches of various poets scattered around; he seemed to love Dylan Thomas and Michael's *Over Celtic Ponds* was a hoot. I heard him declaiming it to Charlie. Among several vocal registers, he had cultivated a mellifluous theatrical voice which he could adopt for occasions like this.

It is Autumn, the crescent moon sheds a little light on our glum streets; silent now, enlivened only by my pen: old Wright is staggering home having sunk his share at the Clover and Thistle and given up his last shilling, and no other stirs, stares, or steers his course, or hers, but me. Our town is blind with sleep. Except for Polly, my raven-haired Polly, caught in a photo who only has eyes for me. Babies gurgle and murmur, farmers snore and shake the walls, the cattlemen, the ladies from the school and the gallery – no cash to count again – the copper, the paper man, old Doc, dreaming of catching a giant fish, the man who fixes cars and he who fixes souls, or tries – forgive me Father – are bedded down.

You can hear the creek rippling, then shooting through, and the wind strips the Myrtle of its leaves which bleed into the night, or make work for keen sweepers tomorrow. The little church is silent, home now only of scurrying mice and other rodents that do not curtsy as they should, and the windows that tell old stories hint only at their tales. Spot barks as something scurries across the Paddock. 'Shush, boy.' It's sweet soft Bra ...

I thought it was very clever; the product of a keen observer, outside it all, putting everyone in their place. Should I be offended, being captured as his *dear, near Clar, caring all she can to mind my wayward, haywire soul*? But one disconcerting cameo stayed with her: *one of my joys, he said, is when I play with little boys. Please, please, be pleased that life is such an awful thing?* Nor did she like the smirk that preceded it, did he inject himself into the poem out of ego or self –loathing?

Yet it was Charlie's sketch of Michael's verse drama that intrigued me. For, whereas Thomas' *Under Milk Wood* was in Michael's poem at every twist and turn, Charlie's visual was original. Looking upwards to *Clifton* from the town, the painting, careful in its representation of the village, even down to the glimmer in the church windows, gives up its realism as the eye climbs towards the location of the 'I' that made the tale. Instead of a perspective that was at its broadest over the town – an inverted 'v' – Charlie reverses it and Michael, pen in hand, his papers on his lap, sits astride the bull-nose roof of the big house dominating the scene. Michael is indeed, 'over' Celtic Ponds as Charlie turns Michael's simple theft of an idea from Thomas into the psychological reality of what has gone on.

* * *

We'd agonized over our decision to resist Michael's desire to attend *Riverview* for his senior schooling. I knew he'd been boasting to the kids at school that he'd soon be attending the great school but, while we were convinced of the merits of keeping him in the loving environment at home, we didn't want to hold him back academically. 'Our only concern is for Michael's welfare,' I'd said to the new Parish Priest, Father Patrick McCusker when I asked his advice about our decision to send him to *St Patrick's* at Broadwater. 'I worry about what could happen to him if he was left to his own resources,' I'd added, as the priest nodded. I didn't elaborate, but I was worried about his moral core; thought it could be better nurtured in our loving family. 'You're getting to know him, Father, are we being selfish?'

'Well now, the Jesuits – and you know, I'm one m'self – versus the Brothers; there's a difference, of course, my lot think they are educating the intellectual elite and the future leaders of the world, the other is trying to give their charges the tools to break out of poverty; for getting on. My sense of young Michael is that he's a very bright lad, you won't be holding him back intellectually, and' – and he smiled, knowingly – 'he has a healthy sense of his own importance. I don't think he needs that fire to be stoked. I watch the three of you all together, it's beautiful the love you give him … even as I'm equally sure he doesn't know how to give it back. He certainly won't learn to do that in the boarding dormitories, no matter how glorious and dignified their fine stone walls!' And he smiled: 'No, no. I 'm thinking you made the right decision.' While so far as Michael was concerned, as bitter as his disappointment was, once the decision was made the subject was off-limits.

For his part, the priest was pleased to be involved. He liked Claire. Oh, he knew she wasn't locked on to the Church, but she had a beautiful heart. While, Bran, he noticed, took his own counsel – 'did he think I might get between him and the boy?' – but, as he liked to say, 'my Father's house has many rooms.'

He had first met Michael when he was serving as an altar boy. Old Father Donegan might have been taken in by his fawning to him, mimicking mannerisms, playing loose, but Patrick wasn't. He saw that Michael's service was a performance, had watched him strut and put on a show when in the public eye, acting out a role; perfunctory when not. In fact, Patrick suggested he should relinquish his role at the altar: 'there are others Michael, who want to take it more seriously. If I tell you it's about commitment, not outward show, do you know what I mean?'

Michael was surprised, purred sweetly: *I want to be like you, Father.*

'I don't know about that, my boy. It's not all cassocks and smoke and bells you know. You'd better have a talk to your God; on second thoughts, you'd better have a talk to mine!' The change in emphasis was not lost on the boy. Nor was Patrick surprised when Michael, speaking as though he was giving up childish things, told him that he was too busy at school and would have to step down: *I'm sorry Father, my time'd be better spent on my studies.* Michael knew he wasn't fooling the priest, but he went ahead with his ritual resignation as though he was, just in case! Whatever it takes.

'That's a wise decision, Michael; you don't want to get on the wrong side of the Brothers, now do you; don't want them getting out the paddy bat to ye,' he laughed, sensing that Michael was too clever to get off-side with his teachers. He continued to see Michael, as the family rarely missed Sunday Mass, although Bran preferred a more literal reading of the bible than Patrick delivered. But Patrick didn't incline that way, offering one which lent itself to metaphor. He was prepared to rest in the mystery of the Word. 'I'm happy to allow mystery into my life,' he would say: 'who would deny the inexplicable; that contact with a reality outside reason, which defies the planned, the ordered. I'm prepared to allow myself, in my Faith, to live in the enigmas and riddles of the mystery. I am open to the reality of a spiritual life.'

Claire understood, but Bran found it unnecessarily complicated and, having been through what he had in the war, he held out no hope of divine intervention; while Michael thought symbol and metaphor took him into very dangerous territory; far *too open to interpretation. Too risky!*

Patrick kept an eye on Michael's progress at St Patrick's, where he and Charlie Greenwood flourished academically and he wasn't surprised when Brother Tippett, their English master, confided to him that whereas Michael accepted the success and the recognition that flowed from it as a given, it rested uncomfortably with Charlie. Out of a shared interest, Patrick also chatted about rugby with Brother Liam, who ran the school sports programme and, as he began to prepare for the '69 season, spoke excitedly of young O'Connell. 'What a find Pat! Still a bit of growing to do, but he's a natural!' This wasn't an idle conversation however, for Patrick was a former rugby International and Liam was keen to enlist his support. 'Would you look him over Pat? Make him a project, eh? Won't be a waste of time unless I'm very wrong!'

'Well, well! Michael, eh? So you like what you're seeing? He's a fine looking lad to be sure. Mrs Doogue told me you'd put him in the squad. Where will you play him?'

'He could play anywhere! He'll end up at lock the way he's growing but, this year? Too early! Wing or outside centre, he's quick and loves the ball. He's only sixteen; I can't bring him on too quickly, but he'll be in the firsts. It's ages since I've seen anyone so gifted; and knows it', he added as an afterthought.

'You've whet me appetite, Liam. I'm keen to see him play; this'll add a bit of excitement to Wednesday afternoons; school matches still mid-week?'

Michael got to *Riverview*, if only for a State Schoolboy's rugby trial, although I fancied he'd been out there before with his father. I remember the weekend well because we invited Charlie to come along. Bran thought his presence might help Michael take his mind off the trial. In reality, Michael seemed more excited about visiting the school: *You wait until you see the buildings Charlie and the grounds. You'd get a real education here, you know. Not just getting trained for jobs!* Overhearing the conversation, Claire was staggered! Where did he get these ideas? *You can even do debating, wouldn't that be terrific?* I wasn't surprised that Charlie, not one to relish a verbal contest and putting anyone down, was only tepid about the idea, but I didn't delude herself that Michael was thinking about Charlie! But then he lured him back in, describing the fabulous organ – *bigger than the one in Wollongong*! – the choir, and the orchestra. *And drama! I would love that; not a stupid Christmas play; a whole subject. They want you to be great. Have to learn the School motto:* 'Dare to do your best.' *And their rugby teams! Beat the shit out of the proddies,* he whispered.

'Michael!' I couldn't resist it; 'that's unnecessary.' At which he winked and pummelled Charlie in the ribs, shifting the focus. You wouldn't have thought he was about to put his skills to the test. It was Bran who wa up tight, wanting it for him.

***

The trial was going well. Bran was absorbed and although I was interested, it was also a day out. I wanted to have a look around the school. Noticing that Charlie had already wandered off, I caught up with him. 'It's fabulous, isn't it?' He said, as we stood on the rise on which the school is built, overlooking expansive gardens, running down to a bushy headland and a stunning river view. 'I'm so glad you brought me; thank you!' He touched my arm: 'Isn't it magnificent.'

'The rugby was great too, I enjoyed it. I think he's one of the best players there.'

'You don't need to apologise Charlie; I needed a break too! And Michael? He's *daring to do his best*, just what he set out to do!' I wasn't entirely satisfied with what I'd seen. A little too much Michael and not enough team. But he's a damn good player, even in this elite company! 'You obviously like the gardens?' We didn't usually have extended conversations, but I loved him: so gentle and sensitive.

'The grounds? Ah, yes, really like the way the sculptured gardens up at the school gradually become wilder – more naturalized – as you go down the slope to the river; all set off by the sweep of the river. It was a little like what I'd wanted to do down the gully after we'd been reading old Capability.' The plans were in his head, informing his language.

'Oh my; you are interested in this landscape business aren't you? I remember the fun the two of you had last summer; why don't you go back to it?'

'I loved it, but there just seems to be too much else to do …'. He didn't finish.

'It'd be good for Michael, and … just sometimes I feel as though I need a hand with that boy.'

'I don't think you need to worry about Michael; he's a star and today,' he said, grinning self-consciously in anticipation of his poeticism: 'I think he's shining very brightly.'

'Yes, that's what worries me. Anyway, I'll wander back and see if the star is still twinkling.'

'I'll join you: terrific school isn't it?'

'Yes, but don't let's start on that. What's done, is done. We didn't dare let him go.'

***

Father Patrick was standing with Bran when we got back to the sidelines. 'Couldn't stay away, Claire,' he laughed, 'had to see how the boy was doing.

Judging from what I've seen and what Bran has said, he's had a good trial. Liam will be pleased.'

'Well he's been fortunate to have two mentors in our little back woods. He couldn't have done what you're suggesting he has today without you and Liam; despite what he might think. And oh my, he'll be pleased you came.'

'Perhaps, perhaps; but he's a real talent to be sure. They say rugby's a game played in heaven, well I think the good Lord made Michael O'Connell to play on his team,' he joked. 'Look at that physique and it's not finished yet. Oh, my!' For a boy who seemed to have no need for heroes, Patrick was as close as it came. *What did Father Patrick think, Bra?* He asked Bran, when we got to the car, intent upon knowing.

'He thought you were tremendous.'

No! No! He said, a little impatiently. ... *About the plays I made?*

'Ah well, let's see:' he went over their conversation and as usual, Patrick was to the point. 'Well, Bran, the boy reads the play and that takes a lot of self-confidence. You can't be coaching that! He works hard, the selectors will like that I'm thinking; I didn't see him late for anything all day. He did a couple of fine things in open play, hmm, he looks grand; has quite a future unless I'm a poor judge!' I sometimes wondered if Bran was jealous of the intimacy between the priest and the lad and was pleased when he criticised him for possessing the ball too much. 'Wants to own it, rather than share it.' Bran thought it just showed off his class.

Michael made the team and was the least surprised of all. Patrick confided that the selectors thought he was very promising, and they liked that he shows a bit of mongrel.

* * *

'Liam's right Claire,' said Patrick, 'that boy of yours can play and I'm happy to help.'

'Thank you. Bran kicks a ball around with him but God love him, he couldn't kick his way out of a paper bag. Michael gets frustrated and goes off and practices in the paddock on his own. He doesn't even bother to ask Charlie out with him. It's the only thing those two haven't done together. I'd be thrilled if you were involved; in more ways than one.'

As for Michael, he sought Father Patrick out for advice and drills to do in his free time, even if it meant he spent less time with Charlie. *You should see us, Bra. I've marked one of the trees with a bull's eye and when I pick the ball up, I run a few yards with it then angle my pass back to the target; pass, leave the ball on the ground or roll it, pick it up, control it, and pass. I just do it heaps of times.*

'I'd like to help him Claire, but I can't compete with an International.' Bran shrugged.

Father Pat has given me finger exercises. You should feel how strong his are, making a cage around the ball, they hold it, then a long, clean release. He was reciting what Patrick had said: *Throw the ball up, run on to it, control it.*

'Control is very important, I think you might be good at that', I'd chuckled. Couldn't resist it. Bran wasn't so relaxed, wasn't sure who was controlling whom; thought the boy was seeing altogether too much of the priest. While for his part, Michael loved the attention and fed off his mentor. His progress was rapid and as if on cue, he grew another couple of inches over the next year, filling out his beautifully designed frame.

Star of the Future boomed the *Southern Highlands Chronicle* the next year, as he dominated the schools' competition; while Brother Liam thought he was a rare talent. 'Tremendous ball skills, like yours were, Paddy; wish we had two of him: I'd like one in the centre!' Liam sighed.

'Be thankful for your blessings Brother,' Patrick joked. Actually, we've got another one a bit like him up in the local League competition: Ben Temple, but you won't be getting him. His schooldays, whatever they amounted to, are long gone. He's rougher around the edges than young Michael and self-taught, but take my word, he can play, and he's smart. We've got them together in the *Tigers*. Or didn't you know, Michael's playing League on Saturdays as well?'

'He hasn't told me,' he shrugged, 'as long as he doesn't get injured, the more game-time he gets, the better. And I know you'll keep an eye on him. Boy, he thinks a lot of you!'

'Ah does he now!' Patrick mused, for he saw Michael as one of his bigger challenges; and it wasn't all about rugby!

No-one was surprised when Michael was invited to play local Rugby League with the *Ponds Tigers* as they rebuilt after a couple of poor seasons. However, in one of life's ironies, in securing Michael, the club also got Bran Doogue who, keen to watch over Michael and allay some of Claire's fears, was elected to the committee.

Strangely, he was a more valuable acquisition than Michael, for the School and State Trials had first call on the boy's time whereas, in his own quiet way, Bran began to revive the fortunes of a Club renowned for its 'punch and piss-ups' by shaping its presence in the community and putting an emphasis on skills training. President within a year, he turned the *Tigers* into a family club: encouraged picnics at the game, organized foot races and events for boys and girls at half-time, and sausage sizzles after home games, with cool drinks for the kids, he encouraged them to get to know their favourite players after matches. He even had local musicians put on entertainment; and Claire welcomed the players to the CWA's dances. The *Tigers* prospered. The players didn't play any less spiritedly, the reverse probably as they became a side noted more for their finesse than their fists. Bran also encouraged them to put money into player development and support. 'Kids like young Temple? Ben didn't have two bob; may not have been able to come if we hadn't helped him out. It pays dividends.' When Bardy Lewis began to vary his coaching methods and started doing some genuine strength and flexibility training, Bran suggested they build a gym: 'wouldn't that be better than tossing a few medicine balls around outside? We could build one onto the club rooms, I'll back you. Put it up to the committee; the Bank'll help us, and the team's full of labourers of one kind and another – bet there's a bricky amongst 'em – or a few tough cockies; we could do it for about half price.'

Intrigued by Bran's initiative and commitment, I found I enjoyed going to games with him; it added another dimension to our lives. And I did like watching Ben play!

***

In 1970, as a joke we celebrated our 100th birthday – Bran was 51; I was 49 – with a huge bash and, birthdays being occasions to reflect, we took stock. If Australia had been virtually transformed by migration and a population explosion which had seen it almost double in size in little over twenty years, so had our little world changed. From being nearly defunct in 1946, *Wicklow Hills* was back to the kind of pre-eminence in the cattle community, and certainly in the town, that I believe it had enjoyed under Timothy O'Connell. The herd had been transformed and we had revolutionized the way it was managed. The first sire from our collaboration with the Kronenburgs arrived: *Zach Double K* was a fine-looking animal. We also received the initial genetic material: 'This'll keep our prize girls busy', I'd chuckled. One of the first SimAngus bred, *Black Becky* K603, which we named after Mrs O'Connell: so densely black was her coat, seemed to prove the point. She was a stunner: we were on our way!

'To see that herd at sunset, B, with their beautiful black frames set against the horizon is thrilling. Aren't we clever!'

And then there was more good news, having worked on the offer for much of the year, Father Patrick finally convinced *Randwick Districts* to have a proper look at Michael O'Connell. 'Not a bit early Father? We like what we see; it could be jumping the gun.'

'Well, I don't think so, and if you don't pick him up, someone else will. He's a real prospect!'

'What do you think Claire, about Michael trialing with *Randwick*? Liam thinks he's good enough and Bardy agrees, although he's a bit miffed he's not going to League.'

'Of course he should go! Paddy'll look after him.'

'I'm sure he will; that's the only thing that worries me. I just wish he didn't see so much of the priest. Oh, I know you think he's wonderful; anyway, I won't hold the boy back. He's been hankering after it.'

'I've never heard you so judgmental Bran. You've got Paddy all wrong, you know. Now to … practical things. Does a "trial" mean summer training?'

'At least a month, pet. Perhaps we could go up. Could we stay at Edward's and keep an eye on things do you think? I wouldn't like to leave him on his own.'

'Well …, it'd be lovely to have a couple of weeks in Sydney. Will you contact Edward?'

'Stay here? Not much room Doogue. Come up if you must; I'm sure we could find a place somewhere, but Michael told me he thought it would be better if he didn't have any distractions. I really think it would be better to hold fire; I'll manage.'

Telling me of the conversation, I thought it was one of the better brush-offs. 'It's clear Michael discussed it with him' I sniffed. 'He'll manage, will he? No place at the Inn! Bet there would have been if I was going up on my own. God, he's an ignorant bugger. And Michael's not much better! He's worked this all out!'

A fortnight later – we would never forget it – it was Tuesday the eighth of December: Father Patrick drove Michael to Sydney where they were to stay at the Coogee Seminary for a fortnight, and Patrick would introduce Michael to the *Randwick* officials, make sure he was settled in, after which, with Edward already in Sydney for the Summer, Michael said he would move into the apartment with him until his trial had finished; however long that would take.

When Bran came in for a cup of tea on the morning of Michael's first training session, wondering out loud about how the trial might go, he stopped. Molly was in the kitchen sobbing on my shoulder. I couldn't hide my confused mixture of emotions, anger and hurt, shading into compassion for Charlie. 'What's happened? Is it Herb?' The question hung in the air, 'Oh, Mol!' I exclaimed. 'How could he… what were they thinking? … Poor Charlie. How is he? That darling boy. I'm sure he didn't want to hurt you.'

'Tell me what …!'

'Charlie planned to run off with Michael, this morning …' Molly exclaimed. She caught her breath: 'but Michael didn't turn up.'

'Of course he didn't Mol, hasn't Claire told you: he's in Sydney?'

'She just told me, what do you think that means?'

'Not to put too fine a point on it,' I interjected, 'it means our Michael set him up, stood him up … and abandoned him. Argggh!' she wailed.

'My God! He went off with that bloody priest.'

'For God's sake, B, don't be stupid, and … melodramatic, Patrick just took him, Mol.

We knew all about his going. Oh, I'm so sorry; I can't express my anger with that boy. Charlie adored him; would've laid down his life for him. Oh! Oh! Mol.'

'Shush darl.' Molly said, regaining some composure. 'It's not your fault, but Charlie's devastated. 'Silly, silly boy. Hare-brained scheme. How did he think it was going to work?' She mumbled.

'Wasn't Michael's problem dear. He's been working on the *Randwick* Trial for months.'

'But he told Charlie he'd done all the bookings, made all the arrangements. Why, why?'

'We can only guess at that, but Charlie's going to need help; you know that, don't you?'

'Oh yes; I realise that. I'm not angry with him. Sad, bewildered, terribly disappointed, but, angry? No!' And then she gave a melancholy laugh. 'What fun he must have thought he was going to have! Golly, if Herb had tried to sweep me off my feet like that when we started going out; I would have leapt at it too.'

'Yes, but that was different Mol; you and he were courting. Whereas this is two …'.

'B, darling, don't be thick! Charlie thought they were eloping, I'm sure!' Claire said.

'Anyway my dears; thanks for your shoulders; I'd better get home and have a chat to Herb. My-o-my, this'll send a ripple around the town. Ben

Temple got caught up in it too, did I tell you? Nothing serious, he was going to drive 'em out of town.'

'What a business.' No less than me, I'm sure, Bran looked as though he'd been physically hit, the blood draining from his face. But he couldn't cut Michael adrift. As for me, I was overtaken by grief. My body wracked with tears. 'Oh, B ... he's gone you know.'

'There, there, sweetheart. It's only for the Trial. I'll go up on the weekend.'

'Yes, you go; not me ... I'm disgusted and ashamed.' I could hardly speak, was releasing a despair that Bran hadn't seen since the loss of their babies. 'You're wasting your time, my good, good man' I sobbed in his arms. 'After the example you've set him – honest and straight – shown him the way all his life; pah! You can apologise for him if you like; I'm done! See what his father can do. My word, he won't like that, but ... Ugh!' I was groping for words. 'There's something dark in his heart. Mine goes out to poor Charlie. I'll go over and see them later this afternoon, but there'll be no simple consolation. He must feel bereft.'

***

As he said he would, Bran went up to Sydney to see Michael on the weekend. 'That was a bastard of a betrayal you worked on Charlie. Anything to say for yourself?'

Huffing and puffing like that, Bran! Sound like my father. He'd never called him 'Bran'. *I thought you'd come to see how the Trial went. Pretty well, so far. They want me to keep training with them; at least to the end of January. A good sign, would you say? Should be able to turn this into a place in the University First Fifteen!*

He paused, looking sideways at Bran. Was he goading him?

Bran was tense, returned the look. Unblinking. But Michael continued. *I don't want you to go on about this. The matter's finished as far as I'm concerned. I'm sorry there seems to be some collateral damage.* 'Collateral?'

Bran spluttered, but Michael kept talking. *It makes sense for me to stay here until term starts?*

'Yes; I don't think it would be wise to come home just yet. "Collateral damage", you say! That could be your father speaking! It's you who sounds like him, not me.'

Don't liken me to him. It was as passionate as he'd been all day. *And what do you mean: 'Home!' Home? This place'll do me until I go into College. I lived in Celtic Ponds; let's not kid ourselves, I boarded there; that was the contract; now I'm going to stay here.*

Relaying the conversation to me later, Bran was incredulous. Disturbed. His anger mounting. 'He's not even doing the right thing by Randwick; shows no remorse about any of it. Not a beg pardon; nothing. I lost it with that final insult, Pet. Damn near struck him. You've broken Claire's heart; she was your mother, or, as near as anyone could be; loves you like a son; we both ... do!'

'Thankless little bugger. He's spitting in Father Paddy's eye as well; you realize that, don't you!' Claire paused. ... 'What we are seeing, my darling, is Michael in the raw. He's shed us like a skin. My worst fears are being played out. He has a highly developed sense of entitlement, but no sense of obligation; thinks everything is there for the taking; can be bent to his will. He will yield nothing. God ..., has he no conscience? Feel no guilt? Patrick warned me that he seemed to lack a moral centre. That kind of spiritual and emotional emptiness enables him to isolate himself. It sends a shiver down my spine. He burns people off, excludes, discards them. I've grown to distrust him for it, for his overwhelming self-centredness.'

She had her hands up in a defensive position in front of her chest. 'Oh, B, I think you were oblivious of it; and he knew it, and – darling, this isn't a criticism – he put you in situations enjoyable to you and him. You take everyone at face value. Not like cynical old me and, and, ... God knows what he's done to poor Charlie! Michael's ego must seem like a battering ram to him, seeking to overwhelm and master. You both trusted him.'

'Well! I saw a side I'd not seen. I was shocked. But he simply skipped around my anger, like a crack in the pavement; a nuisance only!'

Look, Bran, he'd said, testily. *It's done. Don't be so sentimental. We all knew the deal. My father made it quite clear! I'd have been off in a couple of months anyway; you knew that. Your job was finished. I wasn't going to hang around the Ponds, for Christ sake. Guess I'd better organize to come down and pick up my things.'*

'Job! Job!' He could barely speak. 'We gave you all the love we had. Were we just doing a job? Not everything can be measured in commercial terms, Michael.' Then he sighed. 'Collect your things? Yes, you should. I'd do it quietly if I was you. There's a few folk in that quaint little town that you so easily disparage, who might wish to cut you off at the pass. I'll let you know a date. Claire may not wish to be there!'

O dear; I thought she was tougher than that. My father thinks a lot of her, he smirked, letting the insinuation hang in the air. *Let's know the best time. Discretion, hey!*

'I can't believe it, B; not … no remorse.'

'Agh, Pet. But, look, I can only think he wasn't himself!'

'I disagree; I think, perhaps he was. Anyway, if he's going, we'd better get it done with.' I was whispering, my eyes brimming with tears. 'I have to go to Canberra on the 21st; he can come down then. Molly and Charlie may wish to join me.'

And he did. 'Took just about everything that wasn't nailed down, Mol.' I was distraught; my mind churning through their relationship. My darling child. I could find no solace. Molly thought I loved him too much: 'showed your hand, love. Like Charlie.'

'Oh, Mol, I'm neglecting Bran, the Girls at the CWA; and the *Stud* books. Can't recall ever dropping my bundle like this. You know, even during the war when B was going through hell in New Guinea, or when we were losing our babies. I knew we'd get by because we cared so much for each other; in Michael's case, though, there's an air of futility about it; he absorbs our love, all of us, but gives nothing back. One day,' her smile was bitter, 'he'll have to wring out that sponge; it won't be a pretty sight.'

'He didn't even leave a note. He's seen Father Patrick off. I had a letter from him. What with the scurrilous rumours floating around, he's going back to Ireland. The dreadful Marj Nelson is orgasmic, serving the story over the counter at the News agency! Makes my blood boil! Even Bran can't get rid of Paddy quickly enough; thinks he shouldn't have been involved; blames him for everything that's happened and, like some of the other fellows around here, insinuates all sorts of filthy rubbish about him. Oh, in Bran's case, I'm sure it's a part of assuaging his own pain. But, that's no excuse. I've no sympathy for him on this one. Thank God we don't disagree on much; you could cut the air with a knife at home at the moment.'

So it was, two-and-a-half months before his 18th birthday, of his own volition, Michael returned to his father. *I'll stay here for the summer,* he told him, '… *and then move into College. I won't cramp your style will I?* Edward was laughing when he recited the conversation to his cronies at the Yacht club. 'Take more than him to cramp my style!'

We ached with loss. 'Oh, darling, there's hardly been a day when he wasn't with us; the object of our love. It feels like a death in the family. It's as though he'd been hatching the plan for ages,' I couldn't help kneading away at my sorrow. 'Couldn't wait to get out!' But, how does this happen? I stopped, hugged Bran, and we did what we always do, tendered to each other and got on with things.

'It's alright, it's alright, sweet! Let it rest for a while. Come and give us a hand with a couple of cows in the *Gulaga* paddock; they're having a bit of trouble.'

* * *

When Bran came in that evening, I looked him in the eye, put on a smile: 'Anyway,' it was as though I was breaking into the middle of a sentence: 'As I was thinking, before this eruption! Without blowing our bags too loudly it's time we started bragging about what we're doing at the *Stud*. Give these photogenic beasts of ours a bit of recognition; they are stars. Look at them.' He joined me as I pointed out across the rear verandah, down to the first of the large paddocks.

'Oh, my darling!' He put his arms around me and kissed me on the lips. 'Yes; let's think about something real. What do you have in mind?' And I explained I'd been thinking about publishing a newsletter. 'Not a roneoed pink sheet. *The Stud News*. Targeted at everyone in the business. We can use Michael's old room as the editorial suite. I'd like you to keep your office as it is; it's a nice place for you to relax, and I've got my sewing room.'

'Well, that's moving on! Great name.' He was grinning. 'Of course, we are THE stud!'

By the end of March, the first number of *The Stud News* was at the printers. Featuring our black Simmentals and incorporating photographs and thumbnail descriptions of the prize stock, an idea I'd borrowed from their Busselton friends, I outlined the *Stud's* philosophy, including the centrality to planning of our profiling of each animal, and capped it off by advertising the *Stud's* next sale. *Follow us: our animals are sought by breeders and commercial cattlemen alike.*

The Stud News was a hit and drew a bumper crowd to the next sale. Within two years, we were publishing it twice a year, coinciding with *Wicklow's* on-site sales, and *Wicklow* was setting the agenda, publishing practical and learned articles on a range of industry topics. Cattle breeders from all over Australia attended the sales and followed the newsletters, which provided a forum for questions and answers. And, to help pay for itself, included advertisements. 'Little could I have thought,' I'd joked, in a moment of reflection in the '90s, 'as a besotted Romantic and a lifetime reader of novels that my literary debut would be as the editor of a newsletter about cattle. Puts another kind of "stud" on the news-agency shelves, though.'

* * *

As time passed, the Doogues, individually or as a team, were in demand to serve on panels and committees and as speakers at Cattlemen's meetings all over the state: Claire, on data collection models, and Bran, on their breeding programmes. They were authorities and *Wicklow Hills* was an exemplar. By the late '70s, their bi-annual sales were not to be missed by any serious breeder. But Michael did not visit.

I'd had three years as local president of the CWA and done a similar stint on the State Committee, while Bran, as a partial consequence of his growing reputation in the cattle industry, but also because of his success in turning the *Tigers* around, was elected to the Shire Council in 1978 and was quickly elevated to the presidency, which he held for a record nine consecutive years, seeing it through the Bicentennial celebrations, before standing down on his seventieth birthday. And, due to Bran's popularity, I was 'Madam Pres!' Throughout it all, Reg died, followed soon after by Maude who, after all she'd been through, didn't want to leave him, and darling Elspeth, still wonderfully exuberant if a little pickled in sherry by her 95th year, passed away to our great sorrow, and Bran kept in touch with Michael.

'You're an extraordinary man, Bran Doogue,' Claire mused one day, as they wandered around the property. 'You just can't desert him; regardless of ...'

'Of what he did to us? Well, pet; it's just the nature of the beast, I guess. You know what I'm like. I am what I am. He doesn't know it, poor devil, but he's a lost soul.'

'But darling ... agh! I love you. Don't you need something back from him?'

'Look, I get it in a strange kind of way. He doesn't know how to love but, in what he's asked of me there is, I think, an implicit recognition, that he needs me. He seems only capable of expressing it in financial terms.'

'Isn't he using you?'

'I never see it that way. He virtually gave us *Wicklow Hills* ...'

'But, but ...!'

'I know. We had a free hand when Edward was around, but we always had to go cap in hand to Threadgold, or him, like any salaried employee. Michael changed all that, took his 7%, or *O'Connell* did. Now, you know all this dear; there were no more Threadgolds or Edwards, the only thing we didn't have was freehold ownership of the land. We've become very wealthy. We've got that beautiful house to live in; we would never have moved to *Clifton* under Edward, and thanks to Michael we have those couple of 15 per cents in *O'Connell* and they are not to be sneezed at!'

'Pah. He should have let us buy the place if he was so generous. Oh no; wouldn't do that! He would have lost control of us. It's not that I don't love living in the big house, I adore it and the garden and those lovely dividends, yumm, yumm, but, oh, you know how I feel; he's a cunning piece of work.' She paused but hadn't finished. 'If I sound ungrateful; p'raps I am; but you watch, … he's tied up Ben and Charlie and us; Susannah will be next; mark my words. He'll get his clutches into her. Won't want her leaving Charlie in the lurch; now they're so close: now there's a dripping irony for you! Knotting up any loose ends you could say. He'll make it worth her while, don't you worry! There aren't many in town that aren't beholden to him in some way.'

'Ah darling, on the matter of Michael: if 'I say day, you say night: You say I'm wrong, I know I'm right', smiling, he said, you see I think he looked after Charlie and Ben: businesses, houses, gardens …'.

'Oh, B! It's as though he wanted everyone to be caught in time; caught in a web of his making. No-one must escape the place it would seem he doesn't much like. Looked after Charlie, did he? Pah! And I'm sorry; you do his dirty work for him!'

'*Dirty work's* a bit tough! I do what I can to help him, I couldn't abandon him.

'And he knew that, played on it. That's how he's got us dancing to his tune. I'm not having a go at you, love.' If naïve, she thought. 'It's all so cynical. He showered us with money, but he couldn't love us…sorry!' Her laugh was bitter; I'll not change my mind. But damn it, I'll take his filthy lucre!'

'That's too cynical.' He replied. 'What about the Memorial Garden? That was entirely Michael's idea.' *This'll give Charlie something creative, something useful to do,* he'd said. *His music's come to nothing. Anyway,* he'd said. *Here's what you'll do: convert the old Greenwood house into a Pioneer Museum, and the former Manager's cottage into a tourist shop and café, with offices attached for the centre manager and staff. There: together with the two new houses, that covers most of the bases! You'd better run the show. Will that be a problem, since you're Shire President? No, shouldn't imagine so, make it easier really.*

'Condescending devil wasn't he? But, there's a touch of selective memory going on here, isn't there! His idea? What rubbish. Ben and Charlie were already working on it! And what was its hidden agenda, given who was to develop *HIS* idea? It was to keep us all locked in to Celtic Ponds just at a time when the younger ones might have been thinking of leaving? Very neat! Unless I'm mistaken, he'd already set the wheels in motion before he shared it with you!'

He knew she was correct. He had forgotten the planning they'd done as kids. 'But, love: I was amazed at the detail. He hadn't been back since 1970, but he recalled it as though it was on a map in front of him.'

'It probably was B!' I hooted. 'I'm sure he took those old plans when he left. Very clever; he's thought of everything and discussed it with no-one! We are all to do his bidding and I guess we will! I presume you've accepted? And he'll have Charlie wielding the shovel … lovely touch; that's Michael!'

***

When Natasha strolled through the Memorial Garden with me in '98, she couldn't help remarking on the peace and tranquility of the place. 'You know Claire, for all his attempts to shape and control the development of this glorious garden' – oh, she knew about that, just as she knew she was deliberately excluded from being involved in the project – 'Michael couldn't have imagined what has been achieved. I know I'm being just a little bit naughty,' she said, making a gap between her thumb and first finger, 'but there is something deliciously ironic about this garden.'

I looked sideways at her, interested: 'Go on.'

'Silence, ... peace, ... tranquillity, ... contemplation? They were anathema to Michael. If there's a lull in a conversation, he must fill it. Sometimes I wonder if he's not frightened of what might fill the gap, so he closes it; or is he provoking someone to interrupt: contradict him? Always a risk! If a room is quiet he'll start talking, put television on or a disc; anything to block out the quiet! He gets fidgety, will wheel himself around the place, picking things up, placing them somewhere else, fiddle with the paintings, furniture; oh anything; it's still that way: worse!'

'Would've done him good to spend some time here! It's impossible not to find peace in this garden; oh, what pleasure I've taken – take – in it Natasha. What amazes me about it is that, apart from blasting a spot towards the top end of the creek to make a larger, more dynamic waterfall, adding to, and reshaping the huge boulders that rise above a tranquil pool, the site hasn't been unduly fabricated: Michael never mentioned Apple Pocket?'

Natasha looked questioningly at her. 'No, but then, he didn't talk about the garden.'

'Well, the decision to dynamite the Pocket was fraught. Certainly was for Charlie. I knew he had a huge emotional investment in it. He agonised over the decision.'

'Now, this is a mystery! What do you mean? I know Michael felt deeply for Charles.'

'Really? That's interesting in itself! Well, let's say that Apple Pocket was a kind of initiatory site for them and any decision to destroy it was ...'

'I understand; ... highly charged.' Natasha nodded as she spoke, smiling at her unintended pun. 'I follow. But, er, ... chalk and cheese, those two?'

'Very, very different, and perhaps nowhere more than in this decision. Bran told me that he'd warned Michael of the plan to dynamite it, but said it evoked little reaction. *Sure, sure; whatever it takes. I'm happy for it to go. I'll wager Charlie won't go through with it anyway.*

'My, we are trampling over a lot of ground, aren't we?' Natasha murmured, conspiratorially.

'In the end, though, Charlie said Apple Pocket lived in his memory as much as it was a physical place. Dynamiting it was a difficult choice but, with the Indigenous custodian, Mrs Williams, having agreed to it, he felt it would serve the garden better by being transformed. Besides, it allows a spot, once part of a miniature landscape secret, known only to a few, to become part of something grander which will give pleasure to many. It wasn't malicious, in fact he kept the flat rocky outcrop, the spot where they used to sunbathe, the pool, and of course the Myrtles and their glorious red tears, while the stronger overflow enabled the construction of streams which would include picturesque overflows and ponds as they wind around the rocks.'

'Now, we can all enjoy it.' Sighed Natasha. Andrew wants to take me through it; perhaps we should ask Charles to guide us.'

'If you need a guide, dear!' Claire chuckled fondly. 'Oh, it's a joy. I never tire of it.'

'I'm dying to see these two majestic gardens in autumn; I can imagine the radiance, the yellows and golds, burning down to burgundy, to shades of orange and ochre.'

'Simple, my dear; you must make sure you come again; in the autumn!' Natasha took her hand, and they strolled on.

* * *

As much as I grumbled about Michael's behaviour – although I was just trying to get the history right – I couldn't deny how much I loved moving into *Clifton*. From that moment the big house was again a centre of social life for the community, as it had been years ago. When he and a couple of the other oldies had been up for afternoon tea one day, old Dwyer said how much they'd enjoyed the occasion: 'Mr Timothy used to have happy gatherings up here – *soirées*, he liked to call 'em, being a bit of a toff – but Mr Edward ignored us all. The wife would be very envious of me, Claire.'

I revelled in returning the place to its previous simple elegance. It was once again a home that was warm and light on the inside, its high ceilings and French windows in almost every room, creating a sense of spaciousness and flooding natural light, but it was also a house that seemed to delight in looking out. The vine clad verandahs were furnished for comfort and relaxation and cushions and throws were a feature of the bedrooms where she'd made only minor changes. Sensing it had always been a happy room, with the bed positioned so that the garden was in full view, and apart from refreshing its pastel tonings, I left our bedroom as it had been when Timothy was in residence. 'Hidden pleasures in here,' I'd joked on occasions; 'delights for all to share out there. Don't you love it?' Rebecca's bedroom, sans the photograph, and two other bedrooms, were just touched up, and a fourth bedroom was converted into her office-cum-sewing room-cum-nest.

We spent hours in Bran's book-lined study. For, while the library was constructed around the O'Connell collection: covering the three generations of *Australian* O'Connells, and my random collection of novels and poetry. The shelves nearest Bran's large armchair are filled with Second World War histories and diaries. Except, in the move from the Manager's Cottage – or, was it earlier? – his own diaries were misplaced, only for Natasha to find them in Michael's library in Sydney and return them. 'God, she's adorable; like the daughter we never had, B; don't you think?'

Although the huge kitchen is still the focus of our day-to-day lives, as it had been in the cottage, the centre-piece of the house is 'the big room'. Painted in a warm, soft grey, with burgundy tints on furniture and in the long drapes, and abundant glassware – much of it a part of Timothy's antique collection – deflecting the light; the room seems to twinkle with delight. With O'Connell photographs and paintings and an assemblage of rare photos of the village covering the walls, it combines a quite formal dining room where twenty can sit comfortably around the long, polished cedar table with a salon or sitting area. The two parts are linked by a large sliding wooden panel which can be drawn back, turning the space into a small ballroom for special occasions. As it had been when Timothy was in residence, it once again became a place for celebrations; wedding receptions and anniversaries, 21ˢᵗ birthdays and engagements, or massive shows like that held for the Centenary of the *Stud* or more recently, the 'Millenial Party of 1,000 Years' which saw the whole town milling around, were common. At Natasha O'Connell's request, Sir Michael's wake will also be held in the room.

As old Timothy had been, the Doogues became synonymous with the house at *Clifton* even after Charlie became the estate's fifth manager. He wouldn't have it any other way and they developed a wonderful partnership. Oh, they helped Charlie along the way it's true; and he's never been neglected: but, it's only what he deserves. He's never asked for it, and as Andy put it recently, having watched over him from the moment he arrived: 'Time and place have been the healer I think, and the stability of being here in a caring community, where his talents have had the freedom to flourish, can't be underestimated. Rather than being tied down by Michael's strangely construed generosity, I think it enabled him to fly … imaginatively.'

'Oh my; you have watched him closely, Andrew.' Claire murmured.

***

And then they got the news from Andrew: 'Michael has died.' As *The Australian* put it in a brief note:

Sir Michael O'Connell Dies in London
    Accidentally, in a pool accident at his home in London, Sir Michael O'Connell, K.C.M.G., AC: the British-Australian entrepreneur was drowned. There are no suspicious circumstances. Sir Michael overbalanced at the pool side and could not be revived when found by his valet several hours later. Lady O'Connell, who was not home at the time, is in mourning. There were no children.

'Poor Natasha!' Claire said to Andy as he gave her the news. 'She'll need a hand, settling business in London and Sydney ...' She hesitated. 'Sorry, no disrespect. Of course, she'll need our sympathy as well. I shall phone anyway, I like her very much.' They were standing at the door. 'Come in, come in, we must find Bran. He'll be shocked. One thing, unless I'm very mistaken – oh, I know, I'm being thoughtless and jumping the gun – his affairs will be in tip-top order. Nothing will have been left to chance. There will be no surprises, no unwelcome disclosure; everything will be, as they say, carefully sanitised.'

'Hmm, Claire, that's for Natasha to tell.' Now that did interest me, but my reply was lost as Bran burst into the room. 'Charlie told me. What dreadful news; oh, ... Natasha! What a shock ... so young, so young!'

Over the next few days, fielding numerous phone calls, receiving flowers and messages of condolence at *Clifton*, it became known that Michael had requested a burial in Celtic Ponds. Natasha was in discussions with the Premier's Office; while at the same time, there were rumours that he had taken his own life: 'More like he was rude once too often to Natasha – or the valet; 'Christ, have I heard him slip into that boy!' one of the chaps at Michael's Club was heard to say. While Marj tried fanning the flames of rumour in town, they barely sputtered: the ranks had closed. None of the speculative variants could get any purchase.

The funeral was to be held on 18 September. Someone in the Premier's Office thought it was getting a bit too close to the footy finals, but, fortunately it was on a Friday, they could get up and back in the day. Okay if you're a League man; tough if you going to the 'G', that'll be a rush. Andrew told Claire and Bran, with whom he shared whatever was necessary concerning the funeral and Natasha's visit, that he would drive her down the night before the ceremony, and she would stay at the hotel for the weekend. Separately, Natasha had asked Claire if she could hold a wake at *Clifton* on the afternoon, after the service – she would meet the expenses, of course – and that she would like to have a small gathering – 'I know this sounds a little like the denouement to an Agatha Christie novel', she muttered, wryly. 'Perhaps on the Sunday afternoon, say 6 pm?' Just you both, Charles, Ben, Susannah, and, although it's a small indulgence for me, Andrew. He's been so good to me for years.'

'Whatever you need, Natasha. We'll use the salon, and Ben will have the garden looking gorgeous. Sue might like to think about some music.'

***

Then, as we began to compose ourselves for the week ahead, having wondered since Michael died if there was going to be an obituary, one appeared in Monday's *Sydney Morning Herald*. I had it open on the table when Bran and Charlie came in for lunch. I can't speak for the others but, at one minute, reading the forensic eye of an objective reader, at another, I found myself probing its depths for clues with the urgency of a lover. 'What do you make of this?' Charles' voice was dull, sombre. He'd been drawn immediately to a photograph of a youthful Michael O'Connell in full rugby kit, muddied, his black hair tousled, jubilantly holding a cup aloft, flanked by adoring team mates and fans: the people's hero!

Vale Sir Michael O'Connell (1953–2000)

Merchant banker and philanthropist, Michael Edward Timothy O'Connell, KCMG, AC is to be buried this week. Although born in Sydney, following the death of his mother Rebecca O'Connell, Sir Michael was raised on Wicklow Stud, in Southern New South Wales. He moved to the city at the age of seventeen, commenced his university studies and did not again return to his home town.

Educated at St Ignatius College 'Riverview', Sir Michael was a graduate of Sydney and Cambridge Universities, where he rowed for Emmanuel. While at Sydney University he edited the Commerce magazine Quid Pro Quo, and at both Sydney and Cambridge he stepped the boards in University Reviews rubbing shoulders with some notable artists. It was, while at Riverview and Cambridge, he insisted his lifelong interest in Education was formed, culminating in his appointment as Chancellor of Newhouse University which, under his watch was transformed into a 'Cambridge of the South.'

Following in the footsteps of his grandfather Timothy O'Connell who was responsible for many of the finest London, Sydney and Melbourne inner city domestic and commercial redevelopments between 1895 and 1935, he was one of Australia's youngest CEOs when he assumed control of the family company in 1974 and set about transforming it into the merchant bank O'Connell Pty Ltd with offices in London and Sydney. While not turning his back on development Sir Michael amassed another fortune as a Merchant Banker.

He said his father wielded the wrecking ball, whereas he was in a direct line from his Grandfather, who made elegant buildings. His aim had been to make money as elegantly as possible. Indeed, so masterful was he that under his stewardship O'Connell became one of those names, like the renowned financial houses of London and New York, which cannot be ignored. He will be remembered as one of his generation's titans of business.

It has been said of him that he was difficult, evasive, irascible and unpredictable. Of these claims, he said simply that he was a private man, and saw no reason for others to know his business. If some saw him as irascible or evasive, because he was protecting his privacy, then that was the price he was prepared to pay. He insisted that he was not unpredictable, although he conceded that it may have been a side-effect of his desire for privacy. He found in business, as in life generally, that those who didn't know him had preconceived notions of how he would respond in certain situations. If he did not act in the expected manner, he was often labeled unpredictable or unreliable. He always said however, that those who knew him a little better did not try to second-guess him, and therefore understood that such claims of unpredictability were entirely predictable. He was his own man.

Others found him impatient, which, on occasions made his actions seem brutal or ruthless. Private Eye *once christened him 'The Human Scythe' because of the manner in which he went about the internal restructuring of companies he took over. He called this behaviour, cutting out the dead wood. Is it rude to tell someone who has under-performed that they have done so? Or, is it ruthless to then remove them before they infect others? He liked to say: 'Just as the countryside needs the occasional bushfire, businesses sometimes need someone like me to bring about a revival.' As this suggests, he did not suffer fools gladly, believing they cluttered up the space where something useful could be happening. His motto had always been: 'Clear the space.'*

Yet all of this is belied by the fact that he was a man of great charm and urbanity, a wonderful host and bon vivant, *and his London home in Cadogan Place was renowned for its luncheons and dinner parties over which Sir Michael presided with considerable panache. He was a man of enormous passion, vitality, and brio.*

Although he spent the greater part of each year in the UK, he insisted his heart was in Australia and had been since he was a child. The roots that ran deepest in his life were planted then and while he confessed that he never watered them, he insists he took pleasure from watching them flourish or offering sympathy if they failed. Because of this love for Australia, his philanthropy was felt at National, State and local levels. Among his proudest achievements was to guarantee, by his active support, the continuation and growth of the Western Suburbs Children's Cancer Clinic which he associated directly with the ground-breaking research of Dr Mary Nowak. He also admitted to having a certain respect for the design of the building.

His philanthropy, he explained, was designed to support research into human illnesses like cancer (excluding lung cancer), multiple sclerosis, muscular dystrophy, and spinal injuries causing paralysis, and to give pleasure. In which case, he cited his donation to the State and Commonwealth of his massive Australian art collection; his funding support for the development and design of the Memorial Gardens in his home town of Celtic Ponds, and the commissioning of a major symphonic work by the emerging composer Susannah Beaumont. Or even, he said, the huge redevelopment of the London Docks, which transformed a dreadful eyesore, into what he wanted people to enjoy. He made little of this, or of the gift of his art collection. Of which, he remarked: 'Some make much of gifts like this. The pleasure for me, is in giving it away! It became redundant almost as soon as I began it and has moldered away in my stacks in London and Sydney for too long; it's a mere bagatelle. Others might take an interest in it. And if they do, they should thank John Stocker, who put it together, not me. The man's a genius; he could make a silk purse out of a sow's ear!'

He is survived by his wife: Lady Natasha O'Connell.

Sir Michael O'Connell performed on a grand stage: some will see it as a life fully acted out; he saw it as one that was wasted.

There was a brooding silence after we'd finished reading, as if the elemental gloom outside had invaded the room. 'Extraordinary, isn't it!' Charles murmured, 'For what it includes and what is left out; it leaves us looking for what is not said! He wrote it of course.'

'You think so?' It was Bran, who was baffled. 'So sad! No mention of his life down here or of rugby, and he was such a talent, but Cambridge? Rowing? Education? Newhouse? I guess I can understand the Riverview business; his heart was set on it, you know, and we deprived him of that dream which, ... what can I say, he incorporated into his life.'

I was offended and couldn't hide it. 'It's him and not him. All that posturing and, as you say, B, the fabrications! The Jesuits are in, the Christian Brothers out! London's in, Celtic Ponds is out! Good grief, it was his grandfather who rowed for Emmanuel! "*Stepped the boards*"? The only stage he performed on was in the packing shed at *Glen Cannich*, unless he means the stage of life!'

She brushed off Bran's comforting hand. '"*Raised on Wicklow Stud*"! God, makes him sound like one of the cattle!' She cried. 'A swipe only at his father, and … Natasha? He's stripped her of any identity except as his wife. Why did he marry her anyway!? Pah! He finds room for his mother, whom he never knew and the grandfather with whom, ironically, he identifies. What about us, who loved him?'

Charles was deep in thought, mumbled: 'Yes, he didn't seem to mind if he hurt anyone, either. Did he mean to, do you think?' And, like the others, he wondered about the evasiveness. 'Those careless clichés, and dare I say it, in its second handedness. Oh, he's plundered turns of phrase from obituaries he's read over the years, and I'm sure, if *Private Eye* cast any kind of aspersion, he would have gone for them!'

I was taken over by it; stabbing a finger at the paper. 'I'm sorry, it's not a record of a life. And what about the art collection! Mentions Stocker to put him down, just a trifle: the State can have it! Whereas, Natasha told me that they spent hours in the stacks discussing the works. Lost interest? What rubbish. That was a tilt at you, Charlie,' she said, resting her hand on mine. I'm sorry; he's opened up old wounds.' Her voice reduced now to barely more than a sob.

'Ah, Claire, I know, I know.' Charles touched her arm. 'The landscape collection was one of those things we talked about doing. I'm there, if obliquely, like a puppet doll, held up to be slapped down. Apart from the photo, which has no context, like you say Bran, where's the rugby, his poetry, or things of the mind for that matter? All exchanged for an ugly view of his business operations as if written by an enemy. He was deceiving himself, or hiding, one last time.'

'Hiding, more like. Charlie, the enemy was within!' I couldn't leave it alone, kept getting sucked back into the vortex of this awful document. 'It's one more role he's adopted to save revealing himself, even as he pretends to. In its elusiveness it speaks directly of him, but the greater irony is that in using others' words to shelter him from those who glimpse his soul, I think he hid it also from himself. He may have thought he was his own work of art, but who did he see when he looked in the mirror?'

Quiet. Each one mulling around in their thoughts. 'The kettle's boiling; shall I pour love?' Bran murmured.

'Poor love, indeed, poor ... love ... didn't know how to. Could never show his love, even in the lived moment.' Oh, I felt myself coming undone. 'Why couldn't he ... there I go again, I've simply assumed he was the author, ... have given Andrew and Natasha credit for driving the cancer clinic project? Or celebrated Charlie and Ben for their gardens, even if with his money. There's no place for his generosity for, despite the personal havoc he wreaked, he kept the town alive after his dreadful father would have let it rot. To the end ... such an enigma! Am I being too hard on him?'

Bran rested his arm across her shoulders, gently curling her into him, whispering into her hair, falling now onto his shoulder. 'Poor sad thing. Yet, he made so much of his life.' He looked at them. His lips were quivering, his voice was thick, as though his tongue was stuck on his palate. They were all soul-achingly saddened by the obituary; as much for Michael as for themselves.

After a desultory lunch, they each went our own way. Charles wandered through the *Clifton* garden to the gazebo, giving himself up to the new growth, now fully scented and the colours of spring; Bran, a dark spectre in his old greatcoat and boots, trudged down to the back paddock worrying over the calves, while Claire set off for Broadwater to see Molly for a 'cheer up'.

Ben Temple:
Pick-up Truck Man

I'd had no sooner put my head inside the News agency than I was looking into Andy Buchanan's craggy face. It was just after 10.00. The papers were in: 'Hope you left one for me, Doc,' I joked.

'Of course, Ben; my adage is always to leave something for the next chappie. Plenty left.'

'You're all dolled up.' I was looking him up and down. 'Ready for the funeral?'

'I am. Lady O'Connell asked me if I would accompany her; I'm honoured. *O'Connell* provided substantial funding for the redevelopment of the cancer clinic at the *Western* when I was there in another life,' he smiled. 'I got to know Natasha then. She made it all happen and was often on site. Will we see you there?'

I let the question hang in the air thinking instead how I was looking forward to meeting Natasha again later today, having first met her in 1998 when she made that visit to the Ponds.

'Anyway, I won't hold you up. A few things to do before I'm off to the Kirk. For an old Presbyterian, I probably should be practicing my squats, which I see you are about to do!' He was glancing down at my bag. 'Wish I could get more of you lot into the gym; beats propping up the bar at *The Clover and Thistle*!'

Then he sauntered off. I took a left turn and made my way to the *Tiger's* gym where I did a few sit-ups, rode the bike for a bit and pushed a light weight around; pretty slack, but I'd earned a shower and the usual juice. And yet, with the bells swelling the air, I couldn't help pondering Andy's question. Will he see me later at St Michael's?

Sir Michael O'Connell's funeral had been the talk of the town since he died and the obituary this week fanned the interest. No-one could work out why it was being held here and not in the Cathedral in Sydney, especially if a bloke hasn't been back since he was a kid and left without so much as a *see ya later*. There were mixed feelings! He'd let a lot of people down. But it wasn't as simple as that. There were few in town who hadn't been helped by his generosity; in my case alone the debt was huge: that's where the guilt lay.

***

Memory's a strange thing! Thinking about Michael like this I was sent back years, to when we first played for the *Tigers*. We were the same age, although I always felt like his kid brother and our rugby backgrounds, like our lives, were poles apart. I'd been recruited from the junior competition, having picked up my rugby from here and there and listening to Dad's old radio. And when he showed promise the locals got me a job, found me somewhere to live and put a few bob in my pocket. Happy memories: 'Fiver a game and look in your boot if you have a good 'un.' Whereas Michael was coached from the start by Brother Liam at St Pat's and Father Paddy McCusker. Playing Union for the school on Wednesdays, he stripped with the *Tigers* on the weekend. But, being an amateur, he wasn't paid; no stray fivers in his boot! That's how we got to know each other; yarning away after training, we'd plan moves while waiting for Bran to pick Michael up, and then once I had use of the Council pick-up truck, I'd give him a lift home. 'Very convenient, you having this old truck Ben,' Michael had remarked one afternoon when we were chatting in the cabin.

I'd guess you'd say we were an unlikely pair. Michael, born with a silver spoon in his mouth, accepting membership of the team as his right, made sure he was noticed; and me, brought up kicking rocks with my bare feet, went about my training with no expectations. But I enjoyed Mick's company – always called him 'Mick' – but, if I'm honest, I was surprised he bothered with me. Rugby was our common ground, of course, but I found myself opening up about my life on the farm and the gardening I did when I dropped out of school. To my surprise, when I told Michael I dreamed of going to Tech to do my Intermediate, he encouraged me. *Go for it Benny. Then you could do a horticulture course or something like that. Become a proper gardener. Fix up the garden at Clifton, eh?* He mused. *You don't want to finish up a dum shit like those yobboes in the front bar at the pub.* He was only seventeen, but it was as though he had everything mapped out. *I'm not going to hang around. Education's good for you. Nothing'll stop me going up to Cambridge.*

We yarned about most things, except, when I come to think of it, Michael never spoke about his family. I reckon I shocked him when I told him how things operated at our place! How the old man was a bit of a piss-pot, trying to scrub out a living on crook land settled after the war. How 'Rowdy', as old Temple was known around the place because he was a silent man, was shitty – really sort of bloody angry – most of the time with grog and what he moaned was his 'lot in life', although 'moaned' isn't all that accurate; he hardly ever spoke. Except for when he was with his mates, he barely said anything beyond what was necessary.

Michael said he'd never seen his father with other men: having fun. 'Fun!' Don't think you'd call what my old man and his mates got up to fun; it was more like a kind of torture. They'd been in the war together and after getting stuck into the slops they'd finish up yelling at each other, falling all over the place and fighting; swearing and screaming and crying. Oh, that awful sound! Tough blokes you know: bush men, sobbing their souls out in each other's arms. It sure wasn't fun, but they hardly missed a Friday night. Long necks everywhere, and a huge pot of stew on the stove, cooking all night.'

'At least he went to the war,' Michael had roared! It sounded like a criticism.

Although I'm looking back on these conversations with Mick through the haze of time and a recalcitrant memory, I think they'd helped me understand a little about my old man. The poor old bastard was almost inarticulate. It was as if his tongue couldn't mouth out the anger he had bottled up. I felt sorry for him; loved him in a pathetic kind of way, even though I was lousy and he'd stolen my childhood. Childhood! Christ, as I'd told Michael, from about the age of five, I was his rouseabout! By the time I was fourteen, I'd graduated from protecting the chickens from the marauding foxes, shooting the odd rabbit, looking after the veggie patch or cutting the wood and carting water, to doing these chores as well as earning a few bob doing gardening jobs. Once I had the truck though, I could keep an eye on him doing my rounds. I knew every inch of bitumen and gravel in that country, from the ranges to the sea, dropping off packages and collecting mail and milk churns from front gates.' Although I realized later, I hadn't internalised the country like Charlie and Sue.

* * *

Sitting in the small pavilion we'd constructed on the bluff overlooking the Myrtle Creek gully, Charlie waved as I approached. 'G'day! What do you think?' He'd bellowed, gesturing at the reef of dark clouds hanging on the mountains, hiding peaks from view.

'Looks pretty dinkum this time, Charlie. Probably had half-an-inch already.' I had my eye on the scudding clouds, thinking it was a suitable backdrop to the tolling bell. Sitting on a log, *Chews* at his feet, Charlie was rubbing the palm of one hand with the thumb of the other. Kneading away, he was squeezing the dirt from the network of creases in the skin that age and labour had delivered. He seemed to be following the soil-stained lines, wondering perhaps, if his life could be read from the graffiti criss-crossing his skin. Watching him, I couldn't help contrasting their current condition, burnt by the sun and bruised by work, with the delicate, schoolboy's hands that I saw when we first met. They still had a beautiful shape to them though, those mits. 'Made for the cello,' Susannah had said.

'It'll be fine, Ben. It's those bells that give me the creeps.'

'Yeah, sets you thinking doesn't it.'

'It's inevitable I guess. What with all this fuss and the funeral. I've been in the past most of the morning myself; don't usually go fossicking in that old country. Anything particular on your mind?' The question was genuine.

'I was thinking about Mick and me, as you might expect.'

'Really!' Charlie hesitated. 'I've always wondered about it: you and him.' He was fumbling for words. 'Don't go there if you don't want to. I mean, I could've asked before but I put a kind of wall around him, made him a *no-go zone* and then, when you and I became such good mates, it didn't seem to matter. But I was intrigued because he clearly looked after you.'

'Mick and me, eh? We were never close like you and him and I came to learn that the friendship was very flawed, but at the time I thought we were mates. Anyway, death is a kind of clearing out and you're right, for whatever reason, we've never really talked about him. 'Didn't he tell you about us playing for the *Tigers*; how I'd drive him home after training and the drills we did together?'

'He never mentioned you Ben. Oh, I'd heard your name around town of course; the new star in our little pantheon, but as you know we never met until I was in the cabin of your truck.'

'Yeah, what a time and place to meet eh? Anyway, although I thought it was a bastard of a thing he did to you when you two were going to shoot through; after he left, it was as though he needed to keep in touch. A phone call here and there, a short note or a postcard (mainly about rugby) at first – what they did for training – what good form he was in. Well, you know he made the Waratahs and what that was like. At that time I was playing well too; got my name in the paper a few times which led me to think of trying my hand in the city. Did he think that was a good idea? Not a bleat in reply! It was as though he didn't want me leaving the Ponds. I thought it would have impressed him. But it wasn't only ...'

Charlie interrupted, an edge to his voice. 'Did you want to impress him?'

'I dunno, guess so. I mean, he was a bit of a hero too. Quite apart from being a bloody brilliant footballer, he was an O'Connell! But hey, I'd be lying if I didn't admit I was a bit chuffed he wanted to keep in touch. I mean, who the hell was I? Anyway, like I was saying, despite pissing off like that he still wanted to know our news. It wasn't just footy talk.'

'I suppose I was a part of the provincial news you sent on? But did he talk about his own life?'

'Let's see; not much. Mentioned someone called Madeleine a few times and a few *cool* guys, but hardly anything personal. Didn't tell me where he was living; said Uni was a piece of cake: *Should've gone to Cambridge and got a real education,* he said once. But he was spending a lot of time in the office.'

'Really; do tell!'

'Yeah, he didn't like the way *O'Connell Global* was being run. Reckoned his father was a *lazy bastard,* he said, but he thought he'd pick up more from poking around the office than listening to some dry old accountancy Prof. And that's what he did.'

'Incredible! He would have been about twenty-one; no more than 22 anyway.'

'Then he had that accident. Flattened him: huge news on the sports pages; a lot of good judges thought he might have been picked for the Wallabies.'

Charlie interrupted: 'Yes. I wrote to him. My first contact since he left, asking if there was anything I could do? I received no reply.' He paused, 'he must have been devastated. For someone who was born to rule, he would have felt he'd been dealt a rough hand. A brilliant career now had serious limitations placed on it.'

'Yeah, he was rooted. How do you adapt to a life in a wheelchair? Couldn't even put his boot on a shovel like I could. When I saw him the first time I remember him saying, he might as well slink back and lock himself up in *Clifton. The legs and the old engine room are gone; no more hanky-panky! Rugby's over of course,* he'd said, trying to make light of it, but his voice was grim. If it's not too crude, in the space of a couple of months he'd gone from having the world at his feet, to … well, carrying it on his shoulders.'

'Still, there was the University work, wasn't there? He hadn't finished Honours.'

'That's right. I didn't know much about his Uni stuff, but he said it was the least of his concerns. Told me the Economics Department had given him plenty of time to wrap it all up, that the course work was done and he was using the firm as the subject of his long paper, whatever that is. No, the thing that was really pissing him off was the mess he'd found in the company; said he'd like to take a sword to it. But despite his seeming bravado he looked bloody worried; his face, pale and drained. *God, Benny, the last thing I need at the moment is to be figuring out what to do with the Stud, let alone the other Australian holdings; the houses and office blocks in London, and oh, he groaned, the European properties.*

'Weren't those the things his father should be worrying about?' Charlie asked, engrossed.

'*No!* He'd roared when I asked him. *Everything is tied up with the father-problem!* But as confused and bitter as he was, that's when I thought he started to turn the corner. It was a long time ago and I was sifting through the debris of our shared pasts, but the moment of Michael's accident had an air of heightened reality about it and, drawn intimately into it because I liked him. I found it came back with an unusual clarity.' He paused, shaking his head, as if clearing it. 'It would have been about Christmas I suppose. The accident was in August. *Jesus Benny, what was I thinking? Go back to the sticks, give them that much satisfaction? Not bloody likely! I'll get on top of this, never you mind!* He'd already upped the ante in the gym. *It won't beat me; I'll have to get a man to help at certain times of the day, but I won't be a burden.* Said he'd have a bit of look at the paralysis management programme in Stoke, but you know Charlie, his real concern was with *O'Connell Global. You wouldn't believe the neglect,* he'd muttered. *Someone's got to fix the settings if we're gonna survive the repercussions of the mining boom. Looks like it'll be me! The old man should be helping out but he's not too keen on that. The shit!'*

'What a strange comment,' Charlie offered.

'Yeah, I thought so too, but he brushed it aside. *I'm on my way. My way! You watch, Benny. I'll show any fucker who thinks I'm down and out what I can do. Couldn't give me a loan of your legs, could you?* There was steel in his voice. I didn't know too much about what they called the Poseidon boom, but he seemed on top of any fallout and oh boy, I remember thinking, I wouldn't like to get in his way.'

'So he opened up to you about all of this? Most unusual,' Charlie mused. 'He rarely let the left hand know what the right was doing!'

'Mick just seemed to need to talk. It was as though I wasn't there. I thought he was lonely. Although of course, Michael would never admit to that weakness!' Charlie was looking admiringly at him, thinking how perceptive the insight was. 'And yet each time I visited, nothing seemed to distract him and he generated a furious mental energy. It was as though it took him over. I remember when I asked him if he was planning to go into the office, he just exploded. *Christ, if it wasn't for this* – and he looked at his legs – *I'd set up residence there! That father of mine ...!* God he was in a state. *And those other two buggers ...!* He didn't finish, just shook his head: *I've got a lot of thinking to do.*'

'God Ben, you did get to see him naked, didn't you!'

'Oh, I don't know about that but I can tell you, the flood gates were open and he just swept me along. Naked, eh! Well that sets off another memory. Strange how some things come flooding back. We were at the Rehab clinic. He'd just finished a session and was in a singlet, sweating like a pig, his upper body was glistening; he looked bloody fit. If it wasn't for his legs, I reckon he could've run straight on to the paddock.'

Charlie was overtaken by an image of that rippling torso as Ben gave him Michael's voice. *Decision time Benny old son...decisions! Honours 'll be wound up by May; then it's down to business. I've ditched the MBA; gotta take a chain saw to the Company and decide what to do with the old man. I'll show him a thing or two about running the show!*

'What a transformation!' Charlie couldn't hide his grudging admiration for the drive, the primitive will.

* * *

I had to laugh, it wasn't long before my visits, generated out of genuine concern, became *meetings* and I was *invited* to them. *Bran'll set up our next meeting,* he'd said. *We'll meet at the office. Bent Street. Can't miss it.* Although there was no sight of Bran at the 'meeting.'

No need to be here. Michael explained, dismissively when I asked. This was how he was, Bran told Ben. 'Claire said he keeps everything in watertight compartments.'

I found Michael on the 10th floor, behind a polished cedar desk as big as Victoria and to his left, his desk being at the opposite end of the room to the door, a massive window opened up glimpses to the Bridge. He looked great. A crisp white shirt: absolutely Persil white, cuff links: silver, and what looked like a rugby club tie or something smart, with eagles on the wing and a navy blue suit. His dark eyes didn't leave mine. Greeting me; his grip was firm.

'He had this stunning secretary Charlie; he called her his PA. Hair as black as night down to her shoulders: Becky. *Alright! Alright! Get your beady eyes off her,* he bellowed, as though she wasn't there.'

'Tell me Ben, were there any landscapes on the wall.'

'Not a gum tree in sight Charlie, if that's what you mean. Apart from a photograph on his desk of a beautiful woman, the office was exaggeratedly bare, except for a stunning black and white photograph hanging in the line of sight as you left the room. I'd never seen anything quite like it: the torso of a nude male holding a camera just above a substantial cock drooping down from just below the box of the camera, it was not to be missed. While it didn't turn me on, I was struck by its construction, both the placement of the camera in relation to the figure's hands, the dangling penis, and the way the camera was suggesting that the gazer was about to be the subject. I started to say something about what you'd call the aesthetics of it Charlie, but I was fumbling around for words when Michael cut me off, his eyes intent on me as he whispered: *You like it? It's a real jerk-off, don't you think?*'

131

'Jesus, that sounds like a come-on! What'd you say, Ben?'

'Yeah, could've been. I was surprised. Told him that wasn't how I saw it.'

'*You've been too long in the bloody bush mate,* he sniggered, and wheeled himself out. Left a nasty taste in my mouth. Why did you ask what he had on his walls?'

'Just interested. As kids we spent hours painting landscapes and imagining what we'd put in a collection if we ever had one. And I hear the collection of Australian landscapes he donated to the gallery is priceless. It's strange he had none hanging in the office!'

'Well, you're right. His secretary told me he had some lovely Australian pieces in the apartment, "They'd be gorgeous in here instead of blank walls and that ghastly bit of pornography! I don't know what to make of him sometimes." But, it didn't mean a thing to me at the time you know.'

'Did you meet his father when you were there Ben?'

This was another of those heightened moments. *'Edward's gone. No free lunch for him today. Story hasn't broken yet.* His voice had ice in it: *He stood down last week. Best for everyone.* That shut me up, as with hardly a flicker of his cold eyes, his father was dismissed from the conversation. *Anyway, this is what's going to happen. Bran and Claire will move into Clifton. Been vacant for too long. You'll go into their place, rent free. We'll crank up your gardening job to full time. Take on the garden at Clifton. You'd be up for that wouldn't you, now you've done that course!'*

'Bloody amazing eh! Everything now was about the future. I managed to blurt out something about those other worries he had; you know, properties all over the place and so on.'

All in hand; been clearing some space for good things to happen!

'I was stunned Charlie. But when I started to thank him, he just brushed it off and explained how it would work. *Bran will fix everything up.'*

Charlie smiled. 'God, he gave you a future! I'm not grumbling, mind. It pushed some extra cash my way and gave me something exciting to do. He must have thought a lot of you.'

'I don't know about that, … but I knew it was a big ask; course I knew that. I mean it was a hell of a lot more than mowing the lawn and pruning a few bushes. That's where you came in, mate!'

* * *

I remember the lunch as if it was last week. *Lunch Ben,* he'd said, banging his hand on the table: *Bec, do they know we're coming?* Several years later, purely by accident – a photograph in the social pages – I learned Bec's name was in fact Sylvia Manning. Strange eh? Anyway, Michael spun his chair around and headed for the door, I almost had to jog to keep up. Lunch wasn't sandwiches and a cuppa! *Oysters to start eh? You must've had some at Broadwater. And you'll like the fish … and, er, what will you drink?*

I didn't care. The oysters were fat and salty: took me right back; I hadn't had oysters since Dad and I used to pick 'em off the rocks down at Broadwater; and we certainly didn't have them with a vinegar sauce! We had a white wine, French; sounded like 'sincere'. Nice drop, not that I knew much about it at the time. I now know it was a Sancere and it was delicious!

So, how does that all sound? He said.

I'd no sooner nodded my agreement and started to tell him what I might do in the cottage and at *Clifton*, things I thought would interest him, than Michael was mumbling, *umm, good, good, … good,* and his gaze was wandering around the room, nodding to contacts here and there; he wasn't listening: *hmm, hmm,* but then, he stretched across the table, his head close to mine and held me with those steely eye; as tight as any grip. He spoke quietly but there was an edge of threat in his voice: *You will do something for me. No ifs or buts – it's not a favour – it's an obligation.* I was shocked, surprised; couldn't look at him, went dumb. *You won't disclose this agreement to anyone; never: no-one! It's between you and me; it's your 'duty'!*

Shit, what's this I thought; but when Michael slowly said, *I want you to look after Charlie Greenwood;* I relaxed, stopped strangling the stem of my wine glass: 'That's no sweat,' I mumbled and started to say something … but he spoke over the top of me… *Good, good. It'll work out; it's all for*

133

the best, believe me but, and the hint of a threat remained: *but, he must never know. I'll provide you with whatever you need, given that I trust you not to screw me around on this, to help him financially and to be sure he has what he needs when he's in Celtic Ponds. It's agreed? If he leaves: nix, nothing, nada.*

With that Michael thrust out his hand, turned his wheelchair and headed for the door, calling back over his shoulder, *Bran'll talk to you about the money. You know where the lift is!*

* * *

When we met a month or so later to confirm the plans were in place, I asked him again about his father. Bran had shown me an article in the *Financial Review.*

> *Michael O'Connell takes over* O'Connell Global Holdings
> *To the surprise of the financial world, Edward O'Connell announced he is stepping down as CEO of O'Connell Global Holdings, effective immediately, in favour of his son, Michael O'Connell. After nearly thirty years at the helm of the prestigious family company, there was a view that it was time for a fresh approach.*
>
> *In spite of his youth and recent crippling rugby accident that has left him in a wheelchair, Michael O'Connell indicated he was ready to assume control.*

Including a summary of the history of the business, the piece concluded with a waspish glance at the young CEO.

> *Announcing an imminent name change to O'Connell Ltd., he explained that its two earlier formulations, foregrounding 'design and construction', and then its 'Global' status, were inappropriate in the current commercial world, where the*

entrepreneur is pre-eminent. With a confidence belying his youthful years, the new CEO indicated that O'Connell's ongoing presence and relevance will be as a hedge fund. In this capacity, he is pleased to announce that O'Connell is open for business and with a massive war chest at its disposal, it will not be a bit player.

Time will tell.

Michael snorted. *Pretty half-hearted coverage. Gave 'em a piece of my mind. 'Time will tell' indeed. I'll show those condescending bastards what a new broom is!*

'What did happen at the end, between you and your father?'

Very simple, Benny. I had a succession plan; he didn't! He just thought he would coast along with his two lazy cronies: Ronnie Threadgold and the execrable Sam Withers, and hand over to me when he was ready, but he'd taken his eye of the ball hadn't he! And YOU know what happens then. You drop it!

I was hanging on every word. 'I'd like to hear the story.'

Why not; it's between you and me, mind. Bec! Can we have coffee and a piece of that date slice. An hour later he escorted me to the lift, having told me how he had his father over a barrel since he did an analysis of the *O'Connell* companies for his Honours paper. Said, after that, he knew every twist and turn of the company's history. What a story it was! Going right back to 1938, Michael told me a meandering tale of Edward's fraud and malfeasance, of companies floated and run down, then fleeced and started again; of buy-backs and name changes; of greed and corruption, manipulation and collusion. In the process, the once distinguished private company *O'Connell Constructions*, founded by Timothy O'Connell at the turn of the century, was turned into a listed Company: *O'Connell Public Pty Ltd*, which had a brief and sordid existence before being again privatised as *O'Connell Global Holdings Pty Ltd*, as it set out to play, extensively on an international stage, Edward having greased his way into the lucrative post war reconstruction with generous kick-backs. He and his new bride Rebecca were the principal shareholders of the new company, holding 90% equally between them, while Withers and Threadgold, in repayment for their loyal service and in lieu of any insurance policies covering length of service, were ceded 5% each of the new entity. It was also agreed that in the event of any O'Connell progeny, on attaining the age of twenty-one in each case, the major shareholding held by Edward and Rebecca O'Connell and existing progeny, will be diluted to accommodate all parties. It would require a 51% majority to take over the Company.

There it is Benny. My father was very proud of his piece of legerdemain, which he boasted was his business acumen. 'Watch and learn,' he'd roared; 'there must only be one winner.' I've never forgotten it, the only thing he taught me! After he had finessed the O'Connell Global deal, he purchased a suitably prestigious property in London with OGH funds and largely but not entirely, left the running of the Australian side of the business to Withers and Threadgold. He visited Australia annually and made irregular and cursory visits to Wicklow, although his wife Rebecca, rather liked staying in the big house and often lingered there or in Sydney after he'd gone back to Europe.

I was stunned as we walked to the lift. Speechless. 'Amazing, Mick!'

It's not for publication, okay! I'll know where it's come from if it gets into the public domain he said, shaking my hand. His grip was steel and seemed to carry a warning, which I thought was an insult, and although Michael's lips creased into a smile, it was ambiguous; ugly: a slash. Was there something like self-loathing in it?

***

And yet, Michael had kept in contact; cards and letters would come in from all over the world. One of the first was from Cap Ferrat, it must have been about 1977. I remembered it because I'd never heard of the place and Michael seemed to have lowered his guard: *Ah well, Benny, I'm tripping with the beautiful people, having a few days at the Grand Hôtel. The sights here, and I'm not talking about the landscape, have to be seen to be believed. Sun-kissed boobs and the beautiful flat bellies of the boys and their tight little bums are everywhere, cavorting among themselves; taking their pleasure however they like it! Simply delicious. I'm afraid I'm like the little boy with his nose pressed against the lolly shop window, lusting after the mouth-watering treats inside which sadly, I can't taste to the full.* Other notes followed, but rarely with such rare candour that left me wondering. From New York, Chicago – *brilliant architecture* – Berlin, from Brussels, later Strasbourg – *just love these hare-brained Eurozone schemes; money for jam!'* and Moscow: *Benny! Smoke and mirrors. My kind of place; a killing to be made there.* And of course many from London, one of which stays with me because the Australian papers were full of how our entrepreneurs were rampaging through the City. *Bloody yobboes,* he'd scribbled, becoming quite expansive, even witty, as he wrote them off. *Fleet Street tries to tar me with the same brush as those 'Aussie Buccaneers' who they loved to hate: the Elliotts and Bonds of this world. I keep my buckin' ears under my buckin' hat; I stay under the radar. I don't run with that pack, all paper and hot air, no value. A good pal of mine will have Bond for breakfast; you mark my word. You don't mess with Mr Roland. I wine and dine him and have enjoyed his hospitality, cruising around the south of France, but I don't cross him. I know what makes him tick!* This would have been '86 or '7.

Charles was interested in the correspondence. 'A glimpse into the new Europe, and, dare I say it, Michael!'

'Yeah! Opened my eyes, I can tell you. Yet, there was nothing about his rehabilitation; did he get to Stoke? Nothing about his houses, his knighthood, not even about his marriage. *Oh! Didn't think it was any of your business.* Not a word about Natasha; I mean we knew she was a famous ballerina!'

'He was overseas more than he was in Australia but, even when he was here he never visited or tried to meet. Strange, eh? It was as though he'd tied up all the threads when, as a 24-year-old, he saw him off at the lift. 'Yet, from first to last Charlie, he never stopped asking about you and your folks. It was a long time ago, but I remember that: ... *how was the orchard going, were they battling?* He mentioned Bran and Claire and the Stud, and Bran's work as Shire President and his involvement with the *Tigers*; but it was you Charlie, who was on his mind. Not that I had much contact at first when you were in Sydney, but hell, he could easily have contacted you; he seemed reluctant to do that.'

'Of course. Far too risky, exposing himself like that! What did he want to know?'

'Ah, Charlie, … well, I remember he asked about your music, about you and Sue and what you were doing. He did make some snide comment about *our happy little threesome*, although I'd not mentioned our shared friendship. Did he feel guilty about how he had treated you? I'd wondered.'

'Guilt? Not in his vocabulary Ben. It was about control, not compassion. He was keeping tabs on me, but at a distance. It's been a strange feeling: all my adult life I've felt as though he had me under surveillance, was manipulating me and you my old buddy; and Bran unwittingly enabled him to do it. Oh, I know about that as well! Didn't you understand?'

* * *

'There I was all those years ago Charlie, trying to digest what was happening around me. And here I am now, having this strange, belated conversation with you. At last I've broken his confidence! God, we've been tending that garden together for over 25 years and we've never talked about how I came to be doing it or the circumstances that brought us together to do it.'

Charles looked up, sharply: 'So that's how you could afford to pay me so well for my-labour?'

'Labour? Creativity more like, anyway it became our garden Charlie.'

'Too right; it's been a wonderful team effort. But … well I never, well I bloody never …; so that was what's been going on! Did you know your benefactor once described me, among other things, as *a vegetable farmer growing food for chooks!* Shit, he must've thought you were a live one!'

'You're not shitty at me are you Charlie, not blaming me? I gave him my word.'

'No, me old mate; you're very loyal.'

'Let's face it, I was naïve. It wasn't until much later, after he'd cut me off, that I realised he'd turned me into his agent reporting on the comings and goings around town. But at the time, I was in his debt in so many ways I was vulnerable and he exploited it. I came to understand our correspondence wasn't about him. His business was his business and so was ours! I didn't wonder if others were in touch with him. I knew Bran was, because of the *Stud* and that he handled all the financial matters relating to the garden at *Clifton* and my salary. It wasn't until we were gearing up for the gully garden project and you referred to our contact as a kind of reporting back, that I understood that even if unintentionally, I'd been feeding him!'

'Don't beat yourself up about it. He was a past master at looking for weak spots and striking at them. But look, I said I'd meet Sue down at the cottage, I'd better be off.' As he shambled off, mumbling about a puppeteer's strings, I couldn't help reflecting further on the meeting with Michael that had set me on this course. Rather than his responsibility: his obligation, Charlie had become mine, and a mate. We were knitted together, not by Michael's forced conjunction, but out of shared interests and a common spirit; some might say, a compatibility of souls. Yes, I'd acquiesced, but he'd played on my loyalty and laid a sense of obligation over everything. I had no choice, although I now realize it was those very traits Michael exploited. Still, that's who I am and I'd also felt sorry for Charlie, not in a patronizing way, but knew he'd had the stuffing knocked out of him. I wanted to help.

* * *

Having seen smoke wafting out of the *Clifton* chimney, I wondered if the kettle might be boiling. As I strolled across, I remembered, contrary to what I'd told Charlie, that I did see Michael again. When our book on the Myrtle Gully Memorial Garden was published in 1991, I'd taken two copies up to him, not that they generated any interest. Glancing at the cover – *Bit flash!* – he set them on a side table, unopened. *Lucky you caught me. Can't hang around here;* O'Connell's *going to Moscow. Christ Almighty, they're selling the family jewels; it's too good to miss. Don't suppose you've got any Russian mates,* he guffawed, *seriously though; there's a killing to be made!*

Surprised at the turn of the conversation, I wasn't sure what he meant.

Glasnost, me old chum. The great opening up. Yeltsin's got rid of Gorbachev and the wolves are in the hen house. He's handing out shares in the state-owned companies to the great unwashed. Christ, they'll be buying vodka and Aussie beef with 'em! O'Connell *can go in, I just need a front man; get hold of those shares: pure gold!*

'Can't your wife help you?' I wasn't up on Russian internal politics, except that I thought it was exciting to see stirrings towards democracy. My suggestion about Natasha was innocent, but it seemed to catch him off guard.

You'd think so, wouldn't you? He mumbled as he turned, dismissing me. *Bitch.* But that was that. *I'll get Bec to catalogue the books. Find you own way out.*

It wasn't until much later I understood what he was talking about, but I had arrived at *Clifton* and Claire was busy over the stove. 'Very productive places, kitchens', she'd once told me. Said it was where she did her best thinking.

'Come on in, pull up a chair.' she called. 'We're going to get another deluge any minute, by the look of those clouds, black as sin. Hope B's got his greatcoat.'

I told her I'd been owning up to Charlie about some of the Michael stuff and I needed a cuppa. She was like a mum to me.

'Ah, my dear, I can't think of you now without including Sue. All rosy in that garden?'

She was smiling, 'Sorry! Am I putting you on the spot? But there'll be altogether too much talk about Michael O'Connell today for anybody's good! Dear Susannah: where would we have been if she hadn't been around when that awful betrayal occurred? And now she's got you to…' she didn't

140

finish: ...look after, knock into shape, mother, love? I could have finished her sentence for her as I let the reference to Michael lapse.

'Could've knocked me over with a feather when you two got together,' she smiled at the simple rhyme. She was inviting expansion, and on this day of reflection and confession, with my shield of reserve well and truly lowered, I was happy to talk.

'Yeah, that set the tongues wagging.'

She laughed. 'Well, the poor old biddies didn't know quite what to make of you: inseparable you seemed to be; the three of you. I remember in one of Michael's notes to Bran, the cynical devil asked how the *ménage à trois* was going: always had to soil it somehow, that Michael. Bran, bless him, told him it was a despicable thought.'

'Michael? Really? Filthy bugger.' I'd been around enough to know what he was hinting at. 'Some of the guys at the club prob'ly thought the same thing. It wasn't like that at all!'

'Oh, I know, but all that tut-tutting around the place was amusing, especially when you and Sue hitched up: "She's quite a bit older than him, you know and what can they talk about? He wouldn't know Bach from a bassoon, must be all in the bedroom Norm." Which left Norm thinking: half his bloody luck!'

'Oh, yes ... but, I'm very happy; and it didn't happen overnight.'

'Why did it take so long? The first I noticed was when you had the odd dance at our Friday doos.'

'Well, we were the crutches on either side of Charlie, trying to keep him upright. We didn't give each other a thought in the sense you mean. It was a bit more complex than that, really!'

Claire nodded. She liked it when Ben opened up and had learned early on that he had a sensitive mind, if belied sometimes by his bluff appearance and manner.

'Neither of us had much idea of what love was to be honest. You know how I was brought up. Don't worry, I remember you coming around with some tucker, pieces of clothing, a toy – not that there was much room for them in our place – oh yes, and that real footy! What a terrific gift that was, but gee, there wasn't a lot of love around there, and I don't know what you know of Sue's background ...?'

'Very little, she's very private. She never talks about it but, it's strange isn't it? The only one of her famous family to visit is her younger brother.'

'Well, it's not for me to say; except it left her badly bruised. But, looking after Charlie didn't give us much time for ourselves. We didn't push our feelings forward. I was in love with her a long time before I said anything and honestly, she was terrified of showing how she felt.'

'I could be soppy and sentimental and say love will out but I know that's trite. I'm just glad you stuck at it and found a way to express yourselves. Ours was so simple by comparison.' She had a misty look in her eye. 'But, why keep your own places, I don't get it. Don't you want to be together all the time?'

'We don't need to, but we don't get hung up on what people think. Even Marj Nelson,' he laughed. 'The same goes for marriage. Yours is a beautiful union but it can be a bit like the Church: a way of controlling the rabble. I want her to be as free as a bird. We are just lucky to have found each other. Her mother's marriage was a kind of imprisonment and mine fled from what was perhaps, a reign of terror! We are a couple, though!'

'You certainly are, and she's very lucky. Sometimes I think of you as a philosopher.'

'Can't even spell it! It all started during those strange, troubled years after Michael tossed a bomb into Charlie's world. Although I'd witnessed the cause of his depression – God, as you know, I was there that awful morning – but it was Susannah who picked up the pieces. Oh, I felt sorry for him but, at first, I didn't know how to help.'

'I know darling, he didn't really want anyone to help him; he was enchanted by Michael and just wanted to curl up and die like a sick dog when he was so let down.'

'Yes it seemed that way and we were totally different sorts of blokes and once Uni started, he was off to Sydney, and if I wasn't working or playing rugby, I was training. There was nothing much I could do. I looked in on him occasionally when he was in town but he couldn't have cared less whether I was there or not if I'm honest. He was responding to Sue, but really, it wasn't until he came back permanently that things began to happen between the three of us. I remember it clearly. She came to see me wondering if I could help out on weekends when he seemed at a total loss. He just has no friends', she'd said, bleakly, 'God knows how he got on in Sydney!' It wasn't a prospect I welcomed. Ironically, apart from the fact that we'd both narrowly missed the call-up ballot, the only thing we had in common was Michael! Now I'm not the sharpest tool in the shed but when Michael offered me the gardening job at *Clifton*, and muttered something about enlisting Charlie's help, I thought I had a solution.'

'Yes, quite cunning, don't you think,' Claire said, patting the side of her nose. 'Forced you two to get to know each other. Reckon you probably found out you weren't so different?'

'Yeah I liked him. He was a strange bloke, kind, shy, sensitive; certainly hurting; but quite good company, and the garden became what we shared. Sue was wonderful with him, getting us to talk about our plans for the garden and its gradual re-shaping, all the time trying to engage him and draw him out of himself. She even began to make me feel as though I had something to offer as she pushed us to think deeply about landscaping, while showing me how to advance that other 'project': Charlie. I thought she was pretty smart, but as you've suggested, that wasn't the only place I saw her!'

'Ah, the dances! That's when I noticed,' Claire grinned. 'Sue rarely missed a chance to have a dance with you. "What about me …?" She'd gesture, pouting and putting her hands on her hips like a strumpet and you'd whirl her around the floor. Oh, it was gorgeous!'

'You sticky beak! I used to love going to those hops and when she joined the band, I met her as soon as she arrived in town: well before "Charlie". We'd smile and shyly greet each other and have a dance now and then whenever I bucked up the courage to ask. Well, she was the music teacher and I was just a shit-kicker around the place … you know?'

'But you sure could dance Ben! Everyone wanted to dance with you.'

'Oh maybe, it just kind of came naturally. Pretty well the only chance

I had to cuddle up to a dolly-bird as well, Claire!'

'Oh I don't know about that. I reckon that Michelle Wellham would have put her shoes under your bed any time, if you'd asked,' she was chuckling. 'But, seriously, I noticed you and Sue. You didn't make a show of it but I could see you slowly, tentatively, beginning to relax with each other. Made me think of Bran and me: we met at a dance. I wondered if you'd be as lucky as me.'

He was blushing. 'Anyway, so we started working together with him. At first it was a damn sight easier to get results from the garden! But we stuck at it and cautiously as he began to trust us, we started doing things together, the three of us. We'd have a coffee at the tea rooms with old "Phyllis", or we might potter down to the coast for a real coffee or a meal, if fish and chips can be called dining out!'

'You don't have to explain to me. I was so thankful it was happening. I mean, I took some of the blame for what Michael had done of course. He just seemed to have no moral centre.'

'We became a kind of family of the lame and the wounded. Sue's ties to her home were always tenuous – "home: what's that," she would wail ironically, and you couldn't call me and the old man a family. As for Charles, he was as lonely as a crow out of its country; and really, I guess he was also coming to … you know, he was getting used to the fact that he was gay.'

'Oh, so you knew he was gay?'

'Well, I had a pretty fair idea; figured it out on that rotten morning I guess. But as time went by, even as we knew he was having a battle with it, we didn't want him to see it as a dead-end. Look, I probably shouldn't say this, and I don't to open that can of worms, but I wondered about Michael, too, but, … we were talking about Charlie.'

'That's pretty special Ben; a lot of men around here wouldn't have had anything to do with him. Good Lord… look at my Bran; although he saved his abuse for poor Patrick until I gave him the rounds of the kitchen and told him he wasn't welcome if he wanted to talk like that. Not his fault; it's the way a lot of them are brought up to think, but that doesn't mean he shouldn't know better! Oops, hobby horse! As to the other matter, let's not go there!'

'Charlie and I'd rattle on for hours about what we could do with the garden, poring over the magazines and specialty books Sue used to bring us. I'd moved into the Manager's cottage by then and we used to sit on the verandah in summer looking out across the gully or inside by the fire in winter on Friday nights. We'd found we didn't enjoy the Friday swill at the pub, instead we would have a beer or open a cask or a bottle of wine and yarn.'

'I'd see you occasionally; it was so nice.'

'Sometimes he'd put some music on. He would tell me something about the piece we were going to hear and then we'd listen to it in silence and then chat about it. It gradually brought out another side to this reticent man.'

'How wonderful,' Claire remarked.

'Oh, yeah! He'd get really excited: "Just listen to the patterns ..." and he'd mark them with his hands, "listen to the language of the music, not our apology for sound! Listen to the moods of the instruments, think of them as a bunch of friends chatting together. Try to recognize their different voices. Which ones are singing, or whispering, laughing ... even shouting. It's a bit like wine tasting", he'd say, "this kind of appreciation; it doesn't matter if the wine you like is a Lafite, or a Grange, or a Bloggs from Bulli; but when you nose it or roll it around in your mouth it's a matter of treating it with respect and letting its flavours give you pleasure. Nose this music," he'd say with a grin. Sometimes, when we were out in the bush, he'd suddenly stop, put his open palm on my chest and we'd listen to the landscape's music. It was a part of his recovery I think, a kind of therapy, but for me, it was all grist to the mill: those years were a part of my education.

'If Michael taught me how to speak and write, encouraging me to go to Tech, Charlie and Sue showed me how to feel and really ... that it was okay to do so. We'd often go to the dances when Sue was playing and I took them to see some rugby – only the good stuff – and although I'd been a League man, we went to Union games and I taught them a little of how it worked. I introduced them to *its music*, and I don't mean the hideous gyrating and twanging guitar before the game. God, I still remember one game, early '80s; we'd gone up to watch the Wallabies play Scotland and got there early and this kid from Queanbeyan, just up the way: Campese, was playing in the curtain-raiser against New Zealand under 21s.' Claire was smiling; had heard of Campese. 'The crowd was milling around, getting their pies and beers ready, when suddenly a hush came over the stadium and everything stopped: this young bloke, got the ball at the end of a line of passes, and with a series of goose steps, these weren't your ordinary jinks or sidesteps … these were huge and a chip and chase for good measure, he left the opposition all ends up, left them 'legtied' as Charlie excitedly said later. We were laughing and yelling like the rest of the crowd. Sue even confessed that she found some of the movement was memorable. We went periodically to other games in Canberra or Sydney, once or twice in the Gong, but I hated that place, sunk in its despair.

Talk about first time for things for this boy from the bush.' Claire was nodding, smiling. 'We'd go to the more accessible galleries in Paddington, or to the movies. You know, somewhere like the *Dendy*. We even went to the opening of the refurbished *Chauvel*. And books, oh how I got to enjoy reading! Poetry was written in a code I could never crack, that's more up Sue's alley, but there was one I really liked. Charlie read 'Tintern Abbey' to me when we were landscaping the Creek. "I used to knock around here with Michael." He'd said. "You might like this, it's what it's like to come back."'

Claire rested her hand on his arm. 'Hang on a minute.' She returned with a worn book, marked with pieces of faded paper. 'Now where is it? "Five years have past; five summers," is that it? "With the length / Of five long winters! And again I hear / The waters, rolling from their mountain springs, / With a soft inland murmur."' She lifted her head, a wistful look in her eyes. 'That takes me right back. I loved Wordsworth at school. She lifted the book and slowly read,

For thou art with me here upon the banks
Of this fair river; thou my dearest friend,
My dear, dear friend; and in thy voice I catch
The language of my former heart, and read
My former pleasures in the shooting lights
Of thy wild eyes.'

'Ah yes, that's it. It's moving, isn't it? But Sue and I also read a lot, together. She's just finishing a piece on Judith Wright's *Woman to Man*. I'm into novels and with her gentle nudges I have pretty wide tastes. I'd missed out on these opportunities, growing up. Anyway, I'm rabbiting on Claire, sorry.'

'Don't be sorry; it's lovely to have this sort of chat; it doesn't happen all that often; where you just stop and yarn. I'm sorry B and I didn't move ourselves a little more over the years; oh, we went up to Sydney and heard some wonderful choirs. Hey, what about that *Stones* concert? The five of us; remember? Oh, and *Hair*! B couldn't believe his eyes, or his ears.'

'And *Les Mis*: ...?'

'Course I remember. Gosh, Bran hummed *Do you hear the people sing* ... for the next month! Used to put a lump in my throat.

'But we didn't do as much as we could 've, yet you know, once we were settled at the *Stud* and then with Michael, they took over our lives and, well ... Bran loved it ... I loved him and we'd made our choices. Besides, at the outset, what a wonderful place to get over the war, and heal those dreadful welts on his soul that he could barely speak of. This place is Edenic of course – how many times do you hear one of the locals say "Ah, 'nother day in paradise"? But it's easy to become complacent.' Looking at him, a vague smile on her lips she couldn't quite leave it alone. 'I'm not having a grumble! We had things to do. I didn't want to escape.'

I was still thinking about our little threesome. 'As time went by, Sue and I grew together out of what you might call mutual concern for our "brother".'

'Compassion, I'd call it.' Claire muttered.

'Really! Not easy, but we also had heaps of fun together and to Sue's great joy, she got to know Melbourne again and delighted in showing me around. She would often get tickets to some of the big classical concerts, and when Bennets Lane opened in the early nineties, we'd drop in for some classic jazz. Andy has come down with us once or twice but we were eclectic in our tastes,' he laughed. 'In Sydney, we're just as likely to go to a disco or a club, even a pub, when one of her pal Cynthia's groups had a gig in Sydney, the Opera house. Of course, we never miss what's on in the Ponds.'

Claire let him talk; a rare expansive moment.

'We were sharing meals by now, quite the little foodies, particularly if Charlie was having a weekend away; it was a happy time. 'So this is what love is', I thought as Sue, never one to be rushed, came to trust me and I came to understand her.'

'Did Charlie ever feel left out?'

'I don't think so. We never needed to live in each other's pockets. He thinks one of the strengths of our friendship is that everyone has their own space. I'm sure he never felt overtaken and I certainly didn't. We didn't really analyse what was growing between us, but he was emerging from his exile and would quite often disappear up to Sydney or Canberra. After a while we used to joke with him about when we might meet some of his fellow travellers: Jay and his dyke pals?'

'And one thing led to another?'

'You could say that! Sue was no pushover though.' But I left it at that. 'And we are happy! Everyone thinks Sue... ah: Susannah Beaumont: the torch singer, didn't start singing until the Doc came along and got us hooked on Jazz; but really it did start around this time. Charlie was keen on jazz – had a taste of it at the Con and his friend Jay played double base in a group; so between the three of us we'd put together a good collection of Jazz standards'.

Did he ever think how far he's come, Claire wondered, this kid that had turned up like a Banshee from the bush? 'Jazz standards.'

'So, she started to sing to them. Well to me at first, and then to Charlie and me and then of course to a wider audience with the *Ponds Alive:* God we were knocked over by her voice; throaty and oh, I don't know, just plain sexy. Let's face it we had heard some great female vocalists at Bennetts, as well.'

'Well, that's wonderful, it's amazing, what you two have found. Another cuppa?'

* * *

'Did I hear cuppa? What's this about another one? Have I been missing out on something?' His grey hair falling down over his eyes and his big open face, like his hands, tanned by years outside, Bran burst through the door. 'So son, keeping my lady wife from her daily toil, eh?'

'I didn't know what your plans were love or I'd have given you a call,' Claire said affectionately, as he took his boots off, puffing a little. She looked at him, a shadow of concern creasing her brow. 'Why don't you let Ric or Ernie do that sort of thing, that's what they're around for, or leave it for Charlie.'

'I'm fine, just went down for a squiz in the Galguna and got caught up with a couple of calves; one of them's not too good. You know, the one that lost its mother. I'll be surprised if it sees tomorrow's dawn, poor bugger. I've put a spare hide over him to see if I can trick that other dame into taking him on the teat. It's his only hope; otherwise, he's done for. A bit like me, eh! I still might try and get to the burial. Are you sure you're not being a bit tough on him, not paying your respects?'

'*Pay my respects*! Now come on B we've had this out plenty of times over the years. Did he ever try to earn my respect? The full requiem mass might be asking a trifle much of the great Redeemer. But I bet he'll have the full ecclesiastical catastrophe!'

'I guess you and Ben weren't talking about Michael then, when I came in?'

'No, certainly not: about Sue and Ben and love as a matter of fact.' She said.

'And why not! What a nice couple you make; but it would not have happened if it hadn't been for Michael, keeping you here with that good job. You probably would have shot through, hey: given League a go in Sydney?'

'Maybe, may- be! Claire and I just touched on that, but I reckon it was Charlie who kept me rather than Michael; although, he had something to do with it; but not how you meant Bran.'

'Ah yes, strange business, I'm still trying to fathom it out.'

'Because you've never wanted to, you old softy,' she chided, gently. 'You just didn't want to believe it of him.' There was an edge to her voice. 'We've gone over this piece by piece, well … not quite; there's one bit I've never shared.'

Ben started to get up from the table but Claire stopped him: 'no, stay, Ben; it might fill in a few of your gaps as well. We've talked about how agitated Charlie was that morning; his expectations torn asunder. By the time you two were sitting in your truck, Michael was settled at the Seminary where Patrick had got him a bed.'

'I was never comfortable with the "got him a bed bit".' Bran added, defensively raising his voice. 'Sure, summer training with Randwick Districts was a coup for the lad but why they had to stay together at the seminary I'll never fathom.'

'For God's sake, Bran,' Claire interrupted. 'I've told you it wasn't like that. Damn it! Look, there's been things you didn't know because Patrick asked me not to divulge it, perhaps now's the time to do so. I'm sure the dear man won't mind; there's oceans between us.' For the second time in an hour, she went into the bedroom, returning this time with a dusty old shoe box; she drew out a letter and handed it to her husband: 'perhaps you should read it aloud.'

St Aidan's

Parramatta … 'Parramatta?' He read. 'Didn't they stay at Coogee?'

Dear Claire,

We had an uneventful journey to Coogee, but there are matters that I wish to share with you in confidence. I don't think it's necessary to bother Bran about it, but I trust you to use your discretion in this matter.

You will notice I'm writing from St Aidan's. I did not stay at the Seminary although I was clearly welcome and indeed, for old time sake the Rector seemed pleased to see me. Events occurred with Michael that made it impossible for me, and I've come over here as you can see from the markings on this note. We have spoken briefly of this before and you know my position (and I think I know yours): I worry for the boy's soul. For a child of his tender years, he has found – how else can I say it, as I'm sure he didn't learn it at your feet and it's certainly none of my teaching – a code of behaviour that I find despicable. After we had arrived at the Seminary I went to his room to make sure he was settling in and he made an improper approach. Did he think I would respond or did he not care? Was this a way of thanking me? I sought no thanks as I told him, I would have done the same for any other similarly gifted boy. Was he rather, trying to manipulate me? And this, I fear may be close to the mark. He seemed to think from what he said at the time, that he could bend me to his will. At seventeen! I'm afraid my disgust, showed. I dressed him down and took my leave. I cannot begin to think what the Rector thought, although I made up some feeble excuse about having business other than simply looking after Michael's training.

You will undoubtedly be deeply disturbed by the contents of this letter as am I; but in the light of other conversations that we have had, I felt you should know. As to the rest of this trip – its so-called real reason: the rugby – we shall see. I feel sick at heart but I will do whatever is necessary to get him a fair trial at Randwick.

Sincerely, Patrick

'After all these years! You should have told me Claire, I deserved to know. Oh, I know you said Patrick was innocent; but, Michael!' Bran was embarrassed, flustered and must have felt awkward in front of me.

'I felt dreadful for a while not telling you, but you thought Michael was born of the sun. I didn't want to shatter your illusion, my image had been well and truly degraded over the years and then ... after the accident, it didn't seem so important. So it's finally said and done!'

While Bran gathered himself, Ben picked up the thread. 'Well, it's a day for confessions! I've never come to terms with the way he set his mate up. God, Charlie told me they'd put their hands together in a bond of trust when they last met, only a couple of days before they were gunna do a bunk. And I got tangled up in it as well; I thought I'd been asked to help them because I had access to the truck and there'd be nothing suspicious about me being on the road early in the morning. *5.00 am; on the dot, mate, don't be late.*' Ben was looking intently at them. 'But as I've pondered it over the years, I realize I was there as a witness of the rejection, not as a driver. It was pretty bloody sick!'

'As I told Claire a short while ago: we waited and waited ... and ... we waited; at first it was easy because I didn't know much about Charlie at all and we just yarned about where they might go and what they'd do when they were away. He was quiet, but he was excited; said: and the words stuck in my mind: they were going "to grow up together." But after about 10 minutes, he began to get fidgety and it went downhill from there. After half-an-hour, it was my turn to get worried; I had a job to do and knew I'd get a hurry-up from everyone along the track if I was late and besides, the boys had to be at Broadwater by 7 am for the bus; it wouldn't wait. By then Charlie was a mess; worry had turned to panic. It was clear Michael wasn't going to turn up. It was awful. I wished I hadn't been there. A bastard of a trick.'

Bran was now grim-faced.

'It was worse than that, as you know Claire; he'd hung his mate out to dry. Charlie was prepared to jeopardise everything to be with him. I guess you know Sue had to revive his enrolment at the Conservatorium.' Claire was nodding. 'He'd applied for a year's leave of absence to better prepare himself, he'd said. They weren't to know his plans had nothing to do with music and everything to do with Michael.'

'So callous.' Claire wailed as she was taken back over it. 'Molly should have known but, what with Herb being so ill and all and Charlie such a reliable kid, she may have nodded and he ... well, did what was necessary! But Michael let him do it. Ugh! I'm sorry it is so... so malicious! He was prepared to sacrifice his beautiful young friend; to what end? Didn't he care?'

I wondered if perhaps he cared too much. Or, was he saving his own skin?

The three of them were speechless. 'Oh, lord ...,' Claire murmured, recovering first; 'I've got to get the place ready; put a few flowers around and put some tucker together. Hope everyone's coming to the wake. I know it's unusual if you haven't been to the funeral, but this is no ordinary funeral and certainly, this is no normal day! See you all there; for now: skedaddle!'

I started to say something, but I'd hardly opened my mouth when Bran put up his hand: 'enough for now, Ben.' I could see he was upset, so I paid my respects and set out for my place. Good chance to have a browse at the paper and a snack, before the afternoon unfolded.

***

I'd only just stoked up the stove and put the kettle on than Bran was knocking on the door. 'Sorry, sorry; didn't mean to give you the cold shoulder back there, but that horrible stuff about Michael and the priest set me back in my tracks, after all these years. Set me back alright. I've been a kind of bagman for him over the years you know, and he's been incredibly generous to us. But, I've never understood why he shafted his mate like that and ... and trying to have it off with Patrick. What on earth was on his mind. Christ, the number of times I've bagged that priest doesn't bear thinking about.' 'He sat there shaking his head: 'I just don't know what to make of it all. To find out today, of all days! I don't know whether to drink his health or drown my sorrows! Do you think he was, er … homo-sexual?'

Here he was in my kitchen, old enough to be my father, facing up to the human frailty of one of his idols and confronting some of his prejudices which, did he understand that yet, had nothing to do with sexual preferences and everything to do with personal integrity, and how you honour yourself and other people? The image of Michael that Bran had built up over the years and wanted to respect to the end was crumbling before his eyes and he didn't know what to make of it. 'Life's a hard school, old mate,' was all I could say. I wasn't going to tell him how to suck eggs, but I did wonder what he'd thought about Charlie over the years, because while he'd never flashed it around, Charlie had made no secret of his sexuality: and Bran knew!

'You thinking about Charlie, are you?' He said, as if reading my mind. 'Never a problem; well, that's how he was, wasn't he?'

'But, but, …?'

'But, what about Michael? I didn't think he was that way inclined. In his case it seemed unnatural. That's why I blamed the priest for leading him astray! Oh, shit, Ben: I don't know.' He muttered, still bewildered by his own jaundiced view as much as anything. 'But, right now, I haven't been this knackered since I pulled out of Buna, and I need a break. I would 've liked to talk it over with Michael but,' he smiled weakly, 'he got out before I could; anyway, I'll have a chat with Lady O'Connell over the next few days while she's down. I'd like to take Claire up the coast for a couple of months; go up Byron way. Do the hippy thing, eh.' He laughed; 'might teach me thing or two about tolerance.'

'What a great idea, she'll love it; you might even get her into a tinny, and she can sneak you into a gallery or two. Sue took me to a beauty at Murwillumbah, on the Tweed River. There's some lovely little towns in the hills around there, too. Gee, mate, you've earned it!'

'We've done well I think; don't you? The Memorial Gardens is a real sight to see. This is why I have trouble with the trashing of Michael's image. Wouldn't have done it without him. And…', he looked a little sheepish, '…

and Charlie's doing a great job with the *Stud*, as though he was born to it.'

'Well look, I don't want to rubbish Michael either although, Jesus, he's done some pretty bloody awful things, I think we're simply starting to see him full on and frontal.'

Bran's reply was non-committal. 'We had fun though, didn't we? Remember how it all started?' He was talking about the Memorial Gardens.

'Sure do, but I don't reckon it was much fun for you, you had to manage it all; we just spent the money! Loved it; Charlie's a great bloke to work with.'

'I remember it like it was yesterday, Ben. I admired you both so much.'

'Really, and then out o' the blue, you unloaded Mick's incredible proposition for the Bi-Centenary. You must have told him we were doing some landscaping of the Creek; because I hadn't. I'd only sent him photos of the work at *Clifton*.'

'Yeah I told him just in passing and then: snap! Six weeks later he puts that package to me. *Well, Bran, if we are going to do it, it might as well be done properly. The Bicentenary will be huge you know. I'm on the Bicentennial Council and …* As he took breath I couldn't help noticing that inclusive "we"; it was no longer Charlie's and my project; and then he was off again! Told me he'd organized the practical support and funding and had met with several state government politicians and their bureaucrats and they were on board. It was agreed he said, it would be the focal point of the local Bicentennial celebrations.'

'Bloody amazing really wasn't it? Even though he knew we'd started on the project, he was … well, so it seemed, taking over.'

'No "seeming" about it, like most of what I did for Michael: I did what I was told. He always had such a clear picture of what he was proposing, he was so focused; I never questioned him.'

'He had the money and the power?' Ben stopped for a moment recalling a conversation they'd had. *Power, Benny? A great aphrodisiac, eh! That's how I get my kicks now!*

'Yes' Bran sighed, 'as I'm now beginning to understand, he got a thrill out of wielding power, almost as if he was born to it. Claire said he had this enormous sense of entitlement.' He paused. 'But he did think of everything didn't he?'

'Even if he ignored that there were other people involved!' I was overtaken by an image of us in Michael's office many years ago. *This is how it'll be*!

'As I've said Ben, I didn't see it like that. I thought the gully garden was a great idea, could come off in a major rather than a minor, key! But I'll never forget Charlie's reaction when I suggested Michael's name be associated with it? Christ! What a stir that caused. "If his name is linked to it in any way, shape or form, you can count me out. You two can do it on your own!" Charlie was livid!'

'It wasn't the plan that he was indignant about so much as Mick's assumption that anything could be bought; even other people's ideas and ambition and that everyone has their price. That's what he meant when he told you his acceptance included having nothing to do with Mick and that no strings be attached to the money. So, yeah, it is … well it's been loads of fun; we felt it was a vision shared between the three of us.'

Bran's smile included a strange mixture of relief and satisfaction. 'Now, son, are you going to offer me a piece of that legendary cottage pie you're warming up?'

'Of course, get yourself some eating irons, the Tom sauce is on the shelf in the pantry and I bought a fresh loaf when I was in town. Obligatory, fresh bread and butter with potato pie.'

'Isn't it the *four* of us? Michael was always there,' Bran said, picking up the thread. 'You've never lost touch have you Ben?'

'Oh, he cut me off when he found out what we'd done to the *Clifton* Garden; no need to go into it. But we were in touch for a helluva long time. So, you knew about him and me, then?'

'Course I did Ben, but Michael always kept things separate. I assumed there was a reason for this so I never queried him or divulged to you. We've been stupid; but would it have been any different? He seemed to have everything mapped out.'

My emotions were in a jumble and yet, looking out across the Gully garden – our garden – I wasn't sorry I met him.'

'Claire doesn't see it this way, Ben, but, for us all – Charlie, you, me, even Sue – he's been an enabler. Claire says he's made a cynical use of his money to keep us all here and not test our wings elsewhere. But I reckon he's given us the ways and means to extend ourselves imaginatively in whatever direction we sought except, for some unfathomable reason, geographically. He gave Sue the financial space to compose her symphony and look at the *Stud*. Edward, in his wildest dreams, couldn't have envisaged what we've made of it; even if Claire and I had the vision, (and did it) Michael made it possible. You and Charlie? The house garden and the transformation of the gully, I can't tell you the pleasure it gives us to walk out into the garden at *Clifton*. Ah, the garden,' he sighed, stopping. 'I've never talked to you about it, just taken it for granted. What was in your mind when you took it on?'

Ben laughed. 'Charlie was in my mind. Michael had made him my responsibility, so that's how we got stuck into what was at the time, a garden in need of a lot of TLC.'

'Well, we'd have to cop a bit of the blame for the neglect. Claire made a point of saying that the garden was the responsibility of the *absentee squire*, not us.'

'You didn't have the time mate; and you weren't living in the place, Edward was supposed to be. But this whole conversation raises a point about Michael. For all his managing, organizing, setting in place, he relied on other people's ideas. When he gave me the job, although I asked him if there was anything he imagined we might do, he blustered: *Christ Almighty, Man. You're doing the job!* That's when he threw out the hint that Charlie knew a bit about gardens, so we just got stuck right into it.'

'Go on! What did Charlie say?'

'Well he told me the two of them had done a bit of reading when they were kids and had some ideas about formal gardens. He said he'd always thought the garden needed "acclimatizing" and since it's been neglected: lots of love and care. He was very excited and had a way of talking about the garden as if it was an orchestra. "It's a matter of bringing together all of its parts," he would say. "Some will provide the harmonies, some the contrast, some the drama; some the strong vibrant sounds, others the beauty and sweetness.'"

Bran was engrossed. 'What an extraordinary way of talking about it.'

'I think he could visualize what it might be like. He said, I can hear him now: "one of the wonderful things about music, is that it can have several conversations running at the same time; so can gardens.' And he'd wave his arms as if conducting an orchestra, calling different parts of the garden into play. From the tall trees, like those Lemon-scented Gums you planted Bran, with their smooth, shimmering silver trunks, to the flaming Waratahs and some of the Grevilleas and Azaleas, providing the colour at the middle heights, right down to the tiny purple Barberries and little Geums" – those fairy lights, as Sue calls them – flourishing in the dappled light. Ah, yes, we talked a lot about our garden.'

Ben was now almost talking to himself as he took Bran deeper into the garden, explaining its levels within levels, designed not only to invite a rambler to look back into the garden but also to gaze out to the escarpment and the high country, glimpsing on the way the original Eucalypts of the larger property.

'Ah Ben, it's a poor day if after my morning stroll along the path you've constructed around the garden, I don't feel as though all's right with the world.'

'So, Bran, you reckon it's okay then?'

* * *

No section of the original garden escaped their modifying hands, yet they didn't change anything that didn't need it. They retained the design of the central driveway at the front of the house, bordered on the outer rim by a low Camellia hedge running from the gate, culminating in the circular drive around the lily pond. In Charlie's words, they animated this homely stretch with swathes of ancient heirloom Daffodil hybrids and various species of Rose, while allowing the rampant pink and white *Pierre de*

Ronsard and Timothy's musk Rose on either side of the wide entrance steps to run and mingle.

By way of contrast, they went to work on the highly formalized large garden behind the house with the pick and shovel, not wanting there to be any misunderstanding about the orientation, the philosophical underpinnings of their garden. That doesn't mean they removed every trace of the formal English garden but they set out to design a garden which did not look nostalgically back to an ideal from the old world. They were looking with fresh eyes, eyes accustomed to living here, where the perfect symmetry of the central pathways and the evenly spaced walks, fanning out in straight lines from every corner of the house with formally planted beds and alcoves, was anachronistic; did not suit a landscape in which symmetry was not the informing characteristic. The new design incorporated ideas of hybridity that Charlie had long held, while Ben's plant selections and placement gave the garden its drama, as bursts of massed colour at one moment, give way to serenity at another; as varied panoramas unfold across softly grassed lawns or gravel paths, broken by ponds, a mature tree or groups of Tulips or blue Forget-me-nots dotted with splashes of pink miniatures. For both these men, never ones to put themselves forward, the garden became a means of expression.

It is still, no less than Timothy's more regimented pattern: a creation of great artifice, carefully composed to give delight and contentment. There were merely other hands conducting the music of this garden. For they had in mind a living organism, which structurally gave them the idea of arteries running, by indirection, from the house to the garden's extremities. Yet as any attentive rambler discovers, although the paths are more randomly placed, there are still destinations to be arrived at: the gazebo, furnished with cushions on old cedar benches; the greenhouse; the larger of the ponds with its sitting and lounging areas; the tea garden under the Wysteria; the iron and wood love seats, donated by Natasha, 'so that you two lovers can have a rest as you wander through your Eden'; while the *Stud Garden Path,* circling the entire area, leads ultimately to the sheds.

For his part, still caught up with 'Old Capability', Michael told Bran they'd *royally fucked up a brilliant English garden*, although he only ever saw it vicariously in the pages of magazines and never spoke of it to Ben. Coming in through the garden at the end of a long day, even knowing it as intimately as he did, Charlie found it held endless surprises. 'Everywhere, from its grandeur to its sun-dappled alcoves and nooks, and copious under plantings, it offers respite and pleasure.' It sounds as though Michael didn't understand it, however!

* * *

'Well, I'm in awe of it and of you two. As I think you know, Natasha loved it. From those tresses of white and pink blooms, mingling and then breaking away from each other at the front steps to the greater garden; it took her breath away. She couldn't wait to be back, she'd told Claire, after she and Andy had explored it in '98. And, I presume' he said, winking 'she was referring to the garden! I have a hunch Timothy would have liked the changes.'

'Well, thanks. My old man would have been proud of it too in his funny way I think: poor old bugger; never stop thinking about him you know; he missed out on so much.'

'Yep. That bloody war has a lot to answer for. I was one of the lucky ones; if it hadn't been for Claire, I don't know where I would've ended up. Head full of that shit when I came back but she nursed me, brought me back you know. The farm didn't work for your old man but this place sure as hell helped me put it behind me. The war's never gone, of course, I still whimper like a dog some stormy nights when the heavens are torn apart, but don't you worry, I know I'm one of the lucky ones. Hey! Anymore of that pie, do I have to bang my pannikin?'

'Help yourself.'

'Tell me, Ben. You didn't miss League? You were good.'

'Not really. Yeah, I was okay … for the bush, but I don't know how far I could've gone and then, of course, when Mick came up with the landscaping lark: real money, challenge and … well … I would've been a bloody fool to knock that back. I couldn't see the point! In the end I was getting more satisfaction out of watching the garden grow, than jinking around one more lumbering forward.'

'You didn't want to captain the *Tigers*? You could have. I would've backed you.'

'Not really; not my scene. I'm happy being a member of the team, don't need to run the show. Charlie's the same, we don't need to take the trophies home. Michael on the other hand – there we are, we can't leave the blighter out, can we – would have had to lead it if he'd stayed. Just as he had to Captain the University side and hold the cup up.' The obituary was in his mind. And Natasha!

'You are a perceptive devil, Ben.' Claire had slipped quietly into the room. 'Come on my darling,' she said, taking Bran's hand; 'come and give me a hand. See you later Mr Freud!'

'Yeah, strange day! But I'm looking forward to seeing Natasha. Hope she's okay.'

* * *

Arm in arm, Claire and Bran set out for *Clifton*, she was shaking her head and smiling. 'What an extraordinary journey that chap's had.' She was thinking back to Ben's arrival in town, as raw as an uncut log. Bran had come in one day, telling her the *Tigers* had recruited some kid who'd been pretty special in the Juniors.' She saw him the next weekend after his first game: gangly, he might have been about 5'10" but he was still filling out, hanging off the edge of the team gathering. 'Just didn't know what to do with his hands; if he wasn't pushing them through his tousled brown hair, he was shoving them in and out of his trouser pockets, rolling from one foot to the other. Wouldn't dare make eye contact with anyone.'

'Yes, I remember, love. I was a bit worried about him. Didn't think they should've played him straight off. But, actually, he was more at home on the pitch than he was in the Club House! Seventeen wasn't he, same as

Michael? That's right, but whereas our boy was mixing in with the rest of the team, Ben didn't know what to do, where to go; looked as though he'd drop dead if anyone spoke to him. Shy? God, he looked terrified when I congratulated him on a good first game. "Didn't do much," he mumbled, speaking to his shoe and that was about the extent of it.'

Ben wasn't entirely new to Claire at the time, she could remember when his father, Bert, arrived at his humpy with this poor little pregnant woman. Woman? She couldn't have been more than seventeen or eighteen, whereas Temple must have been near-on forty (in fact, he was thirty-six, she later recalled). Pretty little face in a nondescript sort of way but unkempt and with a look in her eye that bordered on terror. The CWA heard of her arrival on the bush telegraph and Claire called in a couple of times to see if she could help with clothing, bed linen, nappies and baby clothes. She took her some corned beef every now and again, some casseroles and a couple of sugar cakes at other times. 'Hardly ever saw Bert,' she told Bran 'just his mess in the yard; did he ever finish anything? She kept Ben on the teat for as long as she could, giving some kind of comfort to each of them I guess, not that there can have been much sustenance for the baby, she was so scrawny.' And then one day, was the little tyke three, she wasn't there. 'Gone back to her mother,' Bert offered. 'Didn't she mate!' he muttered, looking down at Ben. 'Couldn't take it!' He said into space; his face creased with a bitter smile.

His little 'mate' didn't have a clue of what was going on of course; luckily he was out of nappies and although he was grubby and his feet were filthy and already as tough as a wild dog's paws, he had something that looked like a chop in his hand. He didn't look hungry. Rowdy never made Claire or any of other girls who went out to help feel welcome; but once it was clear that he was going to try to raise the child, she made sure they called in regularly, with hand-me-downs and pieces of warm clothing, a blanket or two, some soup perhaps. She couldn't help smiling; each time they went back, if they'd taken food, there was never a skerrick left, or if clothes; they looked as though they'd hardly been off his back.

'I've just been thinking about him as a toddler. He was a strange little fellow, he just seemed to get on with things. Even as a five or six-year-old, you'd see him rounding up the chooks or taking them left-overs; later he was feeding ducks up, getting them ready to sell at Christmas, and by about the time he was eight, he was never without a rugby ball. Well *ball*'s a bit of an exaggeration! More like something wrapped up in a sock or a pig's bladder; he'd flick it around, swoop on it and step around a tree or feint past his dog and boot it as hard as he could, racing the dog to retrieve it.'

'That's right; that's when I got him an old match ball.'

'My word, he loved that ball; almost got a smile onto his serious little face. If he wasn't a *Tiger* before that, he was locked on after! I know he didn't last too long at Bega High. I asked him about it once: "Well, he said, dad didn't give a stuff whether I went or not. It was pretty easy, I was a bit bored, … and I was sick of kids making fun of the old man, slurring their words and swearing … so I just stopped going and got a job," which, Claire smiled, 'was rather grandly called gardening by his father, when I called in once. "Earning his keep," the tough old bugger said as he glared at me with a look that said, "what the hell are you doin' round here; bugger orf!" Next thing we know he's at the Rugby Club.'

'I think I told you when the kid was recruited, 'Rowdy' said he was "real proud of him; done it tough, you know: I didn't know what I was bloody doing. Crook example but he stuck by me. Must 've been fuckin' mad!" I suggested that the boy loved him. "Love! Christ mate, there wasn't too much o' that around the bloody place. I haven't got a clue what it is!"

'Look at that shy, rawboned kid now,' she said. 'He's still got those rough edges. Oh, he's filled out, but the angles are only slightly smoothed and he's never lost his bushman's gait.' She'd always kept an eye on him. For while Bran was intent on watching Michael, she kept watch on Ben as well. They were both good players, although Michael let it be known he was a little more so! *All talking about Ben today; couldn't have done it without my ball.* It didn't seem to bother Ben and, while the chaps at the Club reminded her over the years she is only a woman, what would she know about rugby, she thought he had wonderful balance, never seemed rushed, and had the knack of turning up at the right place at the right time;

uncanny really. 'You can't teach that Mrs D.' Father Patrick said, in the early days. 'Ben has flair.'

'Nowadays though, he's as comfortable in a tweed jacket as he is in a flannelette working shirt, and have you noticed: he's as happy in the kitchen as he is in the sheds. And he listens to what others have to say! He's a bit like you, you know B. What you see is what you get, but what you get is miles away from that awkward kid who found his way here because of what someone thought he might do on a rugby pitch.'

'You're very fond of him, aren't you Pet?'

'Yes, he's so much his own man and here I am, won't see seventy-five again, and I love it when he turns those big browns on me,' she laughed, 'and, teaming up with Sue! God knows what they thought when she trotted him out at Festival Hall, or the café strip on Chapel Street!' Ah, she thought, what progress he's made! A recent survey of country gardens: 'Men for all seasons: Australia's landscape gardeners' in *Country Style*, found a place for him and Charlie and their garden at *Clifton*. And there's that magnificent photographic record of the making of the Memorial Garden: *The Myrtle Creek Gully Garden*. Who would have thought we'd see them on the coffee table! He's a celebrity of sorts, even if he says it's all unnecessary.

'Our lives are the richer for having him in them my darling girl, but no-one's as lucky as me.' As he spoke Bran put his big arm around her, felt her snuggle into his side.

Susannah:
Songs in a Human Key

Now, half a good lifetime since we'd first met, Charles is again on my verandah. I'd imagined him dodging showers and puddles on his way. He would have come down the zig-zag path across the Myrtle Creek gardens, following the creek into the town, past the bridge and then I heard him fiddling with my creaking gate before threading his way through the wilderness of the garden, just as he had as a young boy. I was playing the *Sarabande*, from the second of the Bach *Cello Suites*; how he loved those suites. 'Come in, door's open!' As we brushed cheeks he whispered, barely audible: 'Is that a new instrument? The tone's exquisite: such depth.'

Made from a piece of flamed maple, the cello glowed I thought, as I held it out from my body, pirouetting it on its endpin. 'It's a Ruggieri Charles, and it's yours, from Michael.' Atonement, I wondered, or perhaps belatedly, an expression of love? But, there was no need to go into it. I guessed he must have paid in excess of £100,000 for it; was it the one that was sold in 1996? I followed the fine instrument auctions.

Charles was barely listening as he gently lifted the instrument out of my hands, his long fingers momentarily reflected in the rich patina of the diaphragm, tears caught in his eyelashes. He sat, straightened his back and began to play, as though for the first time, the *Prelude* from the first of the *Bach Suites*. I met his gentle tears with my own. At the completion of the first movement, with the final notes hanging in the air he sat, emotionally exhausted, but I thought filled – can you say it – with a sad joy as slowly, we unfolded from the sublime.

'Natasha brought it down. She would have loved to hear that I'm sure. There's room for a lot of music in her starved soul, I think.'

He nodded, gratefully, 'yes, but not yet. It will take me a while to get accustomed to this magnificent instrument.' Then he stopped. 'Sue, do you mind? I just need to be on my own.'

'Of course not, darling.' Kissing him, holding his head to mine a moment longer, I knew I wouldn't be the only one today who had him in mind. I could read him well and couldn't help thinking of the state he was in when Moll came to me after that dreadful morning, with the idea that I might be good for him and found myself dwelling on our union in music, shared, was it really over more than 30 years?

* * *

'I'll do anything to help.' I'd said at the time with a conviction I wasn't sure I could carry off; my own demons and all that anger, were barely held in check. I wanted to help but was I able? I liked Charles, having got to know him a little through his music over the previous year or so. And yet really, I thought I was the one who needed therapy! That's what had brought me to the Ponds in the first place: bush idyll or somewhere to hide? At the time I felt I had nowhere to go and look at me now. She was looking out from her studio, gazing out through the mist, lifting her eyes to the purple of the sculptured hills. 'From whence the help cometh!' She murmured. Content. The text had come from afar, but that feeling of ascent I drew from it, while deeply felt, owes less to its source in *Psalms*, and more to this place; to pleasures stemming from the magnificent ranges and the braided harmonies of the bird calls which enter consciousness at first light, singing through numerous tones and contours. Quite Baroque, a form of counterpoint.

When I stumbled into Celtic Ponds however, such elation was anathema, I felt as if my soul was scored with sadness. I'd completed my music studies in Vienna and although the urge to return to Australia was overwhelming, I knew there was no welcome awaiting me in Melbourne: 'A music career? Who does she think she is!' My father had bellowed; nor did I have any desire to return there. It was the late winter of 1968, I'd had a brief sojourn in Paris with my mother then flown into Sydney and was driving with an old girl-friend from the Grammar days, Cynthia Holmes, who had just broken up with her boy-friend: 'I'm running away, would you like to run away with me?' But we didn't run, we pottered: through Goulburn, on to Canberra and saw the foundations of the city we know today; took in the new Library and heard of plans for other monumental buildings along the banks of the lake; visited Parliament House, sparkling in the August sun and the War Memorial, where strangely, for I wasn't someone who had dwelt much on Australia's war stories, I was overwhelmed to the point of tears by Waller's beautiful windows and the sheer peace of that memorial space. And then on to Cooma, through a countryside of rolling grasslands and lucerne paddocks marked by the bare reaching spires of emergent poplars. It could have been a landscape by Gruner. We just chatted, I'd never done this kind of thing and was surprised how easy it was. Cooma did not delay us, save to kip down in a ratty pub, refuel ourselves and the car and plan a route to the coast. 'Could do a lot worse than stop at Celtic Ponds on the way down,' the publican suggested. 'A real nice Devonshire Tea at the tea rooms: the sister runs it.'

What a glorious drive! It was densely wooded but every now and again, winding down the incline from Mt Brown, sweeping vistas of the verdant country below are revealed. I was enchanted. To my untrained eyes the bush seemed virginal, untrammelled. It wasn't of course, but this was new country to me and, while the same can't be said for Cynthia, I took it all in. From the majestic trees, close packed as if strapped together by the vines, to the hills and gullies as the heights give way to the gentle paddocks and grass lands cut by creeks and gullies, broken here and there by massive granite outcrops, as if cast willy-nilly by some local giant. They wound down to Celtic Ponds, tracing the line of a hearty creek on the low side of the road winding its way through the paddocks, now rushing across boulders, white water swirling and skeltering, then spreading wider, as the earlier turbulence settles and the banks widen, before narrowing again to pass under the town bridge on its way through the town and down. While Cynthia topped up with fuel at Wright's Garage, *First and Last for Miles*, I wandered over to the creek, slipped off my shoes, rolled my jeans and paddled in the shallows. 'I'd have liked to dive in: a baptism.' I remarked to a bemused Cynthia as we strolled into the cafe.

'A bit chilly for that, love!' The lady in the tea rooms laughed as she welcomed us. 'Two Devonshire teas, thanks. With all the trimmings. I believe they're to die for!' Cynthia wrapped her up in a big smile.

'You won't be sorry love! Coffee, out o' the jar, okay? Won't be a jiffy!' But I was preoccupied. On my way in I'd noticed among posters and advertisements in the window, a slip of paper: 'Music Teacher Wanted. Contact Molly Greenwood at the *Glen*.'

As we sat down glancing around, Cynthia waved her arm: 'God! Fancy living in a dump like this. Look at it!' All she could see was a worn bitumen road, crumbling at the edges, a bunch of shops, huddling together as though out of desperation and an old wooden bridge. Whereas, I could see hills and ranges of delicate blue and purple tonings reaching to the horizon; lush pastures and cattle grazing, a creek that seemed to be gurgling to me, while the smoke rising from chimneys on the hills that rose gently above the town, spoke of community. Closer, directly across the bridge in my line of vision, I saw a faded wooden church, topped by a quaint old steeple that housed the church's bell. 'Does that ever ring ... the old bell?'

'Not often love; enough to disturb the dogs of a Sunday, and on big occasions; weddings and funerals, that sorta thing, but we don't have many of them, more's the pity.'

'Yeah, I bet they're real humdingers when you do.' Cynthia chimed in, and they both laughed while May didn't.

'Yes, well, we really look forward to them. Er ... as long as it's not one of us, dyin', that is!' That was her joke.

As we paid the bill, I asked about the notice, pointing to it. 'Would that be right?'

'Oh yes, for sure. Molly Greenwood, lovely lady, just up the hill there at the orchard, *Glen Cannich* they call it; can't miss it. Into music are yer?

Her boy plays pianna like an angel.'

'Thanks Mrs ...'

'Diller, love: May. Should I tell 'er about yer interest?'

'No need Mrs Diller. I might just pop in; but thanks. Lovely scones.'

We went for a walk, 'Won't take long,' Cyn giggled. We finished the line of shops in the main drag, found the little school over the bridge, walked around the church's unkempt lawns and little cemetery, all romantically strewn with leaves that might have been there for a couple of months, and wandered past the brick Shire Office with its brilliant rose beds. 'Touch of class here, nice colonial brick work, and the shutters! Someone must have had big plans for this little carriage-stop once upon a time!' Cynthia remarked, dismissively.

Wandering back over the bridge, we passed a wooden cottage of washed-out white and blue, with a garden that once had been someone's pride and joy but was now a weed or two short of a wilderness, as I looked up the hill: 'Do you mind if we go up?'

'I saw you looking at that ad. But, c'mon sweets, get a grip...,' Cynthia groaned. 'You've got one of the best degrees in Europe and been rubbing shoulders with the musical elite for most of your life. Hardly preparation for down-town Ponds, unless I'm terribly mistaken. I think you're crazy!'

'I know, I know, Cyn. But look, I'm daring to hope: beats despair! Let's have another cuppa and I'll tell you about the sophisticated Beaumonts.'

'Back ladies?'

'Couldn't stay away, Mrs Diller. Just coffee this time, thanks.'

They nodded. Susannah was anxious to talk. 'Well, Cyn, you know bits and pieces but that only scratches the surface, and I'm sick of bottling it up.' Cynthia, who had known Susannah since they were eleven, smiled, making space for her friend.

'Melbourne is not an option. I've lost all respect – did I ever have any? – for my father and you may recall, my mother stayed in Europe after that trip we made? But together, they'd betrayed me at every turn; it's clear I'm homeless.'

'What about your siblings?'

'Oh well, darling Jonathon is gone. A beautiful pianist, but he couldn't satisfy my father. Took his own life. Estelle is escaping into art and design in London and Cedric has thumbed his nose and gone to Tech. The Professor doesn't know what to make of that, so he's ignoring it. And then there's Cranbrook.' Her face was grim. 'I can't even call him *the ghastly ... the horrible!* He has literally and metaphorically torn me asunder!'

'Darling, what are you telling me?'

'Yes Cyn, that's what I'm saying: the unspeakable; he never let up, he stole my childhood.'

'But you never said …'.

'Who tells anyone about this sort of thing! What do you say? Oh, by the way girls, my brother is spying on me, touching, molesting, fucking me. No … you shut up.'

Cynthia covered Susannah's hand with her own, only to feel her friend tense up and withdraw from the contact. 'Sometimes when we'd just met, I saw you so sad and pale. Oh, I'm so sorry.'

'It's not your fault, Cyn, but it is his and theirs: the Professor and the Mother. For years, I could think of them only in the third person: characters in an obscene play. They did it to my brain, as he was doing it to my body; my poor little body.' She spoke of it, as a thing apart. 'I was six, … six! when it started. Jono had just gone to Paris; Mother was with him for four months in that first year and went back repeatedly for lengthy stays over the next few years. The Professor was in his study and I was told to play with Cranbrook. But these weren't the playful, inquisitive games of children, had about them none of that sense of fun or innocent experimentation that kids might engage in. The look in his eye was horrible, leering, like some character out of a ghastly nursery rhyme. 'Zannah, Zannah,' he'd call. 'I'm, after you; I want to play with you.' He'd leer.

'Play! Play?' She was gasping for air. 'How I wept, and then … I stopped. His hands would run all over my body like an obscene insect, but I said nothing; didn't touch him … said nothing. I never laughed, had no dolls, no toys, no friends; no hope, no interests except music, and even there my bowing became abrasive, lacerating! He polluted the simplest things like the joy of watching birds frolicking in the hedges; those days when time seems endless and you might watch this play, but you don't in case he comes along. I stayed in my room, waiting … and I turned it into music: ugly, discordant, heart-wrenching.'

He was only ten; how did he know about this awful stuff; but he did; it was as though he felt entitled to have me. Ohhhh,' she shook herself, as if dusting off filth. 'I did hit him once in the balls with my school shoe, so hard I thought they might come out his mouth; he'd tried to touch one of the littlies. I paid for it – "you fucking slut" – but he left them alone.'

'My dreams and day dreams were now invaded by Cranbrook's assaults; his marauding broke into the security even of my mental life.' She stopped, overtaken. Hands, pink fingers, like fat worms crawling, his angry cock, my mind screaming. Shut up they don't care! Screaming! Opening my little lips. Screaming, sobbing, wetting the bed: filthy girl!

'If I said anything to my father, which I had at first, I was being melodramatic and must stop bothering him: he was busy. I think father saw it as a curious side-effect of what he called "Cranbrook's unusual genius." While Mother didn't want to know about it; but, oh she knew, and when she wasn't escaping to Paris she'd sigh: 'I've got my own problems, girl! It could have been my father speaking; 'perhaps it's how he expresses his affection. He's only playing.'

'When you first came to Grammar, we thought you were so stuck up but then you changed; we loved you and forgot about the little girl we first met.'

'It's alright, I didn't know how to be with kids my own age; just didn't know,' she whispered; 'I had nothing. I felt displaced, unwanted, abandoned by God, my parents, even by myself. I'd given up. I could hear my soul screaming for help, but I ignored it; if I acknowledged it the pain would be truly existential: this way it was only physical, I felt like a prisoner of war.' She paused, taken over by wild images, her mouth was dry. Her skin stretched, felt as though it was on fire.

'What about your mother; she must have been grieving Jono's death?'

'He didn't give a damn about her! "It's your bloody fault: you wandering

Jew," he'd yell.' "Snivelling bloody wretch!" She was sent to her room, yes, *her* room. A room without any adornment as, after Jono's futile suicide, Cranbrook's musical tuition was taken over by the Professor: none better, he professed. "You stay out of it Anya; Jonathon ended up on the end of a rope!" Such spite and loathing.'

'Having made Cranbrook aware in no uncertain terms – more like a threat! – that he was blessed by his inheritance and had better live up to it, Havelock secured him a place at the Academy in Vienna, where he could hone those prodigious talents imparted by his father! He couldn't imagine him being prepared in an Australian institution. Now, it's my turn to be ironic!' She paused. 'What a joy it was when he was away; my soul, poor wizened thing, began again to breathe. Oh, he still invaded my dreams, spawning awful overlaid images; all backed by my mad dialogue of hatred and resistance and submission, but ...'

'Oh, you poor darling. I ... I can't imagine it.' Cynthia said, breaking in.

'That's probably when you noticed a change at school. But I also spent a lot of time composing. Made an *Impromptu* on *John, 1:5*: *And the light shineth in darkness*. I was on parole, you see; I'm never done with that piece, the emotions that filled it are still raw!'

'Are you ...? I don't know what to say.' She was fumbling for a response: 'shall we see if we can find *Glen Cannich*?'

'Ah, yes, let's go up the hill.'

'Just follow the creek love; on to the gravel where Blunt Street runs out.' Mrs Diller whispered to Cynthia as she paid for the coffees.

'Now I think about it, you never went to the school dances, did you?'

'School dances! I hadn't even had a boyfriend; couldn't imagine being touched by anyone. Oh, it cost of course; makes them angry if they can't even get to first base. "Frigid!" "Cock-teaser!" "Lezzo!" I've had most of it thrown at me. I never dressed up, stopped wearing nighties at six, no cute panties, all those fun things. Don't you see? I couldn't afford to look attractive; in case it was an invitation.'

'What about later?'

'Men? I avoided them. I didn't dislike men particularly, I just can't – present tense, Cyn – stand being touched. Even girls. I've had crushes – mooned over Jane Letchford all through fourth form – but it stops if it looks like becoming physical.' The rest just hung in the air.

'Now where were we in my grim tale? Ah yes: Cranbrook was off to Vienna. But even then he got his hands on me when he was back for the long recess. God, it was sick; it was as though he was dependent; do you see? An awful need seemed to drive his attacks. A kind of frenzy.'

'Shit! Now I understand those incredible mood swings you had!' Cynthia wanted to hug her, but didn't. Held her eyes in unspoken sympathy.

'*Mood Swings*? If only you could have seen into my haunted mind, seen it in free-fall, swinging, yelling, screaming like some frantic ape. Mood swings? And then, I got my reprieve by default; it was our Leaving Year remember? The Professor couldn't care less. So, all of us, except Cedric, trooped off to Europe. "Bung him into boarding school Anya; it would be wasted on him." The Professor said he'd been invited onto a doctoral panel at the Royal College of Music. We took a flat for a month in London and had another month in Wien; as he tried to bring Cranbrook up to a level which he discovered, was too high for him.'

'Vienna! We were all so jealous. Well … not really: Leaving Exams and all that, but we did think you were pretty lucky. We wondered where your mother was though, when you got back. You just said she got away. I guess that's what she did?'

'Yes, it was a very difficult time for my father and Cranbrook, the truth was sinking in. The boy wasn't coping and Havelock was grovelling around some of his old haunts trying to land a chair: he was seeking, he said, the end of his exile. But nobody wanted him, not even my mother! Unknown to us all, Anya was planning her escape; at least she had something to trade.' She paused, deep in thought. 'But, that's another story. Well, perhaps not! You see I learned that as Anya Levy, she'd had a triumph here in the early thirties; brought the house down. I was told by someone who'd been at the concert: "In contrast to your father, whose Austrian debut" – '29 it was I think – "was a disaster. Having come with glowing testimonials from London he was almost run off the stage. It was very poor: technically lazy and emotionally inept." I couldn't help thinking how appropriate; to reveal these characteristics even at nineteen! He said he stopped performing at a young age because there was nothing more to achieve and took up composing.'

'I soon found out that my father's reputation closed, rather than opened doors; even at the Royal College of Music where he'd been trained and briefly taught. He was no use to me. Whereas strangely, because throughout our lives it had been hidden, my mother's reputation as a violinist had genuine cachet.'

'Whew! What about your schoolwork, though? Not that I was busting a gut!'

'I'd be lying if I didn't say I was worried about the exams. A good Leaving was to be my way out of the mire! Whereas, my father brushed it off: "You'll make it up girl, if not, does it really matter?" I needn't have worried: I got it in different ways, I guess. I spent the entire month in Vienna speaking German and French, fortunately Synge's *Playboy…* was on in London, so I went to that a couple of times.' She giggled: 'Super production. And, in London and Vienna, I extended my music education in ways that I could never have done at home. I'd simply made sure I boned up on maths and physics. I had a ball!

'This is a long story, Cyn; are you ready? Why don't we wander along the creek? I was lucky in London. Nettie Bainbridge, a Reader in music at the RCM, a wonderful Horn player and a fabulous teacher, took me under her wing. She was simply gorgeous. "What are you doing with that aging lesbian," my father bellowed, "She'll have her hands down your pants before you know where you are."'

'Wouldn't have been easy growing up in that house, I fancy, dearie!' Nettie mused. 'What with Anya – remarkable, truly precocious talent – silenced, but I imagine, seething underneath and Havelock elevated beyond his ability just to get him out of this place; it must have been dreadful! And you? I've got a feeling you know your sound-world already; whereas your father had no idea what it was. Anyway, let's have some fun eh; enter into that sound-world and make some music? I'll find you a nice cello in the music room. Would you like to?'

'I didn't need to reply. She linked arms, funny round thing that she was, her eyes shining, busy grey head bobbing, her rosy cheeks alive: "you'll know this dear. Let me hear a bit," she said as she had plonked a score in front of me – heavily marked I noticed – and I played a few bars.'

'Good, good, ah nice! You'll do. In fact my dear, you've got rather a lovely touch' she said, as she reached out to hug me. 'O dear, lovie, sorry, sorry ... No offence.'

'It's not you, Miss Bainbridge.'

'Nothing you want to talk about?'

'I shook my head, no! But, please, it's not you; I've never had such fun with music.'

'You want more; alright – no more Miss B ... Nettie ... horrid: but it's me! And if you want to talk any time, I have big ears and no memory, so it's safe with me.'

'So, for a month – I was seventeen – can you imagine how exciting it was? We played around with music and I found I wasn't completely lacking. In her understated and unassuming way she was teaching me about interpretation and arrangement. What sweet memories.'

'When we said goodbye, Nettie pushed me a little. "It isn't your father, is it?"'

'Not directly, I'd said, giving little away.'

Nettie remembered him as a tall, rather beautiful young man with a mane of silky brown hair, and she remarked on his manner. 'He would glance', she said, 'rarely looked fixedly at one, or anything.' She thought it was the look of a person ingrained in sensuality and sadism; found it sinister. The men were less disconcerted by it, dismissing it as the lazy glance of the dilettante.

'I let it pass; I didn't really know how to talk about my father's role in Cranbrook's abuse. Although, I sometimes wondered if I was a scrap, thrown the boy's way out of boredom. Nettie had, however, given me a perspective from which I could begin to view him and shown me that I had allies. And I had my gorgeous sister, Stella. "Well, Shuh-shuh," she had stopped calling me Zannah because it was Cranbrook's customary address. We ran wild!'

'London must have been fantastic fun, Suze. Swinging into the Sixties.'

'Yes, the place was putting on new rags. Beat was the scene, it was all Joss sticks and vegetarian food and the clothes! Our parents didn't care what we did as long as we didn't bother them. He was brown-nosing around his old department and she? Well ... that didn't become clear until later. He did invite us to an Elgar concert. "Better than that ephemeral tinkling, strident rubbish that passes for music these days", he roared, not knowing we'd been attending a number of concerts full of this rubbish. We did go to the Elgar, I mean who would miss the *Variations*? But, while it was a wonderful musical history lesson, it wasn't the music I could or wanted to make. Here we were, in a London still visibly violated by war in a century of profound upheaval and my father is advocating the opulent, expansive sounds of Elgar as a model! Even Stella, who had found Bacon and Pop Art, was surprised: "What planet are you on Daddy? *Land of Hope and Glory* after Dresden! Gimme a break!"'

'Bacon, Bacon!' He'd spluttered, when she mentioned her interest. 'That degenerate and his vile figures.' It could have been Goebbels speaking.

'And then ... Vienna! It was fascinating. I was the quiet observer. Stella got involved with some radical art movement; went to a couple of rallies and came back wearing black lipstick, no bra, and offering numerous variations in Austrian of "fuck", some of them very inventive! Next day, she had pink hair, the Professor was shocked, the Mother was laughing her head off.'

'Really, your mother?'

'Yes, I began to see Anya in a different light. She adored being back in Vienna; told me she'd never been a mother to me but perhaps in time, she can be a friend! Strangely, she started including me: got me into a composition workshop and took me to a fabulous recital at the Academy where their renowned Professor of conducting, Hans Swarovsky, was putting two of his students through their paces. She didn't bother bringing

Cranbrook. "Over his head!"'

'What an experience. And Cranbrook; after that? Should I ask?'

'Ah, well, the newly radicalised Stella took action and dealt with Cranny: told him *to fuck off, out of my room and my life!* "You know why I'm doing this," she screamed at our parents, "because that fucking son of yours is a pervert." All the Professor did was mumble about her bad language, while Anya apologised: "Oh, Susannah; I'm so sorry!" Yet, whenever I was alone, Cranbrook hung around, but by now, is it strange? I began to pity him.'

'I can't believe it, you softened to him?'

'No, not softened; but there was a kind of futile desperation in his attacks, now I could brush him off. He was a shell of a man; he'd made no friends, had no normal outlets and his music was coming to nothing. I was aware that my emotional life was damaged because of him, but really, he was emotionally crippled! So, resisting him would leave him shaking, in a frenzy. How could he possibly get inside a score when he was so agitated, so horribly pre-occupied?'

'What happened to this rising star.'

'Oh,' she smiled weakly! He's a very pale star in Melbourne's musical firmament. Lands one or two minor engagements a year, does the odd operetta or the Christmas panto if they can't round up anyone else; gets an occasional gig announcing with the ABC, and works part-time behind the counter in a music store, flogging whatever he's told. I don't see him.'

* * *

They had reached the Greenwood's orchard. 'Thanks for listening, Cyn.' Susannah said, as she called at the open front door. 'Anyone home; I've come about your ad.'

'Coming, … coming! The advertisement? How exciting!' A little breathless, her hair escaping from a rudimentary bun, untying her apron and dusting her hands as she scurried, Molly Greenwood's large grey eyes twinkled a welcome. 'Come, come in!' She led them down the passage to a large vestibule; the dog was barking.

'Don't bother about Furphy, he's a sook; all noise signifying nothing!'

'What exactly are you looking for, Mrs Greenwood?' They had been led into a room which, while it was tidy, suggested the Greenwoods did it pretty tough and the sitting room, seen through an open door – it could have been a stage set, circa 1925 – was dominated by an old upright piano. There was music on the stand, with a straight-backed chair placed adjacent to a piano stool, polished by use. There were two worn-to-comfort easy chairs next to a tiny fireplace. 'You have classes here?' It was a simple question; not ironic.

'Yes, I have half a dozen students but several of the current batch are talented. My son, Charles, even though I say it myself, is ready for a good teacher. Then there's Amy Hargreaves, and …' she paused, 'well that's what the ad's about. I've taken some of them as far as I can.'

Sue interrupted her and in answer to Molly's questions, outlined her musical background, which left Molly wondering if she was over qualified?

'Are you serious, dear?' In her straightforward way the question was as much about Susannah as it was about the job.

'Yes, I am serious, I'd need a second job. I intend doing some composition you see, and I'm beginning to feel I might be able to do it here. I won't go back to Melbourne.'

'Oh, well …, it would be lovely … Vienna?' Molly was murmuring to herself; she once would have liked to have taken her own music further. 'There's no rush for an answer? So, you might come to Celtic Ponds? Don't suppose we can interest your friend? Two beautiful young things around the district would cause quite a stir!'

Cynthia's smile was unconvincing. 'No, er … Molly, I'm on the road, discovering Australia and myself.' The allusion to Kerouac wasn't entirely accidental. 'But I'll be sure to visit. For the moment, though, it's the Duke and Ella and the car radio…'. After ambling back into town, they drove down to the watery expanses of Broadwater. 'So, what do you think Suze?'

'It might work. I've got some baggage, but not much luggage.' She said with a wry grin.

'The cello goes everywhere with me. I'll need a piano, oh and a car I guess.'

'You'll need something else, you can't live on the sweet air of this place. Look, there's a little University up the way; they've got this idea of trying to mount a school, faculty or whatever …of creative arts. Or there's a local Conservatorium: Why don't you contact them?'

'You're a brick, Cyn. I'll give both a go. But … you're not convinced.'

'Hmm, I wouldn't say that, but well, it's your life. Just don't become a hermit.'

'I'd like to give it a try. Let's relax here for a couple of days here, murder a few dozen oysters and then, if you'll drive me back up, I'll stay in the pub and suss the place out?'

* * *

'You're as good as your word, love.' They sat at the kitchen table while, over a pot of tea which they drank from china cups, relics of another age, Susannah rushed into the little speech she'd been rehearsing: 'I'll be honest with you Molly. I want to give it a go, but I won't commit 'til I've got something else to make ends meet. It wouldn't be fair but I've got a couple of leads. Now if possible, I'd like to meet some of the locals, and get a sense of what my pupils might be like.'

'Slow down love, no problem. Let's go and meet the Doogues for starters; over at the *Stud*.'

'You can't stay in the pub, my dear. No, no, …' It was Claire. 'We've always got a room ready up at the old house. You'll stay there.'

'She's right Miss Beaumont,' Bran chimed in. 'It's always made up. Now, Mol said you need wheels. What if you use our old FJ; it's got a few miles on the clock but it's lying idle. Borrow that until you're settled, or not, as the case may be.'

That evening, having dined with Molly, Herb and Charlie, who was impressed by how she talked about music; they went across to *Clifton*, which Claire and Bran had opened up for the evening, and met some of the townsfolk. Once she'd been introduced, she took Charles and Amy Hargreaves, who were both advanced students into the salon to listen to them play and have a chat, leaving behind them a buzz of excitement. Anna Liebowicz, a fine Polish-trained guitarist, who had fled Europe during the war and now lives at *Safe Haven,* a mixed farm out of town, said she'd love somebody with her musical background around the place. Urging caution, Doc Eddington wondered if there might be a skeleton or two in her cupboard; to which Molly huffed: 'Skeletons, cupboards? Perhaps she's just shy. She seems keen.'

'My point is. Why would a young woman like her want to set up here:' the Doc replied.

'You did!' Claire hooted. While Anna who rarely spoke out, picked up where the Doc left off: 'Well, if she is ... how you say, *fragile*, this might be a good place for her to settle her demons; it has been for me. What do you think Charlie, Amy, about having Miss Beaumont as a teacher?' She was looking at them as they came back, beaming into the room.

'It'd be great!' Although Charlie immediately added; 'You were terrific, too, Mum!'

By the end of September, I'd moved into the little blue and white cottage – *The Punt House* – the one we'd first noticed when we visited. Keen for me to stay, the Shire let me have the cottage on a peppercorn rent. I turned one of the bedrooms into a music room/study and I was on my way. I had four Cello classes at the Wollongong Conservatorium, was in discussion with the Teachers' College about a *Fundamentals of Music* class and had calling rights at the Sydney Conservatorium. I was still driving the old FJ which Bran said I could have until it fell apart; my piano had been delivered from Melbourne and I had five enthusiastic students, with the promise of another two after Christmas. I was giving Amy and Charlie additional theory lessons as they prepared for their Leaving year and, having eyed off my cello, Charlie spent hours of extra time at it, and indirectly with me. I liked him. I hadn't been down to Melbourne and I'd asked the removalist not to disclose my whereabouts.

Charlie complicated things a little in the new year by taking a part-time job, which meant the theory classes had to be moved to Sunday. And, having been interviewed for a place at the Sydney Conservatorium, it became clear that his lessons would continue through the long vacation until that is: 'the shit hit the fan', as Herb put it.

* * *

'Charlie is coming along beautifully, Molly. There's something about him. You'd know it better than I; a good brain – inquisitive, alert – mixed with a genuine musical facility and a delicacy of feeling, almost a fragility, which could make him vulnerable.' Molly looked closely at her; wondered perhaps if Sue was speaking from experience.

'I think he's talented, but he's in a mess Sue. I'm worried sick about him; Claire and I are wondering if you can help? All Herb and I can do is to be there for him; he's absolutely gutted.'

'Perhaps I can. I've wandered in some of the same dark woods I think he's lost in. I'll try.' In fact, with Dante as a guide, I was exploring that terrain musically at the time. *Dancing with Dante; a macabre fantasy*, was coming together. 'But, oh God, from what you've said I'd like to give that Michael O'Connell a serious piece of my mind.'

Molly looked at her, was glimpsing a side she hadn't seen: outspoken, resolute, feisty; fired on hot coals of her own, by the look of it. Together with Claire, they began to plot a strategy. 'His world's been torn apart. Like a bomb blast!' I said. 'All we can do is help him find a path through the debris.' I looked at them. 'At first, I'm just going to set him simple musical tasks, Molly. There's no need to break new ground or fuss about tidying things up, it only puts pressure on him. His head won't be there.'

'But, I'm playing muck,' he grumbled. The allusion to Melba got a smile out of me: 'But you're playing, Charles!'

In the interim, I smoothed his re-entry into the Con. It wasn't too difficult. My *Impromptu on a Self Portrait by Francis Bacon, for Stella*, had recently been well received in Sydney, and Caroline Lang, the Acting Head at the Conservatorium, took me seriously, I think, when I pleaded Charles' case'.

* * *

In fact, my interaction with the contemporary music staff at the Con had matured, from an original scepticism based on expectations that I would follow in my father's reactionary footsteps, to a welcome and tangible sense of relief that I hadn't. With its radical use of the impromptu form, the *Bacon* piece convinced the waverers that I had my own voice. 'Don't know what your father would have made of that, Susannah,' Caroline exclaimed.

'I could tell you! But that'd be a waste of time. You knew him then? Well, I guess everyone in the musical field in Australia knew of him.'

'I was in his department briefly; saw how he operated at first hand. He was old school British, delivering it to the Colonials. He was supposed to lead us out of the musical wilderness: introduce us to Modernism. What a joke! He came with a well cultivated accent, and as he boasted: a major work – *The Grantchester Pastoral* – in his brief case. It's gathering dust in some archive; a massive anachronism and an extraordinary throwback.'

'I've never heard it. You obviously weren't taken by him, then?'

'You couldn't like him; I don't think he cared. Excuse me, but I found him a vindictive, vicious, psychotic man; anyone who crossed him suffered. Do you want me to go on? It's not pretty.'

'Ah, hidden family history!' I grimaced.

'In the end, we forced a review of the department, exposed how comprehensively he'd trashed it, and yelling into the wind threatening legal action, he was moved aside and sent on leave, while the department settled down, appointed a new Head and started to rebuild from the ashes of his reign! Must have sent shock waves through home?'

'Of course! That's when we went overseas!' Susannah exclaimed.

'He didn't talk about the Department at home, except to complain about attempts to modernise the curriculum. "Don't get caught up in that degenerate rubbish." He'd threaten, sounding like a Nazi.'

'Goodness me; but you were still a kid.'

'Yes, I was, but musically, I knew where I was going. Look Caroline, this is very raw ground for me to be digging around in. Is there somewhere peaceful I can go?' Even as I spoke, Caroline was pointing out her window.

'Five-minute walk. The Botanic Gardens. Ideal!'

My mind was racing. I was shaking; memories of Cranbrook had been released. My hands were sweating, as they used to. I found a bench. But it was my father's rather soft and affectedly measured voice I could hear, rolling his words around in his mouth as if cleaning them before expelling them slowly, as though they contained pure wisdom. And instead of Cranbrook's close-cropped hair, it was Havelock's bony skull which was in my mind's eye. No longer the head of thick hair remembered by Nettie Bainbridge; completely bald now; he looked like a sculpture carved out of bone, with his elongated face, pale, bony and wasted, as if worn down by a life of arrogance and indifference. A cadaver.

* * *

I sat, gripping the slats of the bench. Dismayed at giving way, my mind was out of control. Memories surging, I heard a gentle whimper. Not now! Get away. Why him? Why is it his voice which fills my mind. Get out! They are imprinted. My mother: I couldn't help myself, thinking of her I was catapulted back to Vienna. Eight years ago now when she got away. 'I've planned my escape,' she'd said at the time. That didn't mean I forgave her then; I do now. It was as though she was sharing the bench with me. ...

'It's hard to forgive you! Do you know? Here I am seventeen, and I can't even imagine letting anyone touch me, let alone have it happen. Last week, darling Nettie hugged me. She's lovely; I adore her, but I couldn't stand it. That's how it is; I feel soiled, dirty.'

The earlier conversation with my mother, forever Anya now, was echoing in my mind, emptying it of the shifting, stifling images of Cranbrook and her father, as she began to see Anya as a fellow victim. 'This sounds cruel, Zannah, but that's how it is in the ghetto. I'm defecting.' She looked me in the eye. Her autumn brown eyes glistening. 'I know I can trust you; although why you should trust me I'll never know. I can only say, sorry, sorry, sorry … .' She repeated it, over and over, until she was barely audible. 'O, miláčku; my darling, I love you; I've let you down. But, escaping; I can't take the risk. I can't take anyone with me. Oh, I knew what was going on; I even knew that you knew that I knew. In the closed space of the prison, you don't let anyone into your head. It's taken seven years; ever since Jonathon died. I'll be gone by nightfall.'

'Yes, you go; we'll all get out somehow.' I didn't know where it came from, it wasn't necessarily to comfort Anya. She'd picked up her metaphor. 'Yes, I think, as far as we kids are concerned, he will let us go. He would never have freed you. I understand that, now.'

We had another cocktail at the *American Bar* and then wandered through Spittelberg as Anya told me she thought she had ten years left as a violinist, which were going to be hers, not his. She had a contract with a French recording company to record the modern Czech violin canon. 'I have a lot of work to do on them,' she groaned. 'Havelock banned them during my Australian exile, no less than the Communists denied their existence at home!'

'I'm so jealous, Anya. Where will you live?'

'I have a place, but if I told you, I'd have to shoot you.' I'd never seen her so frivolous. 'I'll let you know when you too, are out. I don't want this remnant of the *fascisti* at my door. I have a little money from the advance on the record deal. It's a good start. I'm not doing it lightly and I won't fail.'

She was so determined, committed, resolved. I hoped some of it would rub off and when I returned the following year to study in Austria, Anya was like a friend. She'd visit regularly armed with chocolates and biscuits, often a nice bottle of wine and clothes: especially, gorgeous French underwear. We played duets together. I even shared some of my dreams and visited her and the gentle Milosz Havelka, her lover of recent years, in Paris. And we talked! She told me about her parents; her music and her exile. About fleeing the jackboots that were soon to echo around the Ringstrasse, only to finish up in my father's arms: another kind of imprisonment. But that's another story; I hadn't forgiven her, but I was growing to like her.

* * *

'Thanks, Susannah,' Charlie was with Molly, 'for fixing things up with the Con. I was stupid. I won't let you down,' he said; bravely I thought.

'Well, Charles, you have the ability, you'd only be letting yourself down … You can't control all the things that happen to you, but you can choose not to be reduced by them.' She could have said more: raising questions about whether Michael was worth it; matters of the heart; the future; but didn't think he needed what small wisdom she could bring.

'I wish I looked forward to it,' he moaned, as Molly shifted the conversation on to safer ground. 'How did you feel when you went to Vienna? So far away. Why didn't you study here?'

'Vienna? Just far enough away from Melbourne!' She grinned ruefully. 'I had to get out. But, that's a story for another day.' She paused, recalling her father's reaction.

'Christ Almighty girl! Vienna? Composition? A female composer? Isn't that a contradiction in terms? What's got into your head! I might be able to open some doors in Sydney; you're a neat little cellist if you really want to do it. Next thing we know we'll have women conducting! Spare me!' He sniggered, sliding into an easy chair by his desk. I was dismissed. I didn't need to share the memory.

'My father wasn't convinced, but I knew I wasn't wasting my time or his money. Besides, I'd been offered a position on my merits and I paid him back: the cash that is!! I adored Vienna. At a superficial level, the hurrying trams – that casual reminder of home – helped me settle. Rattling along the river and over the bridges, the rickety-rack changing to a hollow sound,

I felt at ease. The music scene was brilliant.' What a waste it had been on Cranbrook. I thought.

'Ah, the Vienna Phil,' Molly sighed.

'I used to love going with friends to this little bar my mother had introduced me to – just off Kärntner Strasse – and, if I was feeling wealthy I'd have a cocktail. I didn't usually act the *flaneur*, but sometimes we'd sit outside on the thick cane chairs and watch the passing crowds, and, ah … to go inside, was to have this huge visual fix. It was like getting lost in a Klimt painting or a Schönberg score: glass panels along two walls giving the illusion of a glimmering spaciousness and the ceilings and walls, layered with black onyx and dark marble and the green and white checker-board flooring. You would have loved it Charles; I tried to turn it into music but kept falling over Schönberg.' A happy memory; it drew even a smile from him.

'A hard game for a woman,' the men in the composition department threatened, waiting for me to withdraw from the course. But old Swarovsky, the Professor of conducting, was counselling me to find my own voice. "Tell me what you've been doing. I hope you are still an 'Orssie'? You can't speak of a tradition yet, but I know that you have wonderful young composers who are discovering a local language for their composition. Very exciting! Take what you need from us, but make it new," he bellowed, waving his arms.' He would have hugged me I think, if I hadn't moved away.

'We were talking the same language. Do you see that Charles? I wasn't eschewing the European tradition, I explained to the Professor, but I was interested in opening my music to other traditions. He was nodding – "Go on." – taking me seriously, then we went on to talk about the place of silence and repetition in music.'

'Well, you can't ignore Philip Glass then,' he'd said. 'Those simple repetitive schemes, modified by almost imperceptible shifts … Sorry, sounds like I'm giving a lecture; but, you know, there's that gentle pulse which gestures towards silence but never arrives!'

She knew her Glass. She joked, however, that intellectually, her Glass was only ever half full, for she said she was also open to the way silence and repetition came to her out of Australian Indigenous music and of course from the sounds and silences of the landscape; where the almost palpable silence sings. 'Yes, Professor, I can only be an Australian composer. But ... am I being very bold; some of the men here ridicule me for my ambition.'

'Ignore them! They are caught up with a bunch of "ists" and "isms"; wanting to control and dominate with their reductive theories. Ach, my dear, you are young and lucky, you haven't got this massive burden of tradition bearing down on you. We can't really pick and choose, but you can. You're a double outsider,' he smiled: 'You're a woman and an antipodean.'

'So Charles, I was lucky, but also you know, I made my luck. It's not only rugby players and cricketers who do that!'

Molly simply smiled at her. 'Thank you,' she whispered. 'Perhaps we can talk about what you left out some other time; when ... if ... you ever want?'

* * *

I settled back into the town, and although Charles was away at the Con, I always had time for him. Caroline Lang at the Sydney Con was a sympathetic sounding board for my musical ideas, while the adorable Cynthia, who was back in Sydney gave me a place to crash, while looking after another side of my musical development. By the end of the '70s I knew my Joplin – 'Janis, thank you!' – and Linda Ronstadt and Emmy Lou Harris; we'd sung *Hotel California* so many times together I could just about do it backwards. But. I was only a visitor, my heart and head were in the Ponds; that was my reality, although I did cut a disc with Cynthia's little production company, putting down the early work.

And, in the long summer breaks when Charles came back to Celtic Ponds we spent hours together. I taught him virtually everything I knew about bowing technique and we began gradually to explore arrangement and composition. It engaged him. In a way in which the instrumental practice didn't, I sensed that speculating together about ideas slowly drew him out of his self. Musically, he seemed to be living in two different worlds: a zombie at the Con, while replenished when he was back home. We would often walk in the bush with Ben, listening to the rustle of leaves and the undergrowth, the brush and rush of the breeze, running water, the silences; feeling the texture of leaves, tree trunks, shrubs, the granite outcrops.

It wasn't long after this – was it 1978? – I successfully applied for a Churchill Fellowship. It was time for a sabbatical – was I really thirty-one! – and needed time to advance my musical explorations into silence and rhythm. And I wanted to spend some time with Anya and renew my European friendships and contacts.

'And I want to explore these ideas with you when you get back,' Charles said, excited for me: 'I'll look at my Glass! Oh I know a little of him; he's sent me back to Bach and I'm listening to a lot of Glen Gould. I've also been thinking about John Cage, but really it was my grief that opened up a place for silence in my composition. For me, it stands for the inexpressible, I think Cage's silences are more academic: a statement.'

'I wouldn't argue with that, Charles. For us both perhaps, it touches on the intensely personal, is felt upon the pulse, like Palestrina, perhaps?'

'Don't stay away too long will you, I'll miss you.'

I detected his anxiety, insecurity; he'd been unable to make a secure landing since Michael had cut him adrift. 'Don't let him sink you Charles, he's not worth it, you know. I'm not going to tell you what to do, but why don't you connect up again with your Sydney friends and do a bit more of that group work. Caroline says they all wanted to play with you *musically*', she smiled at her pun, but he didn't pick up on it. 'And, down here: trust Ben, he's real, and keep exploring the bush; think of it as *plein air* musical painting.'

'Ah I do like that idea, in fact, I might take my paints out with me when I wander and paint my musical ideas. Ally might be a help? What will you do in Vienna?'

'I'll be busy, and I will be serious; it's not a holiday. I've been invited to Aspen – not for the shopping! – I'm in a session on emerging composers and will conduct youth workshops in the summer school. And I'll attend the annual *Festival of the Avant Garde* in New York in November; Cage is speaking.'

'And your mother?'

'Anya, of course, in Paris. Oh, very special; she's wangled me a session with the legendary Nadia Boulanger – a composer and a fabulous technician; she taught Copeland and Glass – now that's a real coup; I'll renew my friendship with Swarovsky in Wien; meet up again with the wonderful Nettie in London and,' she smiled, 'I've got something ripening; on Van Gogh's 'Olive Trees'. Do you know it?'

'That's an extraordinary painting! It's as though the paint was slapped on so furiously it hardly holds together.'

'Yes, there's this amazing, almost deranged, energy. I hope Mme Boulanger will workshop it with me. I'm beginning to hear it as a violin concerto. For my mother.'

* * *

Swarovsky organized a working space for her in one of the music rooms at the Academy and she was made a tutor-adjunct. It was all quite unofficial of course, but he and one of the vocal students, Agnes Milkewicsz, who had a gorgeous deep contralto voice like a rich sauterne, made her feel at home and they became good friends. She was also lucky enough to take two master classes with the great Soviet cellist, Daniil Shafran.

My dear Charles: you won't believe who I have just had a class with, the great Shafran. O, what a delight. If you haven't heard him you must; you simply must beg, borrow, even steal one of his records. (GET HOLD of HIM.) I'm not exaggerating when I tell you, he has beautiful long hands like you and his string work is superb – you could do that, you know – and he uses the bow, strung looser than many, at the tip for long periods. His string hand is wonderful to watch, poetic and romantic and, O, so passionate. You would love the palette of his tone colours; there, we are into painting again, you see. I learned so much.

Which is rather more than I can say for the composition. The men around here won't give me the time of day. They set out, I think, to make me feel unwanted and inadequate and, for a while, they succeeded, but I don't allow myself to submit to it. But, I'm not alone. My dear old friend Swarovsky is disgusted by the attitude of the men, and he's got together with Nettie and they have arranged for performances of my two impromptus – the John: And the light shineth, and the one on Frances Bacon – at a concert at the RCM in December after I've returned from New York. It's very good of them. You've got to have people to beat your drum, Charles!

I'm discovering that, while these two pieces sit quite comfortably within a standard contemporary repertoire, I feel less and less reliant upon the Western tradition for my sources and models. That's my battle with the 'boys' here. 'That sort of thing is all good and well, Miss Beaumont, but, where are your touchstones?' I could hear my father's patronizing voice: 'what do you think you're doing, woman? This is men's work!' And yet, as we've been discovering Charles, our 'touchstones' are just as likely to be elsewhere.

I came here to think about sound and silence, and I have, but, the further I went, the more I realized that, in our minor, fumbling way, we may be on the right track. Our silence, my dear friend, is sourced to our own place, which cannot be ignored. The more I compose, the more I realize we must speak with our own voice; must find a way, in the music that we make, of expressing it. It's terribly exciting.

Similarly, repetition: while the great contemporary exemplar might be someone like Philip Glass, rhythmic repetition is fundamental to the music, poetry, speech rhythms, etc., of many traditional communities, not least of our own indigenous

people. Now, we won't be the first to go there – the wonderful Mr
Sculthorpe is teaching us a lot about where we live – but it's a
fruitful path. We are a part of the oldest continent on earth, and
our first peoples made music for eons. And who knows, Charles,
the fruit of all our exploring may be to know the place for our
first time.

Well, well, that's been something of a reaction, hasn't
it! But, as you can gather, dear Charles, there's lots to think
about and do, and I'm hoping we might go some of the way in
harmony. So, my collaborator, when I get back, I want us to go
exploring. And, oh yes, see if you can rustle up some beating sticks
and a (good) didgeridoo player; I think we are going to need one!

In friendship, and with fond thoughts, Charles; I miss you.
Susannah

Give my best wishes to your mother and Claire, and say
hello to Ben. Xx

PS. I'm also singing in the concert choir of the Musikverein,
and, O, yes, how could I overlook it! I went to a superb Onegin,
the other night. Natasha Levinskaya, a young Russian ballerina.
Exquisite. I went with Agnes, I think we floated home.

I couldn't believe how much I'd written. I'd tossed off that cloak of
depression I'd battled with and, oh, the wonder of it, I'd found my own
voice, even if I still had to hide it away in a choir. Yet, like Charlie, I wasn't
ready to go solo.

I've lost Charles' enthusiastic response, but I treasure the etude for two
cellos he enclosed with it.

* * *

When I returned, Charles remarked, not only on how fully engaged
musically I was and eager to apply what I'd been working on, but he also

thought I was less fraught. It was a shrewd observation, for as much as my friendship with Agnes was an escape from the intellectual muggers in Vienna, it also had something to do with my anxiety about my sexuality. Was I more attracted to women than to men, I had sometimes wondered? Or was it, as Nettie said – who had no such doubts about hers! – 'a reaction to a particular kind of man who, unfortunately, you've had contact with for much of your life. But,' she added with a twinkle in her eye: 'unless I'm mistaken, I don't think Agnes will be making the kind of music with you that she'd hoped.' She was right. It was this new-found equilibrium perhaps, that Charles sensed as we resumed our musical explorations and that wasn't all; with Charles and Ben thrown together, the three of us began to see a lot of each other socially.

I was able to talk to Cynthia about these things. At first, it was easier to relate to Charles and I acted out a simple dance that positioned him in the middle of our threesome.

'Of course you did darling; from what you've told me.'

'But gradually Ben thawed me out. Not that he set out to do it I'm sure, he just put me at ease. He doesn't have an ego which needs feeding; and he certainly doesn't meet the criteria of the rugby player I see on the telly news.'

'Other side of the tracks though, Suze!'

'But he was such a gentle man, such a *gentilhomme,*' she whispered. 'I would see him looking at me and he'd smile, but not look away; he wasn't furtive, nor was he undressing me I felt. For the first time in my life, I was pleased that someone wanted to gaze at me. Is this so bad?'

'He sounds delectable! Any good in the cot? Only joking! Anything up top?'

'Oh yes, he doesn't intellectualise, but he has a lovely mind; intuitive as you might expect, but sensitive and, watching him with Charles in the garden, quick. He never fails to surprise me and,' she smiled, 'you're right, he's got a beautiful body. Aaahhh!' I couldn't help thinking how I love to run my hands over his belly and legs, ideally formed, but not over muscled. But Cynthia needed to know that, let her imagine it.

Later, delighting now in the memory, remembering like it was yesterday, I thought about how it had happened! After one of our Saturday meals, holding hands we wandered out on to the verandah: 'Would you mind if I stayed the night?' Oh, the panic! I closed down. 'What'll I do?' I was over thirty, but I'd never properly been with a man. I was overtaken by a shiver like a small death. My mind was racing. Mouth dry, as though my lips were chapped, hands damp with sweat. I laid my head on his shoulder. 'I want you, want you to …'. Then, he put his fingers to my lips, caressing them, tender, as though bringing them back to life. 'Shhhh, Shhhh!' I took his hand that had been caressing my lips – it was almost courageous, do you see? – kissed it and led him into the bedroom. We didn't speak. As he came into me, I felt a tremor run through my body and sighed deeply; it was as if a demon had been exorcised. 'O, my darling. I was terrified, you know.'

'I know; do you want to talk about it.' We lay there naked, my back curled into his belly, his lips brushing one, two, three, four, five … my neck; alive.

'It's terrible, but I want you to know.' He was holding me, his free hand cupping a breast, responding to his touch. 'And I don't want my emotional scars to blemish what is happening between us.'

She told him about Cranbrook, her father and her parents' neglect; spared no detail; told him of the nightmares and her deepest fears. In the morning, over toast and tea in bed, she took his hand and brought it to her lips, tiny tears hanging on her lashes, then falling. Spoke in mid thought: 'I don't … talk of them. They have fled the country, but,' she was weeping, holding her head in her hands: 'They are still up here. Each of them was so self-absorbed they abrogated all responsibility. For years, I detested them; everything I did was for hate of them; but, no more. Charles and I have gone over this very barren ground; so debilitating and weakening.'

'Yes. Nothing can grow in that foul soil.'

'I've come to love my mother, but I haven't made much progress with him. Although, ah Ben, my darling gardener, I'm learning. Can I say, through how I feel for you, for love of you,' she whispered, 'that I have enough courage to say it's over; I don't hate him anymore.'

Ben was momentarily quiet, taking it in. 'Ah, my darling! I've never used the word before. My darling, I've loved you for ages, but was too scared to say it.' Strangely, they were no longer timid. 'You've brought me home.'

'We ... we ... my darling bushman, we are finding how it is to love and I am happy.'

Confessing their love for the first time they indulged themselves: 'I fell in love with you bit by bit,' he said, smiling with her at the memories, 'and while there was no particular event, it was your compassion, your patience and devotion to Charlie; I could call it your empathy, guiding him back to health.'

'Oh my! "Empathy", eh?'

'I know, I know,' he laughed. 'It's a Charlie word! But, that's by the bye, I knew you had your own demons, but I learned so much from watching you give of yourself. Is that corny?'

She kissed him. 'And me? It's easy. Callas, *O mio babbino, caro* ...; do you remember? That "Opera Night" at *Clifton*; we'd listened to Sutherland, Pavarotti, the young Yvonne Kenny, and then Callas. Even as the opening orchestral bars concluded, I felt you gasp, softly like a sob. Felt you shudder, rapt: your hand, hard as bark, searching for mine, almost involuntarily it seemed; my mind was floating; you were stilled. Even reacting to the plucked harp after her voice has stopped: "Heart strings", you said, breathless, smiling, tenderly, searching my face like ... like a lover I thought. For the first time I wanted my body to melt into another's. Oh, it was like listening to my soul. To find I have a soul. You whispered, as if I had sung: "Thank you, thank you!" I knew then ... such was our peace, as if from poles apart we touched and found a centre. We are very lucky. It was as though no-one else was in the room.' She had the poet Rilke in mind.

'Ah, yes, I've loved that aria ever since. I guess it's when I began to hope.'

'Began to hope? What do you mean, began to ...?'

'Well, ... I don't have any tickets on myself. Who am I? I couldn't imagine why you'd bother with me? In my own way, an uneducated ex-rugby playing gardener, I felt as much in need as Charlie; I didn't want to embarrass you.' He was groping around for words. 'Didn't want you to also have to deal with my feelings which I thought were becoming obvious.'

'Really, you duffer! I saw you as a beautiful man, comfortable in your skin – now, I can say, yumm, yumm! – and finding his expression in gardens; you aren't exactly mucking around in a vegetable patch.' She searched his face, 'I love you; you're not my bit of rough you know. What don't you get?' She was pummeling his chest. 'Class, class? Noble obligations! Oh God, it has no place in what we've found. When you are with me my blood sings; I often wonder if you can hear it! I like to think that each is the guardian of the other's soul, their solitude.' She had turned explicitly to Rilke: 'Is it too much to say that, between us love consists in this: *that two solitudes protect and touch and greet each other.*'

She felt him shudder, shy, awkward as a teenager, he lent across and took her hands that were, as if in unison, reaching towards him; and she was in his arms: 'Sssh, sssh.' His lips; brushing her cheek. 'Sssh, sssh! How beautiful, that idea of souls protecting and touching and greeting.'

'Well,' she laughed, her happiness dancing on her lips: 'Why don't we make use of this bed; I've got a lot of catching up to do! And I'm not talking about the sex; I mean the love.'

Once airless, in which I felt embattled and enclosed, the bedroom is now a place where I feel liberated. I could now linger in front of the mirror, as I did on this occasion having just put some music on, letting the robe fall as I looked at myself, it was as if I was reclaiming my body. Her full breasts, the soft pink of her areola, flat belly, the blonde shading of her *mons*, down to her slim legs that sometimes she thought could not support her, she smiled openly, widely at herself. Her hazel eyes and her hair, often lifeless, now shining. I'd never been able to enjoy my body like this? Glancing towards Ben, lying back watching her in what looked like delight, she began to sing, her voice finding a rich timbre: '*You're just too good to be true / You feel like heaven to touch / I wanna hold you so much … / Can't take my eyes off of you.*'

Then she threw her arms around his neck, found his lips, and kissed her lover. 'I've found my voice!' They kissed, softening into each other. What she couldn't know was the relief he felt; felt in his inner being, but also felt as a physical reaction, as though he'd been working out in the gym. As they dressed she helped him with his shirt, humming ..., 'and now, with apologies to Mr Gershwin and Lady Ella: *'I've been a little lamb who's been lost in the wood / I know I could always be good / To someone who'll watch over me!'* She had never been so light-hearted; nor was she a poor little lamb! He knew that.

From then on there weren't too many Saturdays we didn't enjoy a glass of wine or two and have a 'scroungers' for dinner, depending on where we were and soon were sharing our houses. My invasive nightmares ceased; driven out in the end by one beautiful dream, a fleeting moment in which Ben floated past my window, his hands cupping a tiny plant that he was gently transferring from barren, rocky ground where it could not flourish to a plot of rich soil he'd found in her wilderness. I was surprised how literal it was; as if there should be no misunderstanding.

In a peculiar kind of way, we found our lost childhoods together; it wasn't unusual to have a game of marbles, usually when I went up to see him working on the Gully garden or we played cards, scrabble, monopoly: releasing the child in us together. Or, he might sit and read in the music room at my place while I worked. One particular Sunday afternoon sticks in my mind; an afternoon languidly drifting towards dusk. Having slipped out of the room to pour a couple of glasses of wine, he'd come back wearing an old black trilby. Pulling it down over one eye, and putting the drinks down on the table, he started to sing, rough, huskily: *I've heard there was a secret chord / That David played, and it pleased the Lord, / But you don't really care for music do you?*

Then he laughed, placing his hat on the scroll of a cello and waving his arms at her music-laden room; at two cellos set as if in conversation, the piano, a violin, a lectern covered in a score, other scores in various states of completion on any flat surface, the overflowing book shelf and filing cabinet, the polished piano stool, a bench and two worn lounge chairs.

And, on he sang …*The fourth, the fifth / The minor fall, the major lift / The baffled king composing Hallelujah.*

Over and over, he whispered *Hallelujah, Hallelujah, Hallelujah …,* moving to her and kissing her, and she, waiting for him.

'O, you darling man,' she laughed. 'Is that Leonard Cohen I'm hearing?'

'Yep, Leonard; don't you love it. I can't do him but it's just out. I've heard it on the radio a few times and I've been practicing.' He was whispering into her hair: '*I'll stand before the Lord of Song / With nothing on my tongue but Hallelujah …*' Holding her, his eyes towards the heavens; he sang a chorus of *hallelujahs*! 'I'm sure he won't mind me butchering his song in private. I love you, my darling.'

He was a joy to be with. We still had all kinds of adventures with Charles, but we were a couple. I trusted him with my most precious thoughts; could, you might say, do my feeling aloud. And my work prospered. It's sometimes argued that creativity comes out of stress and angst; the old starving in the garret model. I knew I'd always have residual scars, but they were being buried deeper and my composition took on a new life. In musical terms, it was being played out in a different key, had a wider range of tonal colour. My creative juices were flowing; and they weren't the only juices that were flowing! From loathing my body, I was now taking pleasure in it.

Having work-shopped it at the Con, my *Australia Felix,* was featured in a concert of new Australian composition at the Wollongong Town Hall. Based on an ironic reading of the Henry Handel Richardson novel, in which, rather than being alienated from place, Richard Mahony, whose fortunes are carried through the cello solos, comes to terms with it, figured by an extended didgeridoo solo in the third movement. The didgeridoo is backed by bird calls with both recorded sounds fading into a simulation by the orchestra, filling the prescribed silences in the didgeridoo solo. Charles liked it.

'It works I think? I've got my brother Cedric to thank for that. He's developed into quite a techno whiz and provided the equipment and helped with the recording and editing of all the bush sounds. So gorgeous to do something together.'

As a result of this small success, I was offered a three-month Writer in Residency in the Literature Department at the local University. 'You're writing our stories, if musically; we'd love to have you, if you'd like to come. There's a small stipend.' I re-jigged my various teaching commitments and Ben and I mixed and matched our time. 'I can love you, whether you're in Vienna, Celtic Ponds or the Gong,' Ben said. What a time it was. I got to know the local Kooris and we made some music together, and I mapped out four etudes – for piano, cello, violin, and guitar; all drawing on the local landscape: *Keira Rising*; *Coal Cliffs*; *Lawrence at Thiroul*; and *Rock Pools* – which were performed a year later in the new Faculty.

***

And then a letter arrived from Michael O'Connell.

> *Dear Ms Beaumont*
>
> *I've read the reviews of your* Australia Felix *and know a little of your other work. I am writing to you to invite you to make another major work, a symphony, for the Bi-Centenary. I know a little of the creative processes; if possible I would like the work to have some relevance to Australian history; if not, I understand. The work should be completed by October 1987, and, for the most part should be composed in Celtic Ponds. I will make available $25,000 per year for the four years, or part thereof, of the project. Should you agree, please inform Mr Bran Doogue.*
>
> *I hope you will give my offer your serious consideration.*
> *Sincerely,*
> *Michael O'Connell, KCMG*

'*Serious consideration*? Make it here? We are not going anywhere are we?' I knew what I wanted to make. Indirectly, I'd been moving in this direction since my sense of displacement in Vienna and having taken a few tentative steps towards it in the *Australia Felix* piece and the *etudes*, within a couple of months I had put down an outline, a narrative of a work. It was to be a symphony and although it was very rough and still gestating, I'd only scored the piano and a few parts of the cello, while the broader orchestration was fermenting, I wanted to give the ideas some air and share a little of the music. 'So, my darlings, if I bribe you with a cabernet and some good cheddar, can I inflict my tentative scribbling on you?'

'Your guinea pigs, eh?' It was Ben trying to help her relax. She was nervous.

And so it was, one Sunday afternoon Ben and Charles gathered in the studio and for the next hour, sipping their wine and glancing at some sheets of paper I'd given them. They listened, as I played and talked to my *Symphony of Lost Voices*; stopping often to elaborate a point, repeat what I thought was an important musical phrase, add some stretches of cello, and suggest the placement of the work's four movements, or indicate which instruments might be carrying the underlying themes at any given time.

At the conclusion, the two men stood and hugged her, delight and awe on their faces. 'Alright, alright, enough of that! Now ...will it work? Has it got a life?'

Charles, thoughtful but enthusiastic, liked the way in which a hint of an old colonial song or some thematic phrase echoed through the entire piece gathering additional emotional significance with each repetition; but he was surprised there was no place for Aboriginal chant; 'it's an absence in the first movement at least, and could work like those other leitmotifs.'

'Yes, yes! Ah, I'd wondered about that.' While Ben, conscious of her limited resources suggested she could get around the problem of the bugle in the war sections by having Cedric record it, and cut and paste whatever she wanted from the *Last Post* and the *Reveille*.

'It would have that eerie sense of coming from afar; it's really only a hint and an echo of the dead. Lovely! Even with a full orchestra, it might come from off stage.'

Charles could see there were inherent musical risks in the work and they weren't all solved yet, but thought it was exquisite, and daring, 'and the emotional colour!' He exclaimed, lost for words.

'And our recently anointed knight, Sir Michael O'Connell? Will it appeal to him? I once said I'd like to give him a piece of my mind,' I couldn't help grinning, 'now I am, if somewhat differently from what I had in mind at that time!'

'Well, he'll get his money's worth!' Charles offered. 'But, Sue, the beauty of that question is, it's irrelevant. You don't have to please him; of course it would be nice if you did! I wonder if you'll ever know!'

'Hmmm! We'll see I guess,' but my mind was on the music. 'I know it's raw; you have to use your imagination, but ... this is the broad narrative if you like, from pre-invasion to our attempts at reconciliation, with various stops on the way – but I want everything to disappear into the overall experience of the music. I've given you a hint of the surface, but, I want it to plumb the depths; make all the past events live in the contemporary moment.'

'Now that's where you'll leave Michael behind, Sue. I don't think he's got a clue about that. His *history* was this single entity safely locked away in the past, whereas I see it as something of many parts, shedding light on the past and the present and shining into the future. Christ, I wish our politicians understood that! But ... back to your music. You seem to have this need for content, for ideas, perhaps you should have been a novelist,' he chuckled. 'So different from me, where I'm after tonal atmosphere.'

'Very interesting Charles; I feel so sorry for the novelist. I'd forever be wanting to splice in song or sound, a score, long elongated pauses, a sketch here, a painting there and O God, my poor characters would always be talking over the top of each other. The wonderful simultaneity of music. I do like stories though, never had any growing up; had to make them up by myself. I guess you could say, this desire for content and simplicity makes me a bit of a maverick in our contemporary musical world. But, being á la mode is only useful when it's true to the idea. And, really, music is the most pure embodiment of an idea. That's what I'm looking for!'

'We aren't the only happy ones I gather,' she said to Ben one evening. 'Claire tells me she'd read somewhere – in *The Weekly* I guess – that our benefactor has married a ballerina: Natasha Levinskaya. Now my darling, you're going to be impressed, I know her, well I exaggerate, but, I saw her dance in Vienna and again in Paris; she's superb, but sadly, I believe, she's had a terrible accident. I can only hope he'll be as happy with her as I am with you. Should you congratulate him?'

Dear Michael: I heard that you have recently married. I would like to congratulate you, very sincerely. For, although I'm not married, I might as well be, and therefore understand a little, I think, of how you must be feeling. As I've told you, Susannah Beaumont, whose work as a composer you obviously know, and I have been together now for several years and are very happy. But this is not about me, although, I hope you understand that I feel very lucky; it is about you and your bride. Perhaps, now, you might consider bringing your wife down to Celtic Ponds? We would love to meet her and see you again, for that matter.

Regards, Ben

PS: Any photographs?

[So you can look her over. Not bloody likely! Michael had hissed when he received the letter.*]*

* * *

On Australia Day 1988, to an audience of some thirty locals – a few present under threat, others so eager to hear it that they came early – and a few folk up from the coast, *Symphony of Lost Voices*, commissioned by the *O'Connell Cultural Fund*, had its world premiere in Celtic Ponds.

On the simple cyclostyled programme, the audience saw, among the performers:

Piano	Molly Greenwood
Cello	Charles Greenwood
Guitar/Mandolin	Anna Liebowicz
Drums	Eric Wright
Didgeridoo	Ernie Bennell

Supplemented by players from the small Broadwater orchestra, there were places also for Ethel and Ally and Eddie Williams, and four of Susannah's music students playing the tympani, while Cedric Beaumont managed the recorded bird calls, bush noises, chants and the bugle passages, and Susannah conducted and played the violin. Oh, there were some glitches, mostly to do with timing and experience, but, apart from Sue and Charles, no-one noticed!

As the music moved to its closure, to a person – and the delight of the kids – the audience stood and cheered the players as they took their bows, until, quietening them as he came forward, Bran presented Sue with a massive bouquet selected from the garden at *Clifton*. The *Southern Highlands Gazette*, while clearly surprised by the '*unconventional orchestra and orchestration*,' thought it, nevertheless, '*a tremendous success. When did we last see so many townsfolk in the one place!*'

Three months later, a combined city orchestra, including staff and students from the University, joined by Ernie on didgeridoo, men from the local Koori people, Sue's sought-after oboes, Charles, on the cello, and the English Department's David Lance on piano, performed *Lost Voices* in the Wollongong Town Hall.

On this occasion, Sue merely conducted, and the *Illawarra Mercury's* Eva Lukits gave it an enthusiastic and comprehensive review, while remarking also on '*the beauty and delicacy of her Serenade: A Love Poem*,' which opened the programme. Knowing a little of her expanding body of work, she thought '*it showed her in a new light, with shades of joy and contentment only rarely before in evidence.*' While it needed a full orchestra, particularly expanded string and wind sections, she believed The *Symphony* was '*an important addition to contemporary Australian composition and embellishes Susannah Beaumont's growing reputation.'*

Later, back stage, sipping champagne with Ben, Charles, the Williams' and the Doogues, she had in her hand a single rose and a note scribbled on the programme:

> *Dear Ms Beaumont/Susannah; I hope I can call you that. Michael and I want to congratulate you on your wonderful* Symphony of Lost Voices. *I attended tonight's performance and was very moved by it. I also thought your* love poem *was simply exquisite; a beautiful cameo that one might wear close to the heart.*
>
> *I hope that we will have the opportunity to meet in the future. I have even the little dream – I used to dance once upon a time – that we might be able to put together some movement and music, for my heart has never left the ballet, although it is now being preoccupied by more routine things.*
>
> *Congratulations; I look forward to hearing more of your music.*
>
> *Sincerely, Natasha O'Connell.*

'Well, well, well. That's very nice of her. And Mick …?' Ben remarked. 'She should've dropped in and shared our champers.'

'She wouldn't have wanted to disturb our pleasure, I think. Grander in her hey-day than our few happy bubbles I guess!'

To cap off the year, in a programme which also included new works by Peter Sculthorpe and Ross Edwards: the *Symphony of Lost Voices* received the full orchestral treatment at a concert given by the Western Australian ABC Symphony Orchestra, in the new Concert Hall. Susannah (and Ben) had a long weekend at Cottesloe, enjoying the late spring sun and the after-glow of another wonderful reception for *Lost Voices*. Reading the review to her in the morning – *Australian Music in Good Hands* – Ben was elated. Carrying her to the window as she covered herself with a sheet dragged from the bed, he showed her the beach. Gentle breakers were kissing the sand

and reaching to Rottnest, the water glistened. 'All yours!' That evening, they sat on their small balcony and watched the disappearing sun slipping through clouds, showering them in every shade of pink until suddenly, breathtakingly it was gone and night, like a velvet blanket, arrived. 'We miss that little drama in the Ponds,' she said, her arm across his shoulders, 'there's music in it…Charles would love it.'

'Music in it?' Ben echoed her: laughing, 'not with those teeming Lorikeets squealing like larrikins in the Norfolk Pines! What a sound sight!'

'I love you,' she breathed. 'When I was in my teens, my greatest hope was that I might laugh as much as I cried, a reckless dream. I thought my music would always be made out of despair. Now, I wake up with a smile on my lip; I've learned to love and to accept it. My music has all the necessary tones.'

* * *

And then, another missive out of the blue: a letter arrived from Cranbrook.

Dear Susannah: I have heard of the success of your Symphony; congratulations! I would have preferred to write, 'please accept my congratulations', but I fear that you would reject such a request. So, my best wishes are more peremptory. They are, however, sincerely sent.

I have been offered a six-month contract to conduct the Brunswick Orchestra, here in Melbourne, while their resident conductor is in Europe. Brunswick is a semi-professional group, but it has a good reputation. We will give three major concerts during my tenure and, while two of these have been planned in advance, the third is left up to me; I would like to mount a programme featuring a survey of your work up to, and including Symphony for Lost Voices, *which, for what it is worth, I think very fine.*

Ben could see she was disturbed. 'Sue, … are you alright?' She handed him the letter.

I intend, also, asking Cedric to do the sound production. If you agree, the concert will be held on 1 and 2 June, with a matinee as well as an evening performance on the Saturday. I hope you will give this offer your considered attention.
> *Sincerely,*
> *Cranbrook*

'What will you do?'

Her voice wavered. 'I'll accept, of course. It would be cowardly … well at least timid, to refuse it and it would suggest that he still has something over me. He hasn't! I'll make sure of his intentions however. I won't be jerked around by him; I could put this more strongly, but I think you understand.'

Rehearsals began in March and increased in tempo after the orchestra's April concerts. I went down for the first of the May rehearsals and was pleasantly surprised that Cranbrook was sufficiently sensitive to the occasion to arrange for Cedric to be present when we met. It was a good rehearsal and it was apparent Cranbrook was not going to trash the music. In fact those who knew his previous work remarked on his application which, in the past, had been rarely on display.

Afterwards, having supper in Brunswick Street; if Susannah was watchful and wary, Cranbrook, his pasty complexion marked by crimson blotches flaring and fading, was clearly uncomfortable, and embarrassed, revealing, perhaps, an embedded social awkwardness. He seemed to be at ease only when the conversation was contained within the boundaries of the rehearsal and the eventual performance. There was enough there, however, for her to believe they could work together and they were civil which, as she said to Ben, doesn't mean he has to share our table. 'Just think though, if indirectly, I have Sir Michael to thank for this modest reconciliation.'

In its review of the concert, *The Age* thought it was – *A night out for the Beaumonts.*

> *In a pleasing performance, Cranbrook Beaumont had the Brunswick Orchestra at their peak for what was, in effect, a retrospective of his sister's output to this date. A complex body of work, Susannah Beaumont must have been pleased with the interpretations.* [Going on to cover each of the pieces on the programme in an extensive review, noticing Cedric's competent sound recordings in the major work, *The Age's* music critic, hoped,] *on the basis of what we heard last night, that we might see more of Cranbrook Beaumont in the future, for his is a talent not fully realised. As for Susannah Beaumont, we will certainly hear more from her. She sits comfortably within the emerging group of young Australian composers. Indeed, one may say, she has arrived.*

* * *

With a new commission – from BHP, wanting something relevant to the region – I was able to stop teaching at the local Conservatorium. Ben and I were joyously happy and although Charles was spreading his wings, we were still invariably a threesome, and indeed, if my reputation was growing, so was theirs as landscape gardeners. And we were often at *Clifton*, where Claire and Bran hosted a regular *Salon in the Salon* as Claire called it, having fun with the affectation, I think. It was a chance for Charles and Susannah to show off work in progress, to play the classics and when Andrew Buchanan arrived, he also came.

'Oh, Andrew, what a delight to have you involved. I haven't tried your medicine yet, your music is a huge bonus,' Claire gushed; 'you simply must stay.'

***

Once Andrew had settled in and held several jazz sessions with the music club, Charles suggested they might try '*Summertime*', what do you think?'

'Isn't that a wee bit ambitious?' Andrew laughed. 'Here goes anyway, I'll give you the chord and play a few bars; wonderful song. Pity we haven't a vocalist.'

'S-uu-mmmer-time and the livin' is easy …'. Sue hung on the opening.

'Ah, my dear; that's a beautiful instrument you've got there.' He meant it but couldn't help thinking what a lucky chap Ben was, feeling a familiar knot in his belly: 'Well! That widens the repertoire!' He whispered. Within the month, Sue had sung *Cry Me a River* at the CWA dance and she was on their billboard, while in private Claire exclaimed. 'Sue! You blew me away. Why so secretive?'

'Well Claire it's always been there you know, but it's only recently that we've set it free. I've always sung in my head but I never wanted to share it; the silence was a factor of my sadness. You don't know much about this, but I was symbolically mute, although I couldn't have put it that way when I was growing up. Oh, this is getting very deep. [Claire nodded, "No!"] I was always careful not to expose myself. I did some choral work in Vienna, but it's taken me a long time to sing solo, and I was so nervous; couldn't you see my legs shaking?'

'Well, hooray to you, for coming out!'

***

As they sauntered up to *Clifton* on the Saturday afternoon in 1998 Ben could sense that Susannah was anxious. 'After that lovely message at the Wollongong Concert I didn't hear from her again, although I sent her several notes and there's been nothing from Sir Michael about the *Symphony*, although I sent him a copy of the score. Not a sound. Do you think she's a fairweather friend; you know: good-naturedly insincere? "Ahhhh darling!

Gorgeous to see you. We must have lunch/coffee/a drink", even as they have no intention of following through. Why bother!'

'You'll be fine!' But Ben watched everything closely when they gathered. Until, having been pulled this way and that, Natasha slipped away and joined them. 'At last!' She held out her hands. 'It's so long ... but', she stammered: 'you didn't contact me.'

'Oh, no, no! I wrote several times.'

'That ... Michael!' Natasha wailed. 'Pardon me ... but he's done this to me before. I know what has happened to your letters ...'

'Don't apologise! In another context, I would have put it more crudely.'

'He has that effect! Anyway, that's water all gone under the bridges now.' She was smiling, and shrugged: 'and Ben; you've been such a good friend to him for all these years. It's lovely to meet you ... both. For so long, I want to talk to you about your music Susannah.'

'And I ... to talk about your dancing. Is that still possible? I saw you in 1978: Vienna, with my mother. Dancing *Onegin*, ...'.

'I was so young.'

'Yes, but you were simply gorgeous. You still are, your complexion!'

Natasha laughed, blushing. 'Ah, *mon cheri*: my secret? I am Russian and haven't lain for days cooking on the beach at Bondi.' Laughing, she wagged her finger. 'And and of course, I never go to bed with my make-up on.'

'Then I was lucky enough to see you with the Nureyev in Paris: *Giselle*. Is it all over? I ...'

'It's over, if with greater finality for darling Rudi.' She dwelt on his name, 'but, you know, something like that is never ... I didn't retire, my career was interfered with ... like an abuse.' She touched Susannah's hand. Did she know she'd hit a raw spot? 'It would be like you giving up composing, it's never over. I may not be able to do a *pointe* anymore, but as far as movement goes, I still think in dance terms. I said in my note to you that I wanted to talk about these things. I still do and now I've heard so much more of your music; it's so visual, I'm always choreographing it. Have you thought of a ballet?' She looked at me. 'I want to ... my life is changing and even more than ever, I need to have dance in it. Can we talk about this sometime?'

'I'd love to: I'm so glad you weren't snubbing me, I felt quite let down. Perhaps we could catch up in Sydney, Sir Michael might like to join us? Ben would love to see him; we are always looking for excuses to come to the city.'

'Yes, yes, we'll do that soon. But, it will be without Michael; and oh it's *tres fastidieux*, but,' she paused, 'like my friendship with Andrew, you must use this email address. Silly, isn't it the games people play! Well, that's the way it is.'

Susannah smiled, understanding what she was saying even as she lingered on the thought that Natasha and Andrew were such good friends. At the same time, Ben was studying Natasha, and he remembered Michael calling her a bitch, on the only occasion he'd met him after they were married. Everything about her seemed to contradict the remark, 'Did you ever return to Russia? I remember your husband saying that he was interested in doing business there?'

'No! I didn't return.' Her voice hardened and she peered at him. 'Michael contrived to get access, although he didn't actually visit himself. He had what he called a bag-carrier, doing his work for him.' In other circumstances, she might have said, 'dirty work', but held her tongue. Ben sensed he'd wandered in to dangerous territory.

'I'm sorry; don't go there if you'd rather not. It was an innocent question.'

'O, Ben. As I think you sense, these are not good memories. Michael and I have very different views of what doing business in Russia might mean! They are my people. I see them drenched in blood. Call it my fatalism, but they need sympathy and support, not exploitation. He would be shocked to know I'm supporting an orphanage for handicapped children. Whereas, he's got people slinking around in the entrails of its chaos, ripping the wealth out of the place since it *opened up*!' She shook her head at the phrase, 'do you mind if we don't go on? I'm not being rude; you weren't to know.' Her mind, however, was slicing through scurrilous and boastful conversations about *O'Connell's* rapacious presence in Moscow.

Segueing back to safer ground, Sue said she was trying to remember when she'd last heard of Natasha professionally. 'It would have been about 1984 or '85? I always looked out for you after seeing you when I was in Europe.'

'Yes, 1984: ominous year! And not just because of Mr Orwell! I hurt myself dancing; very boring, we can talk about it anytime. Tonight, why don't we just get to know each other?'

'Let's go outside then?' Susannah whispered as Ben watched them link arms and drift into the garden. 'Ah, you can feel God smiling on you out here.'

'What a gorgeous thought.'

But Susannah's mind was elsewhere. 'Why do they do it; some men?'

'Ah,' Natasha was attentive. 'I wondered if you might have dealt with it in some of the earlier work. The violence in the *Dante,* and the *Bacon Impromptu* came from somewhere very dark I thought.' Natasha hugged her, held her close for a moment, running her hand over her hair, as she told her about Cranbrook: 'Couldn't let anyone touch me, when he'd finished with me.'

'You've got rid of him, I think. If I hear your *Serenade: A Love Poem* correctly?'

'O yes, yes! We've sent him packing.' She noticed, as she paused, Natasha was glancing towards Andrew who was on the verandah. He waved.

* * *

'She's gorgeous, Ben. She's had a very sophisticated life but really, she's not so different from some of us down here. She's had her problems: still has a huge one, I'd say! But she is more than a survivor; she wants to thrive and to do so with panache. Bravo, I say. I think I've made a friend. She wants us: you and me, to catch up in Sydney.'

'Oh, me too? That's good. Didn't mean to put my foot in it, earlier!'

Over the next couple of years, we visited Natasha often when she was in Sydney. She seemed at her happiest and most relaxed when Andrew also came, but it wasn't a closed shop. Claire often joined us, although Bran stayed away. 'Won't he come Claire? He's most welcome.'

'Ah … silly old duffer, he thinks we should be at the house! I know, I know, I set him right, but well … he said he'd only have come if Michael invited him; he still opens the car door for me, gorgeous old thing.' She said, as if by way of explanation.

And Sir Michael never chose to join them. *Why do you persist with those yokels, Natasha? What on earth do you get out of it?*

'What... apart from pleasure and inspiration? The delight that comes from minds that are vitally … so vitally engaged with living.'

Are you complaining about our life together?

'Actually, I wasn't reflecting on us at all. Not every conversation has to dock at your harbour. I was suggesting something about the "yokels" I am engaged with.'

Well, don't invite 'em here. Wiping their muddy boots on our Persians, spilling grog on the cushions! As if by denigrating them, he could bring them down. *So, do you make anything, or make anything happen at these little tête-à-têtes?* He couldn't resist the diminutive.

'Not directly. These are social gatherings; there's no agenda, no topics, although it's a rare day that we don't finish up somewhere different from where we started, having picked up something along the way. No-one gets trashed!'

She didn't make excuses for him, but she didn't ridicule him. Simply put, she explained, he'd prefer she caught up with everyone outside the house. Charles was pleased, Ben insulted, Claire angry, Susannah indifferent; and Natasha embarrassed.

'The sad thing is Michael, you might enjoy our conversations. We don't curdle our flat whites,' she giggled, 'but we range far and wide over our worlds and our moments, happening on these things as part of talking about what is on our minds.'

Aren't you giving away your secrets.

'These aren't card tricks, we simply share ideas.'

And the doctor? Still sniffing around is he; guess he's got into your pants …?

'O, Michael, why demean yourself.' She wondered sometimes, if he didn't seek out humiliation. 'Quite apart from that disgusting innuendo, I'm telling you about something – meetings with my friends – that gives me pleasure and all you want to do is debase it. Can't you enjoy it?'

Oh, so you are … screwing him, he called over his shoulder as he wheeled himself out of the room. Abasi! Where the fuck is that boy; never around when I want him. ABA…SI! Just because you're out here. Doesn't mean you're on bloody holidays.

'He might come quicker if you called him by his proper name,' she called after him. 'He's Nicodemus, and aptly named as it is, it seems to me.' She had in mind biblical stories of Nicodemus cleansing Jesus' body at his burial. 'Oh, I know why you call him Abasi,' she replied, contempt in her voice. 'But he's a lovely man. He's entitled to an identity.'

What a lot of rubbish! Like the others, he's Abasi; he abases himself …
ABAA … SSI! Damn you. Get me out of here.

* * *

Natasha had told Susannah a little of her life with Michael, and the role Nicodemus played in Michael's day-to-day living. 'Abasi', whose birth name was Nicodemus Onyango, was the only one of his carers to last beyond two years. Nicodemus however, had tolerated Michael's manner for almost six years. He drove them hard, gave no praise and took no interest in them, while setting traps to make sure they weren't stealing from him. But, needing the work to help support his family and put himself through Medicine, Nicodemus stayed. He even spends a month of the university break in Australia with them. A man of twenty-eight – the gentlest of souls – he would cycle to Cadogan Place daily at 5 am, attend Michael in the gym, run his bath, assist him into and out of it, but never stay with him; make sure all toiletry needs were catered for, and help him dress and prepare for the day, have breakfast with the two of them and drive Michael to work at 8 am. He would then go on to the university, before once again being at Michael's beck and call from 5.30 in the afternoon until at least 8 pm, by which time he waits while Michael visits his club or other haunts and assists him with his ablutions and helps him dress for whatever the evening requires. Throughout which, Michael barely utters a personal word to him, despite their intimacy.

Natasha, however, makes sure he has breakfast and an evening meal and helps him where she can: they are friends. If he is released early from serving Michael they might sit and chat; he would talk about his home in Kisumu and the contrast between the beauty of their great lake and the poverty of his people and how his greatest happiness will be to return to his community to practice his medicine in the children's hospital. She told tell him about her Mamma and Papa and growing up in St Petersburg. She would sometimes find him playing with Pushkin, lying on the ground curled up like the cat, petting him around the neck and head and blinking, calming the cat. 'He loves that, Nicodemus; you're very gentle with him.'

'Ohhh, Nart-arshar,' he sighed, 'he's a beautiful little boy; he's not hard to love.' ...

***

Natasha was attentive to us all when we got together. Turning to me at our next lunch, she asked if I had 'anything ..., you know, gestating?'

'A few murmurs, a gentle kick or two ... I've been listening to the magpies ...!' I left it at that, but their calling and responding, warbling and caroling across their full vocabulary in the mornings is irrevocably mixed with the bliss of waking up next to Ben, with the soft murmur of his breathing, the texture of his flesh firm against mine, nestling, not insistent, with the almost unconscious movement of his hand, finding mine sometimes, at others caressing my cheek, brushing my lips, touching, smoothing, cupping a breast in no pattern of behaviour, except in the desire to give pleasure. But I didn't need to share that; I thought my happiness was written in every movement of my body anyway. 'It might be something quite large, the way I'm hearing it in my head, I'm thinking of it, already, as my *Celtic Ponds Chorale...*'

Then Natasha moved, caught their attention. 'Now my dears, this might be the last Sydney interlude for a while. Michael is due back in London; so, it's *au revoir* – never good bye now – until next year. I've loved this sojourn in Australia more than I can tell you.' She brushed away a tiny tear. 'And I hope the time will fly.' Even as she spoke, they moved towards her as one. Darling Natasha; holding her hand, brushing her cheek with gentle kisses, arms around her waist. And she was gone, into the taxi. A gap opened in their lives.

Andrew:
Hunger Pangs

I stand in the study watching the rain, light now – as thin as mist, slide down the window. I could have been in Edinburgh: 'what a *dreich* day.' The sound of the bell echoes around the hills, yet I need no reminder of the occasion. I'd driven Natasha down from Sydney the night before and settled her at the *Clover and Thistle*, where the publican's wife Sheila Welham, told me she'd 'done up a room specially for her', even down to the Arum lilies. As you can imagine, there was quite an ado about the funeral of this rich and powerful man being held in our little wooden church; for the south coast hinterland had seen few occasions like this in its quiet history. Oh anyone who spent time here soon heard of their famous, if somewhat recalcitrant son; who, though he never came back was woven into the fabric of its local stories. I was a latecomer to Celtic Ponds, but I had met Michael O'Connell in an earlier life. Reflecting on his self-imposed exile from the place, I couldn't help thinking of my own move here. An association stretching now to six years; which some wag suggested would soon qualify me as a local!

The first couple of years weren't easy. But that was understandable, I was grieving my wife Mary's passing and with old Doc Eddington's patients cautious about putting themselves in the hands of a new chum, pink as a cherub and with a toffy accent to boot, I had some lingering doubts about my decision. However, I'd made a commitment and I wouldn't renege on it; I'd give it a proper shot. Besides, it would have been unnatural if I hadn't mourned Mary and Eddington had been the GP here for thirty years; of course they were going to miss him and question me. But things turn and by now I'm content, if a little incomplete. I have this gnawing feeling deep inside, constant, if untreatable. (No, you can't fix it with *Mylanta*, or a good meal!)

It comes from an inner longing and yet to my surprise it didn't take me long to feel as though I could put down roots in this special place.

Bran and Claire held a large party to celebrate *Wicklow Stud's* centenary and they thought it was a good opportunity for me to meet some of the locals. The town band was playing and there was dancing. I was a good ballroom dancer, although I hadn't done much since coming to Australia, but you don't forget those things. 'My word, Doctor Buchanan,' Claire had said, 'you'd be a huge asset at our CWA dances. You must come!'

'God Doc,' Bran chimed in, 'blokes who can dance are scarce as hen's teeth. I'll have trouble keeping Claire's hands off you!' Even Ben, who I was currently treating for a bad laceration on his arm in an accident with a power saw, wanted to know where I'd learned to dance; while Sue, commenting on what she called my sense of rhythm, said she'd be surprised if I didn't play an instrument.

'Not sure you'd call it playing, but I tinkle on the piano and can do a few tunes on the accordion.' Now that got her attention! 'Aha, piano and accordion, that's just what we need; perhaps the *Ponds Alive Four* can become a *Five*! What do you think?'

It wasn't long before I had joined the band, sharing my interests in the Tango and being swept away by Susannah's vocals and her outstanding – quite marvellous – technical skills on the cello and the fiddle, which was what she mostly played with the group. My presence solved one of the band's problems as Molly was ready for a break, but we could never rustle up anyone to play clarinet or trumpet. Practice was on Tuesdays: 'Another happy Tuesday', I mused, thinking back to my student days in Edinburgh.

But, that's another story! We played at the monthly dances and at pretty well all the other dances, weddings and one-off events around the district.

Within a couple of months, we had most of the town locals – from Claire, who was excited about the whole thing, and Bran, at one end of the age spectrum, to a couple of the high school kids, at the other – proudly posturing and sliding around the dance floor, practicing their Tango steps. 'Listen to the music, remember to slide, hold up your head; look very proud; head erect, now e-ex-extend.'

To my surprise, no one was more adept than Ben who, together with Natasha, whom I taught somewhat later, was one of my great success stories. He was instinctive, entering into the music while also responding to its passionate core. 'My word!' I whispered to Sue. 'You'll have fun at home.'

I took a lease on a cosy weatherboard cottage above the town, with a large verandah like Susannah's to enjoy the view. I'd moved several pieces of furniture down from Sydney; favourites, mainly for the study which I'd converted from one of the front bedrooms: an old cedar desk and a pair of rosewood Victorian gentleman's chairs – my 'Rachaels' I called them – which I'd carted out from my digs in Edinburgh. For the most part, it was a fresh start and selling the Five Dock apartment in July was a statement about my desire to reinvent myself.

I had one afternoon off a week to have a piano lesson from Susannah, started a Music Club on Monday evenings, opened a surgery in one of the shops in the main drag down Blunt Street, and with a consultancy in Broadwater, I had sufficient interesting medicine in the practice to keep me motivated. I kept up on my reading of the journals, for I didn't love medicine less; I simply practiced a different kind. In a sense, if the practice was more intellectually isolated than the Clinic, my collaborations were now just as likely to be found in our musical explorations. As I said to Susannah, who understood the delight I took from my involvement: 'In my other life I was rather grandly called a creative catalyst, where I was the ringmaster to a group of talented colleagues in a special environment with shared goals, this also enables me to fit the bits together. It's about team work. Ben'd know.'

I was beginning to settle, and it wasn't long before doors around town began to open, and my patient list filled out: 'seems like a good bloke Mabel, better give him a go!' I was now on the end of cheerios, friendly waves, and invitations to dinner.

Smiling inwardly, for these were happy memories, if never quite appeasing his inner hunger, Andrew unravelled himself from this reverie, took care in dressing in a dark suit and a white shirt, spending a little time over choosing a tie, before settling on a navy one decorated with delicately worked yellow shields encasing a rampant lion, which he thought of as a Buchanan tie. Then, with Natasha not expecting him for a couple of hours, he strolled into town for a coffee and the papers.

'It's a busy village we're going to have this morning Ben, getting in early?' I said as we bumped into each other at the News agency. I knew the place would soon be invaded by black suits and dresses, milling around, gathering in groups and separating, sorting the wheat from the chaff. Deciding who to greet, who to safely ignore. No less than the women in their high heels, the men will carefully negotiate the mud puddles and broken paths; anxious not to spoil the shine of their shoes. Umbrellas at hand, held as if to parry an unwanted attack, they will, however, be alert for a photo opportunity, for the paparazzi would soon be staking out St Michael's.

As for the locals, apart from Ben, who seemed in no hurry, they were scurrying around preparing for any business the crowd might generate, while others were carrying the last chairs across to the church as, nursing my coffee and nosing the smell of the wet grass, I wandered up the hill vaguely watching the blue-black clouds like massive bruises, spreading across the sky. I was taken back to Mary's funeral and what, for all its sadness, was a memorable wake. Mary had wanted that. What would this afternoon bring?

***

Ah, Mary. I'd talked to Natasha about our relationship in the car as we drove down the previous evening: 'Everyone said we had a thoroughly modern, professional, urbane relationship. I know that sounds frightfully clinical but, having decided early on that we didn't want children, medicine was our life's work. It wasn't as simple as that of course, I didn't have any great need to see myself re-produced and Mary – always Nowak, "I'll never give up my polish name; is that okay with you, husband–to-be?" – was born in the ghetto. Her life was filled with stories of the dead and missing and the violently disrupted.'

'Who would want to bring a child into this insane world? I don't want children.'

'Adoption was an option for Michael and me, of course,' Natasha had said. 'I would have. But it was out of the question for him: *Adopt? Who knows how scarred or broken they'll be!* Really, it was a crazy idea, reckless to suggest it. There was little room in Michael's life for anyone other than himself. Did you ever wish you'd had children though?'

'I had regrets. But it didn't affect the marriage and Mary was older than me. We would have had to get cracking as soon as we married and we had careers to forge. The rationalisation is easy in our line of work. We have all these children at the clinic.'

'Tell me a little about Mary? I'm not prying; I'd just like to know. We have plenty of time. I knew it was terribly sad towards the end. So young and perhaps unready?'

'Yes; it was a dreadful time. We live many lives and carry the shards of them with us; these are some of mine and you do know a little of it.'

I was carried back to the moment: it was in the depth of winter in '92, Mary had come home from work early, her face ashen, her eyes sunk deep into their sockets; she kissed me on each cheek and pushed me down into a chair.

'Now this is going to sound like a bad joke,' she'd said, 'but it's not even a little bit funny: I've got a year at the most. Andrew, oh Sandy, I have ...,' her voice wavered, just for a moment, before she was back in control. 'I've had the king hit; Liver and Pancreas! I'm starting chemo: there's nothing you can do ...'.

'I implored her to let me in. I wasn't being selfish. I wanted to help; not be shut out.'

'She didn't see it like that? Perhaps she was protecting you?' Natasha spoke softly.

'Yes, perhaps; but I didn't need a shield. Subliminally, you know, I'd kent it; knew, but didn't! As for Mary, it was the way she was. She insisted – demanded – she go it alone. [Alone into that dark night.] … That was Mary. You see, this was the way it was, I was always in a sense, on the periphery. When I protested, and I can hear her now: "Don't be tedious, Sandy. What good would it have done? Do *you* have a cure? You've got our new building to get on with. It isn't your problem; but it's going to become a little of that as the months pass. I'm just unlucky!" So much to the point. "No moping, I know you won't, but just in case you need to know: I don't expect it. There's heaps to do and I'm going to get as much done as I can; okay?"'

'So matter of the fact. But almost brutal, no?'

'In the ensuing six months, she didn't make the year, she hardly faltered; I think she lived on morphine, largely self-medicating and her intimate diary – a *journaux intime* you might say – of those last six months provides a moving window on the dying process. *Diary of a Disease: from Doctor to Patient*. We published it as a documented guide for specialists in the field, of the experience of the patient, told not by a lay-person but by one steeped in the field. There was not a little irony in that, but I don't want to go into that.' He looked fondly at her. 'I'm immensely proud of what she did. But, of course, you know about *Diary of a Disease*?'

'Yes, remember you'd told me and I mentioned it to Michael who backed it. I think he was more interested in it than the Clinic. *Damned important, people should read this, especially doctors working at the coal-face. Feisty woman!*

'Let's start at the beginning! We met in 1975 after I'd arrived from Scotland to begin post-graduate research in paediatrics. Mary was a young doctor with a stellar degree and a growing reputation as an oncologist, specialising in childhood cancers. It started very casually, a relationship of convenience, perfunctory at times, and just drifted into marriage. 'Look,' she'd said one night, 'I've got a Post-Doc at Boston Children's for a year, why don't you complete your letters and we'll make medicine together, good idea? Isn't it what you want? Surely you haven't been wasting my time; don't tell me you hadn't thought about it?'

Natasha interrupted: 'Sorry Andrei. Love?'

'Exactly what I said. Isn't there a word missing? I can hear her reply to this day.

'"Oh God, don't be so sentimental Sandy; surely I don't have to tell you all the time, of course I love you! We never argue and that's bloody extraordinary, we're both clever, so we probably won't condescend. You're good in bed, damn good; best shag I've ever had; where did a long streak of misery like you pick that up? We'll be a fabulous team: Nowak and Buchanan, oncologist and paediatrician at large. Got a ring to it hasn't it? Now," and she wriggled into me: "let's make that love that you're soooo good at; what more do we want?"'

Natasha smiled at the carnality of it, but still wondered about the depth of feeling.

'While Mary was away I finished my Letters, published a couple of papers – "Oh, clever boy, I even heard about your Helsinki paper over here; you're on the radar!"– and when she returned, with her research drawing a lot of attention, we were being hailed as *stars* in the new Western Suburbs Hospital's firmament. We had few distractions and shared the same work place; had a comfortable, low maintenance apartment in Five Dock and overlapping networks of friends and associates which meant we had a semblance of a social life, or another space in which to talk shop.'

Natasha sighed. 'How did you relax? Holidays? Anything away from work?'

'Nothing!' It sounded hollow. 'Holidays? "What a luxury," Mary had groaned once. Conferences were our vacations, but rarely together. But I played piano in a little trio. Stefan Holderlin, an architect, was exercising his fingers on the double base and we had a spunky hairdresser, Dawn Antrobus, on clarinet and sax. "Hope she's not blowing you as well, husband!" Mary said, disparagingly of Dawn, who seemed entirely fulfilled with her spiky-haired girlfriend.'

'O, dear!' Natasha sighed.

'We didn't do it for the money but got a few gigs. Mary just didn't get the jazz, I'm afraid. 'Why do you bother with those wasters, Sandy? What on earth do you talk about? Or, do they just talk gibberish through a haze of weed?'

'Ah, Mary! Some chaps play football, others have a boat, go flying, have a beer and a bet; I play jazz. It's how I relax.'

'Pah, relax? You need taking in hand,' she'd roared. 'You'd be better off giving 'em a lecture on the hazards of smoking!' But I kept playing and even returned to piano lessons and expanded my range beyond classical and jazz, into dance music.

'Mary was soon running her own laboratory, but the team was beginning to fracture as the increasing daily demands of the Clinic and an expanding and highly regarded research profile pulled us in different directions. And I was administering it, or, at least, trying to hold it all together. It was obvious we needed more space. And then, after a Research Committee meeting, she burst screaming into my office: "Some big-shot magnate has gifted the hospital some land, oh Sandy, it's the clinic's. And you, my sweet, are the one to lead us benighted Israelites out of our wilderness: you're good at that sort of thing."'

'Ah, the big shot magnate with the land,' Natasha sniffed. 'That's a story in itself!'

'So I got cracking, but before I did anything, the way I am I guess, I needed a consensus, both about the direction to take and my role. Mary would have simply bashed their heads together and told them where they were going.'

Natasha looked closely at him. 'But you don't think like that.'

'No! It takes a little longer, but everyone gets to share in the project. That's where *O'Connell* came on the scene, we met and started to choreograph the new clinic.'

She smiled. 'It was so much more than that, I know. But where was Mary?'

'Having urged me on and got me engaged in it, she withdrew to her lab. Sadly, from there, our story unfolds very quickly. I was totally occupied with the building and managing the clinic while Mary buried herself in her research. It wasn't unusual for her to sleep over in the office, where she'd set up a trestle-bed, and if I dragged her out, we might have a coffee together in the canteen of a morning; but only if I insisted. Even at home, while the atmosphere was never cold or bleak – "You understand Sandy, don't you? Of course, you do! I've got a lot to do, and so little time" – we were living separate lives.'

'How did you cope? I could see the stress you were under. It was inscribed on your face.'

'Cope? Not well. I have this peculiar internal mechanism – I call it my hunger pangs, an ache in the pit of my stomach – which is activated when I am soul-shakingly lonely; had it since I was a wee chiel at boarding school and about this time that alarm was set off. We were lucky if we saw each other in passing; she was looking haggard and worn, scrawny even, and her beautiful skin was blotchy. I tried to make sure that she at least had lunch. *Eat*! I'd say. She was courage itself; some say she taught us how to die.'

'What made you leave the Clinic? You were doing some remarkable things.'

As we talked, it was as though I was watching the replay of an old movie. 'It was an easy decision. We'd built it up together, then, with Mary gone our work had finished. But, Natashenka, this is silly, me chattering about myself.'

'No, please; I like to hear your story.'

'Well at first the staff didn't want me to go, but after a bit of blathering and much ado, as though the only thing I could do centred on children under the age of eighteen, I was off.'

'Surely, they were worrying you'd be wasting yourself and all that knowledge lost to the Clinic? 'Pressure cooker specialist to ruminating in the bush? Yes, those things. But it wasn't a reckless decision, I knew the Clinic would flourish, it was all in place. People were eager to work there, and my dear, you do see' – I touched her arm, wanting her to understand

– 'its current strength was due in no small part to *O'Connell* and your passionate advocacy.'

'You're too kind,' she mumbled. Like Andrew, she had little need to be puffed up; a quality acquired perhaps around the table in St Petersburg. 'I remember the collaboration well. It was my first trip to Australia, I was excited by the work you were doing.'

'Yes, it was a combined effort. Do you recall how it all started? Polly – remember Pol, our general factotum, secretary, PA, fund-raiser, chief cook and bottle-washer – had found out it was *O'Connell,* who had donated the land. "It's run by Michael O'Connell," she'd yelped. "He's an Australian, spends most of his time in the UK, but he has this charity arm. Let's see if he'd like to help us." We were desperate, so …'

'I remember her. Like a little terrier dog, yappin' away in her broad Ossie accent,' she replied, trying to put one on. 'To be honest though, my immediate reaction was to wonder if she was the best you could do by way of a front, you must have been desperate! So, I checked you out and she turned out to be a gem. We met often or talked on the phone; she organized it all.'

'Yes, we were excited, but … you were no pushover!'

'I certainly hope not: I wanted *O'Connell* to be involved but I had to satisfy myself you were worth it. I did my due diligence, she smiled ironically at her use of the technical term. It *was* my first big job for the Company.'

'Well it took two years! You were so thorough, I didn't think I could ever satisfy you.'

They looked at each other. 'Do you remember our initial meeting? Polly had arranged for you and Michael to visit the clinic. Pushing him around all afternoon, you explored every corner of the place, asking questions as you went. You didn't just want to know what we did, but what we didn't do and would like to. It wasn't an examination; I mean we had the bare bones of where we wanted to go but you helped me understand how to put flesh on them. And I remember you saying, very business-like but with a smile: "Always have a wish-list in the bottom drawer."'

'That's what I learned from Michael. He didn't seem overly interested in the project, but when I told him about our conversation he sniggered, disparagingly: *Ah, that lot,* he liked lumping academics and medicos together, *all the bloody same in business: too timid. React, instead of lead!* Then he muttered; *what's the fellow's name? Buchanan is it?* But, he knew!

'Michael also wondered if you – and your colleagues – had thought about the dynamics of the split you were wanting to engineer. He thought that there'd have to be some *pretty vigorous head-bashing. Can your fabulous Buchanan do that?* I told him that you didn't come across that way to me, at which he snorted. *He'll have his bloody time cut out then.* He wore cynicism like a piece of national dress: *I'd want to know he can manage that before I pushed too much of the hard-earned his way. Looks like you've got your work cut out!*'

'I remember saying to you: "Alright, let's put our heads together", and you, smiling at the expression, nodding. But, if Michael wasn't interested why did he let you proceed with it?'

'Ah, that's a story in itself. When we started out, in fact it was 1987, I remember it well because Michael was making sure I didn't get involved with the late stages of the Memorial Garden project, so he wanted me occupied with something, anything. At the time I didn't understand but now I think I do.'

Andrew sighed. 'We were surprised how quickly you got back to us. Pol was so excited: "They're hooked!" she chuckled. And it was on. You were on site immediately and involved in every facet of the project, even down to negotiating for additional funding from the Government. I mean you were overseeing *O'Connell's* major involvement, but it was so much more, for you basically ensured the direct support of the State Government for up to six years.'

She shrugged. 'Part of the job. And Michael was happy because I had something to do. But, to mention Michael raises the question of the land, which needs some clarification. *Mon Dieu!* Michael operating at his very best; what a killing he made from it!'

'But, but…I was told he donated the land adjacent to the hospital for the development!'

'He didn't "give" you anything, Andrew. I won't go into every cut and thrust of the deal, but he swapped the land, which was purchased solely for this deal, for a plum piece of Government real estate in the inner city. It cost him some stamp duty and the contents of a few brown paper bags,' she grimaced: 'the price of the strongest voices in the Cabinet room.' [*Whatever it takes!*] Andrew frowned. 'You see, he'd acquired the so called "hospital" land much earlier, having had a nod from one of his cronies that the Government was beginning to formulate plans for a major extension of the Western Suburbs Hospital. Oh, I'm talking ten, twelve years ago; don't talk to me about patience! It was well before my time. He simply bought up the mixed farming land adjacent to the hospital before it was rezoned and waited! When the development was confirmed in the early '80s he was on hand.'

'Shrewd. Did he tell you this?'

'Tell me? Michael didn't ever tell anyone, friends or enemies, more than he thought they needed to know. He never breathed a hint about where the land had come from. I found out about the deal from documents I read at home when he became very ill. But, the building. How did that come about?'

* * *

'A satisfying confluence of forces, really. It was an exciting prospect. I got Stef Holderlin, our double base playing architect, to help me visualise what I had in mind and he became the lead architect, produced some drawings I could take back to my colleagues, and got his principal interested, and he fed into the project.'

'Yes, you see that was another piece of good fortune for Michael held *Ronald Bearne and Associates* in high regard, and there weren't many he was prepared to say that about! *Bearne has a good mind; let's hope Holderlin's in the same mould. Bearne saw him as something of a protégé, so there's a chance you might be onto a winner.'*

The original brief was for Holderlin to design a modern, functional building, with as few secrets as possible. It would have two interlocking areas, linked, physically and philosophically … two parts of a whole in harmony… discrete but together, with communal spaces at the centre uniting them all. When people came for treatment, I wanted them also to enjoy the place as a creative space, which I hoped would be flexible, incorporating further interactive and interdependent spaces. I also wanted large see-through areas which would be a literal statement of the desired philosophical openness.

'Ah, interlocking solids and voids,' Holderlin exclaimed. 'I like it!'

***

'I'll never forget the excitement when you first showed me the plans and explained the logic behind them, Andrew. It was like watching a piece of modern dance coming together with something of the same, how do you say, imperatives?'

'And, Michael?'

'Oh, you know. He affected an off-handedness, even as he noted everything. *You like it? Will it do what they want? Better give me a copy of the plans.*

'I told him that you wondered if he would like to visit. *No, why? You seem to be seeing enough of Buchanan for the two of us!* Then he laughed mirthlessly and turned away, speaking as he did so, as if offering an afterthought: *My, aren't you a cunning devil, my dear. Plans that you like and a sweet little property deal for the firm!* He was sliding the land deal onto my plate. Oh Andrew, am I talking out of turn?'

'I don't think I have many illusions about Michael, Natasha!'

'It was his manner you see, to seduce people into his way of thinking – the spider and his web – and then, snap: it's your idea, not his. You are the one who is implicated if anything goes wrong, if not, you are beholden to him. I tried not to let him play those games with me, even at my lowest. I was never his pawn. *You should take credit for the deal; it's brilliant.*

'But, Michael it was your idea, not mine. On behalf of *O'Connell*, I'm committed to a development I believe in, I can't take any of the credit for the land deal. O, I was being provocative. What you do with the proceeds of that deal is entirely up to you.

I see; intense, his mouth a bitter line. His anger was extravagant. *I guess you are fucking Buchanan; is that part of your deal?* It was as though he was frightened and was trying to stage manage his fear.'

'You accused me of that once before, as in the case with darling Rudi: you were wrong then, you are wrong now. It doesn't become you. Leave me alone, I have work to do. I added the latter, as I knew he couldn't stand being dismissed and put down, and rarely was of course. O dear, he just couldn't help himself sometimes. The irony of that crude accusation was that when we were married he said he didn't mind if I had outside arrangements. I rejected the suggestion for a variety of reasons, but I came to realise that it was also a good strategic decision, as I saw how he could use it as a means of control. Awful! But, you good man, all this was of no matter to what we were building, which gave – gives? – me enormous and consuming satisfaction.'

* * *

From the first pour in 1988, to the attachment of the innovative external mesh and the internal fit-out five years later, the project went with barely a hitch. I was surprised how often Natasha was on site when she was in the country, and what a sight she was; always elegant, usually in tailored slacks, shirts or jackets. Occasionally, if the weather turned bleak, in an overcoat all topped off with a yellow hard hat. She seemed to rather enjoy the incongruity of it!

By 1993, The Children's Cancer Clinic was a reality and throughout it all, at Michael's insistence, Natasha had received Board minutes: *It's just good business, my dear. Don't give up control if you don't have to! O'Connell: 101.* While to cap it all off, as the Clinic began to plan the establishment of a new unit to work with cancers in under-privileged children, Natasha made a one-off donation of $1,000,000 from her own *Foundation*, providing for the establishment and maintenance of a professorial position in the field.

'The only difference of opinion between us, and it was only minor, do you remember, was over the naming of the Clinic? You thought it was a chance to commemorate Mary. 'Oh no, no! ... It was never about her or even us,' I'd said. 'Besides, we have the *Nowak Oncology Laboratories* and ... da-da, the *Buchanan Playground*: internal memorials to each of us. How Mary would have loved that, "I'll do the work, husband", she used to say, "you play around with the kids." It was our joke. In all honesty, almost from the moment we began to lay down the plans, I've thought of the building, in its elegance and practical beauty, as being a monument to you. You were much more than the bag lady! But even then, I never saw Michael on the site; didn't he want to see where the *O'Connell* money was going?'

'Well; Michael was a strange man. He knew what was happening, followed the entire project right down to having someone take photos of it, but he wouldn't let anyone know he cared, not even me, although I'd learned to read him by then.' She paused, thoughtful. 'I'm not sure if he saw it as a weakness. I think it was a part of that shield he had erected around himself.'

'How odd. Why demean yourself like that ... it's so, so... ungenerous!'

'You are right. But he didn't see it that way; not, perhaps until the end. I think the project was just one more victory. He made a lot of money out of the land and he thought he'd, how do you say, ... hoodwanked ... the Government.'

'It's ironic. I feel sorry for him. I think you meant "hoodwinked". Although ... it wasn't an altogether erroneous slippage!'

She laughed wildly, 'he wouldn't have liked to hear you pitying him either!'

'And then, just as the project was reaching its culmination, Mary died.

It was over, just like that!' I left unspoken the harrowing couple of months before her death when I tried to give succour; and the cancer and its humiliating side-effects, but thought Natasha may have intuited something of that. What is it? "We make plans and the gods laugh!"'

'Yes, horrid, I understood what you were going through; and … the speed of it in the end, as though she was in a hurry … the awful irony of it; the Gods can be cruel. But, *mon docteur*, … we don't stop making plans, we just make others: we open other doors!' Yet even as Natasha was being wise, she thought back to her own black night and Rudi yelling at her.

'For God's sake, Natasha Yakovlevna Levinskaya, get off your arse, and get on!'

* * *

Natasha was waiting in the hotel foyer when I arrived.

'Good morning, *moya dah-ra-gho ya*.' I spoke slowly – a foreigner feeling his way in a new language – and touched her hand in greeting.

'And to you Andrei.' She nodded, thanking him. 'You have Russian?'

'Oh, only a smidgen,' I chuckled. 'Actually, I've just been thinking about our conversation in the car last night, finishing as we did on your notion of doors opening.' He was picking up her expression: a kind of homage. 'We were trampling through questions of irony and fate; not the least of which is the extraordinary coincidence that we should find ourselves in Celtic Ponds …' I hadn't meant to be ambiguous but as we spent more time together, there was the sense, buried in the banal metaphor of discovery, by which, of course I'd meant no more than a coincidence of place and time: of myriad possibilities.

'Ah, yes, I've found myself …,' she smiled at the echo of his words; 'have often thought how strange that you should move to Celtic Ponds. Did you know about Michael's links to the place?'

'I don't think so; it may have come up in conversation, but I've no recollection.

Michael O'Connell was definitely mentioned at the interview I had when I was offered the job.'

Natasha looked at him. 'I remember coming home from my first meeting with the Clinic Board after you'd left; it would have been March '95 I guess; we were back in Sydney earlier that year. When I told him you'd accepted a position here, he grinned sourly. *Yes; amazing, isn't it.* It was a statement, not a question: he knew! *What a waste; he'll die of boredom. The previous doctor went fishing.* That's the overarching irony of the man; he knew nearly everything about everyone and yet he hadn't set foot in the place since 1970.'

'Then you visited: 1998, I remember it well. It was like royalty coming to town!'

'Oh, don't exaggerate!' She laughed, brushing it off like fluff on a sleeve as they left the hotel. 'But, I had to come, Michael was starting to develop his ideas for a Celtic Ponds Millenial Gift project and yet he wouldn't visit. I thought it was rude, but enough! This is about you, not me,' warmth in her smile: 'the humble Scotsman.' She might have said, 'my', but refrained! 'You never talk about yourself. Gracious, when I think of the number of inflated egos ... oh, not just doctors, but some of them take a bit of beating!'

'Be gentle now,' he whispered, 'Some of them have been told all their lives how clever they are and they believe it. Well generally they are smart, but it's like academics you see, they have very specific knowledges, just think they can pontificate on anything!'

But, she wasn't inclined to be charitable. 'It's their consuming arrogance, but you're not like that. ... How was Celtic Ponds so lucky to get you?' She asked as they crossed the road to the church she took his arm.

'Well let me see, a month or so after Mary died I found an ad in *The Medical Examiner* ...'. She finished his sentence, reciting: '*Pleasant country town seeks a medical practitioner who will devote himself to the community.* Or something like that. I'd seen the advertisement you see, among Michael's papers!' She paused, let it sink in. 'But, how did they – who – convince you to give up everything and set up here?'

'Well, as you know, if you have seen the advertisement, old Eddington had died and the town was having trouble attracting a replacement. Celtic Ponds isn't on everyone's lips. I made contact and within a couple of weeks I was on my way to meet Mr Sanders, the Shire President. I made a holiday of it, pottered down that glorious piece of coastline south of Sydney, armed with my favourites, Cleo, Roberta Flack, of course, Oscar and Buddy, and the fabulous Blossom Dearie, sighing through *Once upon a summertime*. I stayed overnight at the old *Dromedary*, in Tilba, and traveled up in the morning.'

The priest was at the doorway to the porch when they arrived, but the Monsignor had not yet arrived, they waited in the gardens. 'Don't stop', she whispered, lifting her short veil and looking at him; *Once upon a summertime* in her head. 'I'd like to hear your story. Let's wait for the Monsignor.'

'I turned away from the coast and began to wind my way through the foothills. If it can be said that landscape is persuasive, everything – the gently billowing clouds, casting pale shadows across the pastured fields, the drifts of trees spilling down the slopes, issuing dappled light and the burst of sunlight that lit up the village as I descended into the valley – worked to welcome me.'

She looked at him again, as he continued. 'As if to reciprocate nature's welcome, as I tootled past the little gallery, a woman – I know now that it was Nina Oakley – who was sweeping the path, looked up and waved. Corny isn't it, or is it a human need for good omens? As I crossed the town bridge and glimpsed the sign directing visitors to the Shire Office, with Buddy and Oscar doing *Someone to Watch Over Me*, an old fellow tending the roses greeted me. Looking me up and down, he said: "You'll be looking for Bill Sanders I reckon, straight ahead mate, through the glass door. Melissa'll tell him you're here." That was my first experience of the bush telegraph!'

'Go on. There's no sign of him yet.'

'Well, next thing I was in the office, sharing teacake and a cuppa. Within forty minutes, having been given an energetic tour of the village and surrounds on a large wall map and met Bran Doogue: "the grandfather of the district" as Sanders called him; it was clear that I had the job if I wanted it.' Talking about it, I lingered on the memory, even as I was surprised by her interest.

'"Now Bran, Dr Andrew Buchanan; he's looking us over, be nice to him eh! Andy [I was Andy already?] this old codger was the long term Shire President before me; sits on, or has done, most of the committees and boards around the place, and he and his lovely wife run *Wicklow Stud* for the O'Connell family; have done for nearly fifty years. Real show piece; p'raps you know it?"'

'I confessed that I didn't, but, almost speechless at the extraordinary coincidence, I told them I'd worked closely with you and *O'Connell* in developing the Clinic.'

By then the fully festooned Monsignor in his purple trimmed black cassock and matching stole had arrived and together with the priest, welcomed the crowd as they filtered into the church and were dispersed in a suitable pecking order by the ushers. Saying a quiet hello, Natasha and Andrew walked to their pew at the front of the church and as the buzz of whispered conversations petered out, the Monsignor and the trailing priest strode down the central aisle in front of the casket which was wheeled down and parked close to the sanctuary. Because the church was so small, it was almost beside Natasha's pew. She could have patted it but didn't! Instead, as if to answer my concern that it was so close, she leant in my direction: 'Michael doesn't spook me!'

The candles were lit and the coffin was sprinkled with holy water, then the Monsignor called everyone to prayer. With a gentle expiration, I slid down into a kneeling position, my long legs meeting the footrest of the pew behind. I could feel Natasha next to me. 'Eternal rest give to them O Lord; and let perpetual light shine upon them.' I was thankful to rise and add my voice to the mutilation of *On Eagle's Wings* that was being enacted. Although Natasha had the words in front of her, she did not – could not? I wondered – sing.

You who dwell in the shelter of the Lord,
Who abide in His shadow for life,
Say to the Lord, "my Refuge,
My Rock, in Whom I trust.

And then, after more of the ritual, they were at the doorway.

As Natasha, flanked by the newly planted Monsignor who had arrived in Sydney recently from Cork, and the priest farewelled the mourners and others who were departing, temporarily redundant, I was thinking about Natasha's visit to Celtic Ponds in 1998. I had finally made contact with her, having unsuccessfully tried to do so since I'd left the *Clinic*. On this occasion, having sent a note to her care of the *Clinic*, rather than to the Hunter's Hill house, she called me.

'When the build was finished Andrew, I thought you'd severed all contact. Perhaps, like a business deal, you know, it had run its course. It's so lovely to hear from you, can we catch up? We're here for a couple of months. I thought I'd lost contact.' He thought he heard her sigh.

'I have an idea; why don't you come down to Celtic Ponds? That's where I am. It's time you saw where your husband grew up and what he spends some of his money on! So, Natasha, I'm not taking no for an answer, would Michael like to join us?'

'O Andrei ... Michael won't come, but I would love to. I've asked so many times to visit, I can predict his response and I can tell you there are few occasions when I am able to do that! He didn't even visit for the Bi-Centennial celebrations. But also, he's not well; do you know that? It'll take a little bit of arranging and Michael won't like it. We'd better do it soon, before he can disrupt our plans. I want to visit, apart from seeing you again; there are others who I want to get to know.'

'Ah wonderful, I'll make sure you meet everyone you should. They will love seeing you; I can tell you that!'

'I'll drive myself, I have some business in Canberra. Just give me some dates to work with.'

A couple of days later I got this glorious card: a gaily dressed ballerina performing a soaring leap, a huge smile on her red lips. 'So looking forward to seeing you all: organise me!' …

I can't understand why you want to go down there, Natasha. I forbid it. In fact, I've done all I need to here and have been thinking of heading back. His mood was black. *How the hell did you get in touch with Buchanan, anyway?*

'O Michael, such a performance. I plan to visit as I have to wind up the Canberra business.' He was to receive an Honour in the Queen's Birthday list. 'I can do the two in the one trip, and as I've explained before, you may find some way of disrupting my plans, but you will never "forbid" me to do anything; I thought you understood that. I will arrange for your casual nurse to attend you full-time, together with Nicodemus. I won't be gone more than four days. Perhaps, if you'd like to share with me the millennial plans you are hatching, I could advance them with Bran, who is still only a name to me!' She paused, furious, because it was clear Michael had intercepted Andrew's previous letters. Wheeling himself away he bellowed over his shoulder. *There are no plans to share with anyone. Fuck off then and leave me alone!*

And that's how she came to visit, spending a long weekend in March with the Doogues, who wouldn't hear of her staying anywhere but at *Clifton*. They also held an afternoon tea for her on the Saturday, inviting, as Charlie put it with tongue in cheek, 'all the likely suspects,' while Charlie and Ben took her on a tour of the *Clifton* garden on Saturday morning. She was flushed and excited when she came in: 'O, Andrei,' turning to him as if involuntarily: 'the colours, the variety and design, the scents. It's so subtle, everything has a place to shine, it is so beautifully choreographed. I adore it.' Her response was intensely emotional, visceral.

'Come, look!' She extended her arm towards him, fingers outstretched. She could have been leading him into a *pas de deux*. 'Do you know it? Come!' She was joyously relaxed, then, tightening her grip of his hand she whispered: 'Let's walk, perhaps we can lose ourselves!'

I found the afternoon tea strangely fractured, but, as Susannah put it: 'you can't be surprised, Andrew? You and I stand outside, our faces at the window, distanced, like a narrator perhaps, watching the narrative unfold, interpreting it but not being a part of it, while the others, each in their own way are, … are … feeling their way around the absent character; for as always, Michael is at the centre of the story. What does Natasha know that they don't? Or paradoxically, does she know anything at all about Michael's Ponds *family*?'

Natasha seemed oblivious of any such tension as she circulated or, if stationary, was greeted: 'Do you miss the ballet Lady O'Connell, you were so very good.' Molly Greenwood enquired, a little overwhelmed, as she struggled to make conversation.

'*Natasha*, Molly please! I have another life now, but … every day, there is a gap.'

'Oh, I can understand that. Ah, another life. Was it hard to leave Russia?'

'Not Russia: as I once said to my Maman, Russia is hard to love but, like my ballet, there are times when I long for St Petersburg's pearly nights; it's in my soul you know and my darling parents are buried there. I know you can't have everything and yet I ache for it sometimes; I have no *myehs tah*, how you say, no place!'

'But you've got London, Sydney – Hunters Hill, unless I'm wrong – they don't come much better than that,' Charlie said, interrupting, 'and, of course, Clifton!'

'O, I have houses or Michael does, and I share them, but I'm not rooted down anywhere like you are here. I can see it in your body. A dear Russian friend of mine used to say when we were lamenting this very thing: "well, my darling, stateless is our state." He was braver than me though, I need to belong … somewhere! I don't enjoy being homeloose; as he used to say.'

'I'm sorry, I misunderstood, I know what you mean: I'm sorry!' Charlie felt he'd embarrassed her as Andrew changed the subject.

'Did you once tell me you played the clarinet, Natasha; do you still? We have a little group you see and don't have any wind instruments.'

'You're naughty! My clarinet,' she giggled, 'makes dogs bark. I used to play with my Maman and Papa as a child, but now I would blow hot air rather than musical sounds. But who knows, if I brushed it off … one day I might make music with you.' She smiled at him.

She was not only the object of conversation; she wanted to know everything about the *Stud* and was delighted to hear of Charles' involvement, Michael hadn't told her.

'Do you need for anything, Bran?' But even as she engaged with everyone, she was casting her eyes around the room, and then seeing Ben and Susannah together, she excused herself. 'You are Susannah? I've wanted so much to meet you…', and then they were off, heads together, deep in conversation. Ben soon left them and joined Andrew: 'she's been hanging out to meet her.'

A little later, I saw her leading Charles into a quiet corner. I could only hear snatches of their conversation. 'He cared for you, … but', and then it was lost … fragments only, floated above the general chatter and bustle. 'We had no contact … his choice … not mine,' Charlie offered. 'I never… like he thought … stopped playing, for gardening…'

'Perhaps, he couldn't understand … Paintings…?' 'May I see them?' And so they went on.

As the sun faded into a pink light and night was just over the hill, the chatter, like the day, meandered to a gentle close. Natasha walked Andrew to his car, making plans to meet the next day with what almost looked like a spring in her ageing step, Molly left with Charles for his eyrie on the hill and Sergeant Heenan offered the tipsy Wrights a lift into town. While Sue linked arms with Ben and they ambled across to his place, Bran, his arm resting over Claire's shoulder, smiled as they waved good bye: 'Well, did you ever; isn't she lovely; just lovely!'

* * *

At home, a couple of lamb chops and tomatoes on the griller, I put together a small green salad and poured a glass of red and let my mind wander back to my childhood: 'Well, laddie, it's off to big school you go tomorrow.' I was seven, and Father had called me into his study; I was to leave Glasgow for boarding school in Edinburgh in the morning. 'There's not a lot I can give you – you'll understand that as time goes by – except a good name. Be proud of it my boy, it's an ancient name in Scotland and the line has worn it well.' Not that he bothered to elaborate, although Mother had told me a little of the family history of the Buchanans at Bannockburn, Baugé, Flodden Field, and the devastation at Inverkeithing: 'Scottish warriors!' Actually, I thought it was all faery, but I wouldn't have told Father that. 'And, I can make sure you have a good education. I hope you realize it's a privilege; one of the few left for our class as we rot away.' He seemed sad when he said that. 'I'm sure George will keep a bit of an eye out for you.' George, my fifteen-year-old brother, had commenced at the school the year before I was born. 'And,' my father said adopting a grave posture, making me think of what he must have been like as a Colonel in the army: 'Ahem, I like to think that the black lion on the crest, you see it here', he had in his hand a copy of the school prospectus, 'propping the shield up with that strutting deer, is taken from our family crest. You know what that is, I hope.'

This tale was apocryphal, but I loved that black lion rampant in the Buchanan crest, although I'm afraid I didn't wear the yellow and magenta colours with distinction on any of the playing fields. 'Bit different to your old man; tremendous front row forward. Like an ox, he was!' And my brother George, warrior blood throbbing in his veins. If anything, I imbued the school motto, *Industria*, and could always be found in the library or on the piano in the music room: sanctuaries shared with a couple of pals. Fortunately, I liked Edinburgh, with its Georgian buildings and mews, old town and new.

'Hmmm, so … good luck, my boy – *Clarior hinc honos* – make the honour glow ever brighter. And don't forget – it'll save you a lot of trouble, as a young chiel at school – take whatever's given, eh; your day'll come.' I soon learned what he meant, but I would be a bum-boy to no-one. My brother may have had a reputation for buggering half the preparatory school by the time he left, but I would not play those games! And when

I threatened Arncliff Harris with the small dirk that I kept for just this eventuality, word travelled that I was not easy game.

'I'll see you at the end of the Michaelmas Term; let you settle in a bit, eh!' It's one of those images of my father that I recall. Ever the Pater and the Colonel, he stood erect as a post, his shoulders squared, his hand protruding as if to keep me at a fair distance as he shook my hand, ushering me out the door; closing it behind me.

* * *

My meal on the table and a glass topped up, I gave in to the reverie set off by the memory and with no sense of irony, explored how this awkward, studious Scottish laddie should find some sort of peace in the deep south of New South Wales.

Competent in a uniform, the modern Buchanan men could boast of distinguished combat engagements reaching from the Crimea to North Africa. They were, in that wonderful old Scots word, *feckless* out of it and declined into less eminent 'careers' in the law, notable mostly for their boredom and inattention, and a touch of the midday tipple which was known to extend into the earlier evening. Indeed, there was an old Glasgow joke that went through the chambers: 'When is the Law not a career? When the Buchanans practise it!' To a man, they carelessly added their weight to the gradual erosion of the estate which, through various misadventures over two or three-hundred years – I love that word, *misadventure*, hiding incompetence, inattention and naivety – had shrunk, from a share of major estate holdings across Scotland, to the great house in Glasgow and *Buchanan and Carlyle's* Chambers in Buchanan Street in the heart of the city. But with what was left of the estate to go to George, I accepted that was the way of things.

In ten years at *College*, my parents rarely visited. I'm sure my mother would have liked to see me, but Father didn't believe it was important. I quickly learned not to expect anything of George: 'Bugger orff, Buchanan

Minor,' he would roar: 'Get back to your books.' I did enjoy watching him play rugby though; he bowed to no-one and I know he was a fearsome Cadet Warrant Officer, lauding it over his charges. But I didn't envy him and nor, when I was old enough to demonstrate it, did I wish to emulate him.

The small circle of boys with whom I mixed were mostly misfits, foreigners or 'swats' and as such were bullied, ridiculed or spurned by the rest. Between us, we shared most of the annual academic prizes and would spend hours together reading and sharing our knowledge; while Dong Hyun Kim, a wonderful violinist who would go on to study under Menuhin, Alastair MacCausland on clarinet, and me on the piano, formed a small music ensemble. They were the closest I had to friends, but in reality these were allegiances of necessity; bulwarks against the mob. None of them were so close that we shared our deepest secrets. I was rarely without a gnawing empty feeling at the pit of my stomach, which, I knew by now, having explored my loneliness, had nothing to do with a physiological hunger.

By the time I was ready to leave school, by sheer dint of my performances, rather than any competitive urge; I was awarded the medal ahead of my best pal, James Abercrombie. I'm not sure what my parents thought, but Dr McAdam my history teacher, moved from her seat at the presentation to shake my hand as I retreated to the modest applause of the auditorium – 'wonderful, wonderful effort!' Then, smiling, she whispered, evoking the Buchanan motto: 'In the future the honour shall grow ever brighter.' For a moment, I felt nourished.

'My word, my boy,' my Father said over dinner one evening back in Glasgow, in what sounded almost like enthusiasm about my prize in history: 'You'll be able to join George in the practice.'

After ten years of neglect, I felt no compunction to act out the dutiful son. 'You obviously haven't spoken to George Sir! But, to save you the trouble, I have no intention of reading Law, or of propping up the firm while he gallivants around the globe acting out his fancy for war.' Poor Father looked bemused. 'Edinburgh has offered me a scholarship and I shall take a part-time job. I leave next week.' Rather than triumphant, I was desolate.

Mother came to my room the next morning. 'I want you to have this, my darling boy.' I'd never heard her offer such affection, as she handed me a kilt of the Buchanan tartan, prominent in its reds and muddy greens and yellows. Lying on top of the cloth was a sporran carrying the family crest, and in the pouch: £200. God knows where she got it, Father never gave her that kind of money. 'My young hero. I should have left years ago.' She hugged me, her good luck wishes – '*Sealbh math dhuit*' – muffled by tears.'

'I'll be braw.' I mumbled.

* * *

As I poured another glass of the Bannockburn red – how could I resist – there was a knock on the door. 'Natasha! Tashenka ... what a delight.'

'You don't mind, Andrei? I have no excuses, except the moon and the country air.'

'No, no, come in. I'm ruminating on red wine and life. Would you like to join me?'

'I would!' The ambiguity hung in the air. 'The wine, yes, thank you. Life? Perhaps a little too much already today. But you: where are you up to?'

'I've just abandoned the family and like some wayward picaro – although it would take quite an imagination to see me as a rogue – have set out on the rest of my life.' They grinned.

'Tak.' She said, taking the offered glass. 'Now, tell me more ... Signor Quixote!'

'Not too much tilting at windmills in this yarn. I was a scholarship student at Edinburgh University, reading Medicine and taking French to keep sane. "You must be mad, sonny," my tutor had said. "But, if you must, that's up to you. You'll know when such an indulgence is too much, I vouch. If not, I guess I'll have to tell you!"' I muddled through.

'*Pourquoi Français?*'

'*Ah, facile … la literature; c'est trés bonne.*'

'We could converse sometimes, do you think? I haven't used it much since I stopped dancing but when I was in France with Rudi, we spoke French all the time. That was where we were, we had the language, so we honoured it. There is not too much choice in this strangely mono-lingual place, no? But enough. Tell me more about you Docteur, so buried in his work when we met.'

'There's not much to tell. After graduation, I was offered a Residency in the Children's Hospital in Aberdeen. It was as a bird to the open air: I loved it and the kids and I could just be myself with them. I'd never really had a childhood, and they probably thought I was a wee bit goofy, but … well,' I felt like that shy boy uncomfortable talking about himself, but she was attentive. 'So, when I'd completed my two years, I was encouraged to take it further. My Registrar thought I should go to Sydney: "Excellent Paediatrics and what's more, you can get out there for Ten quid." So here I am! Now that's enough from me, see what you think of this? He put on a record.'

'Ah, *Sketches of Spain*,' she said as soon as she heard the opening bars, 'I have to stop what I'm doing and listen.' They slid down into Andy's grandfather chairs, sipped their wine and listened. 'Thank you,' she sighed when it was finished … it was as if I'd played it. 'But you can't get away that easily.' She smiled. 'What did you do for fun?'

'Well!' I looked closely at her. 'Fun might be easy to find for a gorgeous creature like you but for a gawky Scottish boy just coming out of his teens, as tall as a bean pole, with a face that frightens children at night, and who knows only books, *fun was* not in large supply! I remember loneliness, not good times. Strangely enough, my history tutor from school, Rachael McAdam, understood this and said something similar after I'd been at Edinburgh for a term. She was wonderful. She helped me find digs in Cowgate among the maze of houses, half houses, flats, and rooms, and cobbled streets and alleys that surrounded the campus. Tucked away in the basement of the old town, I found it was a congenial place where I, and sometimes with Rachael, would weave a path under bridges, feeling all that life overhead. It suited my solitariness.'

Natasha, savouring the wine, was listening attentively. 'She also lent me several pieces of furniture, including these two old grandfather chairs we're sitting on; made suggestions, without making too much of a dent in my stipend, about what I needed to furnish my tiny digs. "Take care with the bed; they're such personal things: you need to be comfortable." We found the local market and filled the larder. Then, as a house-warming present, she gave me a bottle of whisky. '*Balvenie*; it's a good whisky Andrew; save it for special occasions but enjoy it!' Whereupon, she splashed a measure in two of the glasses we'd just purchased: 'Slàinte!' And, ever the practical woman, she shook my hand: 'For the first six months I'll set a place set for you once a week at our table; let's say: on Tuesdays? After that, we'll see if you still need us.' Muffling my earnest thanks, she reached up and kissed me on the cheek, leaving me with a memory of her delicate perfume that I was never to forget. 'Until Tuesday, then.'

'Ooh, la!'

'When she left that day I had never felt so lonely, and yet things needed doing. I found work as a part-time proof reader with a printing firm: the hours were flexible and the pay kept me in food for the week. I purchased a bicycle, a bakelite radio, a record player, an old pine table and four country chairs. And I looked forward to the regular 'Tuesday' dinner. While not an introduction into society, between them, Rachael – "please just call me Rachael" – and her husband, Mr Hetherington – never Gilbert – taught me how to be comfortable around a table and how to enjoy and respect good wines and food. "Well, old chap, one thing we say for your old school, you've got a jolly nice English accent there. You're not the sort of Scot I feel like calling Jock. Good accent like that can take you a long way; be a great asset in my line of business. Don't look bewildered," he laughed: "that's a compliment my boy!"

Tuesdays passed, wine classes continued in their modest way when Mr Hetherington was there; but he was often away: "He's on the Europe desk." On these occasions Rachael raided the cellar: "He can't take it with him," she giggled naughtily, and I enjoyed my best meal of the week. French was providing the leavening to an otherwise heavy study regime; and I stuck at my part-time job, where the quality of the proof-reading tasks improved. But, as we relaxed with each other Rachael wondered if I was getting out much. "Sounds like all work and no play to me," she had remarked as first term drew to a close. "Do you have any recreation?" I looked at her empty glass: 'Another?'

'Please; a delicious nightcap.' Did she only mean the wine? Her hand touched mine as she took the stem of the offered glass. 'Ah, Andrei. So, your *divertissement*?'

'Well, I told her I went to the local with a few of the lads from work and a couple of different pubs with the Med School chaps but I don't have to drink the place dry like they seem to want to do every time. She shook her head. "Look. I'm just about to start fortnightly ballroom dancing classes. It will be my treat: 7/6d; think of it as your Christmas present. No experience necessary, will you join me?"

'Dancing classes? I'd love to, but won't it spoil your night? Mr Hetherington? Are you sure?'

"For God's sake, Andrew, don't fuss! Gilbert? Not in a fit. Besides, he's got China! It'll be fun. Thursdays, 7.30, Cheyne Road. I'll pick you up. It's settled."

'Thank you. Can I tell you how kind and generous you are to me!'

"Oh, Andrew; please don't tell me I've been like a mother!" She laughed. "You may not know it … you sweet, awkward, precious man; I like your company. You have a beautiful mind."

'She certainly didn't smell like my mother! Oh, that perfume.'

Natasha, so attentive., winked, smiling. 'Well, well, Andrei, your old history tutor?'

'Not so old, Rachael was thirty-six.'

'And, the husband; what did he say about the dancing?'

'Oh, he said he was well passed that sort of lark: "That's for you young folk".

Actually, very senior in his office, he spent a lot of time away. And, for almost two years, until Rachael took a position in Surrey, we learned to dance. After she'd gone I continued to take classes and play the piano, even began to play in another small trio. I guess you could say that, finally, at twenty one, I was out!'

'You weren't out with Rachael?' She was being playful.

'No, we were definitely not *out*! But we were definitely at home with each other, as I think you are beginning to guess. Now, come my lady', he put his hand within her reach, 'Enough of my inane chatter, I'll escort you home.'

'Thank you,' she whispered, as they stepped through the door hand in hand. Ambling past Susannah's she stopped. 'Oh, listen, it's Schubert: The String Quintet in C, are we at heaven's gate? It's the Adagio. I adore it, the exquisite beauty and sorrow: death was stalking him you know when he wrote it.' She held his hand tighter as they made their way towards *Clifton*, the countryside lit solely by the massive autumn moon.

* * *

On my way back home, picking up from where I'd left off talking to Natasha, I thought of Rachael McAdam and the gentle love that developed between us. It began with the dancing for, oddly, given that I had two left feet in games, I had good rhythm. Perhaps it was the piano? 'You'll be teaching me soon, Andrew,' she'd laughed, as we drove home from our first class.

Now, the Lent Term that year: 1968, was bitter and February in particular, was marked by night after night of frozen rain, leaving everyone exhausted. Calling for me as usual, having tolerated the weather for a month, Rachael was in no hurry to leave. 'Aargh! Such a *dreich* night, can we have the night in? Do you mind skipping the quick step? I've been naughty,' she'd said. 'I've brought the chocolates and wine you gave us for Christmas. What do you think?'

'Super, great, but here? Well, actually this is really good because …

look!' He waved his arm across the room. 'Not that you can miss it! It's an old Broadwood.'

'Andrew! Play my maestro!' She exclaimed, sitting back in one of the grandfather chairs. 'It's wonderful, complete with candle holders no less!'

I felt light hearted, flexing my fingers, miming a master, flicking my imaginary tails over the stool and pausing melodramatically; my hands poised above the keyboard. 'Rubinstein I am not' I laughed, as I began to play what I hoped was discernibly, Chopin.

'Well, it's one of the *Etudes*,' she said as she came over to the piano, put her arms around my neck and kissed me, full and intensely on the mouth as I turned to look at her. I felt my lips move with hers: I wanted to kiss her. "Oh, my precious Andrew," she sighed, "more, please?" She whispered, as she slid off the seat and glided to the table, gazing back at me over her shoulder.

'What is this, then?' I asked.

"Ah, well, there's *Air on a G String* in there, but what's going on? You're improvising on it."

'Very good! It's M. Jacques Loussier, do you know about him?'

She shook her head, 'No.' I had put *Loussier* on the record player while she busied herself with the wine. My skin was alive. She reached up and put her hand on my shoulder raising her glass. "Tae, ye; ye wondrous thing! Come here." She slid me into one of the Grandfather chairs and slipped onto my lap, one hand around my neck guiding and comforting, the other holding her glass, from which we sipped. "What can you discern in there, boy?" She was miming Gilbert's overly grave voice.

'Well ma chére, I think it's the delicious full taste of red lips,' I couldn't believe myself. She turned again to me and again we kissed. My hand, trembling, was caressing her tight curls and briefly touched her naked ear. And the glorious scent of her: 'your perfume …?'

"As you will no doubt learn my dear, no discerning girl can be without her Givenchy," she laughed. Then she fed me a chocolate – dark, rich – washed down with our wine, there was no hurry to break the moment. Cuddling in and listening, for the first time in my life I didn't feel hungry.

I kissed her: innocent, opened, filled with joy … alive.

"I don't need any more," she gestured to the wine. "What a beautiful night; thank you." She was looking at me candidly, her eyes shining. I could feel my long face soften with happiness, felt almost handsome as I took her hand and walked with her to the door.

Next week at dinner, she gave me two candles: "For the piano," and within a month, we were lovers. She let out a ripple of laughter when she saw my single bed: "Oh you dear innocent, I knew I couldn't trust you to buy a good bed! Ah well, come here", and she slipped my jacket off, opened my shirt, and kissed my chest: what a memory! "Dear Andrew," she whispered slipping out of her dress. Fevered, inarticulate and hasty in the end, despite her gentle guidance, I made love. Afterwards, our bodies intertwined, she took my hand: "I want to be pleasured too my darling," she whispered, leading my hand over her body, to her breasts and her nipples, large and taut now, across her flat belly, down, resting it then, sighing gently, our fingers interlocked – they hardly seemed to be a part of me – entering her wetness. I felt her body arch against mine as I kissed her neck. The soft scent of her!

We were very gentle with each other and for the next two years made love often. Gilbert knew nothing of it and we didn't flaunt our love. We knew, as if implicitly, we were very lucky and treasured what we had, confident that neither would do anything to restrict or exercise any hold over the other, nothing to mar the simple generosity of our strange love. We even knew, unstated again, that circumstance would eventually separate us. It was beautiful.

I dropped French after third year, as my medical studies intensified, but not before we had a rapturous 'Bastille' weekend in Paris. "Where is that dour Scottish birkie I first met," she laughed, hugging into me, as we sang, and bellowed along with a swelling crowd flowing through the Tuileries. And then, filled with love of her, I kissed her full on the lips, and murmured into her ear: 'I've stormed your barricades before, but tonight, I'll ravish you until you have to call for a *Gendarme*.'

"Oh, goodie! Let's not delay this challenge to my virtue?" She kissed me, her tongue searching.

And then it ended. "Gilbert's been given Russia. I'm part of the package. We are moving south." Rachael took up the Senior History post at St Margaret's and I asked if I could keep the two old grandfather chairs, for that was where it had started. Gilbert was happy to see them go: the chairs, that is!

* * *

I was back home, having ambled, pleasured by the cool air and my reverie. I slipped into one of those treasured old chairs, put Loussier on again and as if 30 years had vanished in a trice, finished the Toccata and Fugue. Is it strange I wondered, that I think more about Rachael than I do of Mary, now that time has passed. Life with Mary had been in a way lived in the daylight hours. She didn't want to know anything about me and shared little of her past. 'Nothing there Sandy, nothing for you to worry about anyway. Let's make the best of things,' she would say, as she slid away from the personal.

"If you understand her sadness at the death all around her in the ghetto, then you go a long way to knowing what drives her," her father, Lucasz, had said. "She doesn't have to bear this burden, but ...". Now, I recognised that, but she wouldn't open up to me. And, strangely, whenever I thought about Mary this was where I wound up. I'd spoken with Claire and Natasha about her but it was always as a remote figure. She had ignored Natasha during the construction of the Clinic and there was a sense from the start, that the building was nothing to do with her: 'That's your job husband; I'll stay in the lab.'

* * *

I had arranged to pick Natasha up mid-morning, as planned: 'You'll need to wear slacks and tough shoes. Do you have anything like that with you?'

'I'll make do, sounds like hard work.'

'*Au contraire*! Pleasure, I hope.'

'Ooooh, I can't wait,' she'd flirted, touching my hand. She was dressed simply in a pair of Levis, a white linen shirt under a loose deep green v-neck jumper, which, she was vain enough to know picked up some of the darker tones in her eyes, and Claire's worn, chipped leather boots. 'You look just right, let's go!'

'Where do we go for our pleasure?'

'Wait and see,' he said, smiling as they headed out of town, winding towards the upper reaches of the creek. 'Have you ever been mushrooming?'

'What joy,' she clapped her hands, 'take me!' After they'd pulled off the road she ambled beside him as they filled a small basket, leaving something for the next fellow. 'Well,' she licked her lips, moist and radiant. 'Do we eat them?'

'We do at home.'

I left her in the study riffling through my library and record collection, while I went into the kitchen. 'Hope you like risotto. I should have checked.'

'I love it, as long as it *is* risotto.' I knew what she meant, fifteen minutes later, she stood at the kitchen door. 'Can I come in? I can't wait. Ahh *délicieux*. The shallots, and that musky smell of the mushrooms ... and asparagus,' she gasped, watching him chop and feed them into the stock, stir in the butter, parmesan, a dob of cream, parsley and chives, some truffle oil, lemon.

'*Voila*! *La nourriture pour vous*.'

'*Mille merci*! Can we eat in here? I want all these gorgeous aromas to surround me.'

I opened a chardonnay, and we ate. Afterwards, we flopped into the big chairs again, let a suite of adagios flow over us, dozing. At about four, we sauntered up to *Clifton*, 'I'm replete,' she sighed, 'I can't remember when I was last so complete. Now, Andrew,' she stopped and turned covering my hands with hers. 'We must not lose touch again.'

I didn't stay when I dropped her off at the big house. 'I've stolen enough of your day, the others will want to say goodbye.'

She looked me directly in the eye, and grinned. 'Well if that is theft, then I'm all for petty crime: thank you.' I kissed her cheeks, right, left, right. Did she sigh or, was it an emanation from my soul? It was probably just the breeze in the trees.

* * *

We kept in touch. When I received no reply to the first of my letters – oh, how tedious – we reverted to email. There was hardly a week we didn't have some kind of contact: a note, a relayed joke, or something more expansive, thoughtful; even the occasional one in French or a phone call. But, I hasten to add, that these exchanges, these regular missives between friends, were not love letters, although I cherished our closeness. And, within a couple of weeks, having to go up to Sydney, we were daundling along the little beach at Bronte; 'One of my favourites,' she'd said. Over coffee at the little café at the end of the beach, she apologised for the clandestine meeting.

'I'm sorry we have to resort to this subterfuge Andrew, but wherever anyone close to him is concerned, Michael has a kind of scorched earth policy. He tries to burn off all contact until the individual is isolated and surrenders to him.' She could have been giving a tutorial on battle strategy: 'Aware of the casualty rate, I refuse to engage with his tactics; as it is, knowing that we have defeated him, he still tries to pervert the nature of our relationship. And things are tense at home.'

She looked drawn; had lost weight perhaps; her face pale and cut back to the essentials.

I raised an eyebrow.

'When I got back from seeing you all, he made a point of not asking me anything about the trip. As though it hadn't happened. And when I mentioned that I would have liked to share the development of the Millenial Gift with them; "surely they are entitled to know." He exploded.'

It's my gift to bestow! He shouted. You once asked *if I was Caesar astride the globe, you were wrong, but if you want to stay with Shakespeare, the hated Coriolanus is closer to the mark.* His mouth, barely a slit was set in an ugly smirk. *I know they envy me and will chortle at my passing.*

'I asked him what that had to do with the gift.'

Everything. I'm thinking of setting *everyone free; you and them, all of you! Well, damn you all! You will have to manage it Natasha. But, then, you seem to have them eating out of your hand. No need to go through it now. It's still taking shape, that can be done later. It's very straight forward, everything is to be sold up.* Oh, Andrew, it was such an extravagantly malicious thing to do. I felt as though I'd been physically struck. I could find no words for my disgust.'

'Michael looked surprised, continued. He could have been at the office explaining a project as he told me that the thrust of his *Millennial Gift* would be to sell all the freehold properties he held. Where they could not be sold, they will lie vacant. He intended, he said, to oversee the demise of Celtic Ponds.' She subsequently discovered that he had also made provision to sell her Notting Hill property, forging her signature to do so and had sold the London apartment, renting it back for the previous six months.' *It is my intention also that O'Connell itself will cease to exist.*

I didn't know what to say; reached for her hands. She held them tight, curled her fingers into mine as if drawing sustenance.

'I felt as though I'd been physically hit. Of course you understand!' She paused, drawn back to the moment. (Screaming, 'keep your ghastly gift. I want no part of it.') But, you know, by now he was overtaken by a numbing depression, deeper than despair, a profound desolation, and I thought he had succumbed to it. I couldn't deny him; he needed consolation; would never ask, but he was bereft I thought. And it was being played out in this horrible plan. Can you understand? She was pleading, he needed me. He had no-one. I couldn't desert him' She glanced at me, her eyes searching mine, while I was shocked, stunned, overcome by a conflict of emotions from anger to sympathy, in awe of her compassion and forgiveness.

I could barely speak. 'I know, I know, but … Jesus! Having worked to keep everyone there, he would then rip it from under their feet! But you know that, … moi Tashenka. I'm here however you need me.' He, too, could provide consolation.

'Ah, yes, Andrei, but he was so desperately sick; could not think straight. ... But, enough of this morbid stuff, I'll get through it. We are going back to London next week; please don't lose touch.

* * *

And, from then on, wherever she was, we kept in contact and when she was in Sydney we'd go to the Art Gallery or to Paddington, take a ferry ride or drive out to Bondi, to Mosman or, like Bronte, one of the gorgeous bays for a coffee, occasionally to lunch, and we would chat. Even if a couple of weeks or months elapsed before we met again, we'd pick up from where we'd left off. ... 'Didn't you have regrets, Andrei; parting from Rachael, it seemed such a lovely relationship?'

'Of course, I missed her but we knew it couldn't go on forever and in a sense, it was an emotional life raft. And, I hope it is also clear, it wasn't just about sex. The sex was wonderful, God, it was my initiation, but we would also stroll through the parks in Morningside or wander out from my digs in Cowgate, exploring my warren. We cared about each other, I loved her, she was my first love!'

'Did you have any other contact?'

'The break had to be clean, we always knew that, but we sent – still do – send cards on our birthdays, and I have one absolutely memorable card from Paris; not a word on it except a splash of her perfume and my address: it was an image of a man firing pink hearts at the ramparts of the Bastille. I contacted her, and we spent a beautiful day together before I came to Australia and I sent my condolences when Gilbert was found dead in London. It was very mysterious and I know Rachael took early retirement; but that's a story that gains nothing from the telling.'

'O, the things one doesn't know! There's something about it in Michael's papers, nothing escaped that man, but he didn't like anyone peering into his world: remarkable!'

'But talking of Michael, in all of our conversations, I still don't know how you met.' 'Well ... it's not so difficult. It's fresh in my mind as he'd recently talked it over with me: *Let's get everything neat and tidy!* I thought he was trying to safely tuck away his history.' She pursed her lips at her memory. 'We met in the early eighties: Rome, the summer of 1982. He had come back stage. I was first soloist in *Sylphides*. At the Teatro dell' Opera: *I muscled my way in,* he said patting his wallet: *where there's a will there's a way.*

'One doesn't easily forget a handsome, elegantly dressed man in a wheelchair. But you know how it is like, in the crush he was just one of many, but I did remember him. He didn't believe me; called me a liar! The cold burn of his black eyes watching me. I looked down at him, but, despite being above him – in ballet talk we call it the Kirov position! – I felt vulnerable. You are unfair. I particularly noticed your cuff links; oval, engraved to look like Moire silk. Good taste. I'd thought.'

'We met next in Nice and Marseilles a year later, I was dancing around the south of France and I couldn't help thinking how strange and such a coincidence that he should also be there, leaving me flowers, chocolates or bubbles after performances. He said it was no accident. *I was stalking you by then*, he'd joked, not too pleasantly I thought. Actually, he wasn't much in my mind but I didn't like the sound of "stalking".'

Andy was frowning as she continued. 'But that wasn't the end of it. The Company then went up to Tours for four nights, where I had a terrible time with my dancing partner, Oleg Golemnikov. Ah, I haven't told you about the dreadful Oleg; life stories are difficult to tell: pull a thread and you unravel others. To talk of Michael is almost in the same breath to talk of Nureyev, Golemnikov, and a host of others. But,' she shrugged. 'I try. ... Then, without Oleg, it was on to Paris, where Michael made sure our engagements coincided, before the tour moved on to its completion in London and, although Michael and I had arranged to meet, it was not until a lot of waters had flowed under the bridges, because that was when I defected.'

'Levinskaya Flies Her Nest', the terrible dailies had roared in London.

Driving out to Watson's Bay for lunch a few days later, I asked her about London. 'Hmm, London, what a mixed blessing! Once the dust had settled after my defection, I was incredibly busy in what was left of 1983 and into '84. I had to prove myself to my new Company and in a sense, to myself, that I was indeed, worthy. I was also becoming better known in the ballet world and had become someone to be seen, and seen with, and a busy social life became the inevitable accessory to the ballet. I had little time to myself: "that's what it's like my Levinskaya; they want every piece of you," Rudi had warned. "Keep something for yourself, and," he laughed. "I think I'm really talking to myself darling; you're too sensible. Just be true to yourself!"'

'Then, he invited me to dance the Paris season of *La Bayadère* with him. "Oh my bird, we'll show that rhinoceros, Golemnikov, stomping around the stage, how to dance this ballet with passion and grace instead of the way you two did it last year," he grinned "with him mauling you with his clumsy hands. We will make it very beautiful."

'And we did, our performance was acclaimed and I loved what I was doing, but I had no wish to be thought remarkable. I was wary of this new situation Andrew, but nevertheless, I enjoyed Paris. Unshackled from minders, staying at Rudi's new *Quai Voltaire* apartment looking across the Seine to the Louvre and the Tuileries Gardens, I could watch the sun rise over Paris, while the line of sight from the kitchen window led to the spires of Notre Dame. After the austerity and shabbiness of our apartment in St Petersburg, Rudi's was brimming with excess, offering a sensual overload of lavish rugs, oriental carpets and tasseled cushions, of brocaded silks and satins, piled one against the another. 'So much?' I suggested it looked like greed.

'"Ah, moya Levinskaya," he lisped humorously, "it's not greed. I never had anything, nothing, and now … I'm gathering everything up and I don't want to let them go."

'He wanted me there, and yet I felt in the way while he settled in and had to close my eyes some of the time at the goings-on.' Andrew grinned, didn't need to say a word.

'So, you see,' she said, laughing and spreading her arms. 'I have a pleasurable Paris story too, although not enjoyed quite the way you had yours! There I was, not chased by the paparazzi like Nureyev, but, well, I was in the Paris 'season'. And Michael made sure he was at the same cocktail parties I attended. Am I being terribly naughty? There he would be, feigning surprise, flirting: *How delightful to see you here!* As if it was an accident?'

'You don't seem to need me,' I said, batting it back to him with a smile, glancing across the room to a tall, slim, gamine-eyed brunette who had come with him. Elegant and sexy, almost boyish, but with her black dress cut just low enough and off one shoulder, she seemed to offer a decidedly, feminine promise: 'She's looking over at us, is she jealous?'

Lovely isn't she. He said, distractedly, looking at her as one might gaze at a statue or a painting. *Jealous? I wouldn't think so.* Instead, he was watching her with such intensity that anyone looking on may have wondered what he had in mind.

'We met again at a Sponsor's cocktail party for the Opera Fund; he was with the same Audrey Hepburn look-alike who, all evening, seemed to be waiting to attend him. He didn't reciprocate and watching them together, as attentive as she was, he seemed more interested in working the room. It was an elegant gathering; from the conservatively tailored evening suited men – not much off the rack here – to the finely cut, rather than modish, gowns of the women, matched by exquisite, but understated jewellery. I couldn't help noticing that Michael's partner had on a similar, surely not the same, off-the-shoulder black dress and onyx ring set in silver and a matching necklace, as that worn on their previous date. Michael had my full attention.

"You seem busy tonight Michael, don't neglect your beautiful partner; she's exquisite."

Rebecca? He mumbled absent-mindedly, but his eyes were on me, intense, direct, until I felt uncomfortable and had to move to break the moment. I noticed I had brought my hands up to my throat as if covering myself. Did he intend to disconcert me?'

'I must circulate,' I said, breaking away but his dark eyes followed me; more than flirting. Then he too, launched himself into the gathering, meeting and greeting and parting, brushing of cheeks and handshakes; exchanging a word here, a whispered remark there. It was a performance.

'Isn't that unusual, Andrew? He's in a wheelchair, but he seemed so … so able, working the room; he was infecting my language. I tried to break the spell – had he cast a spell over me? – and wandered across the room to catch up with Rudi. As I did so Michael's partner caught my eye and we nodded; … coolly was it, or just in passing?

'As I stopped to say hello, I remarked on her jewellery, thought the necklace was exquisite. "You like eet? Does eet suit, *n'est-ce pas*? I'm not sure that my colouring is right for zis and the black dress, but Michael wants that I wear them. Do you know eem?" She might have said, what's he to you?'

'Know Michael? I was still reflecting on the fact that he had asked her to wear the jewellery. "O, no, no, only in passing, a few compliments and just see him at functions like this," I laughed, throwing my arms back in mock surrender: 'I'm no threat.'

"Eez no matter,' Rebecca replied, picking up the tone. "It's nice of you to talk wiz me; I was getting lonely. The others ignore me. I know you are a great ballerina, it must be wonderful to have the gift."

'No no, not great… not a gift … may I call you Rebecca?'

"I'd prefer Sophie," she made a hopeless gesture with her hands. "That's my name."

I was taken aback; probably showed it. 'Not a gift, … Sophie, it's a hard mistress. I have to give it all my attention. A bit like you with Michael, can I say that?'

"Non, non; it's my job to attend to 'eem.' (Job?) I'd love to dance. But," and she paused. "I must go and stroke my man." (His neck or his ego?)

'She did go to him, and yet Michael made sure we met one more time in his perambulations, for I watched him manoeuvre into position. *You are solo? Can you ever be lured?* I ignored the comment and gave him a quizzical look at which, as if caught out, his tone changed. *I hear it's London next for you. Could we have dinner before? I'm in Paris for another week, may my secretary arrange?*

'I said I'd wait to hear but, at the risk of being rude, suggested it would be nice if he called, rather than someone from your office: "It makes it a little less like a business appointment."

You accept my approach? He couldn't help himself.

"Well; I know you a little and," I tried to catch his shifting eyes. "... it's a dinner invitation. Nothing more ... is it?"

'He said he liked my honesty but I wasn't sure he was being honest with himself, and I was to learn he wasn't very good at that. Did he really like such candour? Nor was I sure how I felt about this approach, but he interested me. Anyway it was his PA who contacted me and, sweet Sophie/ Rebecca, where does this, whatever this is, leave her? I decided that was not my problem or my question to ask, and by the look of it, if tonight's display is any indication, not his! And, display or not, he had me wondering. It was as though he was orchestrating some old dance, where partners meet and part, to meet and part again. I thought about him turning up in Rome, in Marseilles, leaving gifts at Nice and Tours and in the same social whirl in Paris where, even on the dance floor, a similar pattern was enacted.

'His attentions had however, been noticed. *"Monsieur le banquier* shows an unusual interest, Natasha," Rudi remarked. *"Oui, tres étrange!* M. O'Connell is usually more discrete."'

"You know him?"

"But, yes, and no! I see him around, that creature who's sniffing at you. He's been at my dinner parties, leering at my boys, wanting to play. But I see him in other places, lurking in dark corners watching, watching, running his hand over a smooth thigh here of a boy brought to him, a sweating back there, furtively taking him in the mouth; lusting to be in it. Never on show, although he knows my haunts like the back of his hand. Ignoring me, sneering; throwing mud at me when he talks to you I'm sure, pah! You ask him about the leather bar at the *Coleherne*; watch him slink around Poland Street. I've seen him, I wouldn't wipe my feet on him, for all his filthy money. What's he doing chasing you? I'd watch him, my darling!"

'It made me think of the beautiful Sophie, and I put it aside as one of Rudi's petty jealousies. Besides, the picnic, the little 'dinner' was so very chic, such a different thing; and so public; there was no hiding away on the lawns of the *Place des Vosges*. *Louis Treize*, you know, the trees in blossom, all surrounded by the lovely arcades. And, the pikneek, is impossible to describe. When I try to it sounds like something out of *Roman Holiday* and no-one would believe it: Was it an indulgence or a farce? It lent itself to either at different moments. It was a performance that few would have had the power or the audacity to carry off. But, throughout it all, there was clearly something on his mind: *I have something to put to you*, which, for all its air of mystery made me think of my reaction to the initial invitation, is it a business proposal? Is that what this is all about? Yet, it was not put.'

'Why?' Andrew asked. 'Did he have second thoughts, do you think?'

'Michael? You joke. He bowed to no man or woman. It might have just got lost in the *Attaque*, the *Parry* and *Ripostes* of our conversation!'

'At once, exhausting and fascinating, I guess.'

'That's right, there was a carefully orchestrated sense of occasion. People milled around this public space, but they were not permitted to intrude on "our" space which Michael had ... perhaps purchased for the occasion at a substantial cost, as a statement of his power? It was as though we were on display, creating a curious tension between the private and public, which added to the suspended agitation that, despite the expensive bubbles and beautifully presented meal, and the repartee, circling around exposure and concealment, shadowed the entire evening. Or was he simply marking out his territory? I wasn't sure what was going on: surprised that he wasn't in the car when his valet picked me up, I was appalled when, on Michael's behalf, the poor fellow asked that I wear certain pieces of jewellery. "My God!" I'd screamed, I'd seen the pieces on Sophie only a few days earlier. I was simmering with anger as I told the poor fellow I thought it would not be a good idea if I wore them, although, my God I did love that ring.

'He didn't join me at the table immediately, arriving as the champagne was being poured, Vintage *Krug*; so he was trying to impress. But why the delay, since he must have been watching from the wings, for his entry was perfect to the second. I couldn't help wondering if I was being jigged around like some puppet, that, as I'd felt before, the disorientation was intended? He must have noticed I didn't wear the jewelry, but he said nothing. He was however, attentive in every other way and made light, charming and disarming conversation on everything from the ballet, to French politics; George Orwell's predictions, to Maggie Thatcher unleashing the city or stamping on Arthur Scargill. I came to recognize this seeming insouciance as a familiar tactic, part of his armoury. It made for a fascinating companion.'

She paused as the dishes were removed from the table and they ordered coffee. 'Then I was back in London, into a heavy rehearsal regime and a testing programme which left no time for anything else but, just as the final touches were being put to the season, it was announced to some fanfare that Oleg Golemnikov had accepted an invitation to dance a short season of ten performances with me in a reprise of our *Onegin* which had *"wowed them in the South of France the previous summer."* I was not amused but, my patient Andrei, that's another story. It will keep, although I am still haunted by it.' She paused, sipped her macchiato, looked intently at him.' Am I boring you?

'I don't think you could.' As, bathed in sunlight, with bursts of chatter and laughter filling the restaurant, it was as if everyone was happy to see them. 'Shall we go out on to the jetty?' In a huge black floppy hat and a white summer dress, the sun finding her, as if to kiss she turned to Andrew who sweetly did, as between friends. And they laughed joyously.

Natasha:
Teach me to Tango

'Oh those bells Andrew, a hymn for those gone, but I like to think the echo carries us into the future if we let it. In the end, really much earlier than that, Michael wanted to die and invited death into his room. He spoke a lot about it in the last two years: *Death and life are in the power of the tongue and those who love it will eat its fruit.* But you don't have to go to *Proverbs* to know of death and the dying, which, from what you've said, Mary didn't welcome in, no?' She touched his arm.

'Yes, we were acquainted.' He said, covering her hand with his own; briefly, but not casually. 'Although for some, I think the time can be right.' He was thinking of Michael but turned to his beloved Frost: *I have been one acquainted with the night.* 'Mary didn't open her arms to death, but she knew,' he sighed, 'that he was knocking at her door.' While, as though reading his thoughts, although she knew no Frost, Natasha murmured: 'Some of those who look on may want to make a judgment about Michael's death (or even his life),' she whispered as an afterthought, 'whether it was wrong or right it was not carelessly taken, I know that.' She slipped her arm through his as they walked to the doors of the church. And, in one of those paradoxes of life, in this moment of death, the bells took her back to Rudi's apartment on the Seine with the carolling bells of Notre Dame filling the air. Listening to them, she thought of her own mortality and wound her hand a little tighter on Andrew's arm.

Dressed in black with a small veil, although it is unnecessary for there are no tears, either real or feigned, she is wearing a single row of pearls at her throat with simple earrings to match. Her dress, beautifully cut, square at the neck with a close-fitting bodice, before flaring ever so slightly to three-quarter length. She wore sheer black stockings and tiny heels.

People may have been a surprised to see me arrive on Andrew Buchanan's arm and to see us talk so intently, to see me lift my veil occasionally and look closely at him as we waited in the gardens. These observers may have misconstrued the tenderness of our exchanges, the intimacy, but to those who mattered, they knew that as yet we were just good friends, one giving unconditional comfort, the other receiving it gladly.

I had lost control of the ceremony to the State soon after it was announced the funeral was to be held in Celtic Ponds. Frankly, I thought another type of gathering would be more appropriate, one where the private rather than the public Michael was buried. To this end I insisted the ceremony by the graveside be private, for immediate family and friends only.

On the day, the main service was too grand, introduced by a sublimely misconceived reading from *Daniel* by Father Gabriel, the Phillipino Parish Priest:

> I, Daniel, mourned and I heard this word of the Lord: / At that
> time there shall arise
>   Michael, the great prince, Guardian of your people....

There followed a full mass with attendant pomp and ceremony and praise for a life, as the Monsignor intoned 'so richly and selflessly lived,' orchestrated to suit the occasion but with little of the human about it. Michael may have quite liked that I had thought in a subversive moment. Although the steady incantation of the rain on the roof seemed more appropriate, it was a satisfactory public event, serving the needs of the State, providing photo opportunities for dignitaries and a chance to market philanthropy. The town had seen nothing like the procession, except that few of the locals who knew Michael well attended the service in the church. At my insistence however, it had been agreed that, immediately after the thanksgiving hymn following the sermon – for I had guessed the tenor of it – I would read a variation on *Psalm* 51. 'Totally inappropriate dear lady,' the Premier's secretary told me between pursed lips, 'and out of context, and your editing of the original ... mutilates a great psalm.'

'On the contrary, you know the text well, do you?' I felt sure he didn't. 'What I am doing is simply intensifying the meaning and shaping it to suit the person being laid to rest. And, ... on this matter, I will not budge.' (Nor will I be bullied.)

She gave the reading with a clear voice, her gentle accent guaranteeing that she was listened to, and looking out intently at the gathering, she laid Michael bare before God. In her subtle editing of the old text, it became as much a psalm of atonement as it was one of forgiveness.

She'd hardly stepped down from the lectern, even before she regained her seat, the Monsignor led the mourners in a rousing rendition of *Holy, holy, holy...* 'Now, that is inappropriate,' she whispered, as she settled in beside Andy, 'moreover ..., as the coffin was incensed and sprinkled with holy water while the *Libera me, Domine* was sung: *Deliver me, O Lord from eternal death ...*' he wouldn't have sought the deliverance and absolution being offered up.' The rest was smothered beneath the *In Paradisium* as the coffin was wheeled away.

As the suits and black dresses disappeared through the old church gates, having been sent off with easy platitudes by the Mons, the four of them were left in the formal line. 'Well, that's that then,' I heard the Mons whisper to Andrew: 'with respect, didn't know the fellow, although,' he added, 'I did contact Paddy McCusker in Dublin, but he was pretty busy and said he wouldn't like to speak ill of the dead. To be sure I didn't have a clue what he was talking about. I'm only here as a matter of fact because, as you probably know they're going to make an Eminence out of the Archbishop; now that's a jolly good thing isn't it!' He clearly loved to natter.

A few of the old families, including Bran, Claire – much to her surprise – and Charles, Ben and Susannah who had also changed their minds, had just arrived and were milling around. The Oakleys closed the gallery for the day, the Wellhams, Dillers, and the Nelsons and even old Ted, who had someone looking after the garage, were all there: 'least you can do,' they agreed. To one side was a nicely dressed couple, if they are a couple, Natasha was musing as the Mons turned to her: 'well Lady O'Connell can I be of any more help to you?'

I was a little startled by the question, but couldn't help smiling: 'Ah, Monsignor, not wishing to sound like someone who has just overseen a murder, we have to get rid of the body!'

'Oh dear, dear me, of course. That's what this other lot must have come for. Yes, yes, ...', his Reverence barely missed a step. 'Where were we now? Yes, yes, I believe it's all in order ... a lovely plot I'm told ... and the casket, now where would that be,' he muttered.

'I think' Andrew offered, 'in the absence of the pall bearers who fled with the rest of the limousines, you'll find the Funeral Director and his lads have it at the rear.'

In a ceremony which was as perfunctory as the other had been elaborately drawn out, Sir Michael O'Connell's body was interred. I don't like the word but didn't think I could yet say he was laid to rest. The thought came to me as I looked across at what was already a friendly landscape that quickened my soul. I was sad that in his cold box, Michael would not be similarly warmed.

Hurrying his way through this brief ceremony, the Monsignor seemed surprised when I moved forward as the casket was lowered into the ground, sprinkled soil upon it and cast the black onyx ring after it, followed by my handkerchief. 'It's bad luck to take the handkerchief away after the funeral,' I whispered to Andrew when I was back at his side: 'it brings sorrow into the house.' Following her lead the other mourners sprinkled soil or dropped a flower on the casket, although, of the nicely dressed couple (had she seen him before?) I noticed she didn't go to the graveside. I hadn't finished however, even as the Monsignor rushed towards an expedient close, I stepped forward. 'I was asked by Charles Greenwood to read these lines by the Irish poet, William Butler Yeats.' She lifted her head and read what he had prepared:

Had I the heavens' embroidered cloths,
Enrought with golden and silver light,
The blue and the dim and the dark cloths
Of night and light and the half-light,
I would spread the cloths under your feet:
But I, being poor, have only my dreams;
I have spread my dreams under your feet;
Tread softly [into death], you tread on my dreams.

With a negligent petition, 'Mayhissoulandthesoulsofallthefaithful departedthroughthemercy of GOD restinpeace': it was over.

* * *

'You must be exhausted Natasha,' Andrew said, concerned, touched her hand.

'No, no I'm comfortable, but pleased that part is over; it was so far from Michael's final agony and despair. We say in Russia that he had a *Bad Death*, you wouldn't have thought that in the first hour and a half would you? The last part was more suited to the reality. But well ...,' I was momentarily wrapped up in other thoughts, 'that's another story which doubtless may be explored over the weekend. Speaking of which I am looking forward to seeing everyone again. You know, although they would be surprised, there are few in this immediate circle who Michael didn't talk about in the last two years of his life, giving me little vignettes, all coloured I'm sure, with the shades of his own prejudices, feelings of guilt, and desires for atonement; if that is not too grand or absolute a way of capturing the complex emotions which overwhelmed him at the end.'

'Overwhelmed... really?' He couldn't hide his scepticism as he returned them to the moment.

'So, this afternoon? Without wanting to worry you,' he said congenially, 'they'll all want a piece of you.' He hesitated, 'but I've brought a smile to your lips?'

'It's an echo of darling Rudi, lost to me in '93 yet never far away. There's plenty of pieces of me to share! You'll look after me just a little though, *n'est-ce pas*. Not that I'm a poor little lamb, it's just comforting to have you …'. I wasn't quite sure what I meant: 'we'll make it a happy farewell, can one say that so soon after …?'

'You'll be braw, just grand. They'll love you all over again.'

I felt slightly disembodied; didn't need to be on my own just yet. 'Andrew do you mind if we take a walk – a little *passeggiata* – before going back? I'm not a bit tired.' I took his arm as we ambled over the bridge.

'I've told you about my school days,' he said; 'but, where did you go to school?'

'The Academy attached to the Ballet School. I loved it and well I have the big appetite to learn. Oh Maman, I'd say, you never know when I might need it; I can't be a famous ballerina for ever. I hung out with other kids from the Academy and had my first boyfriend. Sergei – Sergei Demidoff, he was gorgeous my 'Babi', not Baby – Baabi with the long European 'a'. We were sixteen. He looked so forlorn, I told him I would call him 'Babi' until he smiled; he learned to smile, but it became our name. Do you know St Petersburg?'

He nodded; 'a wee bit. I've been there, *L'Hermitage*.'

'We made the area between the Fontanka River and the Neva our own, dancing across the footbridge over the canal if the lights were on and sitting and cuddling on the benches in Conservatory Park, or following the embankment to the White Palace. On sunny weekends we might lie on the grass at the Summer Palace or in winter head for Ekaterina Square, blowing into our hands, hopping from foot to foot, hugging and rubbing backs in the cold, trying to ignore the patrolling black cars; "wasted on us," we'd giggle.'

'By the time we were seventeen, although I was getting the occasional solo opportunity, Babi was never going to rise above the corps, yet we adored each other. My mother thought he was a lovely boy-friend, "but, oh, you're so young."

Watching her, Andy felt a little like Babi. It was as though she was reliving it.

'Mamma, Mamma! I adore him but I'm not going to marry him (not yet anyway!). He's gorgeous and today, I love him this much.' She laughed, stretching her arms out wide. 'Please don't worry about me ... I love you.'

'My darling friend Vera knew what was going on, had been watching us holding hands, kissing and wrapping arms around each other. 'Ooh la, are you fucking Natashen'ka?'

'Darling!' A cascade of laughter getting lost in her mouth.

'You can always use our place if you need somewhere more comfortable,'

'Oh, Verushka you're so sweet,' adding more seriously now: 'wouldn't want those black cars that track the Levins around, cruising down your way, what would your father think?' Natasha shook herself emerging from her reverie. She did not like Vera's father, Anatoly Dmitriyevich Velen. Called him the little big shot! Always immaculate in his expensive Italian suits and leather shoes, slip-streaming on whoever's draft would take him up the ladder, on the lookout for his best chance. 'But, enough of him.'

Absorbed by her story, Andrew murmured: 'Ah ... wasn't Babi a lucky fellow, I guess he finished up back down the mines though, or did he turn into a frog?' They smiled and he guided her back to the hotel, 'we've dawdled too long my Tashen'ka. This is your doctor speaking, a bath and a rest, perchance to dream. Shall I collect you at four?'

He wasn't the only one who knew a bit of *Hamlet*. 'Now that *is* a consummation to be wished for,' she laughed. As he left he could be heard mumbling something about having his appetite back.

* * *

'Go on up Doc, room six, she's ordered tea.' It was 3.30.

'Ah, you're up then.' It wasn't a question and he would have liked to say more. She looked beautiful in tapered black pants, with oat-meal coloured ballet flats and a loose-fitting jumper, hardly beige, champagne perhaps; casual and elegant. Her green eyes shone and her hair fell to her shoulders, a little wild. She wore a tiny pair of silver earrings glimpsed occasionally through her cascading hair…the craggy Scot may have sighed.

'You look rested. … Your jumper! What an exquisite colour.'

'Ah you like? I bought it in Milano because of the colour. They called it *cane che scappe*, where I bought it,' she smiled.

'The runaway dog,' he said, 'how so?'

'You know, because it's running so fast, it's a flash of colour that they couldn't describe. And, I also had a luxurious bath.' I was always surprised how easy it was to talk to him, with him, he didn't talk over me. 'At home, when I was growing up, we were lucky if we had hot water, but if by a miracle it happened we'd pour a bath, Maman and me and Papa would sit in it, singing and splashing around, sipping tea from a giant Samovar which we kept next to the bath; it was delicious.' She hugged herself. 'What joy.'

'Where did you live in St Petersburg …?'

'We lived in the first of several blocks of communal apartments off Nevsky Prospect, a blindman could find them: just follow the stink of stale cabbages and festering paint. Once fine buildings, the Soviets had turned them into massed housing, partitioning the large rooms so that a small family like ours could live in one of the old rooms. We were fortunate, we had a wireless, it was our only luxury but it meant we could listen to music. Papa would play his violin and Maman the piano and sometimes I'd blow my clarinet, but mostly I'd show them my steps in front of the mirror and we'd have a little concert.' I hoped he understood it wasn't narcissistic, I didn't linger in front of the mirror, it was about technique; getting it right under my mother's watchful eye. 'It didn't spoil our fun, but I wanted to be as perfect as possible, as she moved a foot an inch or two, quietly shifted a knee or hip. It helped make my movements look effortless and spontaneous, no matter how much work and pain has gone into them.'

He gazed at her. 'Your parents…they sound remarkable.'

'I adored them. As best they could, they made life's music together; always with a certain panache. Which makes me say, we should probably go and face the music; leave Maman and Papa for another day.'

I took his offered hand as we walked down the stairs and he eased me into the car.

***

'A penny for them …' He whispered, as he drove up the gravel driveway to the big house.

'Ahhhh Andrei, I was listening to Maman and Papa and their mad friends arguing politics in our smoke-filled kitchen, all washed down with lashings of vodka …,' but she paused, sighed: 'O, just look at those glorious roses, I'd forgotten how beautiful …' A deep breath and then, just a little nervous, I rested my hand on his arm, felt as though, not in a possessive way, he was there for me.

'We heard the car, come… come on in!' Claire kissed her on both cheeks while Bran put out his hand but closed his other over hers as their hands interlocked. 'Andy … you're superfluous to requirements I'm afraid. We all know you.' He laughed.

She went forward, part of a threesome: self-conscious but contained, quiet eyes followed her progress. And then Charlie came forward: 'Charles, I've been so looking forward to …' The rest was lost as they brushed cheeks. Ben joined them, then Susannah, while Bran stayed by her side. Condolences, sincere as they were, were nevertheless dispensed with quickly, albeit with an eye on her reaction. She gave nothing away, did she have anything to hide anyway Andy wondered, as he watched her thanking people modestly and discreetly before engaging Charlie and Ben in a conversation and disappearing with them into the garden.

'I adore it.'

'But, it's your garden now, do what you will with it.' Ben said, as they went back inside.

There must have been more than fifty people milling around now and the room was buzzing; bottles were being opened, glasses filled and finger food was being sent around. Although I was accustomed to a room full of people, I whispered, smiling into those blue, blue eyes and rough-hewn face which, I thought could have been cut out of highland granite: 'Don't go too far away Andrei.'

With the guests flowing around the room, into others and out to the verandahs giving the house a going over, conversations, interspersed with friendly pops of laughter, swelled and shifted. I could hear Michael's name above the commotion. There were times when I would have liked to butt in but restrained myself, perhaps I only half heard. Then I heard Claire: 'Michael and Charlie? Oh, they had endless fun as kids although I always felt I had to protect Charlie, you know Sue ...?'

'Ah yes, I think so,' Sue remarked, as Claire continued: 'Truth was ...,' but their voices were lost in the buzz echoing across the room. The more I listened, the less certain I was that I heard correctly. Then there was a tinkling of a glass and Bran was calling for: 'a bit of shush. Lady O'Connell would like to say a few words.'

'Thank you, Bran, and a special thanks to you and Claire for arranging this little gathering for Michael, I appreciate it. I won't speak for too long today, just a few words. The image I have in mind comes from the Hindu cremation ritual. I think what we are doing today is putting the fire in his mouth to release the soul. Talk about Michael, give him voice, release his spirit, for without being too mysterious and those who loved him will know what I mean; he had little idea of how to do it himself. Raising my glass, I wanted them to name him: 'Fly, Michael, fly! Please, join me in the toast.'

The room rang with Michael's name, while outside, the sun had escaped from the troubled clouds and was disappearing behind the mountains as the velvety shadows crept down the slopes, enveloping them in a gentle fading light. A moment later, the room was stilled as Charles with a barely perceptible smile passing across his lips, sat at the side of the room and began to play Bach: 'For Michael.'

Heads nodded to the delicate harmony in the prelude and a hush fell over the room as he reached to the depths of the music which seemed to touch everyone as an almost physical thing, dying and then swelling to a joyous finish, as though a soul is released. He smiled, bowed his head and stepped away. Susannah couldn't help wondering what might have been, but for Michael.

Soon, Andy was on the piano, Charlie was tuning his new cello, and the rest of *Ponds Alive* had assembled. The party had a life of its own. Sue sang: *'Every time I say Goodbye'* it seemed appropriate, and later, when she gave them *'Can't take my eyes off you'*, singing to Ben perhaps, Bran slipped over to Claire; 'still can't!' He whispered and she kissed his cheek.

'They won't be leaving in a hurry sweetheart, do you think Natasha's alright with it?' Bran nodded to the middle of the room which had become a dance floor where, as the band played the opening bars of a fandango, she was posing with Ben and they started to dance. 'Oh God, she's a delight, yes I think she's alright,' he beamed as Ben, instinctual and naturally responsive and Natasha, lithe, long-limbed and as one could see, more schooled, set the tone.

'You're gawping Bobby,' Sheila cautioned. Young and old, the room was alive with slipping, sliding, archly posturing bodies, some knew what they were doing some were trying to catch on, others had given themselves to the mood while some simply hummed or sang or clapped as the band played on. After they had finished, sitting with Claire, my head was filled with happy echoes of Paris.

'You don't think it's disrespectful?'

'Ah no, no, no! I rather think Michael would have been pleased if not dismayed, to think he is being remembered.' She turned directly to Claire and rested her fingers on her arm. 'He told me towards the end that he had treated you and Bran, very badly'.

'Yes, he disappointed me enormously. I gave him my heart and he trashed it,' Claire, replied, an edge to her voice. 'I wasn't altogether sorry he chose to leave me out of his adult life. But there was always that contradiction: financially he looked after us. How do you balance that?'

'Yes, he would often orchestrate that ambiguity. At the personal level though, I know this is a strange thing to say, I think he might have worried you knew him too well, saw too deeply into his heart. What about Bran?'

270

'Oh, he took him at face value. You couldn't afford to do that, Michael exploited it.'

'Would have seen it as a sign of weakness?'

'Perhaps, Bran didn't, he's never one to tell you how to behave, he tries to show by his own manner what he expects of others. He saw through Michael in the end, understood a little more of his complexity, but he could never cast him aside.'

'Yes, Michael was complex, he made it difficult for anyone to love him. He didn't know what it is to abide with love; enjoy its daily rhythms.'

'It is strange, isn't it? Given that we surrounded him with it: past, present, and if he'd have allowed it, future.'

'I'm guessing, putting things into his mouth perhaps; the only person he ever loved was his Mother. I saw a photo of her you know; very beautiful.'

'You've seen it? He didn't ever know her ...'

'When I asked him about the photo he insisted she was talking to him while dressing. It was as if there was always that childlike search for his mother who only had eyes for him and was never released from the trauma of her death, or from the past.'

The conversation was becalmed. 'There were other secrets, but he was always there between us,' Claire sighed, 'and his father?'

'Ah, a different story altogether. Edward was a rival like anyone who threatened Michael's control of whatever interested him.' I had in mind any number of male rivals who spoke out against him or got too close, from Charlie to hack reporters, to business associates: they littered his past. I was overtaken by one particular memory. 'One didn't want to get between Michael and a business deal, and his operations were carried out anywhere; nowhere was off-bounds.'

Claire looked quizzically at her: 'How so?'

'As you might imagine, given his position, we used to entertain a lot. Dinner parties mostly, large cocktail parties less often. Not that he liked people all that much, not like my darling Rudi, but he could cover a room. He thought he could manage everyone better if he had them captive around a table. He was a great one for having dinner parties after the festive seasons, when everyone was a little reckless, inattentive, you know, wanting to relax and he might catch the unwary off guard, turning any such moment to his advantage.' Claire gasped.

'Anyway, with Mrs Thatcher having let loose on the economy and property development at its epicentre, the hogs were at the trough and table-talk was dominated by conversations about property. In fact, conversations is hardly the word, for these exchanges were guarded and strategic. I found it fascinating to watch the sparring, the legerdemain which went on and learned early on in our marriage, that Michael's little gatherings were no place for the faint-hearted, naive or unwary. I felt, at times, as though I was needed as a kind of terrier, there to rescue the innocent or lazy from the lurking fox; that I had to protect guests from Michael's carefully planned attacks which, when matters moved onto contentious ground, were designed to demolish and humiliate, to emotionally devastate. ...

'But I couldn't protect everyone. This is not a pretty story, Claire, but it is exemplary. Lord Peters, an excessively suave, oily man, was one of the stars in the City in the late eighties. He had made a fortune riding on Maggie's coat tails and although he was a business rival of Michael's, he was, perhaps for that very reason, a regular at his dinner parties – despite my discomfort with his roaming hands. There was a conversation going on around the table about a particular deal when suddenly, Michael threw his serviette on to the table and pushed his wheelchair back, and went for him: *Are you groping my wife again, you shit?*

'I'd seen him execute manoeuvres like this before, but the savagery of this attack caught even me unawares and Peters' wife, Lady Alice, shrieked and blushed crimson as, in this instance, his hands were on the table: indeed they were shaking so violently that he spilled his wine, spluttering inarticulately as he fumbled with a serviette.

'"Michael; there was nothing ..." I was too late, he had tasted blood. Cold, calculating: *George, get out, damn you! Bloody rake. Take advantage of my wife would you! You may muck in your nest at home, but don't go soiling mine.*

'It was so calculated. *Take no prisoners my dear.* I knew however, although Peters was dismissed from Cadogan Place, their business dealings continued and the property deal which was being obliquely played out in the incident, concluded to *O'Connell's* considerable advantage.' When I asked him about it later, he looked closely at me. *Watch and learn.*

'What about poor Alice,' Claire asked, 'and the other guests?'

'*Call it collateral damage*, he sniggered. *Why is Alice still with that despicable creature, and the others? A warning shot, it's never wasted! Anyway, my dear you won't have his fat pink fingers pawing you again!*' He made it sound as though he'd done it for me.

Claire was quiet, thinking. Spoke again as if in mid-thought: 'But you're such a delight. Even if at the time we thought you must have been one of those Russian gold diggers who are flooding Europe.'

'Do we have time?'

'Let's get another drink and you can tell me. They look pretty happy in there.' Where, curiously, instead of Michael O'Connell's name rising above the surface noise, the chatter was now filled with the usual banter about rugby, the weather, stock numbers, politics, from Howard to Bush, jokes, fuel charges, what was on at the movies, recipes, fashion, Kathy Freeman, and aches and pains.

And they continued where they'd left off. 'We know you were being spoken about as someone to watch; don't be modest. We hoped we might see you out here.'

'That I should have been so lucky; no, it all came crashing down: kaput! That's how it was, but Claire it's a beautiful party; let's not go there. We can have this conversation any old time, at the risk of sounding like the merry widow: let's party shall we?' She rose taking Claire by the arm, guiding her back into circulation.

* * *

'Lady O'Connell, you may have wondered who I am?' It was the elegantly dressed man from the funeral, 'Jeremy Bainbridge.' He held out his hand,

I looked closely at him as I met his soft grip, still pondering that face with its reckless brown eyes – or a younger version of it perhaps. 'You stayed for the burial, thank you. And your friend?'

'We were at university with Michael, I wanted to pay my respects. Maddy couldn't stay. I guess you could say we helped the country boy settle into our great metropolis,' and then I remembered the photograph from the obituary. She had found a copy among Michael's memorabilia of an elated Michael in rugby kit, holding up a trophy surrounded by his team mates; it had first appeared in the Sydney University rag. The photo also included a beautiful young woman marked in Michael's hand: *Maddy, main course*, and to the front left, at the edge of the group, a young man dressed in jeans and a duffel coat looking back and up to Michael, smiling; above him was scribbled: *Jeremy, entrée. A good time to be had by all.*

'We knew so little about him. He crashed into our lives, then after that terrible accident he was gone, leaving us to read about his brilliant career.' With that he left to re-join a small group, including Sue, Charlie and his friend Jay, to whom Sue was talking animatedly about jazz.

'So, did you meet Michael when he went to Uni Jeremy?' Charlie asked, interested.

'Earlier, through a girlfriend Maddy, one of those private school girls who he got to know when he made the Schoolboy's team.'

'So, Madeleine, *Rugby chicks*!'

'Not Madeleine Charlie, nice pun, Maddy Lane … Matilda, one of the Hunter's Hill Lanes as they were then: wild child. I was great mates with Maddy but, never like that. I knew where my sweets could be found right from the start.' His smile collapsed into an ugly grin. 'He'd come up and stay at my place.'

'Oh really, I think Michael constructed it somewhat differently.' Charlie was remembering conversations when Michael regaled him with tales of staying at Maddy's.

'No,' he snorted, 'no place at the Lane's for a boy from, where was it, St Patrick's Broadwater? Wouldn't get through the door. But whenever her folks were away, oh brother,' he giggled. 'Constructed it differently you think,' Jeremy continued. 'Yes, could have. For all his rugby bravado and brains, he was in a quandary about some of his urges I think. Quite a little *ménage à trois* we were! Aren't I being a naughty bitch?' He smirked, seeming to enjoy himself. 'Although Maddy came to regret it. Eventually Michael screwed old man Lane something horrible in a business deal and turfed them out of the house. Brought Lane to his knees. Caught him out shorting some stock or other. Got himself a lovely house out of it. Well, as you know: absolute water front, and made it his Sydney residence. Suited him I guess, single story, impeccable address, private: but, not nice. One obviously didn't get in Michael's way!'

'On a night like this it's all grist to the mill.' It was Susannah, pricking an awkward silence and protecting Charles as she looked out for Ben, finding him with Andy putting on some music. 'A Tango for me Ben, would you?' Already, he was moving towards her. While elsewhere … 'Ah, Andrei, may I have this dance?' I was at his side, bowed, lifting his hand to strike a pose, and we began: what joy. Fluid, finely balanced as if one, then flamboyantly resistant, our heads back, taken over by the sensual play of the music. Finishing, my back arched and head resting on his shoulder, hair cascading onto his upper back, we were laughing.' Protectively perhaps? '*C'est trés touchant,*' I whispered as we unfolded.

With groups still forming, breaking up, reforming in different patterns, we wandered onto the verandah after their dance. 'Beautiful timing Andrei, you were in my head, I thought you were doing my thinking for me, I haven't had that sensation for ages. You know… you and not you.'

He blushed, 'but, tell me a little more of Levinskaya, the ballerina.'

It was lovely to hear my name again. 'You want more?'

'As much as you like to give … or is it too painful?'

'Well as I think you've guessed, to speak of dancing, beginning, middle and the end, is to talk of Oleg Golemnikov; it is all mixed up with him!'

We sat and I told him about my dancing partner. 'So, we danced together from when I was seventeen. A graduate of the Kirov, they put him on a high pedestal; strong, clean lifts and his jumps were pretty good! He rose quickly through the ranks of the Company, he wanted to be as good as Nureyev, kept talking about him.'

We had been paired several times by the time I was in my final year at the Academy, not only because of our potential, but also because we were physically compatible. I was tall for a ballerina – I owned up to 175 cm but was much taller *en pointe* – and had been taught how to use my height, not be shy of it. Then on the eve of my eighteenth birthday, I was invited to partner him in a Christmas 1971 production of the new John Cranko-choreographed *Eugene Onegin*. After an untimely defection and an injury to another of the likely leads, the Company had turned to me, what a gift!

'I loved that ballet from the moment I saw it. But being partnered with Oleg wasn't easy, he wanted to dominate me. He was always by my side at the barre, posturing in front of me at the mirror, on the floor, "I'm grooming you," he'd whisper in my ear. I didn't need it and as for grooming me for anything else: the thought appalled me. 'We share the ballet,' I'd said, 'nothing else.' God, I thought I'd run a mile before I tripped to his tricks! "Oh, Natasha," darling Vera would say, "Oleg never takes his eyes of you, watches every step: a lion stalking."

'Despite this, rehearsals went well and surprisingly, if not the triumph we were to make of it later, our first *Onegin* was well received. *Izvestia*'s ballet correspondent, taken more by what he clearly saw as my virginal beauty, gushed,' she giggled. 'Even gave Golemnikov a tick, likening him to *'the aging Nureyev.'*

'You must have celebrated your success.'

'Oh, we did and Babi got a job moving the scenery. Taking me out of Golemnikov's grasp as we backed through the wings he gave me a hug, "ah you flew." He was so happy for me, Oleg was forgotten … then, suddenly Babi was sent back to the Urals.'

'Of course!' Andrew remarked. 'You seem surprised, Tashen'ka, it was inevitable.

The Golem had him carted off back home to the Urals. No?'

'How did you know? I found out he had called on the ghastly Velen – oh, he's nothing like my lovely Vera – and between them they had his Leningrad visa cancelled and saw him off.' It made me shiver: 'O, he was

…', she left it unspoken. 'We used to say about him you know, that he had shit smashing feet,' and she laughed, as if disposing of an evil spirit.

'After that things got worse, with Babi gone, Golemnikov was all over me. Posturing, asking me out, he had about him the stink of a randy cat and his small, hooded, grey eyes left me with a feeling of threat. And yet we still danced well together, even if I was pitting myself against him. When he saw us dance, Nureyev told me he wanted me to dance like that with him, "I don't want the hate my bird, but I want you to try to beat me if you can. We could have a lot of fun, eh?" Now! Isn't that enough of my story? I love it out here with you and the glorious scents being released around us, but, are people missing us?'

'We call this a *lorg*, in Scotland, a tale of mystery and intrigue. I think we can hide for another few minutes before they start whispering about us.'

'Ooh-La, do you think we might make the gossip pages of the *Southern Highlands Gazette*? Let's do it then. So, as you know, I was often in Europe over the next few years.'

'I'm amazed you got permission to go anywhere? I mean, what with Nureyev and Baryshnikov, and Makarova escaping, the last two so recent.'

'Well, I was young and was never far off the leash and the State wanted to publicise itself as being still at the centre of the ballet world. My star was in the ascendant and Golemnikov was being hailed as the next Nureyev, so we were seen as carrying the Soviet flag into Europe. They wanted to show us off. The calls were stupendous! I was back in '79 with the Kirov and again in '82, when Michael and I met.'

'What did the other fellow think of you dancing with Nureyev?'

'Golemnikov? He was jealous, said we were hi-jacking Europe. Rudi was amazing. The delight he took in running "the next Nureyev" ragged. "Pah, this one's not done yet; I'll run that elephant all over the studio until he can hardly spit."'

'I can't imagine he took too kindly to the humiliation,' Andrew surmised.

'*Mais oui*, but really that was only a half of it. When we were in Europe again in '83 with the Mariinsky he thought he had rights and the floodgates opened in Tours.' She paused, 'after the last performance, scoffing the special *Godivas* from Michael with a note: *See you in Paris,* washed down by buckets-full of bubbles, Golemnikov was sullen yet didn't leave my side and when the party broke up he followed me to my dressing room. As I reached for the door, he roughly grabbed my arm pushing me in, I could feel his hot breath on my neck.'

'Let me ... go!!'

'By then, he had his hand inside his tights, smirking, as he grabbed me with his other hand, thrusting his body into mine, I lashed out. The crack of my hand on his face echoed through the cavernous back stage as I screamed, pivoted and kicked forward into his crutch. "Bitch; you'll ..." he bellowed, as he pushed me back over the dressing table, half-empty bottles, brushes, tubes of makeup, a hand mirror scattered across the floor. He was ripping at my leotard trying to pin me to the table top. I slapped at him again, arms and legs flailing, yelling ... let ... me ... go! And then the air was rent with a piercing scream as Vera, her day-shoe in her hand, flew at him and drove the shallow heel into his partly exposed buttock. It was as though everything was in slow motion. "Get out rutting dog, you're disgusting, get out!" She followed through with another blow, opening the flesh. "Go and fire your weapon somewhere else." She was magnificent.

'With him rushing away, holding his leotard and trying to staunch the blood oozing from the wound, she stooped to help me... fussing.' "All that hatred and lust darling, aghhhh, boys and their penises," she groaned. "I've watched him leering at you; it was just a matter of when ... he was marking you out as his territory."

'I sat down while Vera restored some semblance of order to the dressing table and helped me remove my make-up, she was wonderful: hugging me, brushing my hair. After we'd calmed down we began to giggle, which broke into uncontrollable cascades of laughter each voice rolling over the other. "What a sight, Tashen'ka; did you see him slink off? That horrible tail hanging limply between his legs, oh, what a picture!"

'Strangely, I recovered my composure quickly. I was worried about

Verushka and suggested we stay together that night, so arm in arm we took the long way round to our hotel. "Do you think they know what's occurred?" Vera asked, nodding her head to the minders trailing us.

'Of course they do, probably think I need a big buck to bring me into line,' I replied, half meaning it. Pity of it is darling, I haven't had a good romp for ages, I think I might have forgotten how to do it, but not with … ugh, not with the ghastly Golem. Ah well, perhaps there'll be someone nice in Paris.'

'Now Maestro,' she was holding Andrew's hand, and had been she realized for most of her story, 'the guests want to dance. I'll just rest here for a moment.' She raised her hand, wrist bent, posturing for him to kiss her fingers; willingly giving him the Kirov position.

When he left, I kept thinking of Vera and that strange night we spent in Tours, sipping champagne cuddled up in each other's arms and chatting, for this was the last occasion we would do it. Vera left the ballet, went to live with her mother in Kiev and began working with orphans, and handicapped and under-privileged children. She was rarely out of my mind; the dynamics simply changed. At first, she was a conduit between me and my parents and later, the recipient of funds from my personal foundation, to help her continue her work with orphans.

* * *

Rested, I wandered inside, where the room was alive with swirling bodies. 'Aah my dear, I've been looking for you, would you be so kind as to have this dance with me? I have two left feet but it would be my pleasure.'

'Bran, I could think of nothing I'd like more than to dance with you. Claire once told me that you two met on the dance floor, how romantic.'

'Yes we did and you know life with her has been one non-stop dance.' I could feel him look around for Claire. 'But dance is what you do or did. Claire told me you danced with Nureeyoff, was that a thrill or just one more partner?'

'Dancing with him was exciting and, well, I was very young and just making my way. It was a huge honour, but he was also my wonderful friend, I adored him.'

'What a sensation, him defecting when he did. Even filtered down to us.'

'Oh yes, when I was growing up, "Nureyev" was a name not to be uttered behind our iron curtain; but in ballet circles, he could never be ignored or shut down. He was a wonderful man. I miss him,' she said barely audible. 'I met him when he was a huge star but he liked students, wanted to help them if they had talent and were serious about dance. He told me I had a lot of promise "but", then he let out a huge roar, "you are Russian; you need all the help you can get! You must get out of that country. It will crush you; it's like living in a swamp." I was only young, but I knew I would dance for a career and I started planning my escape. He helped me buy my little house in Notting Hill, "this is good value...buy it. I know you have no money. Well, ... I 'ave too much ... I'm a big star and they all want a piece, of me but at a cost", he giggled. "Pay me back when they are pawing all over you." So, I bought it and rented it out, which he thought was very shrewd. "Rent is good my little capitalist, I like that!"'

'Are you alright to keep dancing, I notice you're keeping your feet away from my clodhoppers.'

'Yes, I'm enjoying myself. Of course I paid Rudi back, unless you think ...'

Bran waved his arms: 'No, no! I'm sure you did.'

'How did Michael feel about Rudolf and you. It seemed a nice friendship.'

'As I think you suspect, he ridiculed it, couldn't understand, couldn't believe you know, that I wasn't sleeping with him; that neither of us was on the make.'

Bran looked closely at her, smiled, and kissing her hand asked if they could 'have a breather, I feel as though I've danced a ballet. But, don't stop.'

'Sit down? Of course. Well, they were both celebrities, and were on an International A List that gets shopped around.' I couldn't help thinking that Michael took his celebrity status seriously and embellished and exploited it in his business dealings. Whereas Rudi had fun with it; played it from both ends; sometimes the celebrity to adorn others' functions, at others he'd throw his own parties at his home; might gather up a few bankers and wealthy businessmen, mixing them up with some of his boys and girls: "Good way of getting a few big dollars for the Company loosened onto the table." Although Michael was in that wealthy lot, he insisted he was only at the periphery. And yet, funnily enough, even as he trashed the parties, I sometimes wondered if he was unsure you know, about which side of the table he sat on.'

Bran sighed and managed a smile, but it was weak, apologetic, it looked as though it could slip off his face. 'I'm wondering what it all means myself, I'm still working through it …foreign territory,' before exclaiming: 'Good heavens, that's taken us a long way from Mr Nuree-yov.'

'Not so far, but enough of darling Rudi for now.'

***

'So, Bran, let me put on my business face; tell me about the Stud. Has Charlie settled in to his new role and are you happy with it? If you are not we re-think it.' But before he had a chance to reply Claire broke in: 'What are you two up to? I couldn't help overhearing you talking about the *Stud*. What a joy to talk to someone who really cares, other than just to ourselves. Michael didn't seem to give a damn, or am I being too frank.'

'I prefer it, Claire. I am interested. I've still got some thinking to do, it's all very new to me because Michael rarely let me into *O'Connell's* engine room, or his mind, but whatever I do, I'm thinking I will come down here to live for at least part of the year, and use it as my base. If you'll have me, that is!'

'My dear, that would be simply wonderful,' Claire and Bran spoke almost in unison. 'But,' and she reached out to them, 'I don't want anything to change. I don't covet *Clifton* nor do I want to disrupt the *Stud*. I'll continue to have businesses in Sydney and Europe, although I'll divest some of the less coherent international holdings. As you are aware, it's a large concern and I have a responsibility and the desire to run it.'

'You sound as though you're up and running.' Claire remarked.

'I am, but not business as usual.' Her look was wry. 'I'm not being mysterious. First I have some things to clear up here in *the Ponds* as you say. Michael muddied the waters and I'd like to see if I can tidy the old pond up a bit. We might commence the clean-up tomorrow. Is that possible? A late afternoon soirée, perhaps. I don't want to try talking about it tonight.'

Within minutes Claire had organized it. 'That's fine dear; I didn't see Andy, will you ask him? Charlie'll bring a pot of Paella that will probably feed the five thousand and we'll dig around in the cellar, there are some things there that need drinking.'

***

With only the nucleus remaining, Bran wondered if it wasn't time to haul out the *Balvenie*? Natasha's eyes lit up. 'I'm sure the pianist would enjoy that!' Within moments, they were clinking their glasses one more time – "Slainte Mhath! Cheers! Slainte! – as Susannah, once so shy of it, grinning, thought she should tell them the truth about love. And she began to sing.

> *Oh, tell me the truth about love.* [She paused.]
> *Some say that love's a little boy.*
> *And some say it's a bird.*
> *Some say it makes the world go round,*
> *And some say that's absurd.*
> *And when I asked the man next door,*
> *Who looked as if he knew,*
> *His wife got very cross indeed,*
> *And said it wouldn't do.*

'That's Auden isn't it?' Claire blurted out.

'Yes, don't you love it. Just right for this time of night,' Sue giggled as she gave them another verse, and then, laughing, turned to Ben: 'C'mon you hunk! Let's find out if it looks like a pair of pyjamas, or the ham in a temperance hotel.'

* * *

As she gazed up at the sliver of moon slipping through the curtain of clouds, Natasha wondered if it wasn't spreading the gentle light of benefaction on their little group. 'Some evenings Andrei, I can go on forever,' she whispered almost purring. Her shining green eyes searching his face: 'Let's leave these darlings, we can carry on anywhere.' The delicious ambiguity of it! She didn't blink! 'A nightcap at the pub?'

As they maundered down the driveway, she gave a shiver of delight: 'I'm accustomed to it now, but when I defected, one of my great delights was to move around at night without feeling I was being watched!'

'You're safe! I don't think our friendly Sergeant will arrest us tonight Tashen'ka.'

Back at the pub, Bob Wellham just back himself, asked if he could get us anything. 'A couple of Scotches would be lovely, if it's not too much trouble,' Andrew replied as Bob, anticipating him, passed a bottle of *Glenfiddich*.

'My tab; medicinal of course!' I laughed: 'will you two join us?'

'Nah, it's a bit o' shut-eye for us isn't it old girl.' He didn't wait for Sheila to reply, 'Pull the door to when you go Doc. Good night. Can I say how nice to meet you, Lady O'Connell ...'

'Thank you.' I was a little embarrassed, but turned to Andrew: 'let's find the little sitting room shall we?'

'You're not exhausted?'

'*Non, non; très calme, très paisible*, even if I haven't stopped talking all the night, opening my soul ... and Michael's. Everyone has been so sweet, I think those gorgeous Doogues – so care full – can I say that, are like my lost Maman and Papa. Michael would have scoffed at the idea.'

'It's not so silly. I've had a vacuum there all my life, a yearning rarely appeased, in want of a selfless love: a parent or some other I guess.' He put his arm around her and for a moment before they sat down she nestled into his shoulder. 'Do you miss your parents' love.'

'Ah, always. It was a gossamer attachment, not bondage! They taught me to fly and to honour freedom. And, you know, although I'm still learning, every day I'm happier in the moment.'

'I hope it's not trite to say, you were lucky to have known love like that.'

'Oui, *cheri*; I know …' her voice trailing off, 'and at the end, Michael admitted, while he'd shaped his life around a search for this elusive love, he'd willfully refused to accept that what he'd been looking for had been there all along. And yours, what of them?'

'Well it's awful but, whatever we had if there was ever anything, it just dried up like a summer creek. I learned to stop knocking at their door very early on. But enough of this maudlin stuff *moi* Natasha. This weekend, I'm in your hands.'

'Oooh-la,' I couldn't help thinking of his big hands, and cupped my own. 'Well we have to be at *Clifton* late tomorrow afternoon. Tell me if I'm being pushy … could I join you for breakfast about nine, have an hour or so going through that big parcel I brought down ready for the meeting, then we head for the hills.' She laughed, gaily.

Nodding agreement, he stood, lifted her out of her chair and they kissed as good friends might but lingered a little longer in their gentle embrace, as people who were just good friends might not. '*Grand merci*', she whispered. 'I feel spoilt and in a strange way, released.' She dwelt on the word. 'Freed, all over again. Thank you.'

***

She was early making her way up his path. Dressed in denims and a polo-necked jumper, her hair, gently played with by the breeze, fell loosely to her shoulders. A little flushed from her walk her eyes glowed. Andy was on the front verandah browsing through a journal; standing, he waved as soon as he saw her. 'Sorry I'm so early, … but I'd rather be here than at the hotel.' Do you mind?'

'Never, I'm glad, tea to start or a pot of coffee?'

'Coffee, long black is good, but I guess a croissant is out of the question in the metropolis?'

'Actually,' he bowed, a sly grin growing: 'just this once; *pour vous*. I brought several down from my favourite Sydney bakery. I'll warm them up; I was hoping we might have something like this. Now come into my parlour,' but she knew it was no trap. He watched her move. 'Are you limping?'

'O, it's nothing, a little from last night. I've been lazy with my exercises, it's nothing, I think of it as Golemnikov's parting gift.'

He gestured towards a chair. 'Please … Sure you are not in pain? The coffee will only be a jiffy. We left off with the Golem sent packing with his tail between his legs', he chuckled.

'That's right, then I returned to London and into the season. *Ballet News* thought I was *a new star in the pantheon*: while the ghastly dailies were yawping that I *was conquering Europe*. Oh, they were giving us curtain calls and yelling "Bravo" and stamping their feet. I was on my way.' She laughed. 'Don't think I didn't enjoy it. But, really, I just wanted to be the best I could be. I didn't need to be the latest sensation out of Russia.'

Andrew poured the coffee and passed her a croissant. 'Madame I have a homemade apricot jam, can I tempt you?'

'O please, tempt me,' momentarily frivolous.

'But, look, this story; you don't have to tell me if it's too painful. In broad brush strokes, I can see what's coming and it must have been devastating.'

'Yes, I'm sure you can guess. It's a long story, I'll tell you, then I'll never mention it again but I want you to know.' She stops and takes his hand.

My mind was full of Golemnikov; his hands threatening, invading, his hissing obscenities: "bitch, blyad, fucking whore". His savage lifts, his face, so ghastly, pushing into my crutch. 'Stop it!' I'm screaming. 'Fuck off!' The audience's mounting boos and hisses, their feet stamping. Then Izzy screams, "Get her out." The crash, crack of bones. Mine. Pain, radiating. Excruciating. Is it me screaming? The curtain barely missing me. A flurry of activity. His grey eyes as in death: stare.

'Ssshh, hush.' Andrew can feel tremors wracking her body, as he holds her; she is sobbing. 'I'd got to trust him you see, rehearsals were good. He was careful, engaged, attentive, and unlike the old days his hands did not wander in the lifts, he sought no unnecessary physical contact and he made none of the salacious overtures that I'd expected.' And the story flowed from her like a torrent. When she had finished she paused; spent, hearing again in her mind's ear the awful thundering of hisses and boos, violent stamping of feet, like an ironic chorus.

Whispering, she looked at Andrew: 'It's more than twelve years ago now and it's as vivid as if it happened last week. It cost me a future, I made another but I wondered if I would ever recover, it was more than physical.'

'God! It was like a rape, the bastard; he wanted to finish you off.'

'And the fuss in the press, look ... here, the *Telegraph* was in no doubt.' She rummaged through the papers she had brought with her to sort. *Sensation at the Ballet ... Natasha Levinskaya Crippled: May Never Dance Again. Golemnikov Disappears.* 'It was an immediate *cause célèbre* with the press framing it as an international incident and Golemnikov portrayed as an agent of the KGB. Or was it more domestic as those close to me thought, with its cause personal to the dancers themselves? I withdrew, ignored the newspapers and gave no interviews.'

'And Golemnikov?'

'Off! He skulked out of the country and his career flourished at home. Maman wrote me that they fawned over him in Russia. He hasn't danced in London since.'

Andrew knew recovery from this type of injury would be slow with numerous false starts punctuated by emotional damage.

'What did I do you are thinking, *non*? I was pathetic.' Her smile was mirthless. 'My recovery was painful, slow, and inconclusive. Like you say,

I was aching to dance, it was as though I'd been imprisoned for a crime I didn't commit and the culprit had got away. Deep down, I felt in my belly, even as I fought against it, that life as I knew it was over.' She spoke slowly, her arms held before her, palms up as if in despair. I slipped irresistibly into an enveloping depression. It was as though I was seduced by sadness and I embraced it, sought it out. I luxuriated in the bleakness of it.'

Andrew let her talk, just occasionally nodding.

'Hunched into a ball, I lay for hours, days, weeks, months, letting the profound sorrow of Górecki's *Symphony of Sorrowful Songs* seep into me; Mozart's aching Fourth, with the sound turned down very low until it was like a pulse, and any adagio I could find as I wept into their sadness and beauty, I wallowed in my sorrow.'

'Did you consider a return to St Petersburg?'

'Andrew, how do you know? Yes, I longed to go home until Maman and Papa, giving me, what I now understand as their most profound love, weeping uncontrollably as they said it, told me there was no place for me, "Darling, *moya milaya moya*; we miss you, but we can't give you a place." Rudi's response was somewhat different. He screamed at me to get off my arse, "you'll get ulcers," and, although Michael didn't intrude he sent small gifts, flowers, chocolates, a scarf, a fine leather wallet. Perhaps he was only keeping his name before me just in case, but he was around! Weeks ticked into months.'

'At last, tired of his banging and yelling at the door, I let Nureyev in. "I thought you came here to fly. Go on then, suck it up damn you, get on with it." His hand, extravagantly on his hip, ever the dancer. "You think I'm a shit don't you, think I should be stroking your sorrow. Well, it's enough. Make a choice, curl up and fade away or … find what else you're good at and take that morbid bloody Pole off your record player."

'I hate you!' I screamed at him. "Of course you do Levinskaya," he purred; "but you're wasting yourself and for us *stateless people*, that's not allowed."'

'Three cheers for Rudi,' Andrew laughed.

'Even Michael sent me a note with one of his many bunches of flowers:

My Dear Natasha, you have a choice. You can languish or, if I'm not boasting, you can do as I did, make your way; it may be a different way but let me assure you, it is possible to start over. Let me help you.

'I was surprised. He had emerged from behind his cloak of anonymity' she shrugged.

'Then Pushkin arrived. Izzy, my ballet friend lifted a little Burmese kitten out of her bag, "he's the runt of the litter Tarsh, but look at him; he's so handsome and nobody wants him… well?"

'Lilac – almost cream really – with huge golden eyes, he was watching me as I moved towards him, watching to make sure I knew what he was asking me to do, as he rolled over to be patted. He began to purr, 'Oh, Izzy, I adore him, but look at me … I can't care for myself.'

"Well, darling that's up to you! He's a neglected little fellow but all he needs is love. Couldn't you do that?"

'Oh, dear me …,' she sighed, smiled, almost helplessly. 'Does he have a name?'

'I was told they just called him puss,' Isabel explained.

'Puss? Oh no, if he wants to stay here, and we'll see if he does, he'll be my Pushkin. Perhaps he can put some poetry into my life as we learn to talk to each other. He would spend hours with me, stretching out beside me, snuggling on top of the blankets or lying on my chest when I was on the chaise. He was adorable. Then I was showing off a *pas de chat* to Izzy as, holding Pushy close to my chest and extending a paw, we executed several tiny "cat" jumps across the room.

'What joy. I never had a pet you know, but Izzy was very clever. This was about more than the cat.' Andrew murmured, watching her intently as she told her story.

'You understand! It wasn't long before I was doing brief extensions at the *barre*.

Although it was only just over a year since the accident the prognosis that I would never dance again was being revised weekly. I dared to hope and then Michael came out of the shadows. He'd been a silent presence but, having been told as a primary sponsor that I was to attend the Royal

Ballet's Christmas cocktail party in what was to be a brief appearance in the line of duty, he also attended and thereafter made his car available for brief outings, often joining me. My voluntary exile was over. He took me to gallery openings, to first nights of the ballet and the symphony, the theatre, occasional dinners which invariably included a business component and he invited me to be his partner at a formal 'Ides of March' dinner for twenty at his home. Isn't that tempting fate I asked?

Ah my dear, a bit of Russian fatalism. It's in your blood not mine. There's always a Brutus or two on the list and an Anthony perhaps but I'm not Caesar. I'll take the risk!

'Not Caesar astride your world?' I had mused, wondered if he didn't prefer to have his enemies in sight. Enemies? Well anyone who challenged him perhaps.'

* * *

Is Levinskaya coming out? Flabbergast asked in its gossip column, noting that she had *emerged from her prolonged period of injury on the arm of the British-Australian tycoon, Michael O'Connell. Is there anything to this?* Not to be left behind, *Wow!* gave me half a page, recycling old newspaper clippings accompanied by a photograph with Oleg in one of the lifts in *Onegin*. It also linked me to O'Connell, wondering if he'd given up his *French dalliances*. While *"Ballet News"*, having done some research, focused on my rehabilitation, noting, I'd started at the *barre*. It was even forecasting I'd be in full work by mid-summer. It was only a few weeks out. I was back in the studio by August, gradually increasing the tempo of my work. Nureyev did sessions with me whenever he was in London. "Push me, push me, bird," he'd yell. I struggled to keep up but, watching Rudi closely, sweating profusely, thinner, more ravaged, I was worried. He wasn't well and I fussed over him. Perhaps it was good for me too; took my mind off my own problems. "Too much of the candle at both ends" he puffed.

Why bother about him, Michael had sniffed.

'We *bother* about each other, it's what friends do!' She retorted.

Although Michael was urging caution – *don't rush it my dear* – I began to plan a return to the stage the next April, roughly twenty months since the accident. And, with my confidence growing the Company began feeding me back into carefully chosen social engagements. "It's about profile," my agent would say, "theirs and yours. You are a story you know. Now we can breathe life into that dormant image." Although I wasn't yet in the social whirl, along with others, Michael made sure I was on his card. Was he courting? Whatever it was, he intrigued me.

'I can't put my finger on it, Izzy, but he generates an enormous, if cold, energy, and he has a mind like quick-silver. I admire his courage and he's been very good to me. I wonder perhaps if I might give him the tenderness that seems so lacking in his life.'

Leading with the header *Levinskaya to Fly Again, The Telegraph* correspondent admitted that his prediction that my career was over may have been premature and thought I might be *a surprise bright light in the new season.* I was surprised then, after a winter in which hardly anyone could compete with me for sheer volume of work, that the expected contract with the Company was not forthcoming. "We couldn't build a season around you, Natasha. What if you broke down. Our programme is underwritten by a very generous sponsorship; we can't put it at risk. I'm sorry; but you must understand."

'I was shattered and Rudi was incandescent with rage but, no longer associated with the Company, he could do nothing and didn't make it worse by stamping his foot. I turned to Michael. I mean, the *generous sponsor* was *O'Connell.* 'Don't you want to see me dance again?'

I know how you must feel Natasha, but our few shekels don't entitle us to interfere in the day-to-day running of the Company. That's not how corporations are run. I have no voice. He held his arms out wide, palms up. *I would like to help you, but,* he paused, *I have a proposition.*

I was dumb, nodded: go on.

We need a … what we might call, a … an intermediary between O'Connell

– 'not me', she thought – *and the various charities it supports; such a person would attend selected functions. You and I do a little of this now indirectly, it seems to work. Ultimately, I hope you would direct our charitable foundation.'*

I noticed the semantic slippage from *a person* to *you,* and hoped it was accidental, merely a manner of speaking. Nevertheless, he'd caught me on the back foot; for, while I enjoyed working with him this was the first time I'd experienced ... what was it? A sense of security with him. I brushed the thought aside, for *O'Connell* had only ever been a stop-gap until a return to the stage. He was watching me intently. 'Let's not get ahead of ourselves. I'm a ballet dancer Michael, that's who I am, what I know, what I do! Is it wise to be having this conversation now? Don't you see I've just been given a body blow.' I could barely speak, my throat constricted. 'They've just threatened to take my life from me.' And yet, I felt my eye flick involuntarily; in the back of my mind, barely formed, were vague thoughts of safe harbours!

Now is precisely the time to have it Natasha. Michael was cool, calm, calculating his target. Had he detected a shift in my feelings, or was he probing her vulnerability? *Of course, you are disappointed ...* 'Disappointed ... pah', I spat, 'that's not the half of it!'. He didn't flinch: *I'm offering you an alternative life* he said quietly, firmly. Gesturing to his own situation as he spoke, ... *think about it. I do know what has happened to you. I know.*

I was angry, inconsolable and lashed out. 'I don't think I'd be much good touting for business, pimping; a, a ... high class hooker ... like your poor French woman, if that's what you have in mind.' But, strangely, my thoughts turned to Vera and second starts. 'O this is the wrong time, wrong, wrong ... but the charity interface' – *ah, a much better word,* he said, as if to mollify – 'that interests me. But, whoa there ... I haven't retired from ballet. The Royal isn't the only fish in the oceans!'

Michael was unruffled; he spoke quietly. *Let's re-convene in a month from today. I'm a patient man, I'm offering you a job, nothing else. You'll be well paid and will report directly to me. The busy-work will be handled by my PA. I've seen you relate to an audience* – 'really,' I thought – *I think you'll be brilliant at what I have in mind.*

'I take it though, the other fish in the ballet sea weren't biting?' Andrew speculated.

'Ah, wise Andrew! It took me less than a month to find out I was on the scrap heap. O they all loved me – "loved your work" – but put it into the past tense and wherever I went – from Manchester to Birmingham to the London Contemporary – I was a risk. "There might be something in management or teaching." Talking each application over with Michael, after the fourth refusal I threw my hands up in despair, went home and wept into Pushkin's fur. He looked at me with his golden eyes, and licked my fingers as though he understood, calming me. In my darkest hour, I think he saved my life, but then he meowed for his food. "Always me, me, me; eh", I laughed pathetically, remembering I'd said the same thing to Rudi.'

'Even as things looked bleak, Nureyev was on my mind – I'd heard rumours about his health – but now, I evoked him: "it's your choice, my bird; curl up in a ball again or tell them to go and fuck themselves and move on."

'"May I speak to Mr O'Connell please, it's Natasha Levin. Hello Michael it's your pimp calling." Childish wasn't it, but he didn't miss a beat. "Can we talk about your job offer?" I said nothing about safe havens but they were on my mind, I was crushed; last resort!

'Within weeks, the *O'Connell Charitable Foundation* was established within *O'Connell* and I was set up with a small staff of two in a lovely old heritage terrace in St John's Wood. I'd no sooner attended my first Board Meeting a month later than *Business Review's* Philip Thirlwell had the story.

> *Off with the Tutu and on with the Power Suit.*
>
> Business Review *notes with interest that the former Prima Ballerina Natasha Levinskaya has her shapely long legs under the boardroom table at* O'Connell, *where she has exchanged her ballet pumps for stilettos and will work directly with Michael* O'Connell *on special projects. Mr O'Connell must know something we in the City don't, for we wonder what this*

Soviet trained ex-ballerina will bring to a table where the fare is distinctly high capital. We are casting no aspersions on her ballet career which, until she was crippled in an accident, promised to be illustrious, however, we can find nothing in her CV which suggests she has a business brain in her elegant head. Has Mr O'Connell lost his? We'll see!

Good luck; we notice also that Ms Levinskaya is now Ms Levin.

We'll teach him to snigger. Michael sniffed. A week later, *BR* recanted:

Apology to *O'Connell and* Ms Levin
We notice that offence has been taken at the tone of Philip Thirlwell's article on the appointment of Ms Natasha Levin to O'Connell. No offence was intended and Mr Thirlwell and BR apologise unreservedly to Mr O'Connell and Ms Levin for any sleight that may have occurred or been inferred.

'Michael acted quickly! I did away with my ballet bun and let my hair grow into a bob. Izzy thought it suited me, "frames your face darling, accentuates those gorgeous high cheek bones." And Michael made sure I had several tailored business suits in my wardrobe. "Thirlwell wasn't too wide of the mark," some of the bowler hats remarked, stopping to gaze. But there were no stilettos, although I'd added to my collection of ballet flats.'

Natasha's story came as a deluge from the past and Andrew had the time and the grace to give her the space, observing, as he did so, that the St John's Wood office was a smart idea; allowing her to settle in on her terms, without him looking over her shoulder.

'Yes, you would have thought so. I did, until I found it had more to do with him than me.' Andrew raised an eyebrow. 'Well you see it's how he liked to work. Everything safely separated except that through his PA, Rebecca, who was also servicing my office, he knew what I was doing while I knew nothing of what was going on in the main office. When I queried him about this, he brushed it off as paranoia: *all you need to know my dear is that O'Connell can fund your charitable projects. Isn't that so?*

'I saw a lot of him, we went to most functions together, and fewer other men asked me out, even those who I liked at first sight didn't hang around. Much later, I was to learn that Michael had burnt them off, how do you say, leaving me on the shelf. But while they were retreating, he was in full advance presenting himself as my only ally. I was so fragile. I was still on anti-depressants, getting used to the new position for which there were few guidelines and trying to change life-gears.'

'Were you paid a salary, or one of those dreadful retainers I've heard about?'

'Oh, a salary ... very generous; Michael had his accountant have a look at my tax returns, *Let him run a slide rule over things, Natasha.* They came up with a figure which I thought was so extravagant it was embarrassing; I felt obligated you know. They knew they wouldn't see any return on the investment for years, but that sounds like an excuse.'

'It does,' Andrew responded thoughtfully. 'I confess, it makes me think of Rachael. I never understood why she married Gilbert, but,' he mused, 'they had their reasons I'm sure. As, my dear, I'm sure you had.'

'Don't give me too much credit.' She replied, looking up at him, smiling weakly. 'I was like a sleepwalker for several years, my eyes only half open. We were married within two years, 14 October 1987, a Tuesday, at the Registry Office. Strangely, he had his stockbroker Angus Ranley, who had taken me out a few times, at his side.'

'Was he pressing home a point?'

'Now I would say yes but at the time I let it pass. I had Izzy attending me, even as she told me she thought it was a dreadful waste. We celebrated with champagne back at *O'Connell Towers*, helped by the beautiful raven-haired Rebecca. Strangely we didn't see Angus again. I learned that Michael withdrew his accounts from Angus' control at *Portland Mason*.'

'How odd,' Andrew was thinking about Rebecca and Ranley, Natasha's focus was on her story.

'I saw it all, the job with the attendant responsibility for shaping it and turning it into something, and the marriage, which Michael had framed more like an extension of a working agreement than a romantic proposal, as a way of giving point and purpose to my life after the breakdown.' She was searching Andrew's face for a response. 'I threw myself into the work and while I didn't particularly like some of what I saw and heard, I was at arm's length from it, even as I came to see more intimately what drove Michael and the dark forces that shaped him.'

'Did it make a splash?'

'Our wedding, do you mean? Well, lasting all of ten minutes the best papers gave it a discerning and considerate mention and although it received titillating attention from society magazines and social pages, intrigued by the relationship, they soon retreated. *I don't expect them to bother you any more my dear* he'd said protectively. And they were silent on the marriage, which despite Izzy's and Vera's concerns, gave me the first sense of security I'd had since the accident.'

'Was there any love in there? Mary's and mine was managed by Mary in such a way that overt love was rarely allowed to surface or be dwelt upon, but it was there. I don't have that sense in anything you've told me about you and Michael.'

She looked closely at him and held her hands out as if in surrender. 'You aren't the first to ask, Andrei. I genuinely thought I could bring some affection into his life you know, but I always felt my response was unconvincing, yet I didn't know how to dress it up. I admired him and had persuaded myself, or had he convinced me, I needed him. I was still emotionally fragile, more than I understood at the time. Now, with the advantage of hindsight and a clearer head ... I'd say the opposite. He saw a weakness and began surgically to open it up.' Andrew was nodding.

'You must have known that you couldn't have a normal fulfilling life with him though, given his injuries. There could be emotional love of course, but no expression of it through the physical.' Andy was being forensic.

'Of course I knew, but this was how I was. Apart from my early love affair with Babi and occasional inconsequential liaisons, everything was shaped by ballet and my ambition. You understand I think, but while Michael said he did, I knew it was a potential battleground. He said he realized I would have sexual needs, managing to make me sound a little like a cat on heat. *I have no expectations of you in that regard, but can I ask you not to meet them at home.* To this end he explained we would have separate bedrooms and *en suites* and that his manservant, essentially a valet, would attend to him morning and night. It was understood however, that I would care for him and enter fully into his social activities. Fortunately, for I came to learn that the *extramarital clause* was one of Michael's trip-wires, I told him I had no interest in testing it. I thought he needed some tenderness in his life but, isn't it dreadful to say this, I think he wanted a permanent girl on call. Much later, I wondered about his own physical needs, but that's barren ground, let's not go there. In truth, in the early days, it was all I could do to perform my social and few domestic duties let alone involve myself in anything outside the marriage. It didn't help matters when Izzy got the long-awaited offer to join the Chicago Ballet and just as I'd lost my darling Verushka, I now had to farewell Izzy … a beautiful uncomplicated friend.'

'He must have thought you were crazy or a saint, committing to him like that.'

'I think he saw it as his entitlement; but equally cynically, I wondered if he was testing my saintliness. In a more sinister way than I recognized then, I was also a part of his elaborate disguise. He watched me like a hawk, but he never gave me the St Agnes award for chastity.'

'You asked nothing of him?'

'Well one didn't ask of Michael; his way was to dispense. Yet I did seek one thing of him. When we were working through our wedding agreement, a formality he insisted on, I asked for a codicil providing me with the start-up funds to establish a charitable foundation of my own: the "NO" Foundation which would provide assistance to rape victims and under-privileged children, to be administered in my own time, and operating independent of *O'Connell* and its charity work. It was only by accident that the title incorporates a version of my initials, for it was not about me, it was about saying "NO". It appealed to me however, and Michael acknowledged the wit by ignoring it!'

'So! Michael will dispense; bestow?'

'Yes, he would assume the right of his gift.' She sighed.

'Very subjective! It can't have been easy accommodating his whims and fancies?'

'Ah moy Andrei, I had warning signals but you know, I just thought we were adapting to our new state. At first, they seemed so minor. What would I bring from my place, which paintings, pot plants – *you won't want for anything here* – and O yes, Pushkin.'

The cat, Tasha! You can't be serious. Pissing and spraying all over the carpets. Give him away or have him put down.

"No room for Pushy! Michael think of us as a package. He's my beautiful boy, we'll make a home for him. He saved me. We feel each other's pulse. You'll come to love him as well," but, he gave Pushkin not a jot of his time, shoo-ed him away; would, if it had been worth a fight, have got rid of him, drowned him in the pool perhaps. *What do you see in the runt?*

'These were only minor skirmishes in the larger battleground of the marriage, but if he gave ground on one front he would seek to reclaim territory on another.'

'Didn't you find that exhausting- emotionally draining?'

'Of course I did and initially my reserves were low. But I knew – I don't know how I knew – that for the relationship to work, I had to stand up to him on matters that directly affected me. I could not surrender.' She paused. 'I soon learned I was dealing with a master; Michael was good and I was a novice. It started directly after the wedding. We were getting ready to attend a formal dinner at Lord Crawley's on the Thursday night. I was in my dressing room putting on my make-up in brassiere and panties, when he wheeled himself in. He was already dressed in his tails. A black dress hung over his arm and what looked like a jewellery box was on his lap.' She was reliving the episode.

Go on: I like to watch he said, his eyes intent upon my body, I felt uncomfortable. But he was my husband. He held the dress up to me: *I thought to please me, you might like to put this on.* It was the dress I'd seen on Sophie in Paris. I was off balance and showed my shock. He was unfazed.'

'My God ...'

'Oh, that's not all, *and wear these,* he said. Draped over his fingers and in his palm, were pieces I'd remarked on to Sophie and had been asked to wear at the Paris picnic! "MICHAEL!" I was shaking, screaming, "what's got into you? I've seen these before, on those women from the agency you've been with."

'*Elite* he said smirking, interjecting, reading my mind – *grande horizontales from one of the better Maisons de Tolérance: not that I can lay them out.* ("It was a soft job," Sophie had said. "I just had to let him watch me dress and wear the dress and jewels he provided…and make a fuss of him. It doesn't come much easier than zat!")

'Andrew can you understand why I was so upset?'

'Did he see no difference, surely it was just a bad joke?'

'If only, well you see, I learned he liked his women to look like that. Good thing I wasn't a blonde, he'd have wanted me to dye my hair or wear a wig.' Her humour was grim. 'I was his woman on that night, his wife yes, but I'm sure I was also his escort – his latest cash-girl – to show off. … or, was I his mother? I covered myself up. I was shaking with rage, sadness, confusion, what was I? "Get out" I hissed. "Out of my room. I have to finish dressing. Get out!"

'To which he shrugged, raised an eyebrow, tossed the dress and the jewelry in the corner and wheeled out of the room. I didn't keep him long, quick re-touch of the make-up, put on something demure grey with tiny silver earrings and a necklace at the throat. It was a ghastly evening. Fortunately, we were seated apart from each other, but I felt his eyes on me all evening. I was near some CEO's wife. "Oh, darling, he's hardly taken his eyes off you. Aren't you lucky! Wish Derek was like that with me." An image of Golemnikov leering at me flashed through my mind.

'No, I didn't trash the dress. With my background you don't look the horse in the mouth: I took the dress to my tailor, who made two lovely LBDs from it. I still have them, although, and now I am being dreadful, now, they're a kind of trophy!'

Andrew smiled ... a little in awe of this woman animating his kitchen with foreign tales.

'I wasn't sure what I was; he'd unsettled me, do you see? My world was out of joint, but I still went to the *barre* four times a week, and the charity work was fascinating. And although his cynicism was like some shallow water table that bubbles to the surface periodically he was a good teacher, he knew a lot and was experienced. *Never go into a position half-baked, Tasha: always be the best prepared person in the room; take the high ground. Try to position yourself to have the advantage.* It taught me a lot about Michael ...'

'And about yourself, I fancy?'

'A lot, but you know I realized for all his coaching, I didn't want to do business like that. I wanted collaboration not combat. But, O my God, it was invaluable in learning how to handle those who wanted to use his approach. I discovered after a while and, certainly after the ballet door had slammed shut, that I was tough, resilient and capable of doing things my way. Despite his attentions I don't think he had a clue what made me tick. Nor did he seem to want to find out! Oh, Andrei, I'm being very honest here, ...'.

'It's alright; sometimes one needs to say these things; I think you do.'

'When we first met, I thought he had a fine mind; I was seduced by it. He let me glimpse it and in my depleted state I submitted to it but, as time went by, he made no room for me; if I dared to try to explore it, like some adventurer climbing a high peak, I was starved of oxygen and he made no attempt to help me. I came to see it as a dark, hard mind, barricaded. I couldn't penetrate to its inner chambers. He wanted me by his side, for whatever reason but he did not want me in his mind. It was a kind of suffocation, as cruel as if it had been physical. I learned not to go there.'

'Did he care do you think? What about that tenderness you spoke of?'

'I was never sure if I was making progress or not. At times I thought he was trying, but didn't know how. It was as though he couldn't articulate what was occurring. There were occasional moments of inclusiveness, a softening. At functions he might seek me out, at galleries or exhibitions and we would chat, almost like a real couple, or among his own collection at home where we often wandered, he would ask my opinion of pieces or explain something of their history; opening the door a fraction onto what genuinely interested him. It wasn't yet possible to call this love, but there was a semblance of affection which was new. There was a hint of emotional growth, suggesting at least he'd granted me a place in his life and that he was groping around for something authentic to share: a real word.' She looked at Andrew as if to say is this too confusing? 'But then the opposite might occur. The door would slam shut. It was almost as though I'd exposed a weakness in his armoury and his visor would come down; that semblance of softness I'd glimpsed would vanish as he worked to make himself unlovable, leaving me riddled with doubt. What did he want of me?'

'I'm not sure that I follow?'

'*Par exemple.* He'd talked to me about Russia ever since we met. I found it endearing, thought it was a part of getting to know me. Who were my parents? Were they really under surveillance? Who were my friends, would I like to see them again? Did I have any connections in Moscow? As time went on he would often come back to Vera's father, Anatoly Velen. By the early nineties, he was becoming persistent. "Why do you ask me about that awful man? I detest him, cruising around like a thug pandering to anyone in power, in his expensive clothes, pah: no threadbare jackets or polyester for him." ...

We're going in my dear. It sounded like he was planning an invasion. *I need someone on the ground. I know it'll cost a bit of gratitude, some* blagodarnost. *Velen could be just what I'm after! Can I rely on you to arrange that we meet?* "Michael!" I was appalled. "Velen's not the sort of man anyone I'm associated with should have anything to do with, even if you pay him a little gratitude as you say. I won't lift my finger to help you." It was a horrible conversation which finished with him calling me an ungrateful bitch, but this time, I stormed off. "'You go to Russia if you will, I'll go to Paris. Rudi's very ill." At times like this, we were watching each other like traitors.'

Looking closely at her, Andrew thought she needed a break. 'Why don't we have another cup as we start sorting?'

'Please, let's get it done! A few more shocks *moi Andrei*, are you ready?'

* * *

Natasha spilled the contents of her large mail bag onto the table and began sifting, spreading and sorting. 'That's a jumble' Andrew muttered, as he brought her a coffee.

'Ah, once they were meticulously filed away, a place for everyone. But today, just make rough piles.' She began calling their names. 'Andrew, a dubious treat: first away. Ben; Bran; Charles; Claire; me – ugh, big pile; Susannah.' All those voices in his head.

Together they sorted through letters and postcards; copied, translated and original newspaper cuttings; maps, drawings and sketches, while keeping larger items separate: books and large printed documents, the meccano set, a christening mug.

Natasha had already returned Bran's war diaries and letters and brought the cello down for Charlie. 'He loved it didn't he? I warn you though, it's an extraordinary collection of memorabilia!'

'Not much on you, you're almost in the clear,' she chuckled. She showed him an annotated set of the Clinic Board minutes and the architectural drawings, topped up with photos of progress on the construction; a potted cv of Stefan Holderlin: and copies of letters he'd sent to Michael and Natasha inviting them to visit the Clinic. 'But he hardly knew I existed,' Andrew exclaimed. 'After the initial introduction, I never again saw him on site, I mean we were spending his money.'

'There's the job advert that you responded to and even this little treasure; just as well you told me about Rachael,' she smiled playfully, waving a newspaper clipping of a letter to *The Times* from Dr Rachael McAdam regarding the Buchanan family in response to an article noting the death of his brother, Colonel George Buchanan in Iraq, correcting the erroneous statement that George was the end of the Buchanan line. '*The line survives in Australia in Dr Andrew Buchanan, a distinguished Paediatrician.*'

'Why bother?'

'He had a mind like a steel trap that man; kept tabs on everyone for whatever reason, no matter how arcane…just in case!'

'I see he has my letters sent to the Hunter's Hill address after we'd completed the Clinic; so much for your privacy.'

'And for trusting me; but how I would have loved to receive them at the time. You write a beautiful letter.' She seemed to take delight in reading it aloud:

> *Celtic Ponds/14 February 1996 (Letter No: 4)*
>
> *Dear Natasha: I haven't heard from you and hope that I'm not merely sending these notes into the ether. I wonder what you are engaged with; what large and small projects you have in hand. I am envious of all those who have your interest.*
>
> *I am beginning to feel a part of my little village. I treat their aches and pains as best I can – it is never dull – and am learning to play with them as well, as our little band is in demand and we have some wonderful country dances. To my absolute amazement, the creative energy around the place is realized in many ways. (I should send you an inventory!) They've taken me to their hearts; I feel very fortunate. It is as rich and lively as any dream and provides succour to my heart. It's a pity you don't know the place and its people, given that you are almost its* seigneuresse, *due to your husband's grip and largesse. We hope that you may see us in our place in the future.*
>
> *I wake in the morning to the caroling of magpies, chattering and mimicking the calls around them and later in the morning black and white cockatoos slice the air with their yahoo calls, and delight the eye with their sheer fun together, for the white ones, do you know, mate for life. And always for us, new to this place, there is the laughing call of the kookaburra to ponder. A*

morning is incomplete if I don't have coffee on the verandah,
gazing across the top of the waking town to the purple hills,
hardly mountains in a European sense, but splendid in all their
variegated blues and purples, softened by green fields in the
foreground and clad by bush (I love the word, so much wilder
than woods), enlivened by wisps of chimney smoke, the lowing of
cattle, and the occasional vehicle winding into town. I never tire
of it and on a good morning, and there are many of them, I go
inside and express my joy and good fortune through someone like
Chopin. I am a lucky man.

I had hoped we might be able to keep up a friendship, I
want nothing more from you than that and I hope that I might
hear from you, rather than prick up my ears to the odd scrap of
news of you that I might hear.

Yours, in friendship, Andrew

'I missed our contact. I didn't know you were there, and see here, Susannah's letters after I'd *wilfully* attended the Wollongong concert.' Andrew touched her hand. 'My pile starts even before I knew him, talk about being stalked!' She had a copy of *Izvestia*'s 16 December 1971 review of her debut in *Onegin*. He had attached to the translation a photograph from *Pravda* at about the same time on which he'd scribbled: *"A star is launched, where will she land?"*

Andrew interrupted her: 'What a fabulous review, and so prescient. He read:

An adorable Tatiana. This innocent girl, who has to deal
with the machinations of the rude and confounded Onegin, is
brilliantly cast. Despite her young years, she understands the
emotional demands of the role and achieves the dramatic tension
which is at the ballet's core. As such, she is an ideal foil to Oleg
Golemnikov who, despite a fine performance when he is trying
to seduce Tatiana in Act 1...

'This says it all ... *that weakening, his loss of face, in the third act.*'

'But, I hadn't even met Michael!' she exclaimed. 'He was still a university student in Australia. He must have gone back over old reviews after we'd met and started collecting me.' She shivered. As she spoke, Andrew was skimming through translations of old reviews from *Izvestia* and *Pravda*, notes in the *Times, Guardian*, and *Telegraph*, of the early tours when for the most part, she danced only minor roles. He waves a photo from *The Guardian* of her and Golemnikov with Dame Margot. 'O this is a riot.' She hooted. 'I'd been dying to go to London and Rudi had the Royal Ballet invite me to rehearse with them. I was permitted to go on condition Oleg and I were photographed together with the great lady, but not including Nureyev, who put on a fabulous tantrum for the Minders.'

'Golemnikov looks like the cat that stole the cream.' Andrew laughed, as he kept sifting. A fine one from *Il Messagio* in Rome annotated: *Met her backstage.*

'There's hundreds of them Andrew. Even that hilarious photo in *Cosmopolitan* of Rudi glamming it up in his cowboy boots and red scarf. No less than Golemnikov, Michael hated seeing me with Rudi. *What does she see in that poofter?'*

'Then his attention turned to the defection.' Andrew was reading front page stories from *The Telegraph* and *Guardian*. Working off a modest statement from the Home Office: Soviet Ballerina defects to the West. The *Daily Mail* however, made a meal of it. Everyone's darling: Natasha pirouettes to the West.

> *A friend of the dashing Rudolph Nureyev, himself a defector and a darling of Paris and London audiences, the Prima Ballerina Natasha Levinskaya, who was whisked away from her London hotel in a black limousine by an unidentified male, glided into the Home Office last evening to announce her desire to remain in the West. Yes, please!*

'Such an exaggeration,' Natasha mumbled. 'But look..." She was directing him to Michael's note on the *Telegraph* piece: *Watch this space*, and on the *Mail*: *Nureyev again*. 'See, Michael has circled Oleg's name, this was before the injury when it all starts to get very sinister. My injury was a disaster, but for Michael it was a chance.' She was agitated. 'Here it is, on the margin of *The Telegraph*: *How to catch a falling star*, it was so insensitive, yet, it was also sinister.' She was shaking her head. 'Golemnikov's trip may have been funded by the *O'Connell Cultural Fund*, I can't prove it; there's a £10,000 payment to the Kirov Ballet at about this time. Was it a payment towards his expenses? A travel grant? I didn't know. I've had it tracked but it's not clear what it's for. Perhaps I'm paranoid, that's what Michael would have said.'

'Are you saying he closed down your ballet career? What drove the man?'

'I'm not guessing.' She waves a contract between *O'Connell* and the Royal Ballet to underwrite their 1985, '86, and '87 seasons and Michael's accompanying letter in which he explains the agreement is subject to the condition that, *due to the seriousness of her injuries, Ms Levinskaya should not be considered for any role.* He said he was looking after me; it's all here. Letters to companies buying them off: Manchester, Birmingham, the London Contemporary, even to Australia. Do you remember when I rushed back to London when we were getting the building going? I'd been having discussions with dance companies in Sydney about a comeback. He let them know I was unavailable and whisked me back to England.'

Andrew was speechless. Mary had liked to be in control but this was evil. He put down the correspondence. 'Are you alright, going through all this again?

'It's horrendous and it broke my heart when I found out. Instead of making a little progress, everything was built on lies and deception. Even minor matters like Thirlwell's apology in the *Business Review* was designed to clear his name, not mine.

Thirlwell, I insist on a full withdrawal of your recent article on staffing changes at O'Connell. *I find your comments personally distasteful and demeaning and it could be argued they defame my reputation. Given that I am open and free in my dealings with Business Review, I expect similar respect. I can of course, should I choose, take my custom to your rivals or seek restitution in other ways. As to Ms Levin; she is learning the ropes. She may be as you infer a little inexperienced but she is an adornment to* O'Connell. *I don't think that can be denied.*

'It was as though having emerged a little to court me, object achieved, he retreated into his shell; pulling his carapace even tighter over himself and over our marriage. His lawyers made sure there was no public commentary about his personal life. He didn't want his *good name sullied by crude conjecture about the relationship.* He sought to give not one rouble of pleasure or satisfaction, to have submitted to this ... this harassment, would have been to lose all self-respect.' She paused, the colour drained from her face as she reaching out towards Andrew who suggested they go for a drive.

* * *

'Yes please, that would be heavenly. You are so patient listening to my story.' She was thinking of Michael's inability to listen, constantly talking over her as though she had nothing to say, as she reached out towards Andrew and relaxed into his open arms. He watched a smile slowly radiate her face, from her wondrous green eyes, ardent, spreading to her lips, slightly parted as if in anticipation of some greater joy. He was surprised by her ardour. 'Let's head for the hills,' she whispered smiling at the idiom: 'somewhere quiet, peaceful ... natural.'

It was a soft day. The showers had passed through and a pale sun was melting the early mist and drying the country-side, issuing a gentle light that was playing on the trees as they drove into the purple curtain of the hills. There in the car's cocoon, she dozed fitfully, twitching, murmuring, waking for a moment, touching his hand, smiling before slipping back into a gentle sleep. Glancing across at her occasionally, he let her rest, the strain of the morning's confrontation and the previous forty-eight hours slipping away, to be replaced he thought, by the intimate shades of happiness: 'a plenitude' she had said later.

As he drove, Andrew thought about their conversation. Together, over the last few years Natasha and he had been unwinding the skeins of confusion that was their history, finding muffled words that comforted, reassured. It was a kind of itching beneath the imagination, exploring those unexplained events that haunt happiness. He had often pondered that idea of happiness disturbed by the past and he'd given himself up to it again. For Andrew, and perhaps for Natasha it fits their fumbling, but essential, search for love. Then, parking, they strolled across to a stream; the high waters of Myrtle Creek. He cupped his hands, and she drank from them. The water was achingly cold but sweet in the mouth. 'Thank you.'

Last Things

Natasha was relaxed when she and Andrew drove up to *Clifton* that afternoon. The others were there, milling around, setting the table, organizing chairs, chatting. Charles set a place for Michael between Natasha and Charles, as he put the finishing touches to his paella. Several good Cabernets from the Doogues' cellar were open, breathing, and a chardonnay and some olives were already on the move.

'Well my dears, may I call you that now?' Natasha touched eyes with each of them. 'You have opened your hearts and doors to me in ways I could not have expected and with this weekend having correctly, but very directly, been about Michael, I thought I'd tell you now a little about the two of us; especially over the last two years since we were all together. It wasn't appropriate that I did it yesterday.'

She gestured towards the large mail bag, 'and then I have some things of his, and also … yours, to share with you. I've already returned a few larger pieces that clearly, he treasured. As well, I have an extraordinary piece of writing, stand alone fragments really. I don't even know what to call it, half tirade, half justification? I wondered if he was shifting ground from guilt to reparation. He rather grandly calls it his *Apologia*. It's not by chance that he chose …'

'Not by chance that he did most things,' Claire sighed.

'It's not as coherent as you might think and if I've read it correctly, it carries in every stroke of the pen his emotional anguish. So long mastered by his will, it was now let loose and overlaid with physical pain which was also out of his control. I want to share it, and perhaps he wanted me to. There we are: enigmatic to the very end! But I have also many other pieces from the past; hoarded artefacts of association. You may draw sustenance from them. Item by item, perhaps they don't amount to much, but in their entirety, they speak belatedly, incompletely and yet I'm sure, evocatively of his vulnerability and powerlessness. For the history that he refused to acknowledge and went to lengths to hide, was vividly alive in his consciousness and on his conscience at the end. I want to share its contents with you. You are entitled to it. I'm not breaking any confidences. It is owed to you.'

'For some, your last images of Michael go back years, for others, they may issue from brief and sporadic contact. Some have never seen him in a wheelchair, others, never out of it. Whatever the contact however, I suggest it was orchestrated and shaped – he would like to say *managed* – by him; even, dare I suggest it, from infancy. My closing image of him is from the day before he died, and while his last day carries its own awful *memento mori*, this one was confronting, ghastly. I found him slumped over these papers lying scattered at his feet, weeping uncontrollably. What once had been so carefully buried in his filing cabinet; annotated and dated ...', she paused, letting the image settle in, 'were now in a jumble, without pattern or order.

'He had not expected me. I'd never seen him so abandoned to his emotions ... so undone. I'm sure some of you can't imagine it; the loss of control. He had also messed himself. Sobbing one minute, he was yelling out for Abasi, the next: *A-bb-aa-si! Where is that bugger?* His valet was not due for half an hour and yet he screamed obscenities into the vacancy: *Abaaaasi!* I wheeled him, a struggling emaciated form, thin as a baton, writhing in his chair, into the bathroom; set the tap running: *Leave me alone! Get out! This is not your job! Fuck off!*'

'Then he went limp, let me undress him and as best he could, helped me shift him into the bath, our arms around each other... bathing, gently washing; you could say, caressing. In all our time together, he'd never let me bathe him. He did not look at me, but held my arms, did not, I think, want me to let him go; seemed for the first time to be accepting the tenderness that all along I'd wanted to give him. Holding him, I ran another bath, sluicing away his body waste and lay him back, letting the fresh warm water wash over him.'

I'm all undone. There's no escaping this mess of a life. He cackled, barely audible, but holding onto me. I held him, wanted to comfort him, but he seemed unable to stop talking. *There's an awful appropriateness about my state today and this mess. I have no dominion over what these files once represented. But, I've tried all my life* – his voice, coming in short gasps, was softer, I held him even closer to hear. Was that what he wanted? – *I've tried to account for them, filed them away, but look! Here I am … There is no tomorrow for this bag of bones.* He looked up and laughed: ugly, ironic, compelling.'

She paused, remembering the moment. As he gazed up at her, a strange, almost bewildered look flitted across his eyes, as if he was surprised by the thoughts which, like some swooping bird, had darted into his consciousness. But unlike the bird, indifferent to praise or blame, was he sundered?

And then his valet rushed in. "Can I help? An accident? I'm not late, am I?"

You're too bloody late to help me, Abasi. He cackled. *Damn …*

'No Nicodemus, you're not late.' Her voice was soft, she smiled at him. *Get me out of here, damn you Abasi.*

'Michael was yelling, his hands clutching at the railings, but then his voice gentled: *thank you, Tarsha … thank you my dear for rescuing me. You should go now.* And then, without a blink of recognition, he murmured: *Nicodemus can finish me off.* Nicodemus looked at me with the hint of a smile on his lips as he bent to help him. I like to think I heard Michael whisper his thanks.'

* * *

She made her way back through the study. Glancing again at the strewn papers and files, unable to erase the image of Michael sobbing over them, awkwardly, in the manner of someone unaccustomed to crying. *The mess … is my life.*

It was as though time was suspended. Putting together a slab of cheese, a few crackers with a bottle of his favourite Beaujolais, she could hear Michael shuffling around among the papers, trawling back and forth from his study, the shredder was chewing away. *A few last things!* He called, wheeling himself into the sitting room: *It's finished! I'm so tired.* As, smiling weakly, he joined her and they chatted. She talked about her day in the office, spoke of the increasing pressure on the charity arm, it seemed like news to him.

Well it's your baby, squeeze a bit out of the Board, there's plenty of room to move. Then he looked intently at me. *Can O'Connell push something Nicodemus's way?*

'Michael, you are a one.'

He Graduates in May you know. I thought, oh, … I'm so … tired. His voice trailed off. *Think about it, will you. He never took advantage …*

She told him she would do it gladly, but that's another story. The conversation was rambling, disjointed. Emotionally drained and distracted they found some relief in the wine but didn't need dinner. After he'd gone to his room and was in bed and Nicodemus had discretely left, she went to him. He smiled and opened his arms and she lay with him. *I haven't been so happy since those glorious summer days, on the sickle shoulder of the hill,* he whispered. She felt him weeping softly, but although she'd told Andrew, the others didn't need to know that. The next day he was dead.

'When we returned to London after the '98 trip, as I've shared with Andrew, it was obvious he was gravely ill and sick at heart, his depression was overwhelming. That unsurpassable coal-black hair and his entire aura that he'd worked so hard to maintain were depleted, as if mirroring his defeated will to live. Even as he tried to conceal them, problems with his deteriorating health – increasing incidents of renal and circulatory failure and frequent infections, which the doctors had warned could be a consequence of his condition – were becoming more obvious as they struggled to contain the resultant pain especially from gout and the kidney

311

failure and a general systemic breakdown.' She paused, musing on how she had even wondered if it could be HIV, but didn't need to share it. She remembered Rudi's stories of Michael in London and Paris, and one of his doctors had raised the possibility, but Michael would not countenance any form of testing. As far as she was told there was nothing in the autopsy. 'Often in the night I'd hear him shouting, groaning, muttering, as though his soul was in protest. He barely slept and his powerful body was ravaged. But he made clear it was his problem, not mine. *I'll manage it.* Yet, he began selectively to unburden himself, admitting to a long list of personal failings including confessing (not his favourite word!) to a self-loathing which I now think, coloured everything like a stain. It was as if he was slowly, warily crawling out from under his carefully erected shell … emerging into the open. And although he was talking through a fog of depression and regret, I think he was trying to bare his soul, even though he boasted he didn't have one and tried to prove it: *A sentimental construct, my dear.*

'But I digress. I'd like to read to you from the fragments of writing he left': *I had hoped to wipe the slate clean but you brought me asunder my dear, brought me to grief on your affection, dare I say forgiveness (?), and I lost myself for a moment!*

'Or found?' Susannah whispered to Ben, as Natasha continued.

Much will be made of the symbolism of this ending, or do I exaggerate? Will it pass as a shadow? I had thought to have a final clearing out. I'm sorry you got caught up in that yesterday, Natasha. So unprepared for your intrusion. … Intruder is not so wide of the mark. You've broken so effectively into my life, I can't get you out of my head. Is this love? There; it's taken a lifetime to make that small admission. You've brought me to the brink.

'He invites us in, I think,' she murmured.

I used to think weak all those who loved me: why should they love me, when I didn't love myself? Couldn't they see how they diminished themselves? I gave no cause to love me; I wasn't theirs to shower love on. It rendered them vulnerable, fallible. Didn't they see the anger and desolation that lay beneath the mask I put on for the world?

'The page is stained with what look like water marks, crossings out. I wonder if he was crying and he has inscribed a huge $+$ over several lines. ~~I'm so tired of pretending to be someone I wasn't.~~

Was this a moment of truth? Then he rushes on. *How homeless I felt, staring into a blank void. The horrors I've carried from the swaddling rug of killing her, my Rebecca, I would let no-one fill the space she left. I've spent all my life loving her in her absence. Yearning for that love. Longing for it. The loneliness. Stop my racing mind. Oh, how I dressed them up in search of her! Some I adored, others, no more than seeing if I could find her likeness in them. My raven-haired Rebecca who only had eyes for me. My Rebeccaa. Oh, I would have gone to war for her! Ha-ha; even now, I fool myself, and will not confess it.* The pen is slashing into the paper. *Even in these last rites ...*

The despicable father. I cast him out early, and everyone caught up in this tangled passion. Poor old Bra thought he could fill the vacancy with his decency, and Claire saw through me I know but out of her love, no less than Bra, tried to force a change, and the beautiful boy, in the honesty of his love. Easy game. There is a gap in the text; some crossing out. ~~*Why need I lie?*~~

In the end, he was just collateral damage. The Gods are cruel! ... Christ, I'm all over the place. We were never going away. Expose myself like that! The rugby trial was a simple side-step. Imagine what people would have said if we'd gone. Together? He was in my private world but to have gone with him would have made it public. I could never have given him that kind of power. I always kept something in reserve; had to take account. It was easy for Charlie, and while I fed off the energy of his love, I couldn't commit to it.'

'*Easy for Charlie*; easy?' Susannah hissed, breaking in.

'*Charlie was the risk taker. It wasn't a difficult decision to abandon him. I knew he would be hurt, but I was protecting myself, don't you see? The risk ...!*

To be honest. My entire existence was a mass of contradictions. Even as a child, deep forces moved me. Wanting people to want me – here's a bit of Proust for Charlie – once I've got them, I don't want them. I'd sweep Charlie along in those moods, then when I tired of him or I looked like being touched too deeply, having played him like a fish and had him properly hooked, I'd chuck him back. He didn't know what to make of it, or how to deal with it. Sometimes I hated myself, but this was about self-preservation. Charlie had brought me to a crisis of identity. The public heroics of rugby or having my way in a boardroom were easy options.

'Options? As though you have choices!' Claire gasped, her hand up to her throat as if grief and understanding, buried for so long, were caught there. 'And that streak of childish cruelty he seemed able to exercise at will. Is he saying this rejection of love was a part of his nature, had infected his relationships from birth?' She looked at Charles. 'Sorry love, is this too painful?'

But, it was he who touched her hand, soothing her. 'Not any more. It's just the tangled weeds of a life, now. Sadly, and this is what is breaking your heart I think, he didn't know what to do with the love we offered, or with his own desires. Did they frighten him? It was as if he couldn't trust them.' Charles was threading his way through the mire of their disrupted relationship. 'I think we are facing the paradox of the man. As I've learned this weekend, he never cut me free. He was the puppeteer to the end; spun funds my way as long as I didn't escape! But is this to simplify it, making it easier to digest? As we've heard today, while he didn't dare let me into his life, couldn't acknowledge what we meant to each other, I wondered if his subsequent behaviour was a muted expression of love, as if he wanted to keep me in a certain place and time; or am I deceiving myself?'

'Well he did say he could never bury that voice inside, tormenting him. But, look, I'm not being unsympathetic Charles, I don't think you should take too much comfort from it.' Natasha was mixing tenderness with a necessary candour. 'For, if this confession was a sign of weakness, he also boasted he had you all in his hand. *Easier to manage them all in the one place.*' She stopped, looked at them: 'O, it took me a long while to work it out, because he tried not to let me into that side of his life, but when I met you lovely people who he liked to think he controlled, I knew he had failed, that I didn't have to worry about you, you'd escaped anyway; I saw how you flew in your imaginations, achieved things you could never dream of and certainly he had not dreamt of.'

Unable to clear her head of his loathing of his father, Claire was chipping away. 'Do you think Michael blamed Edward for his inability to give or receive the love we gave, and which he seems so able to disparage?'

'I'm no authority on what drove him,' Natasha replied, 'but, helpless on the death of his mother, I think Edward's actions added to a sense of abandonment.'

'Yes. He told me he wouldn't have seen his father more than a few days a year when he was growing up.' Ben added, looking out at them all. 'You'd know that Claire; said he hadn't been to St Pat's, never saw him play rugby… not until the rugby trial, then he said he was all over him like a rash. To no good effect, however. While it sounds as though he had regrets about some things, he had none about his treatment of Edward.' Claire and Bran nodded.

'He sacked him.' Ben added, as a murmur of surprise echoed around the room: "Sacked?"

'Well, let's not beat around the bush. Edward didn't go voluntarily. I'd just gone into Mick's office and he was waving a newspaper article at me. *Stuck it to him,* he'd shouted. Given what I've shared with you today Charlie, this is a minor secret. It helps perhaps, to strip away a bit more of that outer casing of his, even if in death. I'm breaking a confidence,' he hesitated, looking at Susannah who touched his arm, protectively. 'But … what the hell, let's get it out: a piece of O'Connell family history. We're talking 1974 or 75.'

'It was one of the last meetings Mick and I had in the Bent Street offices and he told me how he'd conducted a thorough examination of the Company for his honours paper; cast a forensic eye over it, he said. After that there wasn't much he didn't know about OGH and the *fraud and malfeasance* behind the reconstitution of the family company in 1945.'

'I've never understood how he got control of the company though, Ben,'

'Bran probably knows, Charlie, but Mick said he always knew he had a 45% holding, although Edward had tried to keep it secret. *Ways and means*, he'd sniggered, when he told me.'

'Of course he would have known,' Claire remarked, nodding. 'He was one of those kids who had to know everything. He would've wanted to make Edward pay; probably used it as motivation during his rehabilitation.'

'I think you're right,' Ben said. 'Instead of losing focus on the business, it was sharpened and, with Edward inattentive and complacent, Michael was drawn to questions of succession.'

'He didn't waste any time acting did he?' Charles suggested.

'No. Went straight for the jugular. *I have a majority holding, Edward. I'm taking over.* It was as bald as that. "Well … you're a touch premature there, boyo." He'd said, parrying the attack. But Michael had done the due diligence and went for him. *Don't 'boyo' me Edward. I want you out of your office by tomorrow and if you wish to retain the London place, you'll pay for it. If not, it will be disposed of.*

'He said Edward still didn't get it. "You're getting a bit uppity. I haven't stepped aside and you haven't accounted for the minority, the Withers and Threadgold loyalty holdings. Didn't you know about that? Still a touch green are we?"

Ah, the 'loyalty holdings'! I've not only accounted for them but, given that your two henchmen would face fraud charges for their role in the delisting of OPL in 1946, if the circumstances were ever to become public … it wasn't difficult to arrive at a price for their loyalty. So 'boyo' now has 55% of O'Connell Global and as soon as the paper work is in place, and it should be ready after lunch, you will relinquish any day-to-day involvement in the company.

'At which, apparently turning puce, Edward had roared: "You little shit; I'm your father. You can't …!" But he had.'

As Ben related the incident there was a background chorus of muffled gasps and sighs at Michael's audacity. Yet, Natasha knew it as a part of his weaponry. 'At first, I thought he couldn't help himself, had to strike out at anyone who challenged him in some way or he saw as a threat, but after a while I recognized he rarely acted on a random impulse; everything was strategic, planned, calculated.'

'Well,' Ben replied. 'It was brutal; he made no concessions. He was roaring with laughter when he told me. Said his father shuffled out of the office shaking as if he'd been shelled. Isolated, ruined, abandoned; he was obliterated.'

'The exuberance, such delight in crushing him.' Sue sighed. 'I remember it as if it was yesterday. Despite all he did for me, I couldn't see him in the same light again.'

'If it's any comfort Ben,' Natasha said as she thumbed through the document, 'he didn't know what to make of you either! Ah, here it is. Parts of it are crossed out, there are gaps and spaces as though he didn't know quite what to write. I left it out when I was reading.

And then there is Ben; ~~never quite fell for it~~. Gave everything. But never had him ~~hooked~~. A very independent spirit, that one! ~~Enormous regard for him~~. He appreciated what I'd done, but he wouldn't kiss my boots.

Ben looked at everyone in turn: 'Well, fancy that.' He murmured, brushing it off as he returned to Michael's actions, for they were not only audacious – precocious even, but as he said: 'they were so cold-blooded. I mean … I was the same age, no more than twenty-three; an innocent. It's amazing. *It's all about Power and control, Benny*, he used to say. As you've said, Claire, it's as if he was born to it. But he distinguished between the two. *Power's useful. I'm not averse to cracking a few heads or unleashing my temper, but control is what I'm after.* He wasn't shy about it; boasted to me that one of his strengths was he was never embarrassed by or had regrets about using whatever tactics were required; nor did he worry about the effect on others.'

Charles looked at Ben. 'I know what you're saying. I often felt naïve when I was with him, or was it something in his style?' He mused. 'The mind wasn't simply a place for reception and response for him; it was an instrument of combat like a fist.'

Natasha gasped. Her hand clutching the table rim. White knuckled. But she said nothing. Oblivious, Susannah continued. 'It's one of the mysteries. Some say he'd done it all before in another life … that he brought experience with him when he came into the world. Or, is that too inscrutable?' Her comment hung in the air.

'Well, I don't plod around in that strange country,' Ben replied, 'but in terms of his business decisions, he made his choices early. (Was it only business decisions?) He idolised his grandfather and liked to reflect on the beautiful and enduring buildings he created.'

'Here, look, it's in front of me.' Now recovered, Natasha started reading: *I couldn't replicate Timothy's idealism, nor did I want to reproduce those monuments to brutalism Edward built in Berlin and London after the war. They are my father's legacy, he made a fortune dragging the O'Connell name and reputation through the dirt: I'll create nothing and make my living out of doing it.*

'It was a boast. But he was discriminating. For a while he took delight in disposing of buildings associated with his father, keeping intact his grandfather's heritage. I'm getting to know our portfolio, believe me, those grand old buildings are the jewels in the *O'Connell* crown.'

'Yes, yes: he did what he set out to do; he built a great financial empire, but at what cost?' Bran's face was drawn. 'I think he needs our compassion, not our ire.'

In addition to the light breeze wafting in through the French doors as the afternoon began to close in, the cold air of reality also brought a chill into the room.

'When I first read this document,' Natasha confessed, 'I wondered if he was grasping at everything he thought he'd left behind: like salt, tasting it again increases the thirst? But now I don't know what to make of it; I think he turned his love of his mother into an excuse. Or, was it his sexuality? Oh, I wept for him in anger, and in pity. She paused, looked at them all. 'And I think you're right, Bran, be gentle with his poor tortured spirit. In those last few years every corner of his life seemed to expose a crisis that set upon him like crows to a carcass and having shied away from the usual expressions of affection ... there was only one place to look.'

The room was quiet as Andrew, as if protectively, suggested they might be confusing an apologia – 'if that is what this strange hybrid is?' – with an apology. Isn't it strange, he left us with two documents, the obituary on Monday, and this one today. Both hybrids, I'd say. I'm suggesting you read them with caution. There may be a bit of breast beating, a *mea culpa* or two unless I'm mistaken in this last piece but, in its very nature, the form invites evasion and a denial, a passing of blame. It's only another form of story after all and while some may want to argue stories are the guardians of history, of truth, they are only words you know, and paper can lie as readily as the spoken word. Its beguiling formal structure might seduce, but knowing a little of the man, Michael is quite capable of turning it to his ends.'

Natasha caught his eye, smiled thank you, while privately admiring his serendipity; thought it was almost as if he was prompting from the wings!

I wish I had a poem in me to hide behind, a piece of confessional sobbing, but I'm left with this poor dithering hand driven, hardly driven, not even guided. ~~Infected~~. Affected. That's more like it in its ambiguity. Affected perhaps by this wracked brain, a mind now almost unclothed, at last sacked, plundered and wrecked. So what is this? Not a farewell missive. Fuck them all. I left them behind years ago. Soared out of their orbit. Over and above Celtic Ponds. Should I apologise? Damn you all!

I'll play my pipes to them. Put things straight. Is there a need to do that or is this an unwarranted assumption? ~~Oh, this feigning at humility~~! A sort of dies irae! I'll vent my spleen. None more so than on Edward, abrogating his responsibility to everything... ~~to me, his only child, his name, the firm~~. Oh, how I detested him. Why am I going there again? His writing is now a scrawl; slashes on the page torn by the ferocity of his scribbling.

'It wasn't only the neglect,' Natasha exclaimed. 'It was what he called his mediocrity. His waste of every opportunity given to him: *Riverview, Cambridge, the business: he didn't bank them*. He was always comparing him with you Bran. Saw you as a beacon of integrity and industry. He thought you had made so much of your life, having started with nothing and took living in the world seriously. He was enormously proud of your war.

'He said, after reading your diaries, his father's wartime bacchanal filled him with contempt.' *What did my father do? Had a riot through Mayfair, messing around in London's entrails, shagging, and feathering his nest!*

'Such loathing.' Charlie sighed. 'It surfaced very early. Blamed him for not insisting he attend *Riverview* or backing him into *Cambridge*.'

'Ah, *Riverview* and *Cambridge*. This is all very strange,' Natasha revealed. 'From the moment I met him he talked about the wonderful

319

education he'd had. I didn't know what to make of it, as I soon found out he was lying. And he knew I knew, but never acknowledged it. In fact he based an ideal of education on the fabrication: formal, intellectually rigorous, elite, with lashings of philosophy, not some trendy rubbish like management; on the rowing; the stately grounds; the gargoyles. She paused, as an air of collective unease settled across the room.

'You are all surprised? It was one of his big hobby-horses. He'd puff himself up very grandly, very self-important and let loose on the failure of modern education. *Universities bobbing up like weeds. Factories more like, churning 'em out!* On he would rant. *Quotas, quotas? ... not to keep 'em out, but to let the masses in! The world'll be awash with more graduates that we know what to do with before long. Why not take only the best?'* Education's *dead and gone,* he'd roar, I remember it as if it was yesterday. *Business Schools and their diabolical MBAs ruling the roost.*

'So this is where his Chancellorship of Newhouse that we read of in the obituary comes in.' Charles was thoughtful: 'a vehicle in which to practise his idealism.'

'Yes Charles, you might have thought so; but the emperor had no clothes. For all the acting out ... a humanist voice in the commercial wilderness, he wasn't seeking solutions. Just the opposite; Michael wanted to exploit the vacuum that had opened up between the old and the new. With its privatization, Education was big business and a new arm, *O'Connell Educational Services,* was ready to exploit its potential.'

'Newhouse? Off the Old Dover Road. University of *Management and Technology,* wasn't it?' Andrew asked. 'I've heard of it. The management tail wags that dog! Certainly not a *Cambridge* of the south! Although, let's not get too idealistic ...' But he didn't finish, muttering about big money talking wherever it is.

'That's the one. *A hell of a lot to pay for a crimson gown, a Tudor bonnet and the name on a concrete slab,* Michael joked in private, omitting to explain that Newhouse had nothing to do with idealism and everything to do with profit. He went into the details with me; it's a bit vague now, but ... O, enough, *O'Connell* was in on the ground floor. I don't need to go on,' she sighed, looking drained.

Charlie grimaced, an edge to his voice: 'Did he believe in anything?'

'Well it was like his view of the economy, arguing for standards on the one hand, he wanted open slather in his own dealings. I agonized over it but by the nineties, I'd come to the conclusion he was completely nihilistic, and what interested me was not the arguments he was regurgitating but why he felt the need to. Why perpetuate the lie about his education? It was as though he had turned his life into a fiction.'

'Is that how he saw himself?' Susannah wondered aloud.

'I'm sure that was the public face he wanted to present. But, over time I came to suspect that it conflicted with a private version and, I wonder, in the end, if that inner life was forcing its way, almost unbidden, to the surface.' Natasha looked quizzically at them, her musing, a question, rather than a statement.

'I've been thinking about this.' It was Andrew, tentative, thoughtful. 'There is a lot of talk about the paradoxes and the contradictions of his behaviour.' He paused. 'I think we have expectations of human identity being unified, singular, but in Michael's case I didn't think there was any such homogeneity. His identity was conflicted, divided, even fragmented. He saw life as a continual battle ground. I think he saw this fragmentation as a strength. It was used as a part of his armoury. He alludes to it in his obituary. It carries its own conflict, however, and both – can we call them identities? – need to be respected; you can't choose to ignore one or other of them which, if I understand Natasha correctly, is what he had done and, in those last dreadful couple of years, it brought him low; weakened him, mirrored perhaps by that mess, that debris which lay at his feet when she found him: "My life," he'd said. He had lost control and was in despair.'

Natasha was almost whispering, pleading for understanding as she told them he had reached the point where the unconscious, so long restrained by his hard mind, was released and the past was now ever-present in all its mutability, in everything he touched, smelled, saw; it erupted out of certain words or gestures; certain lights or sounds haunted him. She had watched this normally austere man unravelling before her eyes, as the past rushed at him, sent him hurtling, but he could no longer manage it; leaving him tentative, exhausted, bewildered out of futility. 'I think this confusion is inscribed into this document. Listen!

I'm wandering. The mess, yesterday. I want to explain. I've spent my life accumulating things, counting, accounting for them, giving structure, order, even an insane purpose to my life, but what are those things now? They are the offal of a life, evacuated now from their files: do you see? Ah stop! My mind is a chamber of echoes. Ah, clichés won't do it! But like these people I've spent my life trying to restrain and contain, they were never my own. The horror! The horror of it. What was hidden is breaking out! I'd take over others' words and images, digest them as my own, and now it's just waste to be sluiced away.

'He was finding it difficult to concentrate, I think. There's a whole section blacked out, as if audited ... censored? Then he starts off again, at a tangent.

What to make of Clar? I drew up the battle lines very early. You know better where the attacks may come from! Damned woman, never had her measure!

Natasha looked fondly at her as she continued. *She was one of my great failures, along with that holy priest. I released all my wiles on him, and when I couldn't have my way with him he became expendable. It sounds calculating, but it was only a survival tactic. Him or me! Whatever it takes.* 'He's rambling now, the text is barely legible.'

Claire could not contain herself. 'You said he was like a wily fox, Tasha, looking for weaknesses, vulnerabilities. He tried to win me over with little gifts, flowers, a term of endearment, even playing to my interests: dwelling on poems and novels he was reading or tales from the rugby club, but I came to see it as a form of camouflage. I lost trust in him, even as I tried to plumb his depths. It's so ugly. He knew the impact of his actions, but as we are finding out, while he may have admired some of his targets he was still prepared to tear them down. Nothing was sacred.' Claire held her palms out in despair, 'I try to excuse him, but ...what can I say!' She shook her head, winced, 'My word, you learned to read him well Natasha; that would have made him uncomfortable.'

'It was like swimming against an unpredictable current. There's a certain satisfaction in staying afloat. However,' she muttered, grimly, 'my self-preservation lay in trying to fathom him, account for his behaviour. I made progress but, … you must have noticed, when I was here in '98, I was at breaking point, I'd nearly drowned. Yet, as I've hinted, things changed and I stayed with him. I'm not saying I'm a saint. In the end he needed me. But I digress. He didn't have these matters on his mind in his confessional mode towards the end. Far from it. He said he'd become so much like the people he dealt with, he could see into their shrivelled hearts and devious minds.'

'Listen!' Natasha was solemn and began reading. *Some contrition, a tear or two, but not for those dreadful politicians and their bureaucrats I had to deal with. Thank God, we keep electing these dysfunctional, maladjusted monsters. And, their grubby side-kicks! Don't start me on them: God! They are as venal as their masters! And those pin-striped Merchant Bankers and the like. I planned each charted course and exploited those feckless bastards. Had my way with them, all in the name of business and then sent them packing, until next time! I did it my way with them all.*

'By now he was tearing at the paper; his pen biting into it. *Their weedling, sniveling* ~~kissing of my arse~~ *as I pushed a crumb their way. They can kiss my arse.*

'Oh dear,' Claire cried, and held out her hands in despair. 'How awful … all mixed up among his last thoughts.'

'I haven't been able to come to terms with the vitriol in these outbursts,' Natasha sighed. 'This railing at the very world he operated in, wasn't uncommon … but he was a dealer…do you see the contradictions? Along with the money they stalked, they'd all become footloose, those money men, with allegiances to nothing else.'

As she read on, Natasha shook herself as though brushing off dirt, overtaken by a memory of how she'd wept when he told her of the money he'd made out of Russia. He'd come storming into the lounge room one evening after being at his club. Liquor and a wild exuberance colouring his voice. *Vive la Russie*! He'd bellowed. *What a killing*! *Some called it theft!*

Those asset sales…what rubbish. They were there for the taking: give 'em to the workers? Christ, they wouldn't know what to do with them. Ah, better than sex! Did making money fill the vacuum she wondered, but instead turned and left the room as he followed her, calling: *Pity your man Velen had such a sticky end, my dear.*

She knew what he was alluding to. Vera had told her that her father had been found dead in the Moscow Canal, his mouth stuffed with British pound notes. Scowling, she left him roaring in ugly glee at his joke. So much for Velen!

Emerging from her nightmare recollection, she murmured, 'Michael said he was a creature of his time. Oh, I'm sorry …' she put her hand to her mouth, 'thinking aloud. I was thinking about some of Michael's hobby horses. When he was astride them, it was as if I wasn't there. He'd pose and answer his own questions regardless of whether I had a view or not. He might stop mid-sentence muttering *what do I know about that anyway* he'd mumble, but he'd hurtle on, ranging far and wide: money-laundering, the mad global spree going on around him, *astro-bloody-nomical,* he would yell. He's at it here! *Assets, what a ridiculous term! Toxic. And the banks – as safe as a bank! What rubbish, bloody great casinos. It will erupt, it'll sweep away the world as we know it! I guess my race is run! But no regrets, I ran the race and I won. A bit of the old Clash song, eh!*'

'What loathing he had for them. But wasn't he touted as the banker's host?'

'Oh Charles, yes, the number of these men we entertained around our dinner table. He'd fed and liquored them all his adult life wherever he was – from Sydney and Melbourne, a cowboy or two from Queensland or Perth – to London and New York. He'd spent as much time in merchant bank boardrooms as he had at home. *What a lot they were, playing pass the parcel!* He'd bellow. *Unsophisticated and bloody shonky, but the numbers were huge. I had to play but I did 'em over, selling on the risk before they did me in.* It was awful, the delight he took in it.' She paused, pensive, overtaken by an image of Michael, champagned to the gills, careering around the living room in his wheelchair, waving his arm as if wielding a lasso, spilling his drink and hooting: *Fuck 'em: I'm a one-man Merchant Bank. Yee-hah!*

Returning to the document: *You might be appalled, my dear; so few regrets … did it my way …: plugged into the mood of my age and ran with the dogs.*

'The writing is unsteady, falling down the page. There are gaps in the text, words omitted. I was appalled, and yet, …'

'To the end!' Claire exploded, 'he still thought it was all about money! Everything had to do with investment potential, speculative value, no other kind of value mattered.' *Whatever it takes,* she reflected. 'It's so awfully sad Natasha.'

'Well, it seems as though he'd closed off that other side of his being which may have given him alternatives.' Susannah remarked.

'Refills anyone?' Andrew asked, offering momentary relief to the sombre group.

'Have a look at the pot, will you, Doc,' Charles whispered as, strangely detached, he mused on the unfolding revelations. 'It sounds as though he'd so objectified the economy that it was like *Fate*; as though he'd entered a world where everyone is at the mercy of the pagan Gods. Were we just his plaything? Did he feel above it all, do you think?'

'Well, he got angry like the gods.' Natasha replied, with the smudge of a sad smile on her lips. 'The way he vented his spleen and the spite, taking out his petty vengeances. Dealing out random acts of malice or charity! He touches on it here, but it's quite banal.

They all thought they were gods and I played with them, but always on my terms.

Sounds like a confession, eh? ~~*Ah, well, I was never one for Confession.*~~ *But as I face the black tomorrow, with my body rotting in its shell, you, my dear, are as close as I'll ever get to a Confessor. I don't expect it to open any doors for me; it won't lead to the greater salvation the faithful yearn for.* ~~*I'm not after absolution.*~~ *Expiation? I know the road I've chosen* ~~*I have no regrets about the one not taken and deceived myself*~~ *…! Choices, …? Aren't they just alternatives? Yet, I've come to believe some things are not a matter of choice.*

'So late to arrive at this realization! In his case, he may have been able to choose between several alternatives about how he lived his life, perhaps, but some things are not open to choice.' Claire's voice was strained, shading into a whisper. 'He hid from the truth of his being all his life. I think this denial was at the core of those decisions he made. And, as you said Ben, he made them very early. But, finally, it couldn't be denied. We've skirted around it all our lives.' Bran lay his hand over hers, soothing it. 'Oh, Pet.'

'We may not have liked the way he made his fortune,' Natasha reflected, 'and may have worried how it hardened him – oh, don't talk to me about that hard mind – or wished he'd done it in other ways but, the subterfuge, the burial of his true identity – God, I had my role to play in that,' she wailed – was another matter. From the outset I think he thought if he exposed his homosexuality – the word hung in the air like a ghost – it would weaken him, would make him vulnerable; it had no place in the image he had projected from a very early age.' She looked at them. 'Is that too confronting? Yet, it seems to me he wanted it exposed at the end; encoded into this strange document. And I'm sure his gift of the cello was a part of this truth. Some will see it as an act of atonement, I think it was an act of love and, perhaps was a message to you, Charles, confirming that love, even as he could not speak it. But let's not fool ourselves, he could now safely make it, it would have no consequences for he was not much longer for this world and he had no hopes of another!'

Everyone was hushed, absorbing perhaps the doleful chimes of irony and this belated truth. A portrait of Michael O'Connell in its numerous shades was being sketched in broad brush strokes, many by his own hand.

* * *

As Charlie checked the paella, Natasha continued: 'Our late conversations were very moving. Michael needed comforting, he would never ask for it, but letting him talk, I would soothe his hands in mine, running my fingers over the veins, just gentling him. Recoiling from my touch at first, he gave in to it.'

'Gave in, what a strange way of putting it', Charlie murmured.

'I didn't love him, perhaps had never, nor, for that matter, did he let me, but I felt deeply for him and he was in awful pain. He was exhausted, his black eyes were sunk deep and the skin around them had turned a muddy brown; his handsome face was ravaged as he confronted his life, realising starkly now I think, despite his great wealth, how he had wasted it. But he could not stop talking.'

'Did you feel you had to force your way in?' It was Charlie again.

'No, he had to talk and I let him.' She brushed the question off with a smile and a fey nod of her head. 'In a strange way, it was heart-warming and spoke of the thaw that I thought was occurring.' He was dealing with his regrets, uncaring now of how it exposed him, but found that was simple compared to the anguish he felt in exploring the loves he'd had in this tattered thing he called his life.

Now, in my death throes, needing no stimulation on the ceiling to animate me, even my mind has turned against me, keeps sending me a jumble of images as if to haunt; memories come crashing through, unbidden, as they might for someone suffering a terrible trauma. How I deceived myself. Oh Christ ... here they come, wave upon breaking wave of memories as if they are happening now... swamping me. Save me!

'My God,' Susannah gasped, 'that came from a dark place!'

Natasha paused, letting everyone take it all in. 'Yes, by now, I think he was terrified, of his self. He wanted me there while he talked. Like a fear of the dark. I wondered if he'd deceived himself into believing he could simply edit out these relationships from the public version of his life, but at the end had to face that they were closer to the man he was than the public persona so artfully created as he buried his true self deeper and deeper, covering it with all the accoutrements – he might have said – with all the detritus of living purchased with his money and power. It sounds existential, but I think it is an image he'd been crafting ever since he denied the self that Charlie was releasing, if that makes any sense. *I constructed a disguise – very successfully I think – aided by the wonderful prop of my wheelchair, to distract everyone I met from trying to see behind the mask. Or get too close.*

'I think, as Andrew hinted, it's reasonable to ask which Michael is talking out of this document he left behind. But, I think there is a groping towards a kind of truth; a kind of gift, perhaps?' She murmured, as if an aside, putting the papers away, 'let's leave it be, it's done its job!'

'Gift, Natasha? When you were here in '98 you mentioned that he was preparing a Millennial Gift; did that eventuate? I thought, perhaps it might be enclosed with this document? Bran asked. 'It was something of a mystery at the time.'

'Ah, the Millenial Gift!' Natasha smiled. 'I didn't ever think I could ever smile about it, but now I can. Michael had shared an early version of it with me – it was a vile contrivance designed to tear the Ponds apart, and I was to be the executioner', the gasps echoed around the room: "Why?" "What are you talking about?" "Gift?" 'Ssshh, let me finish. I had been haunted by the document since he first spoke of it, but it had lain dormant, like a silent threat, in his filing cabinet until I noticed it scattered among the debris on that dreadful afternoon. When I asked him about it at breakfast the next morning, asking what his intentions were, he smiled openly, his eyes momentarily clear and shining like a lover, and reached for my hand: *I couldn't burden you with that, my dear. Don't worry your head about it. I'll do it my way.*

I shook his hand off: 'But you'll do it!' I wailed. 'Don't condescend to me. Why must you do it?' Once again I had that hollow feeling at the pit of my stomach, my emotions contorted and jumbled by the contrast between this vile action and his benign smile and the tenderness of the previous night, I stared at him. "Do what you will!" I couldn't stay in the house, and went for a walk, seeking out the peace of the *Serpentine*: a familiar retreat, my head spinning, my heart in turmoil, sobbing …

'It happened while I was out.' Her face was grim, closed. 'Poor Nicodemus found him. I mean I wouldn't have been gone for more than an hour. He was devastated, stunned.' Her mind was overtaken by recollections of that last morning. Pale, Nicodemus was shaking, sopping wet, he was kneeling holding Michael's decimated body released from the chair to his shoulder; an embrace. 'But Natasha, he was a good swimmer. I'd help him in and stay w…with him.' He was sobbing. 'And help him out.

He hadn't swum for a while, but he could manage without me. He knew the risks. Why would he do it, fully dressed, strapped in? I wasn't late. I ...'

'Nicodemus, it's not your fault. No-one could have stopped him. Don't blame yourself. He wouldn't want you to; he was very fond of you. Perhaps the chair slipped out of his control. That could happen, couldn't it?'

'After the police had left Nicodemus wondered what Michael was doing with his files beside the pool. "He always kept anything like that in his office."

'I can only guess Michael wanted it to be found. I can guess which one it was. But it was empty, except for the pages I've shared with you today and a ghastly little quotation pinned to the cover.' As she spoke the lines came back at her like a punch: *They will chortle at my death!* But they didn't need to know that. Andrew knew, that was enough, and he could be trusted with it.

'But Natasha none of it has happened. We don't even know what it was?'

'Nor would you, Bran, save to say, he was going to cast you all out. However, as I said, there was no Millenial document. Perhaps it also went through the shredder with a whole lot of other business documents. There was nothing to manage. And, you know, despite my anguish at the time, I can't be sure if there was anything in the file the day before. I have wondered if he'd changed his mind! He was in such a tortured state at the end, anything could have happened. He was just done with it all.'

'But you knew his intention; doesn't that carry some authority?'

'Charles, Charles, *my dear friend*, can't you be satisfied that he changed his mind.' Her face was drawn, closed. 'I like to think he did, that, as in this piece of writing you've just heard, he was reaching out to you. We'll never know what drove him in the end. Do we need to?'

Claire also had trouble letting go. 'Ambiguous to the end! But, oh dear, why push you away if he'd destroyed it? Was it hatred of his self? That you should not care for him?' She was fumbling around for some meaning. 'Even in death; we must not think well of him? Agh, my heart is broken all over again. That poor man and his *apologia!* What an extraordinary collection of warped memories, musings and fixations. Hardly an image of joy or delight among them. Right to the end, he wouldn't let us through his door!' She pushed her hands through her silver hair as if to cleanse them.

Natasha looked fondly at her, then, gathering up the large canvas bag she and Andrew had brought with them, she moved to the table and with a gentle sigh, released the contents onto the table. 'Perhaps this will give you a glimpse into what he treasured but never could display. There are things here that you may have blamed yourself for losing or misplacing, like that old poetry anthology of yours Claire, or the christening mug, the photograph of his mother, the early sketches of the Gully gardens that he made with you Charles when you were young.'

***

'Thank you for returning Bran's war diaries and letters, speaking as they do of war and our fledgling love. We've decided to knock them into shape. With a bit of luck *From Giarabub to Balikpapan* will be in your friendly bookshop next Anzac Day!'

'He cared for them, never trashed them as he did some things; had them carefully shelved. But he had separated this one piece. I hope you don't mind.' She passed them a single letter from Bran to Claire, written soon after they were married. 'I'll leave you to read it together.'

Claire gasped. 'Oh, B! How I cherished it.'

Dearest Claire: What a melancholy day it is. The only way I can talk to you is through this vastly inferior medium, for me anyway, of the letter. As you can see my darling, I am back, lying on my back actually, which I'd much rather be doing with you, perhaps feeding berries, into my mouth …

He was smiling. And they were transported back to an evening during one of his furloughs. Sitting on the floor of Claire's cottage, they were enjoying a feast he'd prepared, topped off with Granny's bottled berries in their juices.

'Can I forget it! Stop, stop! Even now I'm getting goose bumps.' They read on: *but I'm here and will shortly go down to the sick bay where they can look me over. I bet they'll get a surprise, having dined on the food of love, I reckon I'm looking pretty fit! Thank you; thank you. You retrieved me from my dark night; lifted me out of the miasma that one of the doctors at the camp said I had fallen into. In the last year dear, dear girl, you've introduced me to love, lived in the presence of every day.*

They read on skimming through comments about his wrecked father and his Mother, so scared of life she couldn't lift her eyes from her rosary and face it without that crutch. Of his loneliness and lack of a childhood.

'Oh, my darling, B,' she whispered.

I'd hardly ever done anything social. I didn't know much about women. had certainly never had sex. God, from what I saw of those hideous "drums" in Bombay, on our way back from Tobruk, and the stories I heard, I didn't see much fun in finding my manhood that way. So, I always felt a bit different; certainly shy and awkward, as your wonderful Grandmother said.

And then I looked into your eyes – into those wide shining pools of deep, deep gold – and I wanted to be there as a mate and a lover. You've taught me that love is not selfish or weakening or something to be shy of. It is to be in the moment, endlessly. How do you know these things? You wise woman. You have replenished me, my darling: and I use that word not accidentally; I am completely filled with love of you; I am replete; I am abundantly stocked; I am consummated. You are my replenisher. ...

'At the time, my darling man, I couldn't believe it of you.'

Natasha had rejoined them, her eyes glistening; she had read the letter. Claire looked at her: 'Here he was, this fellow untutored in the ways of love, the most private of men, baring his soul to me. What depths he was exploring and ... what an adventurer! In the context of what we've just heard about Michael, he was so courageous, so unafraid, he took on the unknown with no expectations and with an entirely open mind.'

Natasha smiled with them and thought of Michael keeping the letter all this time.

Elsewhere around the room there were gasps of surprise as they sifted through the collection. Just as it was for Claire and Bran, delight was mixed with nostalgia and a sweet sadness at again seeing these pieces, and an understanding that for whatever reason, they had meaning for Michael. Among his notes to Michael after his injury and the death of his father, drawings and water colours they'd done as kids, poems and paintings from their later escapades, Charles found Michael's pastiche on *Under Milkwood* and his own drawing on the theme. 'Even the rough score of my *Weeping of the Mountain Clouds*,' he exclaimed. 'How I've searched for that over the years … extraordinary!' There were copies of old academic calendars, posters, programmes and press cuttings of concerts from near and far; sometimes annotated, rarely generously: *can't they do better than Bega!*

'And here Charles,' Natasha was smiling, conducting him to the card he'd sent to Michael with a line of music: *The Heart's Ease,* I'd love to hear it. There's even a fragment of one of your poems:

> *We dance face to face*
> *dressed only in our ghost shirts*
> *celebrating our music.*
> *As season turns to season, the hillside turns,*
> *the wind leans heavily*
> *on the heart, carries cold messages*
> *from the snow country.*

Listening, Charles shuddered, 'that's from our last year at school. I'd forgotten it. *Cold messages from the snow country.* I must have had some premonition things would end badly.'

'Perhaps, but he could never let you go.' As she spoke, she moved over to the wall and turned around a small painting which she had left leaning face-in.

'Ah …,' Charlie sighed, 'so that's where it got to. He wouldn't have liked this scrap floating around!' He was holding *Taking our pleasure at Apple Pocket:* Charles' cubist painting of the boy lovers, into the corner of which was tucked an old Brownie photo of Michael, dripping wet after a swim, smiling into the camera. 'The paint's faded but not the memories.'

'He may not have wanted anyone to see it, but it hung in the study at Hunters Hill, always close to him. And the photo; Michael's beaming smile!'

Charles smiled whimsically. 'How well it captures a moment in our young lives.'

Ben found letters spanning twenty years. There were prints of photos of the *Clifton* garden that had appeared in *Country Life* and *House and Garden*, as well as feature articles in the specialist magazines about both the *Clifton* and the Gully gardens. There were also newspaper cuttings and photographs from his first game for the *Tigers – Wonderful debut by Temple. Fed generously by another prodigious talent, Michael O'Connell,* – to his last – *Tigers say Farewell to one of their Greatest. Many say Ben Temple's retirement is premature. Anyone at his last game can only agree, watching him lead the backs with a magnificent display of ball-handling and running. For ten years now – he is still only 27 – he has enlivened our weekends, we should not begrudge his leaving. Temple explained that his focus is now on his landscaping business. He hopes those who have enjoyed his football will derive a different pleasure from the work he and Charles Greenwood are putting into their gardens; for no less than in rugby, he will still be entertaining us.* The cuttings were dated and marked. The second, with the gently ironic: *Well, he did do it without me!*

Susannah was looking at several grainy photos of him in his League hey-day, mud spattered in one: *Leader of the Backs,* he appears with his arms around his fellow backs after the victorious '75 Grand Final. 'I've never seen any of these.'

'Neither have I Suze, well not since they were published anyway,' he laughed, 'long time ago sweetheart. Where did he get them?'

Natasha grinned. 'Michael continued to receive the *Southern Highlands Gazette* right up until the end. There wasn't a lot he didn't know! And what about this fragment?

Your strength is not only in body, bone and muscle,
holding your life together,
but in your simplicity of purpose, honed by honesty
not learned from creed or classroom.
It grows from the sweat, pain and small pleasures
of a working childhood where games are beyond the daily
compass.

'It's a work-in-progress I'd say, and the rest is lost, but Ben he's celebrating you.'

'Over all that time and he never responded!' Ben exclaimed, 'but,' he added, shifting the focus and holding a separate bunch of carefully annotated cuttings of Australian rugby tours to the UK: 'this is interesting: *Ella! That's how to play five-eighth!* Right up to 1999: *Burke beats the Springboks with his boot!* 'These explain the silence, I think,' for attached to them, in isolation on a single foolscap sheet, was the *Sydney Morning Herald's* bold headline on his injury: *Promising Career Cut Short.* The article had been torn off.

'How sad,' Claire sighed, 'that says it all. The door slammed shut on those dreams. He might even have played with Ella if he'd kept going.'

'He never talked about rugby, you know,' Natasha added. 'Except right at the end, he told me about you lot going to games and what fun you must have had. He knew you see; but until then not a flicker of interest, as though when it was over, it had no meaning for him. Yet it did, he just bottled it up. Did he think by locking everything up in his filing cabinet he cut it out of his life! *The past is done and dusted,* he used to say. I wondered, was he silencing his regrets?'

By then Bran was quietly going through his detailed batch of correspondence which rarely strayed far from running the stud. Across it Michael had scribbled: *was anyone ever so lucky. Old Bra ... salt of the earth, cheap at twice the price.* Claire blanched, and Natasha smiled knowingly.

'Oh, Natasha!' Claire smoothed Bran's hand as Natasha continued, looking across at her: 'You don't escape, Claire. He kept all your newsletters, but he also had someone from the Sydney office check your data against the press summaries.'

On a smaller parcel of letters focusing on town and Shire and District matters, some of which she hadn't brought, he had noted Bran's election as Shire President: *About time, best head around the place for this kind of thing. And honest! Glad I don't have any rezoning I need to do.* Claire's election as the local CWA president drew a perfunctory: *She'll keep them in line.*

Andrew had already seen most of what related to him but, as they glanced through the collection again, Natasha drew attention to a piece relating to his appointment as their local doctor. 'I always thought it strange that he knew of that, Andrew?' She remarked, smiling as she read it aloud. *What's he doing down there with those yokels.* He'd written. *Bit of a star in his field. Pity about his wife. Don't know what Natasha sees in him? Dour Scot.*

'Yokels,' Claire snorted.

Nor had Susannah escaped his enveloping eye. 'You are here, you might say text and verse, Sue. Given the way you and Ben were supporting Charles, I'm sure he didn't want you getting away in a hurry. He's even tracked down your family. Had met your father in London. *A cadaverously thin man who looked as though it had been stretched out in the sun and left to dry.*' Sue gasped audibly. 'He had a signed copy of the score of *Lost Voices* together with reviews of numerous performances. *Fancy making music in that wilderness* was scribbled on one glowing review of a Sydney concert. But you know he never once brought you out of the cabinet to give you the public support that might have helped your career, even after he knew how much I admired your work!'

There was a kind of potted history of his childhood with Bran and Claire; photos taken at the beach, up in the snow, from trips to Sydney, of *Clifton*: *My House*; the manager's cottage with Bran and Claire sitting on the back verandah, *Their place*. A number taken out in the paddocks, sometimes with Bran, when Claire must have taken them, of Bran, tending the herd, taking him on the old Harley – 'how he loved going for a ride on that with you, B' – standing next to machinery and behind the wheel of an old car – 'that's the FJ,' Susannah called out. Strangely, Charles had been erased and there were none with Bran and Claire as a family.

'There are photos – *Riverview, my school. Dux and Captain of Rugby and Athletics* – of the buildings and the ovals, even of a religious statue in the middle of a rose garden.' 'My God! No photos of St Pat's I bet.' Bran sighed.

'No. But there are plenty of the American trip: photos of cattle ranches, of the Empire State building, and the Statue of Liberty; a postcard of the *Guernica*, the programme from a baseball game, marked *terrific*; programmes from *Disney Land* and heaps of photos of the exhibits but, isn't it very sad, none of you two.' The observation hung in the air.

'I didn't escape of course as I've shared already with Andrew, he had me covered from first to last. But you don't need to know all this, it's very tedious.' She looked around the room and sighed. 'So much, so much. He was like a huge vacuum cleaner, sucking up and then sifting through others' lives. You'll find photos from the university magazine *Honi Soit,* of rugby and inter-varsity teams, group shots always with one particular young man in the shot, who you now know as Jeremy,' playing a different game? she mused, 'and others with assorted women, one of whom, most frequently snapped with him is Maddy Lane, who you've heard about.'

'At that stage,' Susannah observed, 'he would have been quite a celebrity at university, had the world at his feet and perhaps he was prepared to strut openly among the wits and gallants on campus as a counter balance to the macho indulgences of the rugby club; where his exploits on the field were a foil against gossip about other proclivities.'

'Now that is interesting, because it speaks of a Michael who was prepared to play in the open; that wasn't the Michael I knew … rather too risky!' But she didn't elaborate, changing the subject. 'I heard various people mention the obituary last night, this may shed some light on it. Like some of you, I was surprised there had been one, for Michael shunned that kind of publicity. He had not discussed it with me, but among his papers I found a copy of it, with a brief accompanying note and a photographic print. It turns out that he'd left the document with his lawyer with instructions upon his death, to send the package to *The Times*' Contributing Editor, Michael Adamson, with copies to the Editors of the *Sydney Morning Herald,* and *The Age.*

> *Adamson*
>
> *It may be that you get it into your head to publish an Obituary after my death. Should that be the case, to save one of your braying editors or journeyman hacks the trouble, I am enclosing a copy of the notice I wish to appear. I request that you use it as it was developed in consultation with me. Should you decide not to comply with my wishes, I insist that you resist the temptation to cobble one together, instead, I would have you make no further mention of my death. My solicitors have been informed of this correspondence.*
>
> *I am under no illusions that I will be greatly missed, except perhaps for those few coins I passed on to charity. If you do use it, I wish to have the accompanying photograph included and I ask that it not be published until the week of my burial. I trust you will have the decency to keep my wishes private in this matter.*
>
> *Sincerely*
>
> *O'Connell*

Listening to her read was to hear Michael's steely voice carrying threat and innuendo from the grave. Andrew gasped. 'Even when really, he was asking a favour.' While Claire and Bran looked at each other and shook their heads.

***

Charlie could be heard in the kitchen, then, breaking into the subdued atmosphere in the room, he quietly called them to the table: 'I'm sorry, if we leave it any longer we'll be scraping it off the bottom of the pan …! Can I ask you to find a place?'

As he brought the huge pan in and set it down on the cloth runner,

Claire gently brushed the remaining papers from the table. Stepping back, his voice marked by sadness, he spoke to them: 'Today has been an almost sacred occasion. Michael has been brought back to us in his many shades, both as a result of Natasha's painful exploration of his last difficult years, and by sharing those memorial objects that were dear to him. We have set a place for him at our table and I like to think he was ready to join us, but I wonder if we can't go one step further. I noticed, among his papers, he had scrawled across one of the photos of the gully garden, *The Michael O'Connell Memorial Garden.*' He paused, everyone was still. 'Is it too much to ask that we honour the thought?'

Claire turned to him, smiled and nodded her approval, and Natasha, not embellishing the moment, thought: 'he would be thrilled…if surprised.' With each one at the table adding their voice in agreement; there was little to be said as Bran turned to the empty place between Charles and Natasha and raised his glass: 'To Michael.' His name echoed around the room and they solemnly drank to his memory.

'Charlie, it looks superb!' Sue said as that sat. *'Bon appétit*, everyone.'

The table was quiet at first, each lost in their own reveries until quiet murmurs of pleasure at the meal slipped into general chatter between loving friends. Susannah was telling Natasha about her little band of music students. 'Really keen, lovely kids. I'm thinking of writing something for them.'

'That would be fun. There are some gorgeous things …,' Natasha started to say enthusiastically as everyone began offering their ideas. Sue wondered about a Ponds Panto. And Ben, picking up the thread, suggested they should set something in the *Clifton* garden. 'You could use the gazebo as a stage.'

'Yes please.' Sue sighed. The very mention of that glorious garden, which she thought of as Ben's garden, filled her with sensual delight. Whether opening into calming vistas or around the ponds and billabongs or captured by its drama, she adored it. Even thinking of it sent a ripple through her, as if Ben was touching her. Her ability to love, once tainted and chained, now unleashed; with Ben and in his garden, her radiant spirit flies.

'What's this about you getting to Byron at last, Claire?' It was Ben. 'Don't forget to go into the hills, Bangalow's a gorgeous spot. Now, we've got a surprise too!'

'You're not …'

'Oh, don't be boring. No, we're off to Europe. I've never been, and Sue's mother's no spring chicken. … Paris … where she is, then we'll go to Prague. …' There was a brief lull in the chatter. 'It'll be a journey into the past. I'm half Czech, you see,'

Sue finished his sentence. 'I'd like to visit what my Mother called her beloved, mad, lost-for-ever-country.' Natasha gasped, reached for her hand. The table was hushed. 'I'm compelled to go there. I'd like to kiss my grandfather's grave and walk over the Charles Bridge with my man.'

'Looks like you'll be minding the fort, Charlie.' Claire said.

'Well, I've never minded that despite what Michael used to think. I lost my way for a while in that dark wood before I was rescued,' he said, gazing out at everyone; '… and since then I've been able to escape into my imagination. Besides Andy, you're stuck here too aren't you?'

'Funny you should mention that Charlie, I'm going to give Natasha a hand. I'll get a *locum* in, just for a couple of months. Nothing fixed yet, nothing mysterious …'

'I'll have some reshaping to do … in London and Sydney, but I promise not to deprive you of him for too long, besides I want to get on with settling myself into the Ponds.' Natasha added.

Meanwhile, Andrew was buried in thought. He couldn't escape the feeling that he was watching the interplay of a family; a family in this instance, carefully constructed by Michael: a life's work. Was it the family he never had perhaps, but once it was all in place, he was prepared to abandon them. The more he watched and listened, admiring Natasha's artful choreography of the day, he realized how dismally Michael had failed, for while they had set him a place at the table, it was simply as one more member of the family not as its patriarch. And yet, they wanted him there.

And on it went. 'Rhododendrons? Some glorious blooms out at the moment,' Ben explained. 'Paris, Susannah? I've got a divine dressmaker;

Didier. Ask me about him before you go.' 'What's your headline for the next *Stud News* Claire, you can't be off before that's at the printers!' Two hours later, replete, they adjourned to the lounge chairs. As they moved, the gentle zephyr from earlier, now more of a breeze, released the contents of Michael's *life* around the room; those papers, once so carefully sorted and contained, had gone on an abandoned dance and were once more in disarray. Some stalled against chair legs, while others had been whisked out the door and were swirling around on the verandah, caught against pots, or had found their way to the garden and were among the vegetables. Caught by the melancholy of it, Natasha wondered if they shouldn't all be collected up; give his life back to him, she thought, and bury them in *his* Memorial Garden.

'Here's to life after Michael!' Sue said as, with a nod to Andrew, she slipped across the room to the piano. 'I thought, just as a way of closing the day and perhaps to open the window on to tomorrow, I'd sing you something I've been trying to get right. Andy will help me out.'

> *No complaints and no regrets*
> *I still believe in chasing dreams and placing bets*
> *And I have learned that all you give is all you get*
> *So give it all you've got …*

It was as if they were one, smiling they touched, and shared their love in its many forms, mingling with Sue's voice as clear as any bell. … *So here's to life, / And every joy it brings / Here's to life,* they sang. *Here's to love … And here's to you…*

Natasha! One with us. And you … and you … and you …! And here's to Michael, too!' Singing joyously, she pointed to everyone in turn, lingering perhaps a moment longer on her beloved mate, and, as if it had been *Auld Lang Syne,* everyone, everyone, lovers and friends alike, kiss and embrace tomorrow in.

Acknowledgements

The novel is dedicated to Ian Templeman whose ideas set this book in motion. In the early stages, before he became very ill with the cancer that finally took him late in 2015, he was my sounding board; later, he was just there to listen: a generous mate.

The book would not have found its final shape without the assistance of Noelene Brasche, a wonderful editor who believed in the story. I should have been so fortunate. I am also grateful to the care and attention given to me by my agent, Michael Cybulski at NAC, and the literary editor, Denise Harris, whose guidance and advice I have valued. I would like also to thank Nick Walker and ASP for trusting the book; Anastasia Buryak for her congenial and constructive conversations about editing; and Wayne Saunders for his wonderful cover design.

Sally Seward has suffered the book in all its stages, and it wouldn't have been finished without her love and support. Justine Moloney, Geraldine Blake, Jenny Edwards, Tim Clifton, and Sandra Wise have been wonderful readers, although they can't be held responsible for the way the book turned out. Mike Introvigne generously shared his ideas about collecting data on cattle, and about his Simmental herd, and Sandra Wise, Cathy Cole, Norm Dennis, and Ronal Hawkins talked to me about things that they knew and I didn't , while Manfredo Sambuy told me about runaway dogs. My 'Rudolf Nureyev' has spun off Colum McCann's 'Nureyev' in his wonderful fictional biography, *Dancer*; Vincent O'Sullivan's 'Come 1917', 'The past that has still to arrive,' published in the *SMH*, 23–24 July 2016, echoes through the pages; and Helen Young's weekly gardening columns in the *Weekend Australian* were avidly read. Ben Temple is a great fan of Leonard Cohen, and he sings the Master's 'Hallelujah' with delight, and would no doubt have been as sad as I to learn of his passing before this book was finished; Susannah sings Auden's 'The Truth about Love' to her friends; and her rendition of the Artie Butler and Phyllis Molinari song 'Here's to life' closes out the novel, while various poets, artists, musicians and composers, rugby players, and politicians are evoked and, in some cases quoted, or have words put into their mouth.

www.ingramcontent.com/pod-product-compliance
Lightning Source LLC
Chambersburg PA
CBHW051328250626
47155CB00007B/2499